THE COMPLETE FAIRY TALES OF THE BROTHERS GRIMM

Volume I and Volume II of *The Complete Fairy Tales of the Brothers Grimm* are all-new translations of the famous 210 fairy tales collected and published by Jacob and Wilhelm Grimm, plus 32 little-known tales that they omitted during the course of their many revisions and that appear here for the first time in English. Popular taste and mores have taken their toll on the stories as the Grimms first penned them, and many startling and delightful surprises await the reader in this new and faithful translation.

Jack Zipes, Professor of German at the University of Minnesota, is a literary critic and children's literature specialist. His numerous books on folktales and fairy tales include *Breaking the Magic Spell, Fairy Tales and the Art of Subversion, The Trials and Tribulations of Little Red Riding Hood, Don't Bet on the Prince,* and *Spells of Enchantment,* as well as articles on children's theater, Bruno Bettelheim, and German drama.

Ask your bookseller for Bantam Classics by these
international writers:

Aristophanes
Dante Alighieri
Honoré de Balzac
Anton Pavlovich Chekhov
Sidonie Gabrielle Claudine Colette
Fyodor Dostoevsky
Alexandre Dumas
Euripides
Gustave Flaubert
Johann Wolfgang von Goethe
Jacob and Wilhelm Grimm
Homer
Victor Hugo
Henrik Ibsen
Franz Kafka
Pierre Choderlos de Laclos
Gaston Leroux
Niccolo Machiavelli
Thomas Mann
Karl Marx and Friedrich Engels
Guy de Maupassant
Baroness Emmuska Orczy
Plato
Edmond Rostand
Sophocles
Marie-Henri Beyle de Stendhal
Leo Tolstoy
Ivan Turgenev
Jules Verne
Virgil
Voltaire
Johann David Wyss

The Complete Fairy Tales of the BROTHERS GRIMM

Volume I
Tales 1–100

Translated and With an Introduction by
Jack Zipes

Illustrations by John B. Gruelle

BANTAM BOOKS
NEW YORK · TORONTO · LONDON · SYDNEY · AUCKLAND

THE COMPLETE FAIRY TALES OF THE BROTHERS GRIMM, VOLUME I
A Bantam Book

PUBLISHING HISTORY

Bantam hardcover edition combining Volumes I and II / February 1987
Bantam paperback edition of Volume I / March 1988

The present translation is based in part on the first edition
of the KINDER- UND HAUSMÄRCHEN published in two volumes in
1812 and 1815. The first 211 tales in this translation are based
on the seventh and final edition published in 1857

The inside illustrations by John B. Gruelle first appeared in
Grimm's Fairy Tales, translated by Margaret Hunt in 1914

Cover illustration is "Dornröschen (Brier Rose) from Märchen Kalender
from the year 1905 drawn by Prof. H. Lefler and Architekt J. Urban

ISBN 0-553-21238-9

Published simultaneously in the United States and Canada

Bantam Books are published by Bantam Books, a division of Random House, Inc. Its
trademark, consisting of the words "Bantam Books" and the portrayal of a rooster,
is Registered in U.S. Patent and Trademark Office and in other countries. Marca
Registrada. Bantam Books, 1540 Broadway, New York, New York 10036.

PRINTED IN THE UNITED STATES OF AMERICA

OPM   14   13   12   11   10

For my daughter,
Hanna,
and for her grandparents,
Celia and Phil, Bette and Dave,
who share the spirit of
once upon a time

❖ Contents ❖

THE COMPLETE FAIRY TALES OF THE BROTHERS GRIMM

VOLUME I

Once There Were Two Brothers Named Grimm

by Jack Zipes

MANY ARE THE FAIRY TALES and myths that have been spread about the Brothers Grimm, Jacob and Wilhelm. For a long time it was believed that they had wandered about Germany and gathered their tales from the lips of doughty peasants and that all their tales were genuinely German. Although much of what had been believed has been disproven by recent scholarship, new rumors and debates about the Grimms keep arising. For instance, one literary scholar has recently charged them with manufacturing the folk spirit of the tales in order to dupe the general public in the name of nationalism. Other critics have found racist and sexist components in the tales that they allege need expurgation, while psychologists and educators battle over the possible harmful or therapeutic effects of the tales. Curiously, most of the critics and most of the introductions to the English translations of the Grimms' tales say very little about the brothers themselves or their methods for collecting the tales—as though the Grimms were incidental to their tales. Obviously, this is not the case, and in view of their 200th birthdays, celebrated in 1985 and 1986, it is time to set the record straight.

Just who were the Brothers Grimm and how did they discover those tales, which may be the most popular in the world today? Why and how did the brothers change the tales? And what is the significance of the magic of those tales today?

A fairy-tale writer could not have created a more idyllic and propitious setting for the entrance of the Brothers Grimm into the world. Their father, Philipp Wilhelm Grimm, a lawyer, was ambitious, diligent, and prosperous, and their mother Dorothea (née Zimmer), daughter of a city councilman in Kassel, was a devoted and caring housewife, even though she tended at times to be melancholy. Initially they settled in the quaint village of Hanau, and during the first twelve years of their marriage, there were nine births, out of which six children survived: Jacob Ludwig Grimm

(1785–1863), Wilhelm Carl Grimm (1786–1859), Carl Friedrich Grimm (1787–1852), Ferdinand Philipp Grimm (1788–1844), Ludwig Emil Grimm (1790–1863), and Charlotte Amalie (Lotte) Grimm (1793–1833). By 1791 the family had moved to Steinau, near Kassel, where Philipp Grimm had obtained an excellent position as district judge (*Amtmann*) and soon became the leading figure of the town. He and his family lived in a large comfortable home there and had servants to help with the domestic chores. As soon as the children were of age, they were sent to a local school, where they received a classical education. They also received strict religious training in the Reform Calvinist Church. Both Jacob and Wilhelm were bright, hardworking pupils and were distinctly fond of country life. Their familiarity with farming, nature, and peasant customs and superstitions would later play a major role in their research and work in German folklore. At first, though, both boys appeared destined to lead comfortable lives, following in the footsteps of their father, whose seal was *Tute si recte vixeris*—"honesty is the best policy in life." To be sure, this was the path that Jacob and Wilhelm took, but it had to be taken without the guidance of their father.

Philipp Grimm died suddenly in 1796 at the age of forty-four, and his death was traumatic for the entire family. Within weeks after his death, Dorothea Grimm had to move out of the large house and face managing the family of six children without servants or much financial support. From this point on, the family was totally dependent on outside help, particularly on Henriette Zimmer, Dorothea's sister, who was a lady-in-waiting for the princess of Hessia-Kassel. Henriette arranged for Jacob and Wilhelm to study at the prestigious Lyzeum (high school) in Kassel and obtained provisions and funds for the family.

Although the brothers were different in temperament—Jacob was more introverted, serious, and robust; Wilhelm was outgoing, gregarious, and asthmatic—they were inseparable and totally devoted to each other. They shared the same room and bed and developed the same work habits: in high school the Grimms studied more than twelve hours a day and were evidently bent on proving themselves to be the best students at the Lyzeum. That they were treated by some teachers as socially inferior to the other "highborn" students only served to spur their efforts. In fact, the Grimms had to struggle against social slights and financial deprivation during a good part of their lives, but they never forgot their father's motto, *Tute si recte vixeris*, and they became famous not only because of their remarkable scholarship but also because of their great moral integrity.

Although each one was graduated from the Lyzeum at the head of his class, Jacob in 1802 and Wilhelm in 1803, they both had to obtain special dispensations to study law at the University of Marburg because their social standing was not high enough to qualify them. Once at the university they had to confront yet another instance of injustice, for most of the students from wealthier families received stipends, while the Grimms had to pay for their own education and live on a small budget. This inequity made them feel even more compelled to prove themselves, and at Marburg they drew the attention of Professor Friedrich Karl von Savigny, the genial founder of the historical school of law. Savigny argued that the spirit of a law can be comprehended only by tracing its origins to the development of the customs and language of the people and by paying attention to the changing historical context in which laws developed. Ironically, it was Savigny's emphasis on the philological aspect of law that led Jacob and Wilhelm to dedicate themselves to the study of ancient German literature and folklore. This decision was made in 1805 after Savigny had taken Jacob to Paris to assist him in research on the history of Roman law. Upon returning to Germany in 1806, Jacob left the university and rejoined his mother, who had moved to Kassel. Given the pecuniary situation of the family, it was Jacob's duty, as head of the family now, to support his brothers and sister, and he found a position as secretary for the Kassel War Commission, which made decisions pertaining to the war with France. Fortunately for Jacob, he was able to pursue his study of old German literature and customs on the side while Wilhelm remained in Marburg to complete his legal studies.

The correspondence between Jacob and Wilhelm during this time reflects their great concern for the welfare of their family. With the exception of Ludwig, who later became an accomplished painter and also illustrated the fairy tales, the other children had difficulty establishing careers for themselves. Neither Carl nor Ferdinand displayed the intellectual aptitude that the two oldest brothers did or the creative talents of Ludwig. Carl eventually tried his hand at business and ended up destitute as a language teacher, while Ferdinand tried many different jobs in publishing and later died in poverty. Lotte's major task was to assist her mother, who died in 1808. After that, Lotte managed the Grimm household until she married a close friend of the family, Ludwig Hassenpflug, in 1822. Hassenpflug became an important politician in Germany and eventually had a falling out with Jacob and Wilhelm because of his conservative and opportunistic actions as statesman.

While Ludwig, Carl, Ferdinand, and Lotte were young, they were chiefly the responsibility of Jacob, who looked after them like a stern father. Even Wilhelm regarded him as such and acknowledged his authority, not only in family matters, but also in scholarship. It was during the period 1806–1810, when each of the siblings was endeavoring to make a decision about a future career and concerned about the stability of their home, that Jacob and Wilhelm began systematically gathering folk tales and other materials related to folklore. Clemens Brentano, a gifted romantic writer and friend, had requested that the Grimms help him collect tales for a volume that he intended to publish some time in the future. The Grimms responded by selecting tales from old books and recruiting the help of friends and acquaintances in Kassel. The Grimms were unable to devote all their energies to their research, though. Jacob lost his job on the War Commission in 1807, when Kassel was invaded by the French and became part of the Kingdom of Westphalia under the rule of Jérôme Bonaparte. Soon thereafter, the Grimms' mother died, and it was imperative that Jacob find some new means of supporting the family. Although he had a strong antipathy to the French, he applied for the position of King Jérôme's private librarian in Kassel, and was awarded the post in 1808. This job enabled him to pursue his studies and help his brothers and sister. Meanwhile, Wilhelm had to undergo a cure for a heart disease in Halle. Ludwig began studying art at the Art Academy in Munich, and Carl began working as a businessman in Hamburg. From 1809 to 1813 there was a period of relative stability and security for the Grimm family, and Jacob and Wilhelm began publishing the results of their research on old German literature: Jacob wrote *On the Old German Meistergesang,* and Wilhelm, *Old Danish Heroic Songs,* both in 1811. Together they published in 1812 a study of the *Song of Hildebrand* and the *Wessobrunner Prayer.* Of course, their major publication at this time was the first volume of the *Kinder-und Hausmärchen (Children's and Household Tales)* with scholarly annotations, also in 1812.

The Napoleonic Wars and French rule had been upsetting to both Jacob and Wilhelm, who were dedicated to the notion of German unification. Neither wanted to see the restoration of oppressive German princes, but they did feel a deep longing to have the German people united in one nation through customs and laws of their own making. Thus, in 1813 they celebrated when the French withdrew from Kassel and the French armies were defeated throughout Central Europe. Jacob was appointed a member of the Hessian Peace Delegation and did diplomatic work in Paris and Vienna. During his absence Wilhelm was able to procure the position as secretary to the royal librarian in Kassel and to concentrate on bringing out the second volume of the *Children's and Household*

Tales in 1815. When the peace treaty with the French was concluded in Vienna, Jacob returned home and was disappointed to find that the German princes were seeking to reestablish their narrow, vested interests in different German principalities, and to discard the broader notion of German unification.

After securing the position of second librarian in the royal library of Kassel, Jacob joined Wilhelm in editing the first volume of *German Legends* in 1816. During the next thirteen years, the Grimms enjoyed a period of relative calm and prosperity. Their work as librarians was not demanding, and they could devote themselves to scholarly research and the publication of their findings. Together they published the second volume of *German Legends* (1818), and *Irish Elf Tales* (1826), while Jacob wrote the first volume of *German Grammar* (1819) and *Ancient German Law* (1828) by himself, and Wilhelm produced *The German Heroic Legend* (1829).

In the meantime, there were changes in the domestic arrangement of the Grimms. Lotte moved out of the house to marry Ludwig Hassenpflug in 1822, and a few years later, in 1825, Wilhelm married Dortchen Wild, who was the daughter of a druggist in Kassel. She had known both brothers for over twenty years and had been part of a group of storytellers who had provided the Grimms with numerous tales. Now it became her task to look after the domestic affairs of the brothers, for Jacob did not leave the house. Indeed, he remained a bachelor for his entire life and had very little time for socializing. The Grimms insisted on a quiet atmosphere and a rigid schedule at home so that they could conduct their research without interruptions. Although Wilhelm continued to enjoy company and founded a family—he had three children with Dortchen—he was just as much married to his work as Jacob. Since Dortchen had been well-acquainted with the brothers before her marriage, when she assumed her role in the family she fully supported their work and customary way of living.

In 1829, however, when the first librarian died and his position in Kassel became vacated, the Grimms' domestic tranquility was broken. Jacob, who had already become famous for his scholarly publications, had expected to be promoted to this position. But he did not have the right connections or the proper conservative politics and was overlooked. In response to this, he and Wilhelm resigned their posts, and one year later they traveled to Göttingen, where Jacob became professor of old German literature and head librarian, and Wilhelm, librarian and, eventually, professor in 1835. Both were considered gifted teachers, and they broke new ground in the study of German literature, which had only recently become an accepted field of study at the university. Aside from their teaching duties, they continued to write and publish important works: Jacob wrote the third volume of *German Grammar* (1831) and a major study entitled *German Mythology* (1835), while Wilhelm prepared the third edition of *Children's and Household Tales*. Though their positions were secure, there was a great deal of political unrest in Germany due to the severely repressive political climate since 1819. By 1830 many revolts and peasant uprisings had erupted, and a group of intellectuals known as Young Germany (*Jungdeutschland*) pushed for more democratic reform in different German principalities. For the most part, however, their members were persecuted and silenced, just as the peasants too were vanquished. Some leading writers, such as Ludwig Börne, Heinrich Heine, and Georg Büchner, took refuge in exile. The Brothers Grimm were not staunch supporters of the Young Germany movement, but they had always supported the liberal cause throughout Germany and were greatly affected by the political conflicts.

In 1837, when King Ernst August II succeeded to the throne of Hannover, he revoked the constitution of 1833 and dissolved parliament. In his attempt to restore absolutism to the Kingdom of Hannover, of which Göttingen was a part, he declared that all civil servants must pledge an oath to serve him personally. Since the king was nominally the rector of the University of Göttingen, the Grimms were obligated to take an oath of allegiance, but instead they, along with five other professors, led a protest against the king and were summarily dismissed. Jacob was compelled to leave Göttingen immediately and returned to Kassel, where Wilhelm joined him a few months later.

Once again, they were in desperate financial straits. Despite the fact that they received funds and support from hundreds of friends and admirers who supported their stand on academic freedom, the ruling monarchs of the different principalities prevented them from teaching at another university. It was during this time that Jacob and Wilhelm decided to embark on writing the *German Dictionary*, one of the most ambitious lexicographical undertakings of the nineteenth century. Though the income from this project would be meager, they hoped to support themselves through other publishing ventures as well. In the meantime, Bettina von Arnim, Friedrich Karl von Savigny, and other influential friends were trying to convince the new king of Prussia, Friedrich Wilhelm IV, to bring the brothers to Berlin. Finally, in November 1840 Jacob and Wilhelm received offers to become professors at the University of Berlin and to do research at the Academy of Sciences. It was not until March 1841, however, that the Grimms took up residence in Berlin and were able to continue their work on the *German Dictionary* and their scholarly research on other subjects. In addition to teaching, the Grimms played an active role in the institutionalization of German literature as a field of study at other universities and entered into political debates. When the Revolution of 1848 occurred in Germany, the Grimms were elected to the civil parliament, and Jacob was considered to be one of the most prominent men among the representatives at the National Assembly held in Frankfurt am Main. However, the brothers' hopes for democratic reform and the unification of the German principalities dwindled as one compromise after another was reached with the German monarchs. Both brothers retired from active politics after the demise of the revolutionary movement. In fact, Jacob resigned from his position as professor in 1848, the same year he published his significant study entitled *The History of the German Language*. Wilhelm retired from his post as professor in 1852. For the rest of their lives, the Grimms devoted most of their energy to completing the monumental *German Dictionary*, but they got only as far as the letter *F*. Though they did not finish the *Dictionary*, a task that had to be left to scholars in the twentieth century, they did produce an astonishing number of remarkable books during their lifetimes: Jacob published twenty-one, and Wilhelm, fourteen. Together they produced eight. In addition, there are another twelve volumes of their essays and notes and thousands of important letters. The Grimms made scholarly contributions to the areas of folklore, history, ethnology, religion, jurisprudence, lexicography, and literary criticism. Even when they did not work as a team, they shared their ideas and discussed all their projects together. When Wilhelm died in 1859, the loss affected Jacob deeply; he became even more solitary but did not abandon the projects he had held in common with his brother. In addition, the more he realized that his hopes for democratic reform were being dashed in Germany, the more he voiced his criticism of reactionary trends in Germany. Both Jacob and Wilhelm regarded their work as part of a social effort to foster a sense of justice among the German people and to create pride in the folk tradition. Jacob died in 1863 after completing the fourth volume of his book *German Precedents*. In German the title, *Deutsche Weistümer,* connotes a sense of the wisdom of the ages that he felt should be passed on to the German people.

Though the Grimms made important discoveries in their research on ancient German literature and customs, they were neither the founders of folklore as a study in Germany, nor were they the first to begin collecting and publishing folk and fairy tales. In fact, from the beginning their principal concern was to uncover the etymological and linguistic truths that bound the German people together and were expressed in their laws and customs. The fame of the Brothers Grimm as collectors of folk and fairy tales must be understood in this context, and even here, chance played a role in their destiny.

In 1806 Clemens Brentano, who had already published an important collection of folk songs entitled *Des Knaben Wunderhorn* (*The Boy's Magic Horn*, 1805) with Achim von Arnim, was advised to seek out the aid of Jacob and Wilhelm Grimm because they were known to have a vast knowledge of old German literature and folklore. They were also considered to be conscientious and indefatigable workers. Brentano hoped to use whatever tales they might send him in a future publication of folk tales, and he was able to publish some of the songs they gathered in the second and third volumes of *Des Knaben Wunderhorn* in 1808. The Grimms believed strongly in sharing their research and findings with friends and congenial scholars, and between 1807 and 1812 they began collecting tales with the express purpose of sending them to Brentano, as well as of using them as source material for gaining a greater historical understanding of the German language and customs.

Contrary to popular belief, the Grimms did not collect their tales by visiting peasants in the countryside and writing down the tales that they heard. Their primary method was to invite storytellers to their home and then have them tell the tales aloud, which the Grimms either noted down on first hearing or after a couple of hearings. Most of the storytellers during this period were educated young women from the middle class or aristocracy. For instance, in Kassel a group of young women from the Wild family (Dortchen, Gretchen, Lisette, and Marie Elisabeth), and their mother (Dorothea), and from the Hassenpflug family (Amalie, Jeanette, and Marie) used to meet regularly to relate tales they had heard from their nursemaids, governesses, and servants. In 1808 Jacob formed a friendship with Werner von Haxthausen, who came from Westphalia, and in 1811 Wilhelm visited the Haxthausen estate and became acquainted there with a circle of young men and women (Ludowine, Marianne, and August von Haxthausen, and Jenny and Annette von Droste-Hülfshoff), whose tales he noted down. Still, the majority of the storytellers came from Hessia: Dorothea Viehmann, a tailor's wife from nearby Zwehrn who used to sell fruit in Kassel, would visit the Grimms and told them a good many significant tales; and Johann Friedrich (*Wachtmeister*) Krause, an old retired soldier, gave the brothers tales in exchange for some of their old clothes. Many of the tales that the Grimms recorded had French origins because the Hassenpflugs were of Huguenot ancestry and spoke French at home. Most of the brothers' informants were familiar with both oral tradition and literary tradition and would combine motifs from both sources. In addition to the tales of these storytellers and others who came later, the Grimms took tales directly from books and journals and edited them according to their taste.

In 1810, when Brentano finally requested the Grimms' collection of tales, the brothers had copies made and sent forty-nine texts to him. They had copies made because they felt Brentano would take great poetic license and turn them into substantially different tales, whereas they were intent on using the tales to document basic truths about the customs and practices of the German people and on preserving their authentic ties to the oral tradition. Actually, the Grimms need not have worried about Brentano's use of their tales, for he never touched them but abandoned them in the Ölenberg Monastery in Alsace. Only in 1920 were the handwritten tales rediscovered, and they were published in different editions in 1924, 1927, and 1974. The last publication by Heinz Rölleke is the most scholarly and useful, for he has carefully shown how the Grimms' original handwritten manuscripts can help us to document their sources and reveal the great changes the brothers made in shaping the tales.

As it happened, after the Grimms sent their collected texts to Brentano, who was unreliable and was going through great personal difficulties, they decided to publish the tales themselves and began changing them and preparing them for publication. They also kept adding new tales to their collection. Jacob set the tone, but the brothers were very much in agreement about how they wanted to alter and stylize the tales. This last point is significant because some critics have wanted to see major differences between Jacob and Wilhelm. These critics have argued that there was a dispute between the brothers after Wilhelm assumed major responsibility for the editing of the tales in 1815 and that Wilhelm transformed them against Jacob's will. There is no doubt that Wilhelm was the primary editor after 1815, but Jacob established the framework for their editing practice between 1807 and 1812 and even edited the majority of the tales for the first volume. A comparison of the way Jacob and Wilhelm worked both before and after 1815 does not reveal major differences, except that Wilhelm did take more care to refine the style and make the contents of the tales more acceptable for a children's audience, or, really, for adults who wanted the tales censored for children. Otherwise, the editing of Jacob and Wilhelm exhibits the same tendencies from the beginning to the end of their project: the endeavor to make the tales stylistically smoother; the concern for clear sequential structure; the desire to make the stories more lively and pictorial by adding adjectives, old proverbs, and direct dialogue; the reinforcement of motives for action in the plot; the infusion of psychological motifs; and the elimination of elements that might detract from a rustic tone. The model for a good many of their tales was the work of the gifted artist Philipp Otto Runge, whose two stories in dialect, *The Fisherman and His Wife* and *The Juniper Tree*, represented in tone, structure, and content the ideal narrative that the Grimms wanted to create.

And create they did. The Grimms were not merely collectors. In fact, their major accomplishment in publishing their two volumes of 156 tales in 1812 and 1815 was to *create* an ideal type for the literary fairy tale, one that sought to be as close to the oral tradition as possible, while incorporating stylistic, formal, and substantial thematic changes to appeal to a growing middle-class audience. By 1819, when the second edition of the tales, now in one volume that included 170 texts, was published and Wilhelm assumed complete charge of the revisions, the brothers had established the form and manner through which they wanted to preserve, contain, and present to the German public what they felt were profound truths about the origins of civilization. Indeed, they saw the "childhood of human-kind" as embedded in customs that Germans had cultivated, and the tales were to serve as reminders of such rich, natural culture.

After 1819 there were five more editions and sixty-nine new texts added to the collection and twenty-eight omitted. By the time the seventh edition appeared in 1857, there were 211 texts in all. Most of the additions after 1819 were from literary sources, and the rest were either sent to the brothers by informants or recorded from a primary source. Indeed, the chief task after 1819 was largely one of refinement: Wilhelm often changed the original texts by comparing them to different versions that he had acquired. While he evidently tried to retain what he and Jacob considered the essential message of the tale, he tended to make the tales more proper and prudent for bourgeois audiences. Thus it is crucial to be aware of the changes both brothers made between the original handwritten manuscript and the last edition of 1857. Compare the following, for example:

"Snow White"—Ölenberg Manuscript
When Snow White awoke the next morning, they asked her how she happened to get there. And she told them everything,

how her mother, the queen, had left her alone in the woods and gone away. The dwarfs took pity on her and persuaded her to remain with them and do the cooking for them when they went to the mines. However, she was to beware of the queen and not to let anyone into the house.

"Snow White"—1812 Edition

When Snow White awoke, they asked her who she was and how she happened to get into the house. Then she told them how her mother had wanted to have her put to death, but the hunter had spared her life, and how she had run the entire day and finally arrived at their house. So the dwarfs took pity on her and said, "If you keep house for us and cook, sew, make the beds, wash and knit, and keep everything tidy and clean, you may stay with us, and you will have everything you want. In the evening, when we come home, dinner must be ready. During the day we are in the mines and dig for gold, so you will be alone. Beware of the queen and let no one into the house."

"Rapunzel"—1812 Edition

At first Rapunzel was afraid, but soon she took such a liking to the young king that she made an agreement with him: he was to come every day and be pulled up. Thus they lived merrily and joyfully for a certain time, and the fairy did not discover anything until one day when Rapunzel began talking to her and said, "Tell me, Mother Gothel, why do you think my clothes have become too tight for me and no longer fit?"

"Rapunzel"—1857 Edition

When he entered the tower, Rapunzel was at first terribly afraid, for she had never laid eyes on a man before. However, the prince began to talk to her in a friendly way and told her that her song had touched his heart so deeply that he had not been able to rest until he had seen her. Rapunzel then lost her fear, and when he asked her whether she would have him for her husband, and she saw that he was young and handsome, she thought, He'll certainly love me better than old Mother Gothel. So she said yes and placed her hand in his.

"I want to go with you very much," she said, "but I don't know how I can get down. Every time you come, you must bring a skein of silk with you, and I'll weave it into a ladder.

When it's finished, then I'll climb down, and you can take me away on your horse."

They agreed that until then he would come to her every evening, for the old woman came during the day. Meanwhile, the sorceress did not notice anything, until one day Rapunzel blurted out, "Mother Gothel, how is it that you're much heavier than the prince? When I pull him up, he's here in a second."

"The Three Spinners"—1812 Edition
In olden times there lived a king who loved flax spinning more than anything in the world, and his queen and daughters had to spin the entire day. If he did not hear the wheels humming, he became angry. One day he had to take a trip, and before he departed, he gave the queen a large box with flax and said, "I want this flax spun by the time I return."

"The Three Spinners"—1857 Edition
There once was a lazy maiden who did not want to spin, and no matter what her mother said, she refused to spin. Finally, her mother became so angry and impatient that she beat her, and her daughter began to cry loudly. Just then the queen happened to be driving by, and when she heard the crying, she ordered the carriage to stop, went into the house, and asked the mother why she was beating her daughter, for her screams could be heard out on the street. The woman was too ashamed to tell the queen that her daughter was lazy and said, "I can't get her to stop spinning. She does nothing but spin and spin, and I'm so poor that I can't provide the flax."

"Well," the queen replied, "there's nothing I like to hear more than the sound of spinning, and I'm never happier than when I hear the constant humming of the wheels. Let me take your daughter with me to my castle. I've got plenty of flax, and she can spin as much as she likes."

As is evident from the above examples, the Grimms made major changes while editing the tales. They eliminated erotic and sexual elements that might be offensive to middle-class morality, added numerous Christian expressions and references, emphasized specific role models for male and female protagonists according to the dominant patriarchal code of that time, and endowed many of the tales with a "homey" or *biedermeier* flavor by the use of diminutives, quaint expressions, and cute descriptions. Moreover, though the collection was not originally printed with children in mind as the primary audience—the first two volumes had scholarly annotations, which were later published separately—Wilhelm made all the editions from 1819 on more appropriate for children, or rather, to what he thought would be proper for children to learn. Indeed, some of the tales, such as *Mother Trudy* and *The Stubborn Child*, are intended to be harsh lessons for children. Such didacticism did not contradict what both the Grimms thought the collection should be, namely an *Erziehungsbuch*, an educational manual. The tendency toward attracting a virtuous middle-class audience is most evident in the so-called *Kleine Ausgabe* (*Small Edition*), a selection of fifty tales from the *Grosse Ausgabe* (*Large Edition*). This *Small Edition* was first published in 1825 in an effort to popularize the larger work and to create a best-seller. There were ten editions of this book, which contained the majority of the *Zaubermärchen* (the magic fairy tales), from 1825 to 1858. With such tales as *Cinderella, Snow White, Sleeping Beauty, Little Red Riding Hood*, and *The Frog King*, all of which underline morals in keeping with the Protestant ethic and a patriarchal notion of sex roles, the book was bound to be a success.

The magic fairy tales were the ones that were the most popular and acceptable in Europe and America during the nineteenth century, but it is important to remember that the Grimms' collection also includes unusual fables, legends, anecdotes, jokes, and religious tales. The variety of their tales is often overlooked because only a handful have been selected by parents, teachers, publishers, and critics for special attention. This selective process is generally neglected when critics talk about the effects of the tales and the way they should be conveyed or not conveyed to children.

The Grimms' collection *Children's and Household Tales* was not an immediate success in Germany. In fact, Ludwig Bechstein's *Deutsches Märchenbuch* (*German Book of Fairy Tales*, 1845) was more popular for a time. However, by the 1870s the Grimms' tales had been incorporated into the teaching curriculum in Prussia and other German principalities, and they were also included in primers and anthologies for children throughout the western world. By the beginning of the twentieth century, the *Children's and Household Tales* was second only to the Bible as a best-seller in Germany, and it has continued to hold this position. Furthermore, there is no doubt that the Grimms' tales, published either together in a single volume or individually as illustrated books, enjoy the same popularity in the English-speaking world.

Such popularity has always intrigued critics, and advocates of various schools of thought have sought to analyze and interpret the "magic" of the Grimms' tales. Foremost among the critics are the folklorists, educators, psychologists, and literary critics of different persuasions, including structuralists, literary historians, semioticians, and Marxists. Each group has made interesting contributions to the scholarship on the Grimms' tales, although there are times when historical truths about the Grimms' work are discarded or squeezed to fit into a pet theory.

The efforts made by folklorists to categorize the Grimms' tales after the nineteenth century were complicated by the fact that numerous German folklorists used the tales to explain ancient German customs and rituals, under the assumption that the tales were authentic documents of the German people. This position, which overlooked the French and other European connections, led to an "Aryan" approach during the 1920s, 1930s, and 1940s, which allowed many German folklorists to interpret the tales along racist and elitist lines. Such an approach had always been contested by folklorists outside Germany, who viewed the tales as part of the vast historical development of the oral tradition, wherein the Grimms' collection is given special attention because of the mixture of oral and literary motifs. These motifs have been related by folklorists to motifs in other folk tales in an effort to find the origin of a particular motif or tale type and its variants. By doing this kind of research, folklorists have been able to chart distinctions in the oral traditions and customs of different countries.

Educators have not been interested in motifs so much as in the morals and the types of role models in the tales. Depending on the country and the educational standards in a particular historical period, teachers and school boards have often dictated which Grimms' tales are to be used or abused. Generally speaking, such tales as *The Wolf and the Seven Young Kids*, *Cinderella*, *Little Red Cap*, and *Snow White* have always been deemed acceptable because they instruct children through explicit warnings and lessons, even though some of the implicit messages may be harmful to children. Most of the great pedagogical debates center around the brutality and cruelty in some tales, and the tendency among publishers and adapters of the tales has been to eliminate the harsh scenes. Consequently, Cinderella's sisters will not have their eyes pecked out; Little Red Cap and her grandmother will not be gobbled up by the wolf; the witch in *Snow White* will not be forced to dance in red-hot shoes; and the witch in *Hansel and Gretel* will not be shoved into an oven. Such changes have annoyed critics of various psychoanalytical orientations, because they believe that the violence and conflict in the tales derive from profound instinctual developments in the human psyche and hence represent symbolical modes by which children and adults deal with sexual problems. Most psychoanalytical critics take their cues from Freud, even if they have departed from his method and have joined another school of analysis. One of the first important books about the psychological impact of the Grimms' tales was Josephine Belz's *Das Märchen und die Phantasie des Kindes* (*The Fairy Tale and the Imagination of the Child,* 1919) in which she tried to establish important connections between children's ways of fantasizing and the symbols in the tales. Later, Carl Jung, Erich Fromm, and Gerza Roheim wrote valuable studies of fairy tales that sought to go beyond Freud's theories. In the period following World War II, Aniela Jaffé, Joseph Campbell, and Maria von Franz charted the links between archetypes, the collective unconscious, and fairy tales, while Julius Heuscher and Bruno Bettelheim focused on oedipal conflicts from neo-Freudian positions in their analyses of some Grimms' tales. Finally, André Favat published an important study, *Child and the Tale* (1977), which uses Piaget's notions of child development, interests, and stages of understanding to explore the tales and their impact. Although the various psychoanalytical approaches have shed light on the symbolical meanings of the tales from the point of view of particular schools of thought, the tales have often been taken out of context to demonstrate the value of a psychoanalytical theory rather than to render a cultural and aesthetic appreciation and evaluation of the text.

Literary critics have reacted to the psychoanalytical approach in different ways. Influenced by the theories of Vladimir Propp (*Morphology of the Folktale,* 1968) and Max Lüthi (*Once Upon a Time,* 1970), formalists, structuralists, and semioticians have analyzed individual texts to discuss the structure of the tale, its aesthetic components and functions, and the hidden meanings of the signs. Literary historians and philologists such as Ludwig Denecke and Heinz Rölleke have tried to place the Grimms' work in a greater historical context in order to show how the brothers helped develop a mixed genre, often referred to as the *Buchmärchen* (book tale), combining aspects of the oral and literary tradition. Sociological and Marxist critics such as Dieter Richter, Christa Bürger, and Bernd Wollenweber have discussed the tales in light of the social and political conditions in Germany during the nineteenth century and have drawn attention to the racist and sexist notions in the tales. In the process, they have added fuel to the debate among educators, and the use and abuse of the Grimms' tales remains a key issue even today—among educators, psychologists, folklorists, and literary critics.

Though there were debates about the value of the tales during the Grimms' own lifetime, if they were alive today, they would probably be surprised to see how vigorous and violent some of the debates are and how different the interpretations tend to be. To a certain extent, the intense interest in their tales by so many different groups of critics throughout the world is a tribute to the Grimms' uncanny sense of how folk narratives inform cultures. They were convinced that their tales possessed essential truths about the origins of civilization, and they selected and revised those tales that would best express these truths. They did this in the name of humanity and *Kultur:* the Grimms were German idealists who believed that historical knowledge of customs, mores, and laws would increase self-understanding and social enlightenment. Their book is not so much a book of magic as it is a manual for education that seeks to go beyond the irrational. It is in their impulse to educate, to pass on the experiences of a variety of people who knew the lore of survival, that we may find the reasons why we are still drawn to the tales today. Though the Grimms imbued the tales with a heavy dose of Christian morality, the Protestant work ethic, and patriarchalism, they also wanted the tales to depict social injustices and possibilities for self-determination. Their tales reflect their concerns and the contradictions of their age. Today we have inherited their concerns and contradictions, and their tales still read like innovative strategies for survival. Most of all they provide hope that there is more to life than mastering the art of survival. Their "once upon a time" keeps alive our utopian longing for a better world that can be created out of our dreams and actions.

A Note on the Translation

This translation is based on the seventh, or final, edition of the *Kinder- und Hausmärchen (Children's and Household Tales)*, published in 1857. In addition, I have translated thirty-two tales that appeared in some of the other editions before 1857 but were eventually omitted by the Grimms for one reason or another. These tales are appearing in English for the first time, and thus the present edition provides readers with the most comprehensive translation of the Grimms' tales to date.

Although a great commotion was made in the press in 1983 when a tale by the Grimms was discovered in a letter and subsequently purchased and printed by an American publisher, this tale is not legitimately a Grimms' tale, for the brothers did not consider it significant enough to include in their collection. It is very much like the other posthumous tales, which Heinz Rölleke gathered and published in *Märchen aus dem Nachlass der Brüder Grimm* (Bonn: Bouvier, 1977)—interesting, but not appealing enough for the Grimms to stamp their own imprint on it. On the other hand, all of the tales in the present collection were shaped and refined by the Grimms, even those that they eventually omitted.

The tales of the Brothers Grimm have been translated numerous times, and some readers might justly raise the question: Why publish another translation? However, with the exception of the work by Ralph Mannheim, David Luke, and Brian Alderson, the available translations are lacking on two accounts: either they are too anachronistic and imitative of Victorian models, or they seek to streamline the language according to present-day usage and often negate the historical features of the tales. In preparing the present translation, I have endeavored to respect the historical character and idioms of each tale and to retain a nineteenth-century flavor while introducing contemporary vocabulary and terms when they were, in my estimation, more apropos. Furthermore, I have tried to let the different voices within the Grimms' collection speak for themselves.

Although Wilhelm Grimm (more than Jacob) revised and altered most of the tales over a period of approximately forty years to make them more graceful and suitable for children and a proper Christian upbringing, many of the tales are still mixed with coarse and naive expressions of their original lower-class storytellers. In fact, a good number of the tales were printed in German dialect and possess the rustic, natural tone that the Grimms admired and attempted to imitate in their refined, high German renditions. The unevenness and variety in tone and expression are actually qualities that I too have sought to convey without destroying the flow of a tale.

The Grimms tended to make their tales more dramatic and colorful in their revisions, especially by shifting indirect speech to direct speech. I have emphasized the dramatic qualities of the tales even more by indenting the direct speech and creating more paragraphs. In many instances, I have provided smoother transition by adding phrases, but I have not departed radically from the texts. The Grimms had a fine ear for unusual idioms and proverbs and often invented their own. These expressions appeared odd and quaint in their own time, and I have retained them because they continue to be striking today.

If there were inconsistencies in the narrative structure, I have endeavored to resolve them without changing the meaning of the tale or incident. In some cases, I have left the contradictions because they were too minor to change. Here and there the translations of the titles will differ with those in other translations. My purpose in doing so has been to make the titles historically more accurate. The Grimms hoped to find great truths about the German people and their laws and customs by collecting their tales, for they believed that language was what created national bonds and stamped the national character of a people. Little did they know that their "German" collection would transcend their own country and through translations create universal bonds of understanding.

This project was originally conceived with the help of LuAnn Walther, whose advice and gentle prodding enabled me to dare a new translation. Deborah Futter assumed charge of the manuscript at a crucial time and supported me with fine suggestions and encouragement. Cecilia Hunt did a remarkable job of editing the translation and catching my errors, while Anne Greenberg made certain that our productive efforts would reach fruition. During the entire process, my wife, Carol Dines, helped me revise many of the translations, and I am most grateful for the understanding and criticism she has given me.

JACK ZIPES
Gainesville, 1986

The Frog King, or Iron Heinrich

IN OLDEN TIMES, when wishing still helped, there lived a king whose daughters were all beautiful, but the youngest was so beautiful that the sun itself, which had seen so many things, was always filled with amazement each time it cast its rays upon her face. Now, there was a great dark forest near the king's castle, and in this forest, beneath an old linden tree, was a well. Whenever the days were very hot, the king's daughter would go into this forest and sit down by the edge of the cool well. If she became bored, she would take her golden ball, throw it into the air, and catch it. More than anything else she loved playing with this ball.

One day it so happened that the ball did not fall back into the princess's little hand as she reached out to catch it. Instead, it bounced right by her and rolled straight into the water. The princess followed it with her eyes, but the ball disappeared, and the well was deep, so very deep that she could not see the bottom. She began to cry, and she cried louder and louder, for there was nothing that could comfort her. As she sat there grieving over her loss a voice called out to her, "What's the matter, Princess? Your tears could move even a stone to pity."

She looked around to see where the voice was coming from and saw a frog sticking his thick, ugly head out of the water. "Oh, it's you, you old water-splasher!" she said. "I'm crying because my golden ball has fallen into the well."

"Be quiet and stop crying," the frog responded. "I'm sure I can help you. But what will you give me if I fetch your plaything?"

"Whatever you like, dear frog," she said. "My clothes, my pearls and jewels, even the golden crown I'm wearing on my head."

"I don't want your clothes, your pearls and jewels, or your golden crown," the frog replied. "But if you will love me and let me be your companion and playmate, and let me sit beside you at the table, eat from your little golden plate, drink out of your little cup, and sleep in your little bed—if you promise me all that, I'll dive down and retrieve your golden ball.''

"Oh, yes," she said. "I'll promise you anything you want if only you'll bring back the ball!" However, she thought, What nonsense that stupid frog talks! He just sits in the water croaking with the rest of the frogs. How can he expect a human being to accept him as a companion?

Once the frog had her promise, he dipped his head under the water, dived downward, and soon came paddling back to the surface with the ball in his mouth. When he threw it onto the grass, the princess was so delighted to see her beautiful plaything again that she picked it up and ran off with it.

"Wait, wait!" cried the frog. "Take me with you. I can't run like you."

He croaked as loudly as he could, but what good did it do? She paid no attention to him. Instead, she rushed home and soon forgot about the poor frog, who had to climb back down into his well.

The next day, as she sat at the table with the king and his courtiers and ate from her little golden plate, something came crawling *splish, splash, splish, splash* up the marble steps. When it reached the top, it knocked at the door and cried out, "Princess, youngest daughter, open up!"

She ran to see who was outside. But when she opened the door and saw the frog, she quickly slammed the door shut and went back to the table in a state of fright. The king could clearly see her heart was thumping and said, "My child, what are you afraid of? Has a giant come to get you?"

"Oh, no," she answered. "It's not a giant, but a nasty frog."

"What does a frog want from you?"

"Oh, dear Father, yesterday when I was sitting and playing near the well in the forest, my golden ball fell into the water, and because I cried so much, the frog fetched it for me, and because he insisted, I had to promise he could be my companion. But I never thought he'd get out of the water. Now he's outside and wants to come in and be with me."

Just then there was a second knock at the door, and a voice cried out:

"Princess, Princess, youngest daughter,
open up and let me in.
Have you forgotten
what you promised
down by the well's cool water?

♦ 2 ♦

Princess, Princess, youngest daughter,
open up and let me in.''

Then the king said, "If you've made a promise, you must keep it.
Go and let him in."

After she went and opened the door, the frog hopped into the
room and followed her right to her chair, where he plopped himself
down and cried out, "Lift me up beside you!"

She refused until the king finally ordered her to do so. Once the
frog was on the chair, he wanted to climb onto the table, and when
he made it to the table, he said, "Now push your little golden plate
nearer to me so we can eat together."

To be sure, she did this, but it was quite
clear that she did not like it. The frog
enjoyed his meal, while each bite the princess
took got stuck in her throat. Finally he said, "I've
had enough, and now I'm tired. Carry me upstairs
to your room and get your silken bed ready so we
can go to sleep."

The princess began to cry because the cold frog
frightened her. She did not even have enough courage to touch him, and yet, now she was supposed to
let him sleep in her beautiful, clean bed. But the king gave her an
angry look and said, "It's not proper to scorn someone who helped
you when you were in trouble!"

So she picked up the frog with her two fingers, carried him
upstairs, and set him down in a corner. Soon after she had got into
bed, he came crawling over to her and said, "I'm tired and want to

sleep as much as you do. Lift me up, or I'll tell your father!''

This made the princess extremely angry, and after she picked him up, she threw him against the wall with all her might.

"Now you can have your rest, you nasty frog!"

However, when he fell to the ground, he was no longer a frog but a prince with kind and beautiful eyes. So, in keeping with her father's wishes, she accepted him as her dear companion and husband, whereupon the prince told her that a wicked witch had cast a spell over him and no one could have got him out of the well except her, and now he intended to take her to his kingdom the next day. Then they fell asleep, and in the morning, when the sun woke them, a coach drawn by eight white horses came driving up. The horses had ostrich plumes on their heads and harnesses with golden chains. At the back of the coach stood Faithful Heinrich, the young king's servant. He had been so distressed when he had learned his master had been turned into a frog that he had ordered three iron bands be wrapped around his heart to keep it from bursting from grief and sadness. But now the coach had come to bring the young king back to his kingdom, and Faithful Heinrich helped the prince and princess into it and then took his place at the back again. He was overcome by joy because his master had been saved.

When they had traveled some distance, the prince heard a cracking noise behind him, as if something had broken. He turned around and cried out:

"Heinrich, the coach is breaking!"
"No, my lord, it's really nothing
but the band around my heart,
for it nearly fell apart
when the witch did cast her spell
and made you live as a frog in a well."

The cracking noise was heard two more times along the way, and the prince thought each time that the coach was breaking, but the noise was only the sound of the bands snapping from Faithful Heinrich's heart, for he knew his master was safe and happy.

◆ 2 ◆

The Companionship of the Cat and the Mouse

A CAT HAD MADE the acquaintanceship of a mouse and had talked so much about his great love and friendship for her that he eventually convinced her to live with him in the same house and set up a common household.

"But we must get supplies for the winter," said the cat, "or else we'll starve. A little mouse like you can't venture just anywhere, for one of these days you might get caught in a trap."

They acted on his good advice and bought a little jar of fat, but they did not know where to put it. Finally, after long deliberation, the cat said, "I can't think of a safer place than the church. No one would dare take anything away from there. Let's put it under the altar, and we won't touch it unless we really need it."

The little jar was safely stored away, but it was not long before the cat felt a craving for it and said to the mouse, "I've been meaning to tell you, little mouse. My cousin gave birth to a baby boy, white with brown spots, and I've been asked to be godfather. I'm to hold him at the christening. Would you mind letting me go out today and looking after the house by yourself?"

"No, of course not," answered the mouse. "Go, for God's sake. If you get something good to eat, think of me. I sure would like to have a drink of that sweet, red christening wine."

Naturally, none of what the cat had said was true. He did not have a cousin, nor had he been asked to be godfather. He went straight to the church, crept to the little jar of fat, and began licking and licking until he had licked the skin off the top. Then he strolled over the roofs of the city and contemplated his opportunities. After a while he stretched himself out in the sun and wiped his whiskers whenever he thought about the little jar of fat. It was not until evening that he returned home.

"Well, you're back," the mouse said. "I'm sure you had a wonderful day."

"It wasn't bad," the cat responded.

The Cat and Mouse in Partnership~

"What name did they give the child?" the mouse asked.

"*Skin-Off,*" the cat said dryly.

"Skin-Off?" exclaimed the mouse. "That's a strange and unusual name. Is it common in your family?"

"What's there to it?" the cat said. "It's no worse than Crumb-Thief, as your godchildren are called."

Shortly after that the cat felt another great craving and said to the mouse, "You've got to do me a favor again and look after the house by yourself. I've been asked to be godfather once more, and since the child has a white ring around his neck, I can't refuse."

The good mouse consented, and the cat went slinking behind the city wall to the church, where he ate up half the jar of fat.

"Nothing tastes better," he said, "than what you eat yourself," and he was very satisfied with his day's work. When he returned, the mouse asked, "What was this child christened?"

"*Half-Gone,*" answered the cat.

"Half-Gone! You don't say! I've never heard of such a name in all my life. I'll bet it's not on the list of proper names."

Soon the cat's mouth began watering once more for the delicacy.

"All good things come in threes," he said to the mouse. "I've been asked to be godfather again. This child's all black and has white paws. Aside from that there's not a white hair on his body. That only happens once every few years. You'll let me go, won't you?"

"Skin-Off! Half-Gone!" the mouse responded. "Those are really curious names. I'm beginning to wonder about them."

"Look, you sit at home in your dark gray fur coat and your long pigtail," the cat said, "and you begin imagining things. That's because you don't go out during the day."

While the cat was gone, the mouse cleaned the house and put it in order. Meanwhile the greedy cat ate up the rest of the jar.

"It's only after everything's all gone," the cat said to himself, "that you can really begin to rest."

It was very late at night by the time the cat returned home, and he was fat and stuffed. The mouse asked right away what name had been given to the third child.

"You won't like this one either," the cat said. "It's *All-Gone*."

"All-Gone!" exclaimed the mouse. "That's the most suspicious of all the names. I've never seen it in print. All-Gone! What's it supposed to mean?" She shook her head, rolled herself up into a ball, and fell asleep.

From then on, no one asked the cat to be a godfather. But, when winter came and there was nothing more to be found outside, the mouse thought about their supply of fat and said, "Come, cat, let's go to our jar that we've been saving. It'll taste good."

"Yes," said the cat. "You'll enjoy the taste just as much as if you stuck your dainty tongue out the window."

They set out on their way, and when they got there, the jar of fat was still in its place, but it was empty.

"Oh," said the mouse. "Now I know what's happened! It's as clear as day. Some nice friend you are! You ate it all up when you went to be a godfather. First the skin, then half, then . . ."

"You better be quiet!" yelled the cat. "One more word, and I'll eat you up!"

"All gone" was already on the tip of the mouse's tongue. No sooner did she say it than the cat jumped on her, grabbed her, and devoured her.

You see, that's the way of the world.

◈ 3 ◈

The Virgin Mary's Child

A POOR WOODCUTTER and his wife lived at the edge of a large forest, and their only child was a little girl who was three years old. They were so poor they could not have daily meals anymore and did not know how they would provide food for their daughter. One morning the woodcutter, who was distressed by all this, went into the forest to work. As he began chopping wood a tall, beautiful woman suddenly appeared before him. She was wearing a crown of shining stars on her head and said to him, "I am the Virgin Mary, mother of the Christ Child. Since you are poor and needy, bring me your child. I'll take her with me and be her mother and look after her."

The woodcutter obeyed her. He brought his child and gave her to the Virgin Mary, who took her up to heaven. Everything went well for the girl there: she ate cake and drank sweet milk. Her clothes were made of gold, and the little angels played with her. One day, when she turned fourteen, the Virgin Mary summoned her and said, "Dear child, I intend to go on a long journey, and I want you to take care of the keys to the thirteen doors of the kingdom of heaven. You may open twelve of the doors and look at all the marvelous things inside, but I forbid you to open the thirteenth door that this little key unlocks. Be on your guard and don't open it. If you do, you'll be unhappy."

The maiden promised to be obedient, and when the Virgin Mary had departed, she began to explore the rooms of the kingdom of heaven. Every day she opened a new room until she had unlocked twelve of them. In each one there was an apostle in dazzling light, and she was delighted by the glory and splendor, and the little angels who always accompanied her were delighted too. Now the forbidden door was the only one left, and she felt a great desire to know what was inside, and she said to the little angels, "I won't open it all the way, and I won't go inside. I'll only unlock it so we can peek through the crack a little."

"Oh, no!" said the little angels. "That would be a sin. The Virgin Mary's forbidden it, and something awful could happen to you."

So the maiden said nothing more about this, but she could not still the urge in her heart. Her desire kept gnawing and pecking away at her and gave her no peace. One day when the angels had all gone out, she thought, Now I'm all alone and can take a peek. No one will know if I do.

She looked for the key, and when she got it in her hand, she put it in the lock and turned it. Suddenly the door sprang open, and there she saw the Holy Trinity sitting in fire and splendor. She stood still for a while and looked at everything in amazement. Then she touched the light just a little with her finger, and the finger turned golden. All at once she was overcome by a tremendous fear, and she slammed the door and ran away. The fear would not abate, no matter what she did, and her heart pounded constantly and could not be calmed. Moreover, the gold stayed on her finger and would not go away even though she washed and rubbed it as much as she could.

Soon after, the Virgin Mary returned from her journey. She summoned the maiden and asked her to return the keys of heaven to her. When the maiden handed her the bunch of keys, the Virgin looked into her eyes and said, "Didn't you also open the thirteenth door?"

"No," she answered.

Then the Virgin Mary put her hand on the maiden's heart and could feel it pounding and pounding. Now she knew the maiden had disobeyed her command and had opened the door. Once again she asked, "You opened the door, didn't you?"

"No," said the maiden for a second time.

When the Virgin Mary glanced at the finger that had become golden from touching the heavenly fire, she knew the maiden had sinned.

"Didn't you?" she asked for a third time.

"No," the maiden replied for the third time.

Then the Virgin Mary said, "You've disobeyed me, and you've even lied. You're no longer worthy enough to stay in heaven."

The maiden sank then into a deep sleep, and when she awoke, she was lying on earth in the middle of a wilderness. She wanted to cry out, but she could not utter a sound. She jumped up and wanted to run away, but wherever she turned, she encountered thick hedges of thorns and could not make her way through them. She was imprisoned in this desolate spot and had to make an old hollow tree her dwelling place. When night came, she crawled inside and fell asleep. If it rained and there was stormy weather, she found shelter there. But it was a miserable life, and whenever she thought about how beautiful it had been in heaven and how the angels had played with her, she shed bitter tears. Roots and wild berries were her only food, and she went out looking for them as far as she could walk. In the fall she gathered the nuts and leaves that fell to the ground and carried them into the hollow tree. The nuts were her food in the winter and, when snow and ice came, she crawled into the leaves like a poor little animal so she would not freeze. Before long her clothes became tattered, and one piece after the other fell off her body. As soon as the sun began to shine again, she went out and sat in front of the tree. Her long hair covered her on all sides like a cloak. She spent year after year like this and felt the sorrow and misery of the world.

One day, when the trees were fresh and green again, the king of the country came to hunt in the forest and began chasing a deer.

When it fled into the bushes that surrounded the maiden's dwelling spot in the forest, he got off his horse, pulled the bushes apart, and cut a path for himself with his sword. When he finally got through, he saw a wonderful-looking maiden sitting under a tree, and her golden hair covered her down to her toes. He stood still and gazed at her full of amazement. Then he addressed her and said, "Who are you? Why are you sitting in this desolate spot?"

However, she did not answer because she could not open her mouth.

So the king continued to speak. "Would you like to come to my castle with me?"

She nodded her head just a little. Then the king took her in his arms, carried her to his horse, and rode home with her. When he reached the royal castle, he had her dressed in beautiful garments and gave her plenty of everything. Even though she could not speak, she was so sweet and beautiful that he fell in love with her, and it was not long before he married her.

When about a year had passed, the queen gave birth to a son. Immediately following this, in the night as she lay alone in bed, the Virgin Mary appeared before her and said, "If you'll tell me the truth and confess that you unlocked the forbidden door, I'll open your mouth and give you back the power of speech. If you persist in your sin and stubbornly deny it, I shall take your newborn baby away with me."

The queen was given the power to answer, but she remained stubborn and said, "No, I didn't open the forbidden door."

So the Virgin Mary took the newborn baby out of her arms and disappeared with him. The next morning, when the child could not be found, a rumor began circulating among the people that the queen was an ogress and had killed her own child. She heard all this but could do nothing to deny it. However, the king refused to believe it because he loved her so much.

After a year had passed, the queen gave birth to another son. Once more the Virgin Mary came to her and said, "If you'll confess that you opened the forbidden door, I'll give you back your child and loosen your tongue. But if you persist in your sin and deny it, I'll take this newborn baby away with me too."

Once again the queen said, "No, I didn't open the forbidden door."

So the Virgin Mary took the child out of her arms and went away with him to heaven. The next morning, when this baby had also vanished, the people said quite openly that the queen had devoured it, and the king's councillors demanded that she be executed. However, the king loved her so much that he would not believe it and ordered his councillors to stop talking about it on pain of death.

The following year the queen gave birth to a beautiful little daughter, and at night the Virgin Mary appeared before her for the third time and said, "Follow me."

She took her by the hand and led her to heaven, where she showed her how her two oldest children were laughing and playing with a globe of the earth. When the queen expressed her delight, the Virgin Mary asked, "Hasn't your heart softened yet? If you'll confess that you opened the forbidden door, I'll give you back your two little sons."

But the queen answered for a third time, "No, I didn't open the forbidden door."

Then the Virgin Mary let her sink down to earth again and took away her third child too. The next morning, when it became known, everyone cried out openly, "The queen is an ogress! She must be sentenced to death!"

The king could no longer restrain his councillors, and the queen was brought to trial. Since she could not answer or defend herself, she was condemned to die at the stake. The wood was gathered, and when she was bound to the stake and the fire began to burn all around her, the hard ice of her pride melted, and her heart was moved by repentance. If only I could confess before I die that I opened the door! she thought. Suddenly her voice came back, and she cried aloud, "Yes, Mary, I did it!"

All at once rain poured from the sky and put out the flames. A light erupted above her, and the Virgin Mary descended with the two little sons at either side and the newborn daughter in her arms. She said to the queen kindly, "Those who repent their sins and confess will be forgiven."

Then she handed the queen her three children, loosened her tongue, and bestowed happiness on her for the rest of her life.

◈ 4 ◈

A Tale About the Boy Who Went Forth
to Learn What Fear Was

A FATHER had two sons. The older was smart and sensible and could cope in any situation, while the younger was stupid and could neither learn nor understand anything. Whenever people encountered him, they said, "He'll always be a burden to his father!"

If there were things to be done, the older son was always the one who had to take care of them. Yet, if the father asked the older son to fetch something toward evening or during the night, and if that meant he would have to pass through the churchyard or some other scary place, he would answer, "Oh, no, Father, I won't go there. It gives me the creeps!" Indeed, he was afraid.

Sometimes stories that would send shivers up your spine were told by their fireside at night, and the listeners would say: "Oh, it gives me the creeps!" Often the younger son would be sitting in the corner and listening, but he never understood what they meant. "They're always saying 'It gives me the creeps! It gives me the creeps!' But it doesn't give me the creeps. It's probably some kind of a trick that I don't understand."

One day his father happened to say to him, "Listen, you over there in the corner, you're getting too big and strong. It's time you learned how to earn your living. Look how hard your brother works, while you're just a hopeless case."

"Oh, no, Father," he responded. "I'd gladly learn something. If possible, I'd like to learn how to get the creeps. That's something I know nothing about."

When the older son heard that, he laughed and thought to himself, Dear Lord, my brother's really a dumbbell! He'll never amount to anything. You've got to start young to get anywhere.

The father sighed and answered, "You're sure to learn all about getting the creeps in due time, but it won't help you earn a living."

Shortly after this, the sexton came to the house for a visit, and the father complained about his younger son, that he was incapable of doing anything, much less learning and knowing anything. "Just think, when I asked him what he wanted to do to earn a living, he actually said he wanted to learn how to get the creeps.''

"If that's all he wants," the sexton replied, "he can learn it at my place. Just hand him over to me, and I'll smooth over his rough edges."

The father was pleased to do this because he thought, The boy needs some shaping up.

So the sexton took him to his house, where the boy was assigned the task of ringing the church bell. After a few days had passed, the sexton woke him at midnight and told him to get up, climb the church steeple, and ring the bell.

Now you'll learn what the creeps are, the sexton thought, and secretly went up ahead of him. When the boy reached the top and turned around to grab hold of the bell rope, he saw a white figure standing on the stairs across from the sound hole.

"Who's there?" he cried out, but the figure did not answer, nor did it move an inch. "Answer me," the boy shouted, "or get out of here! You've no business being here at night."

However, the sexton did not move, for he wanted to make the boy think he was a ghost.

The boy shouted a second time, "What do you want? If you're an honest man, say something, or I'll throw you down the stairs!"

He really can't be as mean as that, the sexton thought, and he kept still, standing there as if he were made of stone.

The boy shouted at him a third time, and when that did not help, he lunged at the ghost and pushed him down the stairs. The ghost fell ten steps and lay in a corner. The boy then rang the bell, went home, got into bed without saying a word, and fell asleep. The sexton's wife waited for her husband for a long time, but he failed to return. Finally, she became anxious, woke the boy, and asked, "Do you know where my husband is? He climbed the steeple ahead of you."

"No," replied the boy. "But someone was standing across from the sound hole. When he refused to answer me or go away, I thought he was some sort of scoundrel and pushed him down the stairs. Why don't you go and see if it wasn't him? I'd feel sorry if it was."

The wife ran off and found her husband, who was lying in a corner and moaning because of a broken leg. She carried him down the stairs and then rushed off to the boy's father screaming as she went.

"Your boy has caused a terrible accident!" she cried out. "He threw my husband down the stairs and made him break a leg. Get that good-for-nothing out of our house!"

The father was mortified and ran straight to the sexton's house, where he began scolding the boy. "What kind of godless tricks have you been playing? The devil must have put you up to it!"

"Father," he replied, "just listen to me. I'm completely innocent. He was standing there in the dark like someone who had evil designs. I didn't know who he was and warned him three times to say something or go away."

"Ah," said the father, "you'll never be anything but trouble for me! Get out of my sight. I don't want to see you anymore."

"All right, Father. Gladly. Just give me until daylight, and I'll go away and learn how to get the creeps. Then I'll know a trick or two and be able to earn a living."

"Learn what you want," the father said. "It's all the same to me. Here's fifty talers. Take them and go out into the wide world, but don't tell anyone where you come from or who your father is because I'm ashamed of you."

"Yes, Father, as you wish. If that's all you desire, I can easily bear that in mind."

At daybreak the boy put the fifty talers in his pocket, went out on the large highway, and kept saying to himself, "If I could only get the creeps! If I could only get the creeps!"

As the boy was talking to himself a man came along and overheard him. When they had gone some distance together, they caught sight of the gallows, and the man said to him, "You see the tree over there. That's where seven men were wedded to the ropemaker's daughter. Now they're learning how to fly. Sit down beneath the tree and wait till night comes. Then you'll certainly learn how to get the creeps."

"If that's all it takes," the boy responded, "I can do it with ease. And, if I learn how to get the creeps as quickly as that, you shall have my fifty talers. Just come back here tomorrow morning."

The boy went to the gallows, sat down beneath it, and waited until evening came. Since he was cold, he made a fire. Nevertheless, at midnight the wind became colder, and he could not get warm in spite of the fire. When the wind knocked the hanged men against each other and they swung back and forth, he thought, If you're freezing down here by the fire, they must really be cold and shivering up there. Since he felt sorry for them, he took a ladder, climbed up, untied one hanged man after the other, and hauled all seven down to the ground. Then he stirred the fire, blew on it, and set them all around it so they might warm themselves. However, they sat there without moving, and their clothes caught on fire.

"Be careful," he said, "otherwise I'll hang you all back up there."

The dead men did not hear. Indeed, they just remained silent and let their rags continue to burn. Then the boy became angry and said, "If you won't take care, I can't help you, and I surely won't let you burn me."

So he hung them up again, all in a row, sat down by his fire, and fell asleep. Next morning the man came and wanted his fifty talers.

"Well," he said, "now you know what the creeps are?"

"No," answered the boy. "How should I know? Those men up there didn't open their mouths. They're so stupid they let the few old rags they're wearing get burned."

The man realized he would never get the fifty talers that day. So he went off saying, "Never in my life have I met anyone like that!"

The boy also went his way, and once again he began talking to himself. "Oh, if I could only get the creeps! If I could only get the creeps!"

A carter, who was walking behind him, overheard him and asked, "Who are you?"

"I don't know," answered the boy.

"Where do you come from?" the carter continued questioning him.

"I don't know."

"Who's your father?"

"I'm not allowed to tell."

"What's that you're always mumbling to yourself?"

"Oh," the boy responded, "I want to get the creeps, but nobody can teach me how."

"Stop your foolish talk," said the carter. "Come along with me, and I'll see if I can find a place for you to stay."

The boy went with the carter, and in the evening they reached an inn, where they intended to spend the night. As they entered the main room the boy spoke loudly once more. "If I could only get the creeps! If I could only get the creeps!"

The innkeeper heard this and laughed. "If that's what you desire," he remarked, "there'll be ample opportunity for you to get it here."

"Oh, be quiet!" the innkeeper's wife said. "There have already been enough foolish fellows who've lost their lives. It would be a mighty shame if that boy with such pretty eyes never saw the light of day again."

But the boy said, "It doesn't matter how hard it may be. I want to get the creeps. That's why I left home."

He kept bothering the innkeeper until the man told him about the haunted castle nearby, where one could really learn how to get the creeps. All he had to do was to spend three nights in it. The king had promised his daughter to anyone who would undertake the venture, and she was the most beautiful maiden under the sun. There were also great treasures in the castle guarded by evil spirits. Once the treasures were set free, they would be enough to make a poor man rich. Many men had already gone into the castle, but none had ever come out again.

The next morning the boy appeared before the king and said, "If I may have your permission, I'd like to spend three nights in the haunted castle."

The king looked at him and found the boy to his liking, so he said, "You may request three things to take with you into the castle, but they must be lifeless objects."

"Well then," he answered, "I'd like to have a fire, a lathe, and a carpenter's bench with a knife."

The king had these things carried into the castle for him during the day. Just before nightfall the boy himself went up to the castle, made a bright fire in one of the rooms, set up the carpenter's bench with the knife next to it, and sat down on the lathe.

"Oh, if I could only get the creeps!" he said. "But I don't think I'll learn it here either."

Toward midnight he wanted to stir the fire again, but just as he was blowing it, he suddenly heard a scream coming from a corner. "*Meow! Meow!* We're freezing!"

"You fools!" he cried out. "What are you screaming for? If you're freezing, come sit down by the fire and warm yourselves."

No sooner had he said that than two big black cats came over with a tremendous leap, sat down beside him, and glared ferociously at him with their fiery eyes. After a while, when they had warmed themselves, they said, "Comrade, let's play a round of cards."

"Why not?" he responded. "But first show me your paws."

They stretched out their claws.

"My goodness!" he said. "What long nails you have! Wait, I've got to give them a good clipping."

Upon saying that, he grabbed them by the scruffs of their necks, lifted them onto the carpenter's bench, and fastened their paws in a vise.

"I was keeping a sharp eye on you two," he said, "and now I've lost my desire to play cards."

Then he beat them to death and threw them into the water. But, after he had put an end to those two and was about to sit down at his fire again, black cats and black dogs on glowing chains came out of all the nooks and crannies, and they kept coming and coming so it was impossible for him to flee. They made a gruesome noise, stamped on his fire, tore it apart, and tried to put it out. He watched them calmly for a while, but when it became so awful that he could no longer stand it, he grabbed his knife and yelled, "Get out of here, you lousy creatures!" And he started swinging the knife. Some of them ran away while he killed the rest and threw them into the pond. When he returned to his place, he built up his fire again by blowing on the sparks and proceeded to warm himself. As he was sitting there, his eyelids grew heavy, and he felt a strong desire to sleep. Then he looked around and saw a large bed in the corner.

"That's just what I was looking for," he said and lay down on it. But just as he was about to shut his eyes, the bed began to move by itself and raced all around the castle.

"Keep it up," he said. "But go a little faster."

The bed sped on as though it were being drawn by six horses. It rolled through doorways and up and down stairs. Then all of a sudden, *bing-bang!* it turned upside down and lay on top of him like a mountain. But he flung the blankets and pillows in the air, climbed out, and said, "Now, anyone else who wants a ride can have one." He lay down by the fire and slept until it was day.

In the morning the king came, and when he saw the boy lying on the ground, he thought that he was dead and that the ghosts had killed him.

"What a pity! He was such a handsome fellow," the king said.

Upon hearing this, the boy sat up and said, "It's not over yet!"

The king was astonished but also glad and asked him how things had gone.

"Very well," he answered. "One night's over and done with. The other two will pass also."

Then he went to the innkeeper, who gaped at him in amazement.

"I never expected to see you alive again," he said. "Have you learned now what the creeps are?"

"No," he said. "It's no use. If only someone could tell me!"

The second night he went up to the old castle, sat down at the fire, and repeated his old refrain. "If I could only get the creeps!"

Toward midnight he heard a lot of noise and rumbling, first softly, then louder and louder. Soon it became quiet for a while until suddenly, with a loud cry, half a man came tumbling down the chimney and fell right at his feet.

"Hey there!" cried the boy. "There's a half missing. This isn't enough."

Once again the noise began. There was a roaring and howling, and the other half came tumbling down.

"Wait," the boy said. "I'll just give the fire a little stir for you."

After he had done that, he looked around and saw that the two pieces had joined together to form a gruesome-looking man who was now sitting in his place.

"That wasn't part of the bargain," said the boy. "The bench is mine."

The man tried to push him away, but the boy did not let him. Instead, he gave the man a mighty shove and sat back down in his place.

Suddenly more men came tumbling down the chimney, one after the other, and they brought nine dead men's bones and two dead men's skulls, set them up, and began to play a game of ninepins. The boy felt a desire to play as well and asked, "Hey, can I play too?"

"Yes, if you have money."

"Money enough," he answered, "but your balls aren't round."

He took the skulls, put them in the lathe, and turned them until they were round.

"Now they'll roll much better," he said. "Hurray! Let's have some fun!"

He joined their game and lost some of his money, but when the clock struck twelve, everything disappeared before his eyes, and he lay down and fell asleep in peace.

The next morning the king came to inquire about him, and he asked, "How did things go for you this time?"

"I played a game of ninepins," he said, "and I lost a few hellers."

"Didn't you get the creeps?"

"Not at all!" he responded. "I had a lot of fun. If I only knew what the creeps were!"

The third night he sat down on his bench again and said quite sadly, "If I could only get the creeps!"

When it grew late, six huge men came in carrying a coffin. Then he said, "Aha, that must be my cousin who died just a few days ago." He signaled to them with his finger and cried out, "Come here, little cousin, come here!"

They set the coffin on the ground, and he went over and lifted the lid. There was a dead man lying inside, and the boy felt his face, which was as cold as ice.

"Wait," he said. "I'll warm you up a bit."

He went to the fire, warmed his hand, and placed it on the dead man's face, but it remained cold. So he took the dead man out and set him near the fire, then put him on his lap and rubbed his arms until his blood began circulating again. When that did not work either, the boy recalled that two people can warm each other up when they lie in bed together. So he brought the man to the bed, covered him, and lay down beside him. After a while the dead man got warm and began to move.

"You see, cousin," said the boy. "What if I hadn't warmed you?"

But the dead man shouted, "Now I'm going to strangle you!"

"What?" the boy responded. "Is that my thanks? I'm going to put you right back into your coffin."

He lifted him up, tossed him inside, and shut the lid. Then the six men returned and carried the coffin away.

"I can't get the creeps," the boy said. "I'll never learn it here no matter how long I live."

Just then a ghastly-looking man entered. He was old and larger than the others and had a long white beard.

"Oh, you scoundrel!" the man cried out. "Now you'll learn what the creeps are, for you're about to die."

"Not so fast!" said the boy. "If I'm about to die, you'll have to get me first."

"Don't worry, I'll get you," said the monster.

"Easy does it. Don't talk so big! I'm just as strong as you are if not stronger."

"We'll see about that," said the old man. "If you're stronger than I am, I'll let you go. Come, let's give it a try."

He led the boy through dark passages to a smithy, picked up an ax, and drove an anvil right into the ground with one blow.

"I can do better than that," the boy said, and he went to the other anvil. The old man, with his white beard hanging down, drew near him to watch. The boy grabbed the ax, split the anvil in two with one blow, and wedged the old man's beard in the middle.

"Now I've got you!" the boy said. "It's your turn to die!"

He seized an iron and beat the old man until he whimpered and begged the boy to stop and promised to give him great treasures. The boy pulled out the ax and let him go. The old man led him back into the castle and showed him three chests full of gold in a cellar.

"One of them," he said, "belongs to the poor, the second to the king, and the third is yours."

Just then the clock struck twelve, and the ghost vanished, leaving the boy standing in the dark.

"I'll find my way out of here all the same," he said, and groped about until he found the way back to his room, where he fell asleep by the fire.

In the morning the king came and said, "Now you must have learned what the creeps are."

"No," he answered. "What are they? My dead cousin was here, and a bearded man came. He showed me a great deal of money down in the cellar, but nobody told me what the creeps are."

Then the king said, "You've saved the castle and shall marry my daughter."

"That's all fine and good," he answered, "but I still don't know what the creeps are."

Now the gold was brought up from the cellar, and the wedding was celebrated. The boy loved his wife dearly and was very happy, but he still kept saying, "If I could only get the creeps! If I could only get the creeps!"

After a while his wife became annoyed by that, but her chambermaid said, "Don't worry. I'll make sure he gets to know what the creeps are."

She went out to a brook that ran through the garden and fetched a bucket full of minnows. That night, when the young king was sleeping, his wife pulled the covers off him and poured the bucket full of cold water and minnows on him. Then the little fish began flapping all over him, causing him to wake up and exclaim, "Oh, I've got the creeps! I've got the creeps! Now I know, dear wife, just what the creeps are."

◈ 5 ◈

The Wolf and the Seven Young Kids

ONCE UPON A TIME there was an old goat who had seven young kids, and she loved them as any mother loves her children. One day she decided to go into the forest to fetch some food. So she called all seven of them to her and said, "Dear children, I'm going into the forest, and I want you to be on your guard against the wolf. If he gets in here, he'll eat you all up, skin and bones. That villain often disguises himself, but you can recognize him right away by his gruff voice and black feet."

"Dear Mother," the kids said, "we'll take good care of ourselves. Just go and don't worry about leaving us here."

The old goat bleated and went on her way with an easy mind, but it was not long before someone knocked at the door and called out, "Open up, dear children, your mother's back and has brought something for each one of you."

But the kids knew it was the wolf by his gruff voice.

"We're not opening up," they cried out. "You're not our mother. She has a lovely, soft voice, and yours is gruff. You're the wolf!"

The wolf went away to a shopkeeper and bought a big piece of chalk, which he ate, and it made his voice soft. Then he returned, knocked at the door, and called out, "Open up, dear children. Your mother's back and has brought something for each one of you."

But the wolf had put his black paw on the windowsill, and when the children saw it, they cried out, "We're not opening up. Our mother doesn't have a black paw like yours. You're the wolf!"

The wolf ran to a baker and said, "I've stubbed my toe. Put some dough on it for me." After the baker covered his paw, he ran to the miller and said, "Sprinkle some white flour on my paw."

The miller thought, The wolf wants to trick someone. So he refused. But the wolf said, "If you don't do it, I'll eat you up!"

This frightened the miller, so he made the wolf's paw white. Yes, indeed, that's the way people are.

Now the villain went to the house for a third time, knocked, and said, "Open up, children, your dear mother's back and has brought something from the forest for each one of you."

The kids called out, "First show us your paw so we know that you're really our dear mother."

He put his paw on the windowsill, and when they saw that it was white, they believed him and opened the door. Yet, who else but the wolf stepped inside! The kids were terrified and tried to hide themselves. The first kid ran and jumped under the table, the second into the bed, the third into the oven, the fourth into the kitchen, the fifth into the cupboard, the sixth under the washbasin, and the seventh into the clock case. However, the wolf began to find them and make short shrift of them. He swallowed one after the other down his throat, but he was unable to find the youngest in the clock case. When the wolf had satisfied his desire, he tottered off, lay down beneath a tree on a green meadow, and fell asleep.

Shortly after, the old goat came home from the forest, and oh, what a sight met her eyes! The door to her house was wide open.

The table, chairs, and benches were turned over. The washbasin lay on the ground in pieces. The cover and pillows were stripped off the bed. She looked for her children, but they were nowhere to be found. Finally, when she got near the youngest, she heard a soft voice calling, "Dear Mother, I'm in the clock case!"

She drew him out, and he told her that the wolf had come and had eaten up all the others. Well, you can imagine how she wept over her poor children.

At length she went outside, still grieving, while the youngest kid ran beside her. When they reached the meadow, she found the wolf snoring so loudly that the tree branches above him were trembling. She examined him from all sides and saw that something was moving and wriggling in his stuffed stomach. Oh, God! she thought. Could it be that my poor children that he gobbled up for his supper are still alive?

She sent the little kid home to fetch scissors, needle, and thread. Then she cut the monster's belly open, and no sooner did she make the first cut than a kid stuck out his head. As she cut some more all six of them jumped out, one after the other. They were all still alive and had not suffered the least bit of harm, for the monster's gluttony had been so great that he had swallowed them whole. What joy there was! They hugged their dear mother and hopped about like a tailor at his own wedding. But the old goat said, "Now go and look for some stones in the field. We'll fill the godless beast's belly with them while he's still asleep."

The seven kids quickly fetched some stones and put as many as they could into his stomach. Then the old goat sewed him up again with such speed that he did not notice a thing, nor did he even stir. When the wolf had slept to his content, he stood up, and since the stones in his stomach had made him very thirsty, he wanted to go to a well and have a drink. However, as he began to walk, he swayed back and forth, and the stones in his body knocked against each other and rattled. Then he cried out:

"What's that in my belly rumbling?
Could it be my bones are crumbling?
Six little kids I thought I ate;
they're more like stones with all their weight."

When he reached the well and leaned over to drink the water, the heavy stones pulled him in, and he was drowned in a miserable way. Upon seeing this, the seven kids ran up to the well and cried aloud, "The wolf is dead! The wolf is dead!"

Then they took their mother and danced for joy around the well.

◈ 6 ◈

Faithful Johannes

ONCE UPON A TIME there was an old king who was sick, and he thought, This will surely be my deathbed. Then he said aloud, "Tell Faithful Johannes to come to me."

Faithful Johannes, his most cherished servant, had been given this name because of his lifelong loyalty to the king. When he reached the old man's bedside, the king said to him, "Most Faithful Johannes, I feel that my end is drawing near, but I am not worried about anything except my son. He is still young in years and doesn't always know what's best for him. You must promise to teach him everything he should know and be his foster father, or I shall not be able to close my eyes in peace."

"I will not forsake him," Faithful Johannes reassured him, "and I will serve him faithfully even if it costs me my life."

"Now I can die in comfort and in peace," the old king said, and then added, "After my death you're to show him the entire castle— all the rooms, halls, and vaults, along with the treasures that are in them. But I do not want you to show him the room at the end of the long hallway, where the portrait of the Princess of the Golden Roof is hidden. If he sees that portrait, he'll fall passionately in love with her and lose consciousness for a while, and then he'll be obliged to undertake great risks because of her. You must protect him against this."

Once again Faithful Johannes assured the old king he would keep his promise. The king then became silent, laid his head on his pillow, and died. After the old king was buried, Faithful Johannes told the young king what he had promised the old king on his deathbed and said, "I intend to keep my promise and remain just as faithful to you as I was to your father, even if it costs me my life."

When the mourning period ended, Faithful Johannes said to him, "It's now time for you to see what you've inherited. So I shall show you the castle of your forefathers."

He led the young king all around the castle, upstairs and down, and let him see all the treasures and splendid rooms. But there was one room he did not open, for it contained the dangerous portrait, which was placed in such a way that one would see it the moment the door was opened. Furthermore, it was such a wonderful painting that it appeared to be real and alive, and there was nothing more beautiful or more lovely in the whole world. Now, the young king quickly noticed that Faithful Johannes kept passing by one door, and therefore he said, "Why don't you ever open this door for me?"

"There's something in there that would horrify you," Faithful Johannes replied.

"I've seen the entire castle," the king said, "and I also want to know what's in there."

He went and tried to open the door by force, but Faithful Johannes restrained him and said, "I promised your father before his death that you would not see what is inside this room. It could cause great misfortune for you and me."

"No, that can't be!" the young king responded. "If I *don't* get in, it will certainly be the end of me, because I won't be able to rest day or night until I've seen the room with my own eyes. You won't get me to move from this spot unless you unlock the door."

When Faithful Johannes saw there was nothing he could do, he picked out the key from the large bunch he was carrying. His heart was heavy, and he heaved many sighs as he opened the door. He made sure that he entered first, because he intended to cover the portrait with his body so the king would not see it. But what good did that do? The king stood on his tiptoes and looked over his shoulder. When he glimpsed the maiden's magnificent portrait, which glistened with gold and jewels, he fell to the ground unconscious. Faithful Johannes lifted him up, carried him to his bed, and was very concerned.

Disaster has struck, he thought. Good Lord, what will come of it all? Then he gave the king some wine to refresh him, whereupon he regained consciousness. The first words he spoke were, "Oh, who is that beautiful maiden in the picture?"

"That's the Princess of the Golden Roof," answered Faithful Johannes.

"My love for her is so great," continued the king, "that even if all the leaves on all the trees were tongues, they wouldn't be able to express how I feel. I intend to risk my life to win her, and since you're my most Faithful Johannes, you must help me."

It took the faithful servant a long time to determine how they might proceed, for it was difficult to gain access to the princess. Finally, he thought of a way and said to the king, "Everything she has around her is made of gold—the tables, chairs, dishes, cups, bowls, and all the household utensils. There are five tons of gold in your treasury. Have the goldsmiths of your kingdom make one ton of it into different kinds of vessels and utensils and into all sorts of birds, wild game, and marvelous animals that will please her. Then we'll take all this and travel there to try our luck."

The king had all the goldsmiths summoned to him, and they had to work day and night until the most magnificent things were ready. When the golden objects were all loaded on board a ship, Faithful Johannes put on the clothes of a merchant, as did the king so that he would not be recognized. Then they sailed across the sea, and they kept sailing until they came to the city where the Princess of the Golden Roof made her home.

Faithful Johannes told the king to stay on board the ship and to wait for him. "I may come back with the princess," he said. "So make sure that everything's in order. Have the golden vessels set out on display and have your men decorate the entire ship."

He then gathered together all kinds of golden trinkets in his apron, went ashore, and began walking toward the royal castle. When he reached the courtyard, a beautiful maiden was standing at the well. She had two golden buckets in her hands and was drawing water. Just as she turned around and got ready to carry the sparkling water away, she noticed the stranger and asked him who he was.

"I'm a merchant," he answered, while opening his apron so she could see what was in it.

"Goodness, what beautiful golden trinkets!" she exclaimed. Then she put the buckets down and examined the treasures, one after the other. "The princess must see these things," she remarked. "She takes so much pleasure in golden objects that I'm certain she'll buy all you have."

She took him by the hand and led him up to the palace, for she was the chambermaid. When the princess saw the wares, she was delighted and said, "They're so beautifully wrought that I'll buy everything you have."

But Faithful Johannes said, "I'm only a rich merchant's servant. What I have here is nothing compared to what my master has on his ship. Indeed, he has the most artful and precious things that have ever been made in gold."

The princess wanted everything brought up to the castle, but he said, "There is such a huge number of objects that it would take many days to do this. Besides, your palace is not large enough, for you would need many more rooms to display all the articles."

Now her curiosity and desire were roused even more, so that she finally said, "Take me to the ship. I'll go there myself to look over your master's treasures."

So, feeling very happy, Faithful Johannes conducted her to the ship. When the king caught sight of the princess and saw that she was even more beautiful than her portrait, he felt as though his heart would burst. After she climbed aboard the ship and the king led her inside the cabin, Faithful Johannes remained behind with the helmsman and ordered the ship to cast off. "Set all sails so that our ship will fly like a bird!"

Inside the cabin the king showed the princess the golden vessels, each and every piece: the dishes, the cups, the bowls, the birds, the wild game, and the marvelous animals. She looked at everything for many hours, and in her joy she did not notice that the ship had sailed. After she had examined the last piece, she thanked the merchant and wanted to go home. But, when she stepped out on deck, she saw that the ship was on the high seas, far from land, and racing forward at full sail.

"Oh!" she cried out in horror. "You've deceived me! I'm being kidnapped, and I'm in the hands of a merchant no less! I'd rather die!"

But the king seized her hand and said, "I'm not a merchant. I'm a king, and I'm not inferior to you in birth. I tricked you and carried you off by stealth because I was overwhelmed by my love for you. The first time I saw your portrait, I fainted and fell to the ground."

When the Princess of the Golden Roof heard this, she felt more at ease, and her heart went out to him in such a way that she consented to be his wife.

While they were sailing on the high seas, however, Faithful Johannes saw three ravens flying through the air as he was sitting and playing music in the bow of the ship. When they approached, he stopped playing and listened, for he understood their language quite well. One of them cried out, "My, he's bringing the Princess of the Golden Roof home with him!"

"Yes," responded the second, "but he doesn't have her yet."

"You're wrong, he does," the third said. "She's sitting right beside him in the ship."

Then the first raven began to speak again. "What good will that do him? When they reach land, a horse as red as a fox will come trotting up to him, and the king will want to mount it. But, if he does, the horse will ride off with him and soar into the air, so he'll never be able to see his maiden again."

"Is there no way he can be saved?" asked the second.

"Oh, yes, if someone else jumps on the horse quickly, takes out the gun that's bound to be in the saddle holster, and shoots the horse dead. This way the young king will be saved. But who knows that? And, even if someone knows it and tells it to the king, that person will be turned into stone from the tips of his toes to his knees.''

"I know still more," the second raven said. "Even if the horse is killed, the young king will not keep his bride. When they go to the castle together, he will find a ready-made bridal outfit in a basin. It will look as if it were woven out of gold and silver, yet it's nothing but sulfur and pitch. If he puts it on, it will burn him down to the very bone and marrow.''

"Is there no way he can be saved?" asked the third raven.

"Oh, yes," said the second. "Someone must grab the shirt with gloves, throw it into the fire, and let it burn. Then the young king will be saved. But what good will that do? Whoever knows this and tells the king will be turned to stone from his knees to his heart.''

"I know still more," said the third raven. "Even if the bridal outfit is burned, the king will still not be able to keep his bride. After the wedding, there will be a ball, and when the young queen begins to dance, she will suddenly turn pale and fall down as if she were dead. If no one lifts her up, draws three drops of blood from her right breast, and spits them out, she will die. But whoever reveals what he knows will have his entire body turned to stone from top to bottom.''

After having talked about all this, the ravens flew away. Faithful Johannes had understood everything they had said, and from then on he became silent and sad. For if he did not tell his master what he had heard, the young king would be doomed; but, if he did reveal everything to his master, he himself would have to pay with his life. At length he said to himself, "I must and shall save my master even if it means my own destruction.''

When they went ashore, everything started to happen the way the ravens had predicted. A splendid horse, red as a fox, came galloping toward them.

"Well now, what's this?" said the king. "This horse will carry me to my castle.''

As the king was about to mount it Faithful Johannes jumped in front of him and swung himself quickly into the saddle. Then he pulled the gun out of the saddle holster and shot the horse dead. The king's other servants disliked Faithful Johannes and cried out, "What a crime! Why did he have to kill that beautiful creature that was to carry the king to his castle?''

But the king declared, "Be quiet and let him go! He's Johannes, my most faithful servant, and who knows what good may come of this?''

Now they went into the castle, and there was a basin in the hall. The ready-made bridal outfit was lying in it and looked as though it were made of gold and silver. The young king went over and was about to pick it up when Faithful Johannes shoved him aside, grabbed it with gloves, tossed it into the fire, and let it burn. Once again the other servants began to murmur and say, "Just look! Now he's even burned the king's bridal outfit."

But the young king declared, "Who knows what good may come of this? Let him go. He's Johannes, my most faithful servant."

After the wedding was celebrated, the dance began, and the bride took part in it. Faithful Johannes paid close attention and kept looking at her face. All of a sudden she turned pale and fell to the ground as if she were dead. Then he rushed over to her, lifted her up, and carried her into a room, where he laid her on a bed, then knelt down and sucked three drops of blood from her right breast and spat them out. No sooner had he done this than she began breathing again and regained consciousness. The young king had seen all this, but he was puzzled by Faithful Johannes's actions and became angry.

"Throw him into prison!" he declared.

The next morning Faithful Johannes was condemned to death and led to the gallows. As he stood there and was about to be executed, he said, "Every condemned man is usually allowed to say one last word before he dies. May I also have this right?"

"Yes," answered the king. "I shall grant you this right."

Then Faithful Johannes said, "I've been unjustly sentenced to death, for I've always served you faithfully," and he told him how he had heard the ravens' conversation on the sea and how he had been compelled to do all those things to save his master.

The king then cried out, "Oh, my most Faithful Johannes, pardon! Pardon! Bring him down!"

But the moment after Faithful Johannes had uttered his last words, he had fallen down and then turned into stone. The king and queen were greatly grieved by this, and the king said, "Oh, how poorly I've rewarded such great fidelity!"

He ordered the stone figure to be carried up to his bedroom and placed beside his bed. Whenever he looked at it, he would weep and say, "Oh, if only I could bring you back to life, my most Faithful Johannes!"

After some time had passed, the queen gave birth to twins, two little boys, who grew up and became the queen's delight. One day, when the queen was at church and the two children were sitting and playing near their father, the king looked at the stone figure and sighed.

"Oh, if only I could bring you back to life, my most faithful Johannes!" he exclaimed.

Then the stone began to speak and said, "Yes, you can bring me back to life if you're willing to sacrifice what you love most."

"I'd give everything I have in this world for you!" the king responded.

The stone continued, "If you cut off the heads of your two children with your own two hands and rub their blood on me, I shall be brought back to life."

The king was horrified when he heard that he himself would have to kill his precious children. He recalled, nevertheless, the great fidelity of Faithful Johannes and how he had died for him. So the king drew his sword and cut off his children's heads with his own hand. And, after he had rubbed the stone with their blood, it came to life, and Faithful Johannes stood before him once again, alive and well.

"Your loyalty shall not go unrewarded," he said to the king, and he took the children's heads, put them back in place, and rubbed the wounds with their blood. Within seconds they were whole again and were running around and playing as if nothing had happened to them. The king was overjoyed, and when he saw the queen coming, he hid Faithful Johannes and the two children in a large closet. After she entered, he said to her, "Did you pray while you were in church?"

"Yes," she answered, "but I could only think of Faithful Johannes and how unfortunate he was because of us."

"Dear wife," he said. "We can bring him back to life, but it will cost our two little sons, whom we shall have to sacrifice."

The queen became pale, and her heart trembled greatly. However, she said, "We owe this to him because of his great fidelity."

The king rejoiced when he saw that she felt as he did. He went over to the closet, opened it, and brought out the children and Faithful Johannes.

"God be praised!" he said. "He's been saved, and our sons have been restored to us as well."

Then he told her what had happened, and they all lived happily together until the end of their days.

◈ 7 ◈

The Good Bargain

A FARMER DROVE his cow to the market and sold it for seven talers. On his way home he had to pass a pond, and even though he was a good distance from the pond, he was able to hear the frogs croaking *"Aat, aat, aat, aat."*

"What nonsense!" he said to himself. "I got seven talers in the bargain, not *eight*." When he reached the water, he called out to the frogs, "You're nothing but stupid creatures, that's what you are! Don't you know any better than that? It was seven talers not eight."

But the frogs held to their *"aat, aat, aat, aat."*

"Well, if you won't believe me, I can count them out in front of you," and he took the money out of his pocket and counted the seven talers, twenty-four groschen to the taler. But the frogs paid no attention to his calculations and kept croaking *"Aat, aat, aat, aat."*

"That does it!" the farmer exclaimed quite angrily. "If you think you know everything, count it yourselves!"

He tossed the money right at them, and it landed in the water. He remained standing there and intended to wait until they were finished counting and had returned his money to him. Yet the frogs continued to be stubborn and kept on croaking *"aat, aat, aat, aat."* Nor did they return the money to him. He waited for quite some time, until finally it became dark and he had to go home. Now he cursed the frogs and called out to them, "Water-splashers! Thickheads! Goggle-eyes! The only thing you can do with your big mouths is to make loud sounds and hurt people's ears. But you can't count seven talers. Do you think you can keep me waiting here forever?"

Upon saying this he went away, but the frogs kept croaking *"aat, aat, aat, aat"* after him, and he was in a very bad mood when he got home.

After some time he bought another cow, and when he had slaughtered it, he calculated that, if he could get a good price for the meat, he could earn as much as the two cows were worth together and still have the hide left in the bargain. When he got to the city with the meat, he encountered a whole pack of dogs outside the city gate. At the head of the pack was a big greyhound who jumped around the meat and kept sniffing and barking *"Wuff, wuff, wuff, wuff!"* Since the dog would not stop barking, the farmer said to him, "All right, I understand. You're saying *'wuff, wuff, wuff, wuff'* because you want a whiff of the meat. But I'd be in a fine pickle if I gave it to you."

The dog's only response was *"Wuff, wuff!"*

"Will you promise not to eat it and to vouch for your companions over there?"

"Wuff, wuff," said the dog.

"Well, if you insist, you can have it. After all, I know you and I know your masters. But let me tell you one thing: I want my money in three days, or else you'll be in for trouble! You can just bring it out to my place."

Thereupon he set the meat on the ground and turned back home. The dogs scrambled for the meat and barked loudly, *"Wuff, wuff!"* When the farmer heard this from afar, he said to himself, "Just listen! Now they all want some of the meat. But I'll hold that big dog responsible for whatever happens."

After three days had passed, the farmer thought, Tonight you'll have the money in your pocket. And he was quite delighted. However, nobody came, and nobody paid him. "You just can't depend on anyone anymore," he said. Finally his patience gave out, and he went to the butcher in the city and demanded his money. The butcher thought he was joking, but the farmer said, "It's no joke. I want my money. Didn't that big dog bring you all the meat from the cow I slaughtered three days ago?"

This remark made the butcher angry, and he grabbed a broomstick and drove the farmer out of his shop.

"Just wait!" the farmer yelled. "There's still some justice in the world!"

Now he went to the royal castle and requested an audience. So he was led before the king, who was sitting there with his daughter, and the king asked the farmer what wrong had been committed against him.

"Ah," he said, "the frogs and dogs have taken things that rightfully belong to me, and the butcher paid me for some of it with a broomstick."

Then he proceeded to tell them in great detail everything that had happened. The king's daughter burst out laughing, and the king said to him, "I can't provide you with justice in this case, but you shall have my daughter for your wife. This is the first time in her life that she has laughed like this, and you're the cause. You can thank God for your good fortune because I promised to give her to whoever might make her laugh.''

''Oh, no,'' responded the farmer. ''I definitely don't want her. I've already got one wife at home, and she's much too much for me. Whenever I come home, it seems as if I have a wife standing in every corner.''

Then the king got angry and said, ''What a stupid boor!''

''Ah, Your Majesty, what else can you expect from an ox but beef?'' the farmer replied.

''Wait,'' the king declared. ''I shall give you another reward, but for the time being, I want you out of here. Come back in three days, and I'll pay you five hundred in full measure.''

As the farmer was going through the gate, the sentry said, ''The king must have given you a really fine reward, since you made his daughter laugh.''

''Well, I should think so,'' answered the farmer. ''I'm going to get five hundred.''

''Listen,'' the soldier said, ''give me some of it. What can you do with all that money?''

''Since it's you,'' the farmer said, ''I'll give you two hundred. Report to the king in three days and let them pay it out to you.''

A Jew had been standing nearby and had overheard the conversation. He ran after the farmer, seized him by the coattails, and said, ''Wonder of God! What a lucky fellow you are! Let me change the money for you. I'll give you small coins for it. What do you want with those hard talers?''

''Yid,'' the farmer said, ''I'll give you three hundred, but I want the coins right now. In three days you can go to the king, and he will give you my payment.''

The Jew was happy about the little profit he was making and gave him the sum in bad groschen, three of which were worth two good ones. After the three days had passed, the farmer followed the king's orders and appeared before the king, who said, ''Take off his coat. He shall receive his five hundred!''

''Oh,'' the farmer said. ''They don't belong to me anymore. I've given away two hundred to the sentry, and the Jew changed three hundred for me. According to the law, there's nothing due me anymore.''

Meanwhile, the soldier and the Jew had entered and demanded

what they had won from the farmer. Indeed, they were soon dealt their just measure of blows. The soldier bore the lashing patiently, for he already knew how the whip tasted. But the Jew reacted terribly. "*Ow, ow*, it hurts! Are these the hard talers?"

The king could not help laughing at what the farmer had done, and when all his anger had vanished, he said, "Since you lost your reward before you even received it, I'm going to make it up to you. Go into my treasure chamber and take as much money as you want."

The farmer did not have to be asked twice, and he filled his large pockets with whatever he could fit inside. Afterward he went to the tavern and began counting his money. The Jew had sneaked after him and heard him muttering to himself, "Well, that scoundrel of a king really cheated me! If he'd have doled out the money himself, I'd know exactly what I have. Now, since I had to stuff my pocket any way I could, I don't know whether I've got the right amount."

"God help us!" the Jew said to himself. "He's speaking disrespectfully about our king. I'm going to run and report him. Then I'll get a reward, and he'll be punished in the bargain."

When the king heard about the farmer's remarks, he was infuriated and ordered the Jew to go and fetch the slanderer. The Jew ran to the farmer and said, "Our Majesty, the king, wants you to report to him at once, just as you are."

"That's not proper, and I know better," said the farmer. "First I'll have a new coat made for me. Do you think that a man who has so much money like me should appear before the king in an old tattered coat?"

When the Jew realized that the farmer would not budge without another coat, he feared the king's anger would subside, and this would prevent him from getting his reward, and the farmer would also go unpunished.

"I'll lend you my beautiful coat," he said. "It's just for a short time and out of friendship. Just think of how much one will do out of kindness!"

The farmer was pleased by the offer, so he put on the Jew's coat and departed with him. Now the king reprimanded the farmer for his bad remarks, which the Jew had conveyed to him behind the farmer's back.

"Come now!" said the farmer. "Jews always tell lies. There's not a word of truth that comes out of his mouth. Why, that fellow's even capable of claiming that I'm wearing his coat."

"What's this?" the Jew screamed. "That's my coat! I lent it to you out of sheer friendship so you could appear before the king!"

When the king heard that, he said, "The Jew has certainly deceived someone, either me or the farmer."

So he had the Jew given his due again in *hard* talers. Meanwhile, the farmer went home in the good coat with good money in his pocket, and he said, "This time I made a good bargain!"

◆ 8 ◆

The Marvelous Minstrel

ONCE UPON A TIME there was a marvelous minstrel who walked through a forest all alone and thought about all kinds of things. When there was nothing more to think about, he said to himself, "I'm getting bored here in the forest, and I need to get myself a good companion."

He took his fiddle from his back and began playing a tune that resounded through the trees. It was not long before a wolf came trotting through the thicket.

"Ah, here comes a wolf! I don't have any desire to see a wolf," said the musician.

But the wolf came closer and said to him, "Oho, dear musician, what's that lovely tune you're playing? I'd like to learn to play that way too."

"You can easily do it," responded the minstrel. "You only have to do as I say."

"Oh, minstrel," the wolf said, "I'll obey you just as a pupil obeys his teacher."

The minstrel told him to come along, and after they had walked some distance together, they came to an old oak tree that was hollow inside and split down the middle.

"Look here," said the minstrel, "if you want to learn how to fiddle, you must put your front paws into this crack."

The wolf obeyed, but the minstrel quickly picked up a stone, and with one blow he wedged the wolf's front paws in so tightly that the beast was forced to stay there like a prisoner.

"Wait here until I get back," the minstrel said, and he went his way.

After a while he said to himself once more, "I'm getting bored here in the forest, and I need to get myself another companion."

He took his fiddle and played another tune that was heard throughout the forest. It was not long before a fox came slinking through the trees.

"Ah, here comes a fox!" said the minstrel. "I don't have any desire to see a fox."

The fox came up to him and said, "Oho, dear minstrel, what's that lovely tune you're playing? I'd like to learn to play that way too."

"You can easily do it," said the minstrel. "You only have to do as I say."

"Oh, minstrel," the fox said, "I'll obey you just as a pupil obeys his teacher."

"Follow me," said the minstrel.

After they had walked some distance, they came to a footpath with tall bushes on either side. The minstrel stopped, grabbed hold of a little hazel tree, and bent it down to the ground. Then he held the top down with his foot while he bent another little hazel tree down from the other side.

"Well now, my little fox," he said, "if you want to learn something, give me your left front paw."

The fox obeyed, and the minstrel bound the paw to the tree on the left.

"Little fox," he said, "now give me your right paw."

He bound this one to the tree on the right. After he made sure that the knots were tight enough, he let go, and the little trees shot up into the air and jerked the fox up high so he was left dangling in the air.

"Wait here till I get back," said the minstrel, and he went his way.

Once again he said to himself, "I'm getting bored in the forest and need to get another companion."

So he took his fiddle, and the sounds reverberated through the forest. Then a little hare came hopping toward him.

"Ah, here comes a hare!" said the minstrel. "I didn't want a hare."

"Oho, dear minstrel," the little hare said, "what's that lovely tune you're playing? I'd like to play that way too."

"You can easily do it," said the minstrel. "You only have to do as I say."

"Oh, minstrel," the little hare answered, "I'll obey you just as a pupil obeys his teacher."

They walked some distance together until they came to a clearing in the forest where an aspen tree was standing. The minstrel tied a long cord around the little hare's neck and attached the other end to the tree.

"Move lively, little hare," the minstrel cried out. "I want you to run around the tree twenty times."

The little hare obeyed, and after he had done that twenty times, the cord was wrapped around the tree twenty times, and the little hare was trapped. No matter how much he pulled or tugged, he only made the cord cut deeper into his soft neck.

"Wait here till I get back," said the minstrel, and he went off.

In the meantime, the wolf had yanked and pulled and bitten on the stone. He kept working at it until he finally freed his paws and drew them out of the crack. Bursting with anger and fury, he rushed after the minstrel, intending to tear him to pieces. When the fox saw him running along, he began to wail and scream with all his might, "Brother wolf, come help me! The minstrel has tricked me!"

The wolf pulled the little trees down to the ground, bit the rope in two, and freed the fox, who went with him to get revenge on the minstrel. They found the little hare tied up and released him as well. Now all three began searching for their enemy.

As the minstrel walked along his way he played his fiddle once again, but this time he was more fortunate. The sounds reached the ears of a poor woodcutter who was instantly compelled to stop working whether he wanted to or not, and he went to listen to the music with his ax under his arm.

"Here comes the right companion at last!" said the minstrel. "I never wanted beasts in the first place, just humans."

Now he began to play so beautifully and so delightfully that the poor man stood there as if he were under a magic spell, and his heart leapt for joy. As he was standing there, the wolf, the fox, and the little hare came running up, and he could see that they had something evil in mind. So he raised his glittering ax and stood in front of the minstrel as if to say, "Whoever wants him had better watch out, because he'll have to deal with me first."

The animals were frightened by this and ran back into the forest, while the minstrel played one more tune for the woodcutter out of gratitude. Then he moved on his way.

◈ 9 ◈

The Twelve Brothers

ONCE UPON A TIME a king and a queen lived together peacefully and had twelve children, all boys. One day the king said to his wife, "When you give birth to our thirteenth child and it's a girl, the twelve boys shall die so she may have all the wealth and the kingdom for herself."

He even had twelve coffins made and filled with wood shavings. Each was fitted with a death pillow, and all the coffins were locked in a room. The king gave the key to the queen and ordered her never to say one word about this to anyone. She then sat and lamented the entire day. Her youngest son, Benjamin, whose name she had taken from the Bible, was always with her, and he asked, "Dear Mother, why are you so sad?"

"Dearest child," she replied. "I'm not allowed to tell you."

But he gave her no peace until she opened the room and showed him the twelve coffins already filled with wood shavings. She then said, "My dearest Benjamin, your father had these coffins made for you and your eleven brothers. If I give birth to a girl, all of you shall be killed and buried in them."

As she was telling him this, she wept, and her son consoled her by saying, "Don't weep, dear Mother. We'll find a way to help ourselves and get away from here."

Then she said, "Go into the forest with your eleven brothers. I want you to find the tallest tree and take turns sitting on top. You're to keep watch and look toward the castle tower. If I give birth to a little boy, I'll raise a white flag, and then you'll be able to return. If I give birth to a little girl, I'll raise a red flag, and then you're to flee as fast as you can. And may the good Lord protect you. I'll get up every night and pray that you're able to warm yourselves by a fire in the winter and that you don't suffer from the heat during the summer."

After she gave her blessing to her sons, they went out into the forest, where they took turns keeping watch. Each one sat on top of the tallest oak tree and looked toward the tower. When eleven days had passed and it was Benjamin's turn, he saw a flag being raised. However, it was not a white one but a bloodred flag announcing that they were to die. When the brothers heard that, they became angry and said, "Why should we suffer death because of a girl? We swear we'll get our revenge. Wherever we find a girl, her red blood shall flow."

Then they went deeper into the forest, where it was darkest. There they found an empty little cottage, which was bewitched.

"We shall dwell here," they said, "and you, Benjamin, since you're the youngest and weakest, shall stay home and keep house. We others shall go out and search for food."

So they went off into the forest and shot hares, wild deer, birds, little pigeons, and whatever was fit to eat. They brought this to Benjamin, who had to prepare it nicely for them so they could still their hunger. They lived together for ten years in this little cottage, and the time passed quickly for them.

Meanwhile, the daughter that their mother, the queen, had brought into the world had grown to be a little girl. She had a kind heart and beautiful features and a gold star on her forehead. One time when there was a great deal of washing to do, she saw twelve boy's shirts among the things to be washed and asked her mother, "Whose shirts are these? They're much too small for Father."

Her mother answered her with a heavy heart. "Dear child, they belong to your twelve brothers."

"Where are my twelve brothers?" the girl asked. "I've never heard of them until now."

"Only God knows where they are," she answered. "They're wandering around somewhere in the world." She took the girl, opened the room, and showed her the twelve coffins with the wood shavings and the death pillows. "These coffins were destined for your brothers," she said, "but the boys departed secretly before you were born." And then she told her everything that had happened.

"Dear Mother," the girl said, "don't weep. I'm going to look for my brothers."

So she took the twelve shirts and went straight into the great forest. She walked the whole day, and by evening she came to the bewitched cottage. When she entered, she found a young boy who asked, "Where have you come from and where are you going?" He was astonished by her beauty, her royal garments, and the star on her forehead.

"I'm a princess," she responded, "and I'm looking for my

• 38 •

twelve brothers. I'm prepared to continue walking as far as the sky is blue until I find them."

She showed him the twelve shirts, and Benjamin realized she was his sister.

"I'm Benjamin," he said, "your youngest brother."

She began to cry for joy, and they kissed and lovingly hugged each other. But then he said, "Dear sister, there's still a problem. We agreed that any maiden who came our way would have to die, for we had to leave our kingdom on account of a girl."

"I'll gladly die," she said, "if I can save my twelve brothers by doing this."

"No," he responded. "You shall not die. Sit down under this tub and wait till our eleven brothers come back. Then I'll settle everything with them."

She did as he said, and when it was night, the others came back from the hunt and found their meal ready. After they sat down at the table and began eating, they asked, "What's new?"

"You don't know?" Benjamin said.

"No," they replied.

"You're in the forest the whole day," he continued, "while I stay at home. Yet, I still know more than you."

"Then tell us!" they cried out.

"Only if you promise me that the first girl we meet shall not be killed," he said.

"Yes!" they all exclaimed. "Now tell us."

"Our sister is here!" he said, and he lifted up the tub, and the princess came crawling out in her royal garments. She had the gold star on her forehead and was very beautiful, gentle, and delicate. In their joy they embraced and kissed her, for they loved her with all their hearts.

Now she stayed at home with Benjamin and helped him with the work. The eleven brothers went into the forest, caught wild game, deer, birds, and pigeons so they would have something to eat, and their sister and Benjamin made sure that their meals were prepared. They fetched the wood for cooking, herbs to go along with the vegetables, and put the pots on the fire so dinner was always ready when the eleven brothers came home. Moreover, they kept the little cottage in order and put nice clean white sheets on the little beds. All this kept the brothers satisfied, and they lived with her in great harmony.

One day the two at home had prepared a wonderful meal, and when they were all together, they sat down, ate, drank, and were full of joy. Now, there was a small garden next to the bewitched cottage, and in it were twelve lilies, also called students. Since she wanted to please her brothers, the sister plucked the twelve flowers with the intention of giving one to each brother at the end of the meal. But right after she had plucked the flowers, the twelve brothers were instantly changed into twelve ravens and flew away over the forest, while the cottage and the garden vanished as well. Now the maiden was all alone in the wild forest, and when she looked around, an old woman was standing near her and she said, "My child, what have you done? Why didn't you leave those twelve white flowers alone? They were your brothers, and you've changed them into ravens forever."

"Is there no way to save them?" the maiden asked as she wept.

"No," the old woman said. "That is—there's only one way in the entire world, but it's so hard you won't be able to free them. You see, you would have to remain silent for seven years and neither speak nor laugh. If you utter but a single word and there is just an hour to go in the seven years, everything will be in vain, and your brothers will be killed by that one word."

"I know for sure," the maiden spoke with her whole heart, "that I shall save my brothers."

She went and searched for a tall tree. After climbing it, she sat down and began spinning and did not say a word or laugh. Now, it so happened that a king was hunting in the forest. He had a big greyhound that ran up to the tree where the maiden was sitting. The dog began jumping around, yelping and barking at her. The king then went over to the tree and saw the beautiful princess with the gold star on her forehead. He was so enraptured by her beauty that he called up to her and asked her if she would be his wife. She did not respond but nodded a little with her head. Then he climbed up the tree himself, carried her down, put her on his horse, and took her home. The wedding was celebrated with great splendor and joy, but the bride did not speak or laugh.

After they lived together for a few years, the king's mother, who was an evil woman, began to slander the young queen and said to the king, "The maiden you brought home with you is nothing but a common beggar girl! Who knows what godless mischief she's been secretly plotting? If she's mute and can't talk, she could at least laugh every now and then. Anyone who doesn't laugh must have a bad conscience."

At first the king did not want to believe this, but the old woman kept at it so long and accused the maiden of so many wicked things that the king finally let himself be convinced and sentenced her to death. A huge fire was made in the courtyard, and the young queen was to be burned in it. The king stood upstairs at a window and watched everything with tears in his eyes, since he still loved her. When she was already bound to the stake and the fire was licking her clothes with its red tongues, the last second of the seven years expired. Suddenly a whirring noise could be heard in the air, and twelve ravens came flying toward the yard and swooped down. Then, just as they touched the ground, they turned into her twelve brothers whom she had saved. They tore apart the fire, put out the flames, freed their dear sister, and hugged and kissed her. Now that she was allowed to open her mouth and talk, she told the king why she had been silent and had never laughed. The king was glad to hear she was innocent, and they all lived together in harmony until their death. The evil mother was brought before the court and put into a barrel that was filled with boiling oil and poisonous snakes. Indeed, she died a horrible death.

◈ 10 ◈

Riffraff

THE ROOSTER SAID TO THE HEN, "Now's the time the nuts are ripe. Let's go up to the hill and for once eat our fill before the squirrel hauls them all away."

"All right," responded the hen. "Let's go and have a good time."

They went up the hill, and since it was such a bright cheery day, they stayed till evening. Now, I do not know whether it was because they had stuffed themselves too much, or whether they had become too high and mighty, but they did not want to return home on foot. So the rooster had to build a small carriage out of nut shells. When it was finished, the hen got in and said to the rooster, "Now you can just harness yourself to it."

"You have some nerve!" said the rooster. "I'd rather go home by foot than let myself be harnessed to this carriage. No, that wasn't part of our bargain. I'd gladly be coachman and sit on the box, but I refuse to pull the carriage!"

As they were quarreling, a duck came by quacking "You thieves! Who said you could come up on my nut hill? Just you wait! You'll pay for this!"

She charged at the rooster with a wide-open beak, but the rooster was on his toes and threw himself at the duck nice and hard. Then he dug his spurs into her so violently that the duck begged for mercy and willingly let herself be harnessed to the carriage as punishment.

Now the rooster sat down on the box as coachman, and when they set out, he shouted, "Giddyap, duck! Run as fast as you can!"

After they had gone some distance, they encountered two travelers on foot, a needle and a pin.

"Stop! Stop!" the two cried out. It would soon be very dark, they said, and they would not be able to go one step further. Besides, the road was dirty. So they asked if they could have a ride. They had been at the tailor's tavern outside the town gate and had had one beer too many, which made them late as well.

Since they were thin and did not take up much room, the rooster let them both get in, but they had to promise not to step on his or the hen's feet. Later that evening they came to an inn, and as they did not want to travel any farther, and as the duck was not walking well but swayed from side to side, they decided to stop there. At first the innkeeper raised a lot of objections and said his inn was already full. Moreover, he thought they were not a very distinguished looking group. However, they used some sweet talk and offered him the egg that the hen had laid along the way and told him that he could also keep the duck, who laid an egg a day. So finally he relented and said they could spend the night.

Now they ordered some good hot food and had a merry time of it. Early the next morning, as the sun was rising and everyone was asleep, the rooster woke the hen, fetched the egg, pecked it open, and together they devoured it. After throwing the shells on the hearth, they went to the needle, who was still asleep, grabbed him by the head, and stuck him into the innkeeper's easy chair. Then they stuck the pin into his towel. Finally, without much ado, they flew away over the heath.

The duck, who liked to sleep in the open air and had spent the night in the yard, heard the flapping of their wings. So she roused herself, found a brook, and swam off. That went much faster than being harnessed to a carriage. A few hours later the innkeeper got out of bed, washed himself, and took the towel to dry himself. However, the pin scratched his face, leaving a red mark from ear to ear. Then he went into the kitchen and wanted to light his pipe. But, as he leaned over the hearth, the eggshells popped into his eyes.

"Everything's after my head this morning," he said, and went to sit down in his easy chair to settle his bad mood, but he jumped up immediately and screamed, *"Oww!"* The needle stuck him worse than the pin and not in the head. Now he was completely angry and suspected the guests who had arrived so late the night before. But when he went looking for them, they were gone. Then he swore he would never again let riffraff stay at his inn, especially when they eat so much, pay nothing, and play mean tricks on top of it all.

◈ 11 ◈

Brother and Sister

A LITTLE BROTHER took his little sister by the hand and said, "Since our mother died, we've not had one moment of happiness. Our stepmother beats us every day, and when we come near her, she kicks us away with her foot. We get nothing but hard crusts of bread, just leftovers for food, and the dog under the table is better off. At least he gets a good chunk of meat to eat every now and then. Lord have mercy on us, if our mother only knew! Come, let's go off together into the wide world."

They walked over meadows, fields, and stones the entire day, and when it began to rain, the sister said, "God and our hearts are weeping at the same time."

In the evening they came to a great forest and were so exhausted from their grief, hunger, and long journey that they crept into a hollow tree and fell asleep. When they woke up the next morning, the sun was already high in the sky and warmed the tree with its rays.

"Sister," said the brother, "I'm thirsty. If only I knew where to find a spring, I'd go and have a drink right away. Listen, I think I hear one gurgling."

The brother stood up, took his sister by the hand, and set out to look for the spring. However, the evil stepmother, who was a witch, had noticed that the children had run away. She had gone slinking after them in secret, as witches often slink, and had put a curse on all the springs in the forest. So, when they found a spring rushing and leaping over stones, the brother wanted to take a drink, but the sister heard the gurgling spring say, "Whoever drinks of me will be turned into a tiger."

Then the sister exclaimed, "Please, brother, don't drink, or else you'll turn into a wild beast and tear me to pieces!"

Even though he was very thirsty, the brother did not drink. Instead he said, "I'll wait until we reach the next spring."

When they reached the next spring, once again the sister heard what it was babbling. "Whoever drinks of me will be turned into a wolf. Whoever drinks of me will be turned into a wolf."

"Brother!" the sister exclaimed. "Please don't drink, or else you'll be turned into a wolf and eat me up."

The brother did not drink and said, "I'll wait until we reach the next spring, but then I must drink no matter what you say. My thirst is much too great."

When they came to the third spring, the sister heard the babbling of the spring. "Whoever drinks of me will be turned into a deer. Whoever drinks of me will be turned into a deer."

"Oh, brother!" the sister exclaimed. "Please don't drink, or else you'll be turned into a deer and run away from me."

But the brother, who was already kneeling at the spring, leaned over and drank some of the water. Immediately after a few drops had touched his lips, he lay there in the form of a fawn. The sister began weeping over her poor bewitched brother, sitting sadly at her side, and the little fawn wept too. Finally, the girl said, "Hush, my dear little fawn. I shall never forsake you."

She took off her golden garter and put it around the fawn's neck. Then she pulled up some rushes and wove them into a soft rope, which she attached to the little animal. Afterward she led him onward and deeper into the forest. When they had gone a long, long way, they came to a little house, and the girl looked inside. Since it was empty, she thought, We might as well stay and live right here. So she looked for leaves and moss and made a soft bed for the fawn. Every morning she went out and gathered roots, berries, and nuts for herself, and for the fawn she brought back tender grass, which he ate out of her hand. This made him content, and he would romp around her in a playful fashion. At night, when the sister was tired and had said her prayers, she would lay her head on the back of the fawn. That was her pillow, and she would fall into a sweet sleep. If only the brother could have regained his human form, it would have been a wonderful life.

For a long time they lived like this, all alone in the wilderness. However, it came to pass that the king of the country held a great hunt in the forest, and soon horns could be heard along with the barking of dogs and the merry cries of the huntsmen. The fawn listened to the sounds and longed very much to be a part of it all.

"Ah," he said to his sister, "let me go and join the hunt. I can't bear it any longer!" He kept pleading until she gave her consent.

"But make sure you're back here by evening," she said to him. "I'm going to lock the door to keep the brutal hunters out, and when you return, I want you to knock on the door and say, 'My little sister, let me in.' That way I'll recognize you. If you don't say this, I won't open the door."

Then the fawn ran off, glad and merry to be out in the open air. The king and his huntsmen saw the beautiful creature and set out in pursuit, but they could not catch up with him. Whenever they thought they had him for sure, he would burst through the bushes and disappear. When it got dark, he ran back to the little house, knocked, and said, "My little sister, let me in."

The little door was opened for him, and he jumped inside. Then he rested the entire night on his bed. The next morning the hunt began anew, and when the fawn heard the horn again and the *"Tallyho!"* of the huntsmen, he became very restless and said, "Sister, open the door. I must be off!"

The sister opened the door for him and said, "Remember, you must be back by evening and say the passwords."

When the king and his huntsmen saw the fawn with the golden collar once more, they all pursued him, but he was still too swift and nimble for them. All day long they chased him, but finally by evening they had surrounded him. Then one huntsman wounded him slightly on his foot, and as the fawn slowly ran away he was limping. This allowed a huntsman to trail him all the way to the house, and he heard the fawn cry out, "My little sister, let me in." He watched the door open and close quickly and took note of all that happened. Then the huntsman went back to the king and told him about everything he had seen and heard.

"Tomorrow we shall hunt again," the king said.

Meanwhile, the sister was greatly distressed when she saw her little fawn was wounded. She washed off the blood, placed herbs on the wound, and said, "Now, go to bed, my dear fawn. You must let your wound heal."

Actually the wound was so slight that the fawn did not even feel it the next morning. And, once again, when he heard the merry cries of the hunt outside, he said, "I can't bear it. I've got to be there! I won't make it easy for them to catch me."

The sister wept and said, "Now they'll kill you, and I'll be left alone in the forest, forsaken by the whole world. I'm not going to let you out."

"Then I'll die of misery," responded the fawn. "Whenever I hear the sounds of the hunting horn, I feel as if I were going to burst out of my skin."

After he said that, his sister could no longer refuse, and with a heavy heart she opened the door for him. The fawn bounded cheerfully and sprightfully into the forest. When the king caught sight of him, he said to his huntsmen, "Now, I want you to chase him the whole day long and into the night, but make sure that you don't harm him."

Later, as the sun began to set, the king turned to the huntsman and said, "All right, take me and show me the little house in the forest."

After the king arrived at the front door, he knocked and called out, "Dear little sister, let me in."

The door opened, and upon entering, the king stood face-to-face with the most beautiful maiden he had ever seen in his life. The maiden was frightened when she saw it was a man with a golden crown on his head and not her fawn. Yet, he looked at her in a kind way, and after extending his hand, he said, "Would you like to come with me to my castle and be my dear wife?"

"Oh, yes," responded the maiden. "But the fawn must come with me too. I won't ever forsake him."

"He can stay with you as long as you live," said the king, "and he shall want for nothing."

Just then the little fawn came running in, and the sister attached the rope of rushes to him, took the rope in her own hand, and led him out of the house. The king lifted the beautiful maiden onto his horse and brought her to his castle, where the wedding was celebrated with great splendor. Now the sister was queen, and for a long time they all lived together in happiness. The fawn was well tended and ran about the castle garden.

In the meantime, the evil stepmother, who had caused the children to run away in the first place, thought that the sister had been torn to pieces by wild beasts and that the brother, as a fawn, had been shot to death by huntsmen. When she learned instead how happy they were and how well everything was going for them, jealousy and resentment stirred in her heart and gave her no peace. Her one and only thought now was to find a way to bring about their misfortune again. Her own daughter, who was as ugly as sin and had only one eye, reproached her by saying, "I'm the one who should be queen! Why don't I have any luck?"

"Just be quiet!" said the old woman, who gave her reason to be satisfied. "When the right time comes, I'll know what to do."

Finally, the right time came: the queen gave birth one day to a baby boy while the king was out hunting. So the old witch assumed the form of the chambermaid, went into the room where the queen was lying, and said to the convalescent, "Come, your bath is ready. It will make you feel better and give you fresh strength. Quick, before it gets cold."

The witch's daughter had come too. Together they carried the frail queen into the bathroom, put her into the tub, locked the door, and ran away, for they had made such a terrible fire in the bathroom that the queen was soon suffocated to death.

When that was done, the old woman took her daughter, put a nightcap on her, and laid her in bed in place of the queen. She also gave her the shape and features of the queen. However, she could not replace the eye that the daughter had lost. Therefore, the daughter had to lie on the side where she had no eye. That way the king would not notice anything amiss. In the evening, when he returned home and heard his wife had given birth to a baby boy, he was very happy and wanted to go to his dear wife's bedside and see how she was doing. But the old woman cried out quickly, "For goodness sake, keep the curtains closed! The queen must not be exposed to light. She needs peace and quiet."

The king stepped back and was thus prevented from discovering the false queen lying in the bed. However, at midnight, when everyone was asleep except the nurse, who was sitting by the cradle in the nursery and watching over the baby all by herself, the door opened, and the true queen entered. She lifted the baby out of the cradle, took him in her arms, and suckled him. Then she puffed up his little pillow, put him back in the cradle, and covered him with a little blanket. Nor did she forget the fawn. She went to the corner where he was lying and stroked his back. Then she silently left the room, and when morning came, the nurse asked the guards whether they had seen anyone enter the castle during the night.

"No, we didn't see a soul," they replied.

Thereafter the queen came many nights and never uttered a word. The nurse always saw her, but she did not dare tell anyone about it. After some time had passed, the queen began to speak, and one night she said:

"How's my child? How's my fawn?
Twice more I'll come, then I'll be gone."

The nurse did not answer her, but when the queen disappeared, she went to the king and told him everything.

"Oh, God!" he exclaimed. "What's going on? Tonight I'll keep watch over the child myself."

In the evening he went into the nursery, and at midnight the queen reappeared and said:

"How's my child? How's my fawn?
Once more I'll come, then I'll be gone."

She nursed the child as she usually did and then disappeared. The king did not dare to speak to her, but he kept watch the following night as well. Once again she said:

"How's my child? How's my fawn?
There's no more time. Soon I'll be gone."

The king could no longer restrain himself. He sprang forward and said, "You can be no one else but my dear wife!"

At that very moment life was restored to her by the grace of God. Indeed, she was alive and well, and the rosy color came back to her cheeks. She then told the king how the evil witch and her daughter had committed cruel crimes against her. So the king had them led before the court, and they received their sentences. The daughter was taken into the forest, where wild beasts tore her to pieces, while the witch was thrown into a fire and miserably burned to death. When there was nothing left of her but ashes, the fawn was transformed and regained his human form. From then on sister and brother lived happily until the end of their days.

◈ 12 ◈

Rapunzel

ONCE UPON A TIME there was a husband and wife who for quite some time had been wishing in vain for a child. Finally, the dear Lord gave the wife a sign of hope that their wish would be fulfilled. Now, in the back of their house the couple had a small window that overlooked a splendid garden filled with the most beautiful flowers and herbs. The garden, however, was surrounded by a high wall, and nobody dared enter it because it belonged to a sorceress who was very powerful and feared by all. One day when the wife was standing at the window and looking down into the garden, she noticed a bed of the finest rapunzel lettuce. The lettuce looked so fresh and green that her mouth watered, and she had a great craving to eat some. Day by day this craving increased, and since she knew she could not get any, she began to waste away and look pale and miserable.

Her husband became alarmed and asked, "What's wrong with you, dear wife?"

"Ah," she responded, "I shall certainly die if I don't get any of that rapunzel from the garden behind our house."

Her husband, who loved her, thought, Before I let my wife die, I'll do anything I must to make sure she gets some rapunzel.

That day at dusk he climbed over the wall into the garden of the sorceress, hastily grabbed a handful of rapunzel, and brought them to his wife. Immediately she made them into a salad and ate it with great zest. But the rapunzel tasted so good to her, so very good, that her desire for them was three times greater by the next day. If she was to have any peace, her husband knew he had to climb into the garden once more. So at dusk he scaled the wall again, and just as he landed on the other side, he was given a tremendous scare, for he stood face-to-face with the sorceress.

"How dare you climb into my garden and steal my rapunzel like a thief?" she said with an angry look. "You'll pay for this!"

"Oh," he cried. "Please, let mercy prevail over justice. I did this only because I was in a predicament: my wife noticed your rapunzel from our window, and she developed such a great craving for it that she would have died if I hadn't brought her some to eat."

Upon hearing that, the anger of the sorceress subsided, and she said to him, "If it's truly as you say, then I shall permit you to take as many rapunzel as you like, but only under one condition: when your wife gives birth, I must have the child. You needn't fear about the child's well-being, for I shall take care of it like a mother."

In his fear the man agreed to everything, and when his wife had the baby, the sorceress appeared at once. She gave the child the name Rapunzel and took her away.

Rapunzel grew to be the most beautiful child under the sun. But when she was twelve years old, the sorceress locked her in a tower that was in a forest. It had neither door nor stairs, only a little window high above. Whenever the sorceress wanted to get in, she would stand below and call out:

"Rapunzel, Rapunzel,
let down your hair for me."

Rapunzel's hair was long and radiant, as fine as spun gold. Every time she heard the voice of the sorceress, she unpinned her braids and wound them around a hook on the window. Then she let her hair drop twenty yards, and the sorceress would climb up on it.

A few years later a king's son happened to be riding through the forest and passed by the tower. Suddenly, he heard a song so lovely that he stopped to listen. It was Rapunzel, who passed the time in her solitude by letting her sweet voice resound in the forest. The prince wanted to climb up to her, and he looked for a door but could not find one. So he rode home. However, the song had touched his heart so deeply that he rode out into the forest every day and listened. One time, as he was standing behind a tree, he saw the sorceress approach and heard her call out:

"Rapunzel, Rapunzel,
let down your hair."

Then Rapunzel let down her braids, and the sorceress climbed up to her.

"If that's the ladder one needs to get up there, I'm also going to try my luck," the prince declared.

The next day, as it began to get dark, he went to the tower and called out:

"Rapunzel, Rapunzel,
let down your hair."

All at once the hair dropped down, and the prince climbed up. When he entered the tower, Rapunzel was at first terribly afraid, for she had never laid eyes on a man before. However, the prince began to talk to her in a friendly way and told her that her song had touched his heart so deeply that he had not been able to rest until he had seen her. Rapunzel then lost her fear, and when he asked her whether she would have him for her husband, and she saw that he was young and handsome, she thought, He'll certainly love me better than old Mother Gothel. So she said yes and placed her hand in his.

"I want to go with you very much," she said, "but I don't know how I can get down. Every time you come, you must bring a skein of silk with you, and I'll weave it into a ladder. When it's finished, then I'll climb down, and you can take me away on your horse."

They agreed that until then he would come to her every evening, for the old woman came during the day. Meanwhile, the sorceress did not notice anything, until one day Rapunzel blurted out, "Mother Gothel, how is it that you're much heavier than the prince? When I pull him up, he's here in a second."

"Ah, you godless child!" exclaimed the sorceress. "What's this I hear? I thought I had made sure you had no contact with the outside world, but you've deceived me!"

In her fury she seized Rapunzel's beautiful hair, wrapped it around her left hand several times, grabbed a pair of scissors with her right hand, and *snip, snap* the hair was cut off, and the beautiful braids lay on the ground. Then the cruel sorceress took Rapunzel to a desolate land where she had to live in great misery and grief.

On the same day that she had banished Rapunzel, the sorceress fastened the braids that she had cut off to the hook on the window, and that evening, when the prince came and called out:

"Rapunzel, Rapunzel,
let down your hair,"

she let the hair down.

The prince climbed up, but instead of finding his dearest Rapunzel on top, he found the sorceress, who gave him vicious and angry looks.

"Aha!" she exclaimed with contempt. "You want to fetch your darling wife, but the beautiful bird is no longer sitting in the nest, and she won't be singing anymore. The cat has got her, and it will also scratch out your eyes. Rapunzel is lost to you, and you will never see her again!"

The prince was beside himself with grief, and in his despair he jumped off the tower. He escaped with his life, but the thorns he fell into pierced his eyes, so he became blind. Now he strayed about in the forest, ate nothing but roots and berries, and did nothing but mourn and weep about the loss of his dearest wife. Thus he wandered for many years in misery. Eventually, he made his way to the desolate land where Rapunzel was leading a wretched existence with the twins, a boy and a girl, to whom she had given birth. When he heard a voice that he thought sounded familiar, he went straight toward it, and when he reached her, Rapunzel recognized him. She embraced him and wept, and as two of her tears dropped on his eyes they became clear, and he could see again. Then he escorted her back to his kingdom, where he was received with joy, and they lived happily and contentedly for a long time thereafter.

◆ 13 ◆

The Three Little Gnomes in the Forest

THERE WAS A MAN WHOSE WIFE DIED, and a woman whose husband died; and the man had a daughter, and the woman also had a daughter. The girls knew each other and one day took a walk together. Afterward they went to the woman's house, and she said to the man's daughter, "Listen, tell your father I want to marry him. Then you shall wash yourself in milk every morning and drink wine, while my daughter will wash herself in water and drink water."

The maiden went home and told her father what the woman had said. The man responded, "What shall I do? Marriage is both joy and torture." Finally, since he could not reach a decision, he took off a boot and said, "Take this boot. It's got a hole in the sole. Carry it up to the loft, hang it on a big nail, and pour water into it. If it holds the water, I'll get married again. But if it leaks, I won't."

The maiden did as she was told, but the water drew the hole together, and the boot became full to the brim. The daughter informed her father how everything turned out. Then he climbed up into the loft to see for himself, and when he saw she was right, he went to the widow and courted her. Soon after, the wedding took place.

On the day after the wedding when the two girls got up, the man's daughter had milk to wash herself and wine to drink, while the woman's daughter had water to wash herself and water to drink. On the second morning both the girls had water to wash themselves and water to drink. On the third morning the man's daughter had water to wash herself and water to drink, while the woman's daughter had milk to wash herself and wine to drink. And that's the way it remained. The woman became her stepdaughter's most bitter enemy and tried to think of ways to make it worse for her from one day to the next. Moreover, she was envious because her stepdaughter was beautiful and lovely, and her own daughter was ugly and gruesome.

Once, when it was winter, everything was frozen over as hard as rock, and hill and dale were covered with snow. The woman made a dress out of paper, called her stepdaughter to her, and said, "Now put on this dress, go into the forest, and fetch me a basket of strawberries. I've got a craving for them."

"Good Lord!" the girl said. "Strawberries don't grow in winter. The ground is frozen, and everything's covered with snow. Besides, why do you want me to go in a paper dress? It's so cold outside that my breath will freeze. The wind will blow right through the dress, and the thorns will tear it off my body."

"You have some nerve talking back to me!" the stepmother said. "Get going, and don't show your face around here again until you have the basket filled with strawberries." Then she gave her a little piece of hard bread and said, "You can use this as food for the day." All the while she thought, She'll starve and freeze to death out there, and I won't ever have to lay eyes on her again.

The maiden was obedient, so she put on the paper dress and went out with the little basket. There was nothing but snow as far as the eye could see, not even a blade of green grass. When she reached the forest, she saw a small cottage, and three little gnomes were looking out the window. She wished them a good day and knocked politely at the door.

"Come in," they cried out.

She entered the room and sat down on the bench near the stove, since she wanted to warm herself and eat her breakfast. The three gnomes said, "Give us some too."

"Gladly," she replied. She divided the bread in two and gave them half.

"What are you doing out here in the forest during the winter walking about in such a little dress?" they asked.

"Oh," she answered, "I'm supposed to look for strawberries, and I'm not supposed to return home until I've gathered a basketful."

After she had eaten her bread, they gave her a broom and said, "Sweep the snow away from the back door."

Once she was outside, the three gnomes began talking among themselves. "What should we give her for being so polite and kind and sharing her bread with us?"

"She shall become more and more beautiful each day that passes. This is my gift," said the first one.

"Each time she utters a word, gold pieces shall fall out of her mouth. This is my gift," said the second.

"A king shall come and take her for his wife. This is my gift," said the third.

Meanwhile, the maiden did as the gnomes had asked and swept the snow away from the back of the house, and what do you think she found? There were lots of ripe, dark red strawberries shooting out of the ground. In her joy she filled her basket with them. Then she thanked the little men by shaking hands with each of them and ran home to her stepmother, bringing her what she had demanded. As the maiden entered the house and said "Good evening" a piece of gold fell right out of her mouth. Then she explained what had happened to her in the forest, and with each word she uttered, gold pieces fell out of her mouth until soon the entire room was covered with gold.

"Just look at how arrogant she is!" her stepsister exclaimed. "The way she throws money around!"

But secretly the stepsister was envious and wanted to go into the forest and look for strawberries too.

"No, no, my dear little daughter," her mother said. "It's too cold, and you could freeze to death."

However, her daughter gave her no peace, and finally her mother had to yield. She sewed her a magnificent fur coat to wear and gave her bread and butter and cake to take with her.

The maiden went into the forest and headed straight for the little cottage. The three gnomes were looking out the window once again, but she did not greet them. Instead, she tramped right into their house, sat down by the stove, and began eating her cake without even glancing at them or saying good day.

"Give us some," the little men cried out.

But she answered, "It's not even enough for me, so how can you expect me to give you anything?"

When she had finished eating, they said to her, "Here's a broom. Go outside and sweep around the back door so it's clean."

"Do your own sweeping!" she responded. "I'm not your maid."

When she saw that they were not going to give her anything, she went out the door, and the three gnomes began talking among themselves. "What should we give her for being so naughty and having such a wicked and greedy heart that makes her so stingy?''

"She shall grow uglier with each day that passes. This is my gift,'' said the first one.

"Each time she utters a word, a toad shall spring out of her mouth. This will be my gift,'' said the second.

"She will die a miserable death. This will be my gift,'' said the third.

Meanwhile, the maiden looked for strawberries outside, and when she could not find any, she went home in a bad mood. As she opened her mouth to tell her mother what had happened in the forest a toad sprang out of her mouth with each word she uttered, causing everyone to be repulsed by her.

Now the stepmother was even more disturbed than before and could only think of how she might be able to hurt her husband's daughter, who was getting more beautiful day by day. Finally she took a kettle, put it on the fire, and boiled some yarn in it. When the yarn was boiled, she hung it on the poor maiden's shoulders, gave her an ax, and ordered her to go to the frozen river, where she was to chop a hole and rinse the yarn. Since she was obedient, the maiden went to the river and began chopping the hole in the ice. While she was in the middle of chopping the hole, a splendid coach with a king inside came driving by. The coach stopped, and the king asked, "Who are you, my child, and what are you doing here?''

"I'm a poor maiden, and I'm rinsing yarn.''

The king felt sorry for her, and when he saw how beautiful she was, he said, "Would you like to ride with me in my coach?''

"Oh, yes, with all my heart!'' she replied, for she was glad to get as far away as possible from her mother and sister.

So she climbed into the coach and drove away with the king, and when they got to his castle, the wedding was celebrated with great pomp, and this would not have happened were it not for the gifts of the three gnomes.

After a year had passed, the young queen gave birth to a son, and when the stepmother heard about her great fortune, she went to the castle with her daughter as if she wanted to pay a visit. However, when the king left the castle and no one else was there, the evil woman seized the queen by her head, and the daughter grabbed her by the feet. They lifted her from the bed and threw her right out the window into the river flowing by the castle. Then the ugly daughter lay down in the bed, and the old woman pulled the covers over her head. When the king came back home and wanted to speak to his wife, the old woman cried out, "Hush, hush! Now's not the time. She's in a terrible sweat. You must let her rest today.''

The king did not suspect any mischief and came again the next day. When he began talking with his wife and she answered, there were toads springing out of her mouth with each word she uttered, not the pieces of gold that usually fell out. So he asked what all this meant, and the old woman said this came from the terrible sweating and would soon go away.

During the night, however, a kitchen boy saw a duck swimming through the drain, and it said:

"King, my king, what are you doing?
Are you awake, or might you be sleeping?"

When the boy did not answer, the duck said:

"And are all my guests now sound asleep?"

Then the kitchen boy answered:

"Yes, indeed, you can't hear a peep."

Then she asked again:

"How about that baby of mine?"

He replied:

"Oh, he's asleep and doing just fine."

Finally the duck assumed the shape of the queen, went upstairs, nursed the baby, plumped up his little bed, covered him, and returned to the drain, where she swam away as a duck. This happened the next night too, and on the third night, she said to the kitchen boy, "Go and tell the king to take his sword and swing it three times over my head on the threshold."

The kitchen boy ran and told the king, who came with his sword and swung it three times over the ghost. At the third time his wife appeared before him alive and as well as ever before.

Now the king was exceedingly happy, but he kept the queen hidden in a room until Sunday, when their child was to be baptized. When he was baptized, the king said, "What does a person deserve who drags someone out of his bed and throws him into the water?"

"The scoundrel deserves nothing better than to be put into a barrel studded with nails on the inside," said the old woman. "And then he should be rolled down the hill into the water."

"You have pronounced your own sentence," said the king.

He ordered a barrel like that to be fetched, and the old woman and her daughter were put inside. The lid was hammered on, and the barrel was rolled down the hill into the river.

◈ 14 ◈

The Three Spinners

THERE ONCE WAS A LAZY MAIDEN who did not want to spin, and no matter what her mother said, she refused to spin. Finally, her mother became so angry and impatient that she beat her, and her daughter began to cry loudly. Just then the queen happened to be driving by, and when she heard the crying, she ordered the carriage to stop, went into the house, and asked the mother why she was beating her daughter, for her screams could be heard out on the street. The woman was too ashamed to tell the queen that her daughter was lazy and said, "I can't get her to stop spinning. She does nothing but spin and spin, and I'm so poor that I can't provide the flax."

"Well," the queen replied, "there's nothing I like to hear more than the sound of spinning, and I'm never happier than when I hear the constant humming of the wheels. Let me take your daughter with me to my castle. I've got plenty of flax, and she can spin as much as she likes."

The mother was delighted to give her consent, and the queen took the maiden with her. After they reached the castle, she led the maiden upstairs to three rooms that were filled with the finest flax from floor to ceiling.

"Now, spin this flax for me," she said. "And if you finish all this, you shall have my oldest son for your husband. It doesn't matter to me that you're poor. You work industriously and you never stop. That in itself is dowry enough."

The maiden was deeply frightened, for she could not have spun the flax even if she were to live three hundred years and sit there every day from morning till night. Therefore, when she was left alone, she began to weep and sat there for three days without lifting a finger. On the third day the queen came back to the room, and when she saw that nothing had been spun, she was puzzled. But the maiden made up an excuse and said she had been so tremendously upset about leaving her mother's house that she had been unable to begin working. The queen accepted this excuse, but upon leaving she said, "Tomorrow you must begin your work for me."

When the maiden was alone again, she did not know what to do or where to turn. In her distress she went over to the window and saw three women coming in her direction: the first had a broad flat foot, the second had such a large lower lip that it hung down over her chin, and the third had an immense thumb. They stopped in front of her window, looked up, and asked the maiden what the matter was. She told them about her predicament, and they offered to help her.

"We'll spin your flax for you in no time at all," they said. "But only if you invite us to your wedding and are not ashamed of us. Moreover, you must call us your cousins, and let us eat at your table."

"With all my heart," she responded. "Just come in and get to work right away."

She let the three odd women in and cleared a place for them in the first room where they could sit down and begin their spinning. One drew out the thread and began treading the treadle, the other wet the thread, and the third twisted it and struck the table with her finger. Whenever she struck it, a reel of yarn dropped to the ground, and it was always most delicately spun. The maiden concealed the three spinners from the queen, and every time the queen came, the maiden showed her such a large amount of spun yarn that there was no end to the queen's praise for her. When the first room was empty of flax, they moved on to the second and then the third until it too was cleared of flax. Now the three women took their leave and said to the maiden, "Don't forget what you've promised us. It will determine your good fortune."

When the maiden showed the queen the empty rooms and the large piles of yarn, the queen arranged for the wedding, and the bridegroom was happy to get such a skillful and industrious wife and gave her tremendous praise.

"I have three cousins," said the maiden, "and since they've done so many good things for me, I'd like to remember them in my happiness by inviting them to the wedding. Please allow me to do this and let them sit at our table."

The queen and the bridegroom said, "Why, of course, we'll allow this."

When the feast was just about to begin, the three women entered in bizarre costumes, and the bride said, "Welcome, dear cousins."

"Ahh!" said the bridegroom. "How did you ever come by such ghastly-looking friends?"

Then he went to the one with a broad flat foot and asked, "How did you get such a flat foot?"

"From treading," she answered. "From treading."

Next the bridegroom went to the second and asked, "How did you get such a drooping lip?"

"From licking," she answered. "From licking."

Then he asked the third one, "How did you get such an immense thumb?"

"From twisting thread," she answered. "From twisting thread."

Upon hearing this the prince was alarmed and said, "Never ever shall my beautiful wife touch a spinning wheel again."

Thus she was able to rid herself of the terrible task of spinning flax.

◈ 15 ◈

Hansel and Gretel

A POOR WOODCUTTER lived with his wife and his two children on the edge of a large forest. The boy was called Hansel and the girl Gretel. The woodcutter did not have much food around the house, and when a great famine devastated the entire country, he could no longer provide enough for his family's daily meals. One night, as he was lying in bed and thinking about his worries, he began tossing and turning. Then he sighed and said to his wife, "What's to become of us? How can we feed our poor children when we don't even have enough for ourselves?"

"I'll tell you what," answered his wife. "Early tomorrow morning we'll take the children out into the forest where it's most dense. We'll build a fire and give them each a piece of bread. Then we'll go about our work and leave them alone. They won't find their way back home, and we'll be rid of them."

"No, wife," the man said. "I won't do this. I don't have the heart to leave my children in the forest. The wild beasts would soon come and tear them apart."

"Oh, you fool!" she said. "Then all four of us will have to starve to death. You'd better start planing the boards for our coffins!" She continued to harp on this until he finally agreed to do what she suggested.

"But still, I feel sorry for the poor children," he said.

The two children had not been able to fall asleep that night either. Their hunger kept them awake, and when they heard what their stepmother said to their father, Gretel wept bitter tears and said to Hansel, "Now it's all over for us."

"Be quiet, Gretel," Hansel said. "Don't get upset. I'll soon find a way to help us."

When their parents had fallen asleep, Hansel put on his little jacket, opened the bottom half of the door, and crept outside. The moon was shining very brightly, and the white pebbles glittered in front of the house like pure silver coins. Hansel stooped down to the ground and stuffed his pocket with as many pebbles as he could fit in. Then he went back and said to Gretel, "Don't worry, my dear little sister. Just sleep in peace. God will not forsake us." And he lay down again in his bed.

At dawn, even before the sun began to rise, the woman came and woke the two children: "Get up, you lazybones! We're going into the forest to fetch some wood." Then she gave each one of them a piece of bread and said, "Now you have something for your noon-day meal, but don't eat it before then because you're not getting anything else."

Gretel put the bread under her apron because Hansel had the pebbles in his pocket. Then they all set out together toward the forest. After they had walked a while, Hansel stopped and looked back at the house. He did this time and again until his father said, "Hansel, what are you looking at there? Why are you dawdling? Pay attention, and don't forget how to use your legs!"

"Oh, Father," said Hansel, "I'm looking at my little white cat that's sitting up on the roof and wants to say good-bye to me."

"You fool," the mother said. "That's not a cat. It's the morning sun shining on the chimney."

But Hansel had not been looking at the cat. Instead, he had been taking the shiny pebbles from his pocket and constantly dropping them on the ground. When they reached the middle of the forest, the father said, "Children, I want you to gather some wood. I'm going to make a fire so you won't get cold."

Hansel and Gretel gathered together some brushwood and built quite a nice little pile. The brushwood was soon kindled, and when the fire was ablaze, the woman said, "Now, children, lie down by the fire, and rest yourselves. We're going into the forest to chop wood. When we're finished, we'll come back and get you.''

Hansel and Gretel sat by the fire, and when noon came, they ate their pieces of bread. Since they heard the sounds of the ax, they thought their father was nearby. But it was not the ax. Rather, it was a branch that he had tied to a dead tree, and the wind was banging it back and forth. After they had been sitting there for a long time, they became so weary that their eyes closed, and they fell sound asleep. By the time they finally awoke, it was already pitch black, and Gretel began to cry and said, ''How are we going to get out of the forest?''

But Hansel comforted her by saying, ''Just wait awhile until the moon has risen. Then we'll find the way.''

And when the full moon had risen, Hansel took his little sister by the hand and followed the pebbles that glittered like newly minted silver coins and showed them the way. They walked the whole night long and arrived back at their father's house at break of day. They knocked at the door, and when the woman opened it and saw it was Hansel and Gretel, she said, ''You wicked children, why did you sleep so long in the forest? We thought you'd never come back again.''

But the father was delighted because he had been deeply troubled by the way he had abandoned them in the forest.

Not long after that the entire country was once again ravaged by famine, and one night the children heard their mother talking to their father in bed. ''Everything's been eaten up again. We only have half a loaf of bread, but after it's gone, that will be the end of our food. The children must leave. This time we'll take them even farther into the forest so they won't find their way back home again. Otherwise, there's no hope for us.''

All this saddened the father, and he thought, It'd be much better to share your last bite to eat with your children. But the woman would not listen to anything he said. She just scolded and reproached him. Once you've given a hand, people will take your arm, and since he had given in the first time, he also had to yield a second time.

However, the children were still awake and had overheard their conversation. When their parents had fallen asleep, Hansel got up, intending to go out and gather pebbles as he had done the time before, but the woman had locked the door, and Hansel could not get out. Nevertheless, he comforted his little sister and said, ''Don't cry, Gretel. Just sleep in peace. The dear Lord is bound to help us.''

Early the next morning the woman came and got the children out of bed. They each received little pieces of bread, but they were smaller than the last time. On the way into the forest Hansel crumbled the bread in his pocket and stopped as often as he could to throw the crumbs on the ground.

"Hansel, why are you always stopping and looking around?" asked the father. "Keep going!"

"I'm looking at my little pigeon that's sitting on the roof and wants to say good-bye to me," Hansel answered.

"Fool!" the woman said. "That's not your little pigeon. It's the morning sun shining on the chimney."

But little by little Hansel managed to scatter all the bread crumbs on the path. The woman led the children even deeper into the forest until they came to a spot they had never in their lives seen before. Once again a large fire was made, and the mother said, "Just keep sitting here, children. If you get tired, you can sleep a little. We're going into the forest to chop wood, and in the evening, when we're done, we'll come and get you."

When noon came, Gretel shared her bread with Hansel, who had scattered his along the way. Then they fell asleep, and evening passed, but no one came for the poor children. Only when it was pitch black did they finally wake up, and Hansel comforted his little sister by saying, "Just wait until the moon has risen, Gretel. Then we'll see the little bread crumbs that I scattered. They'll show us the way back home."

When the moon rose, they set out but could not find the crumbs, because the many thousands of birds that fly about in the forest and fields had devoured them.

"Don't worry, we'll find the way," Hansel said to Gretel, but they could not find it. They walked the entire night and all the next day as well, from morning till night, but they did not get out of the forest. They were now also very hungry, for they had had nothing to eat except some berries that they had found growing on the ground. Eventually they became so tired that their legs would no longer carry them, and they lay down beneath a tree and fell asleep.

It was now the third morning since they had left their father's house. They began walking again, and they kept going deeper and deeper into the forest. If help did not arrive soon, they were bound to perish of hunger and exhaustion. At noon they saw a beautiful bird as white as snow sitting on a branch. It sang with such a lovely voice that the children stood still and listened to it. When the bird finished its song, it flapped its wings and flew ahead of them. They followed it until they came to a little house that was made of bread. Moreover, it had cake for a roof and pure sugar for windows.

"What a blessed meal!" said Hansel. "Let's have a taste. I want to eat a piece of the roof. Gretel, you can have some of the window, since it's sweet."

Hansel reached up high and broke off a piece of the roof to see how it tasted, and Gretel leaned against the windowpanes and nibbled on them. Then they heard a shrill voice cry out from inside:

"Nibble, nibble, I hear a mouse.
Who's that nibbling at my house?"

The children answered:

"The wind, the wind; it's very mild,
blowing like the Heavenly Child."

And they did not bother to stop eating or let themselves be distracted. Since the roof tasted so good, Hansel ripped off a large piece and pulled it down, while Gretel pushed out a round piece of the windowpane, sat down, and ate it with great relish. Suddenly the door opened, and a very old woman leaning on a crutch came slinking out of the house. Hansel and Gretel were so tremendously frightened that they dropped what they had in their hands. But the old woman wagged her head and said, "Well now, dear children, who brought you here? Just come inside and stay with me. Nobody's going to harm you."

She took them both by the hand and led them into her house. Then she served them a good meal of milk and pancakes with sugar and apples and nuts. Afterward she made up two little beds with white sheets, whereupon Hansel and Gretel lay down in them and thought they were in heaven.

The old woman, however, had only pretended to be friendly. She was really a wicked witch on the lookout for children, and had built the house made of bread only to lure them to her. As soon as she had any children in her power, she would kill, cook, and eat them. It would be like a feast day for her. Now, witches have red eyes and cannot see very far, but they have a keen sense of smell, like animals, and can detect when human beings are near them. Therefore, when Hansel and Gretel had come into her vicinity, she had laughed wickedly and scoffed, "They're mine! They'll never get away from me!"

Early the next morning, before the children were awake, she got up and looked at the two of them sleeping so sweetly with full rosy cheeks. Then she muttered to herself, "They'll certainly make for a tasty meal!"

She seized Hansel with her scrawny hands and carried him into a small pen, where she locked him up behind a grilled door. No matter how much he screamed, it did not help. Then she went back to Gretel, shook her until she woke up, and yelled, "Get up, you lazybones! I want you to fetch some water and cook your brother something nice. He's sitting outside in a pen, and we've got to fatten him up. Then, when he's fat enough, I'm going to eat him."

Gretel began to weep bitter tears, but they were all in vain. She had to do what the wicked witch demanded. So the very best food was cooked for poor Hansel, while Gretel got nothing but crab shells. Every morning the old woman went slinking to the little pen and called out, "Hansel, stick out your finger so I can feel how fat you are."

However, Hansel stuck out a little bone, and since the old woman had poor eyesight, she thought the bone was Hansel's finger. She was puzzled that Hansel did not get any fatter, and when a month had gone by and Hansel still seemed to be thin, she was overcome by her impatience and decided not to wait any longer.

"Hey there, Gretel!" she called to the little girl. "Get a move on and fetch some water! I don't care whether Hansel's fat or thin. He's going to be slaughtered tomorrow, and then I'll cook him."

Oh, how the poor little sister wailed as she was carrying the water, and how the tears streamed down her cheeks!

"Dear God, help us!" she exclaimed. "If only the wild beasts had eaten us in the forest, then we could have at least died together!"

Early the next morning Gretel had to go out, hang up a kettle full of water, and light the fire.

"First we'll bake," the old woman said. "I've already heated the oven and kneaded the dough." She pushed poor Gretel out to the oven, where the flames were leaping from the fire. "Crawl inside," said the witch, "and see if it's properly heated so we can slide the bread in."

The witch intended to close the oven door once Gretel had climbed inside, for the witch wanted to bake her and eat her too. But Gretel sensed what she had in mind and said, "I don't know how to do it. How do I get in?"

"You stupid goose," the old woman said. "The opening's large enough. Watch, even I can get in!"

She waddled up to the oven and stuck her head through the oven door. Then Gretel gave her a push that sent her flying inside and shut the iron door and bolted it. *Whew!* The witch began to howl dreadfully, but Gretel ran away, and the godless witch was miserably burned to death.

Meanwhile, Gretel ran straight to Hansel, opened the pen, and cried out, "Hansel, we're saved! The old witch is dead!"

Then Hansel jumped out of the pen like a bird that hops out of a cage when the door is opened. My how happy they were! They hugged each other, danced around, and kissed. Since they no longer had anything to fear, they went into the witch's house, and there they found chests filled with pearls and jewels all over the place.

"They're certainly much better than pebbles," said Hansel, and he put whatever he could fit into his pockets, and Gretel said, "I'm going to carry some home too," and she filled her apron full of jewels and pearls.

"We'd better be on our way now," said Hansel, "so we can get out of the witch's forest."

When they had walked for a few hours, they reached a large river.

"We can't get across," said Hansel. "I don't see a bridge or any way over it."

"There are no boats either," Gretel responded, "but there's a white duck swimming over there. It's bound to help us across if I ask it." Then she cried out:

"Help us, help us, little duck!
It's Hansel and Gretel, and we're really stuck.
We can't get over, try as we may.
Please take us across right away!"

The little duck came swimming up to them, and Hansel got on top of its back and told his sister to sit down beside him.

"No," Gretel answered. "That will be too heavy for the little duck. Let it carry us across one at a time."

The kind little duck did just that, and when they were safely across and had walked on for some time, the forest became more and more familiar to them, and finally they caught sight of their father's house from afar. They began to run at once, and soon rushed into the house and threw themselves around their father's neck. The man had not had a single happy hour since he had abandoned his children in the forest, and in the meantime his wife had died. Gretel opened and shook out her apron so that the pearls and jewels bounced about the room, and Hansel added to this by throwing one handful after another from his pocket. Now all their troubles were over, and they lived together in utmost joy.

My tale is done. See the mouse run. Catch it, whoever can, and then you can make a great big cap out of its fur.

◈ 16 ◈

The Three Snake Leaves

ONCE UPON A TIME there was a poor man who could no longer provide enough food for his only son. Therefore, the son said, "Dear Father, you're having such a hard time and I'm becoming such a burden that I'd prefer to go away and try to earn a living by myself." The father gave him his blessing but was greatly saddened to see him depart.

The king of a powerful country was waging war when all this occurred, and the young man enlisted in the king's army and went out to fight. When he approached enemy territory, a battle was being fought, and there was a great deal of danger. The air was filled with bullets striking his comrades, who fell dead on all sides. When the commander as well was killed, the survivors wanted to flee the field, but the young man stepped forward and encouraged them to keep fighting.

"We shall not let our fatherland be destroyed!" he cried out.

The others followed him as he charged forward, and they defeated the enemy. When the king heard that he owed this victory to the young man alone, he promoted him above all the others, gave him great treasures, and made him the most important person in his kingdom.

The king had a daughter who was very beautiful but also very strange, for she had made a vow that she would accept as her lord and master only a man who would let himself be buried alive with her if she should die first.

"If he really loves me with all his heart," she said, "why would he want to continue living?"

She was prepared to do the same in return, and if he were to die first, she would let herself be buried in the grave with him. This strange vow had scared away all suitors up to that time, but the young man was so infatuated by her beauty that he did not care about anything else and asked her father for her hand.

"Do you know what you must promise?" the king asked.

"I shall have to be buried alive in her grave if I survive her," the young man said. "But my love for her is so great that I don't care about the danger."

The king gave his consent, and the wedding was celebrated with great splendor. After this the couple lived happily and were contented with each other for some time. But then the young queen fell seriously ill, and no doctor could help her. When she lay dead, the young king remembered the promise he had been obliged to make, and he shuddered at the thought of being buried alive. However, there was no escape. The old king had had all the gates posted with guards, and it was impossible for his son-in-law to avoid what fate had in store for him. When the day came for the queen's body to be buried in the royal vault, he was led down into the crypt with it, and the door was bolted and locked behind him.

In the vault, next to the coffin, was a table, and on it were four candles, four loaves of bread, and four bottles of wine. As soon as the provisions were used up, the young man would perish from starvation. So there he sat, full of sorrow and grief. Each day he ate just a little bit of bread and drank just a swig of wine. Yet, he saw death coming closer and closer. Once, as he was staring into space, he saw a snake crawling from a corner of the vault and heading toward the dead body. Since he thought the snake was coming to gnaw at the body, he drew his sword and said, "As long as I live, you shall not touch her." And he cut the snake into three pieces. After a while another snake came crawling out of the corner, but when it saw the first one lying dead and cut to pieces, it went back to where it came from. It returned shortly, however, with three green leaves in its mouth, and it proceeded to take the three pieces of the snake, put them in their proper places, and set one leaf on each of the wounds. All at once the pieces that had been severed came back to life, and both snakes hurried off together. The leaves remained on the ground, and it occurred to the unfortunate young man, who had witnessed the whole thing, that the miraculous power of the leaves that had brought the snake back to life might also be able to help a human being. So he picked up the leaves and placed one on his dead wife's mouth, and the other two on her eyes. No sooner had he done this than the blood began to stir in her veins, rose up into her pale face, and gave her cheeks a rosy color. Then she took a deep breath, opened her eyes, and said, "Oh, God, where am I?"

"You're with me, dear wife," he answered, and he told her how everything had happened and how he had brought her back to life. Then he handed her some of the wine and bread, and when she had regained her strength, she stood up, and they went to the door. There they knocked and yelled so loudly that the guards heard them and reported it to the king. The king himself then came and opened the door. When he found them alive and well, he rejoiced with them and was glad that their troubles were over.

The young king took the three snake leaves, gave them to a servant, and said, "Take good care of them for me and carry them with you at all times. If we find ourselves in a predicament, they might be able to help us."

Meanwhile, a change had come over his wife after she had been restored to life. It was as if all the love she had felt for her husband had been drained from her. When some time had gone by and he wished to make a voyage overseas to visit his old father, they boarded a ship, but she, having forgotten the great love and devotion he had shown her at the time of her rescue, gave in to her wicked passion for the ship's captain. Then one night, when the young king was lying asleep, she called the captain. After she took her sleeping husband by the head, she ordered the captain to take his feet, and they threw him overboard into the sea. Once they had done their shameful deed, she said, "Now let us return home and say he died on the way. I'll rave about you and praise you so much that my father will let you marry me and make you heir to his crown."

However, the faithful servant had witnessed everything. He unfastened a small boat from the ship without their noticing it, got into it, and sailed after his master, while the traitors continued their voyage. He fished the dead man out of the sea, and with the help of the snake leaves, which he was carrying with him, and which he put on his master's eyes and mouth, he succeeded in bringing him back to life.

Now the two of them rowed day and night with all their might, and their little boat sailed so swiftly over the sea that they reached the old king before the others. The king was puzzled when he saw them coming back alone, and he asked what had happened to them. When he learned about his daughter's treachery, he said, "I can't believe she would do such an awful thing, but the truth will soon come to light."

He ordered the young king and his servant to hide in a secret chamber and not to let themselves be seen by anyone. Soon after, the big ship came sailing home, and the godless woman appeared before her father with a troubled expression.

"Why have you come home alone?" he asked. "Where's your husband?"

"Ah, dear Father," she answered. "I'm returning home in great sorrow. My husband suddenly took sick and died during the voyage, and if it had not been for the support of the good captain, things would have gone badly for me. He was present at my husband's death and can tell you everything."

But the king said, "I'm going to bring the dead man back to life," and he opened the chamber door and told the two to come out.

When the king's daughter caught sight of her husband, she was thunderstruck, and falling to her knees, she begged for mercy.

"There will be no mercy," said the old king. "He was ready to die with you and brought you back to life, but you killed him in his sleep, and now you shall receive your just reward."

Then she and her accomplice were put aboard a ship peppered with holes and sent out to sea, where they soon sank beneath the waves.

◈ 17 ◈

The White Snake

A LONG TIME AGO there lived a king who was famous throughout the entire country for his wisdom. Nothing remained hidden from him, and it seemed as if he could obtain news of the most secret things through the air. However, he had one strange custom. Every day at noon, after the table was cleared of food and nobody else was present, a trusted servant had to bring him one more dish. This dish was always covered, and the servant himself did not know what was in it, nor did anyone else, for the king did not take the cover from the dish and eat until he was all alone. The king continued this custom for quite some time, until one day the servant, while removing the dish, was overcome by curiosity. He took it into his room, and after he had carefully locked the door, he lifted the cover and found a white snake lying inside. Once he laid eyes on it, though, he had an irresistible desire to taste it. So he cut off a little piece and put it in his mouth. No sooner did his tongue touch it than he heard a strange whispering of exquisite voices outside his window. He went over to it to listen and noticed some sparrows talking to one another, telling what they had seen in the fields and forest. Tasting the snake had given him the power to understand the language of animals.

Now, it so happened that on this very day the queen lost her most beautiful ring, and the trusted servant was suspected of committing the theft because he had access to everything. The king summoned the servant and with harsh words threatened him, saying that if he was not able to name the guilty person by morning, he himself would be considered the thief and would be executed. It was to no avail that the servant protested his innocence, for he was given a curt dismissal.

Distressed and afraid, he went down into the courtyard and tried to think of a way out of his predicament. Some ducks were peacefully sitting and resting by a running brook, preening themselves and chatting in a confidential tone. The servant stopped and listened to them as they told each other where they had been waddling about all morning and what good pickings they had found. But one of the ducks was irritable and said, "There's something heavy in my stomach. I was eating too fast and swallowed a ring that was lying under the king's window."

Right away the servant grabbed the duck by its neck, carried it into the kitchen, and said to the cook, "This one's well-fed. It's time you killed it!"

"All right," said the cook, weighing it in his hands. "It certainly hasn't been shy about stuffing itself. Besides, it's been waiting long enough for its roasting."

So he cut off the duck's neck, and when it was being cleaned, the queen's ring was found in its stomach. Now the servant could easily prove his innocence, and since the king wanted to make amends for having wronged his servant, he granted him a favor and promised him whatever royal post of honor he desired. The servant declined all of this. His only request was for a horse and some travel money, for he had a desire to travel about for a while and see the world.

When his wish had been granted, he set out on his way, and one day, as he was passing a pond, he noticed three fish trapped in the reeds and gasping for water. Though it is said that fish cannot talk, he heard them crying in distress and wailing that they had to die so miserably. Since he felt sorry for them, he got down from his horse and put the three trapped fish back into the water. They wriggled for joy, stuck their heads out of the water, and cried out to him, "We'll remember you for saving our lives, and one day we'll repay you."

He rode on, and a while later it seemed to him that he heard a voice in the sand at his feet. He listened and heard an ant king complaining, "If only people with their clumsy beasts would keep away from us! That stupid horse is mercilessly trampling my people to death with his heavy hooves!"

The servant turned his horse onto a side path, and the ant king cried out to him, "We'll remember this, and one day we'll repay you."

The servant's path led into a forest, and there he saw a father and mother raven standing near their nest and pushing their young ones out of the nest.

"Get out! You're nothing but freeloaders!" they were exclaiming. "We can't find enough food to feed you anymore, and now you're big enough to feed yourselves."

The poor young birds lay on the ground, flapped their wings, and began crying, "We're just helpless children! How are we supposed to feed ourselves when we can't fly? All we can do is stay here and starve."

Then the kind young man dismounted, killed his horse with his sword, and left it for the young ravens to feed on. They hopped over to the horse, ate their fill, and cried out, "We'll remember this, and one day we'll repay you."

Now the servant had to use his own legs. After he had walked a long way, he reached a big city where there was a great deal of noise and a large crowd in the streets. A man on horseback rode by and announced that the king's daughter was looking for a husband, but whoever declared himself a suitor would have to perform a difficult task, and if he did not complete it successfully, he would forfeit his life. Many men had already tried and had risked their lives in vain. When the young man saw the princess, he was so dazzled by her great beauty that he forgot all about the danger, went before the king, and declared himself a suitor. He was promptly led to the sea, and a gold ring was thrown into it before his eyes. The king told him that he was to fetch the ring from the depths of the sea, and he added, "If you come up without it, you'll be continually pushed back down until you perish in the waves."

Everyone felt sorry for the handsome young man and left him alone by the sea. He was standing on the shore thinking about what to do when he suddenly saw three fish swimming toward him. They were none other than the three fish whose lives he had saved. The one in the middle held a shell in its mouth, which it set down on the beach at the feet of the young man, who picked it up. When he opened the shell, he found the gold ring, and bursting with joy, he brought it to the king expecting that he would receive the promised reward. But when the proud king's daughter discovered that he was not her equal in birth, she scorned him and demanded that he first perform another task. She went down into the garden, and she herself scattered ten sacks full of millet in the grass.

"He must pick them all up before the sun rises tomorrow," she said. "And not a single grain may be missing."

The young man sat down in the garden and tried to think of a way to accomplish the task, but nothing occurred to him, and he sat there quite sadly, expecting to be led to his death at the break of dawn. But when the first rays of the sun fell on the garden, he saw ten sacks all filled to the top and standing side by side. Not a single grain was missing. The ant king had come during the night with thousands and thousands of ants, and the grateful insects had picked up the millet seeds with great diligence and gathered them into the sacks. The princess herself went down to the garden and was amazed to see that the young man had accomplished the task. But her proud heart could not be tamed, and she said, "Even if he has accomplished the first two tasks, he shall not become my husband until he has brought me an apple from the Tree of Life."

The young man did not know where the Tree of Life was. Therefore, he set out with the intention of going as far as his legs could carry him, even though he had no hope of finding it. One evening, after he had traveled through three kingdoms and reached a forest, he sat down beneath a tree and wanted to sleep. But he heard a noise in the tree, and a golden apple fell into his hand. At the same time three ravens flew down to him, landed on his knees, and said, "We're the three young ravens whom you saved from starvation. When we grew up, we heard you were looking for the golden apple. So we flew across the sea to the end of the world, where the Tree of Life is standing, and we've fetched the apple."

Now the young man was full of joy and started on his way home. He brought the golden apple to the beautiful princess, who no longer had any excuses to make. They divided the apple of life and ate it together, and her heart filled with love for him. In time they reached a ripe old age in peace and happiness.

◈ 18 ◈

The Straw, the Coal, and the Bean

THERE ONCE WAS A POOR OLD WOMAN who lived in a village, and she had gathered a bunch of beans that she wanted to cook. So she prepared a fire on her hearth, lighting it with a handful of straw to make it burn faster. As she was emptying the beans into the pot, one of them slipped to the floor unnoticed and lay next to a straw. Soon after, a glowing coal jumped from the hearth and joined the other two. Then the straw began to speak. "Dear friends, where have you come from?"

"Fortunately, I jumped out of the fire," responded the coal. "If I hadn't used sheer force, it would have been the end of me. I would have been burned to ashes."

"I also escaped by the skin of my teeth," said the bean. "If the old woman had thrown me into the pot, I'd have been cooked into a soup without mercy like my comrades."

"Do you think my fate would have been any better?" said the straw. "The old woman let all my brothers burn up in smoke. She grabbed sixty all at once and put them to death. Fortunately, I slipped through her fingers."

"Well, what should we do now?" asked the coal.

"Since we were so lucky to escape death, I think we should stick together like good comrades," the bean said. "Also we'd better begin heading for a foreign country before there's a new fatality."

This proposal pleased the other two, and they set out on their way. However, they soon came to a small brook, and since there was no bridge or way over it, they did not know how they would manage to cross it. Then the straw came up with a good idea and said, "I'll lay myself across, and then you'll be able to walk over me like a bridge."

So the straw stretched itself from one bank to the other, and the coal, who had a fiery temperament, marched boldly onto the newly built bridge. Yet, when it was halfway across and heard the water murmuring below, it got frightened, stopped in its tracks, and did not dare go any further. But now the straw began to burn, broke in two pieces, and fell into the brook. The coal tumbled after, and as it hit the water, it gave up the ghost. The bean, which had cautiously stayed behind, had to laugh when it saw what happened, but it was unable to stop and kept laughing so hard that it burst. Now, it would have been all over for the bean were it not for a traveling tailor who had been resting near the brook. He felt so sorry for the bean that he took out his needle and thread and sewed the bean together. The bean thanked him most kindly, but because the tailor had used black thread, all beans since then have had a black seam.

◈ 19 ◈

The Fisherman and His Wife

ONCE UPON A TIME there was a fisherman who lived with his wife in a dirty hovel near the sea. Every day the fisherman went out to fish, and all he did was fish and fish. One day he was sitting with his line and gazing into the clear water. And all he did was sit and sit. Suddenly his line sank deep down to the bottom, and when he pulled it up, he had a large flounder on the line, and the flounder said to him, "Listen here, fisherman, I beg of you, let me live. I'm not a real flounder but an enchanted prince. So what would it benefit you to kill me? I certainly wouldn't taste very good. Put me back into the water, and let me go."

"Hold on," said the man. "You don't have to waste your words on me. I would have thrown a talking fish back into the water anyway."

He then put the fish back into the clear water, and the flounder swam to the bottom, leaving behind a long streak of blood. Then the fisherman stood up and went to the hovel to be with his wife.

"Husband," asked the wife, "didn't you catch anything today?"

"No," said the man. "I caught a flounder, but he said he was an enchanted prince, and I let him go."

"Didn't you wish for anything?" asked the wife.

"No," said the husband. "What should I have wished for?"

"Ah," said the wife. "Don't you think it's awful that we've got to keep living in such a hovel? It stinks, and it's disgusting. You should have wished for a little cottage. Go back and call him. Tell him we want a little cottage. I'm sure he'll give us one."

"But there's no reason to go back," said the husband.

"Of course there is," said the wife. "Look, you caught him and let him go. That's why he's bound to give it to us. Now go at once!"

The man really did not want to go, but neither did he want to oppose his wife. So he went back to the sea.

When he got there, the sea was very green and yellow and no longer so clear. He stood on the shore and said:

"Flounder, flounder, in the sea,
if you're a man, then speak to me.
Though I do not care for my wife's request,
I've come to ask it nonetheless."

The flounder came swimming up to him and said, "Well, what does she want?"

"Oh," said the man. "My wife thinks I should have wished for something because I caught you. Since she doesn't want to live in a hovel, she'd like to have a cottage."

"Just go home," said the flounder. "She's already got it."

When the fisherman arrived at home, his wife was no longer sitting in a hovel. Instead, she was sitting on a bench before the door to a little cottage. His wife took him by the hand and said, "Come inside, husband. Look! Now, isn't this better?"

They went inside, and in the house he found a little hallway, a splendid parlor, and a bedroom. There was also a kitchen and a pantry furnished with all the best dishware and utensils, tinware and brass, everything that one could possibly need. Behind the cottage was a little yard with chickens and ducks and a garden with vegetables and fruit.

"You see," said the wife, "isn't this nice?"

"Yes," said the husband. "Hopefully, it will stay that way. Now we can live quite happily."

"That's something we've got to think about," said the wife.

Thereupon they had something to eat and went to bed.

Everything went well for about a week or two, and then the wife said, "Listen, husband, the cottage is much too cramped, and the yard and garden are too small. The flounder could have given us a larger house. I'd very much like to live in a great stone castle. Go back to the flounder and tell him to give us a castle."

"Ah, wife," the husband said, "the cottage is good enough. Why should we want to live in a castle?"

"My goodness!" said the wife. "Just go back to him! The flounder can do this without any trouble."

"No, wife," said the husband. "The flounder has just given us a cottage, and I don't want to go back again so soon. He might be insulted."

"Just go!" said the wife. "He can easily do it, and he'll be glad to do it. Just go back to him!"

The husband's heart grew heavy, and he did not want to go. He said to himself, "It just isn't right." Nevertheless, he went.

When he got to the sea, the water was purple, dark blue, gray, and dense. It was no longer green and yellow, though it was still calm. Then he stood there and said:

"Flounder, flounder, in the sea,
if you're a man, then speak to me.
Though I do not care for my wife's request,
I've come to ask it nonetheless."

"Well, what does she want?" the flounder asked.

"Oh," said the man, somewhat distressed. "She wants to live in a great stone castle."

"Just go home. She's already standing at the gate," the flounder said.

The man went back, thinking he was going home, but as he approached the spot where the house had been, he found a great stone palace, and his wife was standing on the steps just about to enter. She took him by the hand and said, "Come inside."

He went in with her and found a big front hall with a marble floor and numerous servants who opened the large doors for them. The walls were all bright and covered with beautiful tapestries. All of the chairs and tables in the rooms were made of gold. Crystal chandeliers hung from the ceilings, and all the rooms and chambers had carpets. Furthermore, the tables sagged under the weight of food and bottles of the very best wine. Behind the palace was a huge yard with stables for horses and cows and the finest carriages. There was also a wonderful large garden with the most beautiful flowers and fine fruit trees, as well as a pleasure park about half a mile long, which had stags, deer, hares, and everything else in it that one could wish for.

"Well," said the wife, "isn't that beautiful?"

"Oh, yes," said the husband. "Hopefully, it will stay that way. Now let's live in the beautiful castle and be content."

"We'll have to think about that," said the wife, "and sleep on it."

Then they went to bed.

The next morning the wife woke up first. It was just daybreak, and from her window she could see the glorious countryside lying before her. As her husband began stretching she poked him in the side with her elbow and said, "Husband, get up and look out the window. Listen, don't you think you can be king over all this country? Go to the flounder and tell him that we want to be king."

"Ah, wife," said the husband. "Why should we be king? I don't want to be king."

"Well," said the wife, "you may not want to be king, but I do. Go to the flounder, and tell him I want to be king."

"Oh, wife," said the husband, "why do you want to be king? I don't want to tell him that."

"Why not?" said the wife. "Go to him at once and tell him I must be king!"

The husband went but was most distressed that his wife wanted to be king. It's not right. It's just not right, he thought, and he did not want to go but went just the same.

When he got to the sea, it was completely gray and black, and the water was twisting and turning from below and smelled putrid. The fisherman stood there and said:

"Flounder, flounder, in the sea,
if you're a man, then speak to me.
Though I do not care for my wife's request,
I've come to ask it nonetheless."

"Well, what does she want?" asked the flounder.

"Oh," said the man. "She wants to be king."

"Go back home," said the flounder. "She's already king."

Then the man went home, and as he approached the palace, he saw that the castle had become much larger, with a huge tower and glistening ornaments on it. There were sentries standing in front of the gate, along with many soldiers, drums, and trumpets. When he entered the palace, he found that everything was made of pure marble and gold and had velvet covers with large golden tassels. The doors to the hall were opened, and he could see the whole court. His wife was sitting on a high throne of gold and diamonds, and on her head she had a big golden crown and in her hand a scepter of pure gold and jewels. Two rows of ladies-in-waiting were standing on either side of her, each lady a head shorter than the next. The fisherman stepped forward and said, "Oh, wife, now you're king, aren't you?"

"Yes," said his wife, "now I am king."

He stood there and looked at her, and after he had gazed at her for some time, he said, "Oh, wife, it's wonderful that you're king! Now let's not wish for anything more."

"No, husband," the wife said as she became very restless. "I have too much time on my hands, and I can't stand it anymore. Go back to the flounder and tell him I'm king, but now I must become emperor as well."

"Oh, wife," said the husband, "why do you want to become emperor?"

"Husband," she said. "Go to the flounder. I want to be emperor!"

"Oh, wife," the husband said. "He can't make you emperor. I don't want to tell that to the flounder. There's only one emperor in the empire. The flounder can't make you emperor. He definitely can't do that."

"What!" said the wife. "I'm king, and you're just my husband. I want you to go there at once! And I mean, at once! If he can make a king, he can also make an emperor. Go to there at once!"

The husband had to return, but as he walked along, he became scared and thought to himself, This won't turn out well at all. Such arrogance, to want to be emperor! The flounder's going to get sick and tired of this.

When he got to the sea, it was all black and dense, and it began to twist and turn from below so that bubbles rose up, and a strong wind whipped across the surface and made the water curdle. The man became frightened, but he stepped forward and said:

"Flounder, flounder, in the sea,
if you're a man, then speak to me.
Though I do not care for my wife's request,
I've come to ask it nonetheless."

"Well, what does she want?" asked the flounder.

"Oh, flounder," he said. "My wife wants to be emperor."

"Go back home," said the flounder. "She's already emperor."

Then the man went home, and when he arrived, the entire castle was made of polished marble with alabaster figures and golden ornaments. Soldiers were marching in front of the gate, and they

were blowing trumpets and beating cymbals and drums. Meanwhile, barons, counts, and dukes were inside the palace walking around like servants. They opened the doors of pure gold for him, and as he entered, he saw his wife sitting on a two-mile-high throne made from a single piece of gold. She was wearing a golden crown three yards tall and covered with diamonds and garnets. In one hand she held the scepter and in the other the imperial globe. She was flanked on either side by two rows of bodyguards, each man shorter than the next, beginning with a tremendous giant two miles tall and ending with the tiniest dwarf, who was no bigger than my pinky. There were also many princes and dukes standing before her, and her husband stepped up and said, "Wife, now you're emperor, aren't you?"

"Yes," she said, "I'm emperor."

Then he stood there and took a good look at her, and after gazing at her for some time, he said, "Oh, wife, it's wonderful that you're emperor. Let's keep it that way."

"Husband," she said. "Why are you standing there? It's true that I'm emperor, but now I want to be pope. Go and tell this to the flounder."

"Oh, wife," said the husband. "What, in heaven's name, don't you want? You can't be pope. There's only one pope in Christendom. The flounder can't make you pope."

"Husband," she said. "I want to be pope! Go there at once and tell him I must be pope."

"No, wife," said the husband. "I don't want to tell him that. It won't turn out well. That's too much to ask. The flounder can't make you pope."

"Stop talking nonsense, husband!" said the wife. "If he can make me emperor, he can also make me pope. Go there at once! I'm the emperor, and you're just my husband. So, do as I say!"

The man became frightened and went, but he felt rather queasy. He was trembling and shaking, and his knees began to wobble. A strong wind swept across the land. Dark clouds flew by as evening came. Leaves were falling from the trees, and the sea rose up in waves and roared as if it were boiling, and the waves splashed against the shore. In the distance the fisherman could see ships firing guns in distress as they were tossed up and down by the waves. Though there was still a little blue in the middle of the sky, the horizon was completely red, as if a heavy thunderstorm were coming. Then he stepped forward, filled with fear and dread, and said:

"Flounder, flounder, in the sea
if you're a man, then speak to me.
Though I do not care for my wife's request,
I've come to ask it nonetheless."

"Well, what does she want?" asked the flounder.
"Oh," the man said, "she wants to be pope."
"Go back home," said the flounder. "She's already pope."

Then the man went home, and when he arrived, he found a great church with nothing but palaces surrounding it. He forced his way through crowds of people and found everything inside illuminated by thousands and thousands of candles. His wife was sitting on a throne even higher than the one before, and she was dressed in pure gold with three big golden crowns on her head. Numerous bishops and priests were standing around her, and there were two rows of candles on either side of her. The biggest candle was as thick and as large as the highest tower, and the tiniest was a church candle. And all the emperors and kings were taking their turn kneeling before her and kissing her slipper.

"Wife," the man said as he looked at her carefully, "now you're pope, aren't you?"

"Yes," she said, "I'm pope."

Then he stepped forward and took a good look at her, and it was as if he were looking into the bright sun. After gazing at her for some time, he said, "Oh, wife, it's wonderful that you're pope. Let's keep it that way."

But she sat stiff as a board and neither stirred nor moved. Then he said, "Wife, be satisfied. Now that you're pope, you can't become anything greater."

"I'll think about it," said the wife.

Then they both went to bed, but she was not satisfied, and her ambition did not let her sleep. She kept thinking of ways she might become greater than she was, while her husband slept soundly, for he had run around a good deal that day. She could not get to sleep at all and tossed and turned from side to side the whole night, trying to think of ways she might become greater than she was. However, nothing whatsoever occurred to her. When the sun began to rise and she saw the red glow of the dawn, she sat up in bed and watched the sun rise from her window. Then the thought occurred to her: Aha, I could also make the sun and the moon rise! She poked her husband in the ribs with her elbow and said, "Husband, wake up and go to the flounder. Tell him I want to be like God."

The husband was still half asleep, but he was so shocked by what she had said that he fell out of the bed. He thought that he had misheard her and rubbed his eyes.

"Oh, wife," he said. "What did you say?"

"Husband," she said, "if I can't make the sun and the moon rise, I won't be able to bear it. Do you think I want to just watch? No, I won't have any more peace until I myself can make them rise."

She gave her husband such an awful look that a shudder ran through his bones.

"Go there at once! I want to be like God."

"Oh, wife!" the husband said, and fell down on his knees. "The flounder can't do that. He can make you an emperor and pope, but I beg you, be content and stay pope."

She immediately became furious, and her hair flew wildly about her head. She tore open her bodice, gave him a kick with her foot, and screamed, "I won't stand for it and can't stand it any longer! I want you to go at once!"

He slipped into his trousers then and ran off like a madman. Outside a great storm was raging, so he could barely keep on his feet. Houses and trees were falling, mountains were trembling, and large boulders were rolling into the sea from the cliffs. The sky was completely pitch black, and there was thunder and lightning. Black waves rose up in the sea as high as church steeples and mountains, and they all had crests of white foam on top. Then the fisherman screamed, but he could not even hear his own words:

"Flounder, flounder, in the sea,
if you're a man, then speak to me.
Though I do not care for my wife's request,
I've come to ask it nonetheless."

"Well, what does she want?" the flounder asked.

"Oh," he said, "she wants to be like God."

"Go back home. She's sitting in your hovel again."

And there they are still living this very day.

◈ 20 ◈

The Brave Little Tailor

ONE SUMMER MORNING a little tailor was sitting on his table by his window. He was in good spirits and was sewing with all his might. Just then a peasant woman came down the street and cried out, "Good jam for sale! Good jam for sale!"

That sounded lovely to the little tailor's ears. He stuck his tiny head out the window and called, "Up here, my dear woman, you're sure to make a good sale with me!"

The woman, with her heavy basket, climbed the three flights of stairs to the tailor's place and had to unpack all her jars in front of him. He inspected each one of them by lifting and sniffing the jam. Finally, he said, "The jam seems good to me. I'll take three ounces, dear woman, but if it comes to a quarter of a pound, it won't matter."

The woman, who had hoped to sell a great deal, gave him what he wanted but went away very annoyed and grumbling.

"Now, may God bless my jam!" the little tailor exclaimed. "Let it give me energy and strength!" He fetched a loaf of bread from the cupboard, cut a full slice for himself, and spread it with the jam. "This certainly won't have a bitter taste," he said. "But first I want to finish the jacket before I take a bite."

He put the bread down beside him and continued sewing, making bigger and bigger stitches due to his joy. Meanwhile, the smell of the sweet jam rose to the wall, where lots of flies had gathered and were now enticed by the smell to swarm and settle on the jam.

"Hey, who invited you?" the little tailor said, and chased the unwelcome guests away. But the flies did not understand German, nor would they let themselves be deterred. Rather, they kept coming back in even larger numbers. Finally, the little tailor had been needled enough, as they say, and he grabbed a piece of cloth from under his worktable.

"Wait, I'll give you something!" he said, swinging at them

mercilessly. When he let up and counted, there were no less than seven flies lying dead before him with their legs stretched out.

"You're quite a man!" he said to himself, and could not help but admire his bravery. "The entire city should know about this!" And the little tailor hastily cut out a belt for himself, stitched it, and embroidered large letters on it: "Seven with one blow!"

"But why just the city?" he continued. "Why shouldn't the whole world know about it?" And his heart wagged with joy like a lamb's tail.

The tailor tied the belt around his waist, and since he now thought that his bravery was too great for his workshop, he decided to go out into the world. Before he left, he searched his house for something to take with him, but he found only a piece of old cheese, which he put in his pocket. Outside the city gate he noticed a bird caught in the bushes, and the bird too found its way into his pocket. Now he bravely hit the road with his legs and pushed on. Since he was light and nimble, he did not become tired. His way led him up a mountain, and when he reached the highest peak, he came across a powerful giant who was sitting there comfortably and gazing about. The little tailor went up to him, addressed him fearlessly, and said, "Good day, friend, you're sitting there and gazing at the great wide world, right? Well, I happen to be on my way into the world to try my luck. Would you like to come along?"

The giant looked at the tailor contemptuously and said, "You crumb! You miserable creature!"

"Is that so!" the little tailor responded, and opened his coat to show the giant his belt. "You can read for yourself what kind of man I am!"

The giant read "Seven with one blow!" and thought that it meant the tailor had slain seven men. Therefore, he began to show some respect for the little fellow. Nevertheless, he wanted to test him first. So he took a stone in his hand and squeezed it until water began to drip from it.

"Do the same," said the giant, "if you have the strength."

"Is that all?" the little tailor said. "That's just child's play for a man like me."

He reached into his pocket, took out the soft cheese, and squeezed it until the liquid ran out.

"That beats yours, doesn't it?" the tailor declared.

The giant did not know what to say, for he could not believe that such a little man was so strong. Next he picked up a stone and threw it so high that it could barely be seen with the naked eye.

"Now, you do the same, you midget!"

"That was a good throw," said the tailor, "but even so, the stone had to return to the ground in the end. Now, I'm going to throw one that won't ever come back."

He reached into his pocket, took out the bird, and threw it into the air. The bird was glad to be free and just kept climbing high in the sky and never returned.

"How did you like that little show, friend?" the tailor asked.

"You certainly can throw," the giant said. "But let's see if you can carry a decent load."

He led the little tailor to a tremendous oak tree that had been cut down and was lying on the ground.

"If you're strong enough," he said, "help me carry the tree out of the forest."

"Gladly," answered the little man. "You take the trunk on your shoulder, and I'll carry the branches and the twigs. After all, they're the heaviest."

The giant lifted the trunk onto his shoulder, while the tailor sat down on a branch. Since the giant could not turn to look around, he had to carry the entire tree and the little tailor as well. Of course, the tailor was feeling good and was quite merry in the rear, so he began to whistle a little song called "Three Little Tailors Who Went Out for a Ride," as if carrying a tree were child's play. After the giant had carried the heavy load a good part of the way, he could go no further and cried out, "Listen, I've got to let the tree drop."

The tailor quickly jumped down, grabbed the tree with both his arms as if he had been carrying it, and said to the giant, "You're such a huge fellow, and yet you can't even carry the tree!"

They walked on together, and when they came to a cherry tree, the giant seized the top, where the fruit was ripest. He bent it down, handed it to the tailor, and told him to eat some of the fruit. But the little tailor was much too weak to hold on to the treetop, and when the giant let go of it, the tailor was catapulted into the air. After he came down again, unharmed, the giant said, "What's this? Don't tell me that you're not strong enough to hold on to that measly twig!"

"Don't worry, I've got plenty of strength," the tailor responded. "Do you think that something like that is really difficult for a man who's slain seven with one blow? I jumped over the tree because some huntsmen were shooting there in the bushes. Let's see if you can jump over it yourself."

The giant tried but could not make it over the tree. He got stuck in the branches, so the little tailor got the better of him once again.

"Well, if you're such a brave fellow," the giant said, "come along with me to our cave and spend the night with us."

The little tailor agreed and followed him. When they arrived in the cave, the other giants were still sitting by the fire, and each one had a roasted sheep in his hand and was eating it. The little tailor looked around and thought, It's certainly roomier in here than in my workshop.

The giant showed him to a bed and told him to lie down and have a good sleep. But the bed was too big for the little tailor, so he did not get into it but crept into a corner of the cave. When midnight came and the giant thought the little tailor was sound asleep, he got up, took a large iron bar, smashed the bed in two with one stroke, and thought he had put an end to the grasshopper. At dawn the next day the giants went into the forest and forgot all about the little tailor. But all of a sudden he came walking along quite merrily and boldly. The giants were horrified, for they feared he might slay them all. So they ran away as fast as they could.

The tailor just followed his pointed nose and kept going. After he had traveled about for a long time, he came to the courtyard of a royal palace. Since he felt tired, he lay down in the grass and fell asleep. While he was lying there, some people came, examined him from all sides, and read on his belt "Seven with one Blow."

"Ah!" they said. "What can a great warrior be doing here during peacetime? He must be a mighty lord."

They went and reported it to the king and advised him that the warrior would be an important and useful man to have if war broke out and that the king should try to keep him there at all costs. The king appreciated the advice, and he sent one of his courtiers to the little tailor to offer him, after he woke up, a military position. The envoy remained standing near the sleeper until the tailor stretched his limbs and opened his eyes. Then the courtier made him the proposal.

"That's exactly why I've come here," answered the little tailor. "I am prepared to enter the king's service."

So he was honorably received and given special living quarters. However, the soldiers were jealous of the little tailor and wished him a thousand miles away.

"What will come of all this?" they began saying among themselves. "If we quarrel with him and he starts swinging, seven of us will fall with one blow. None of us can stand up to him."

Once they had reached a decision, they all went to the king and asked for their discharge. "We can't hold our own with a man who can slay seven with one blow," they said.

The king was sad to lose all his faithful servants on account of one man, and he wished he had never laid eyes on him. He actually wanted to get rid of him, but he dared not dismiss him for fear that the tailor might kill him and all his people and take over the royal throne. The king thought about this for a long time, going back and forth in his mind until he hit upon a plan. Then he sent a message to the little tailor that contained a proposal for him—since he was such a great warrior. There were two giants living in a forest in the king's country, and they were causing great damage by robbing, murdering, ravaging, and burning. Anyone who came near the giants would be placing his life in danger. However, if the tailor could conquer these two giants and kill them, he would receive the king's only daughter for his wife and half the kingdom as dowry. Moreover, one hundred knights were to accompany him and lend him assistance.

That would be just right for a man like you! thought the little tailor. It's not every day somebody offers you a princess and half a kingdom. So he answered, "Yes, indeed, I'll soon tame the giants, but I won't need the hundred knights. A man who's already slain seven with one blow does not need to be afraid of two."

The little tailor set out, followed by the hundred knights. When he came to the edge of the forest, he said to his escorts, "Just stay right here. I'll take care of the giants all by myself."

After he scampered into the forest, he looked to the right and to the left. Soon he caught sight of the two giants, who were lying asleep under a tree and snoring so hard that the branches bobbed up and down. Since the little tailor was no slouch, he filled his pockets full of stones and carried them up a tree. When he got halfway up the tree, he slid out on a branch until he was perched right over the sleepers. Then he dropped one stone after another on the chest of one of the giants. It took some time before the giant felt anything. However, he finally woke up, shoved his companion, and said, "Why are you hitting me?"

"You're dreaming," the other said. "I haven't been hitting you."

They lay down to sleep again, and the tailor threw a stone at the other giant.

"What's the meaning of that?" the second giant cried out. "Why are you throwing things at me?"

"I'm not throwing things at you," the first one replied and growled.

They quarreled for a while, but since they were tired, they let it pass, and their eyes closed again. Now the little tailor began his game anew. He took out his largest stone and threw it with all his might at the chest of the first giant.

"That does it!" he screamed, jumping up like a madman, and he slammed his companion against the tree so hard that it shook. The other giant paid him back in kind, and they both became so furious that they tore up trees and beat each other for some time until together they fell down dead. Then the little tailor jumped down from the tree.

"Lucky for me that they didn't tear up the tree I was sitting on," he said. "Otherwise, I'd have had to jump like a squirrel from one tree to another. Still, a man like me is always nimble."

He drew his sword, gave the giants a few hearty blows on their chests, and went out of the forest to the knights.

"The work's done," he said. "I've put an end to the two of them. But the battle was a hard one. They became so desperate that they tore up trees to defend themselves. Yet, there's nothing anyone can do against a man like me who can slay seven with one blow."

"Didn't they wound you?" the knights asked.

"It'll take more than two giants before that happens," he answered. "They couldn't even touch the hair on my head."

The knights would not believe him and rode into the forest, where they found the giants swimming in their own blood, with uprooted trees lying all around them. Meanwhile, the little tailor went and demanded the reward promised by the king, but the king regretted his promise and thought up a new way to get rid of the hero.

"Before you can have my daughter and half the kingdom," he said to the tailor, "you must put your heroism on display again and perform one more deed. There's a unicorn running around and causing great damage in the forest, and I want you to capture it."

"Do you expect me to be afraid of a unicorn after facing two giants?" the tailor asked. "Seven with one blow is more my style."

He took some rope and an ax with him, went to the forest, and ordered his escorts once again to remain outside. He did not have to search long, for the unicorn did not keep him waiting: it charged right at him with its horn lowered, as if it meant to gore him without much ado.

"Easy does it, easy does it!" the tailor said. "You won't get anywhere by doing things too hastily."

The little tailor stood still and waited until the unicorn was very close. Then he jumped nimbly behind a tree, while the animal ran with all its might into the tree, thrusting its horn into the trunk so hard that it did not have the strength to pull it out again. This was the way the unicorn was caught.

"Now I've got the little bird," the tailor said, and he came out from behind the tree, put the rope around the unicorn's neck, and chopped the horn free of the tree with the ax. When everything was all set, he led the unicorn away and took it to the king.

The king, however, still refused to give him the promised reward and made a third demand. Before the wedding could take place, the tailor was to capture a wild boar that was causing great damage in the forest, and the king's huntsmen were to lend him assistance.

"Gladly," said the tailor. "This is child's play."

He did not take the huntsmen with him into the forest, and they were pleased, for the wild boar had already given them such rough treatment that they had no desire to chase it. When the boar caught sight of the tailor, it charged at him, foaming at the mouth and gnashing its teeth. The beast tried to trample him to the ground, but the nimble hero ducked into a nearby chapel and jumped right out again through one of the windows. The boar followed him inside, while the tailor ran around on the outside to shut the front door. Thus the raging beast was trapped, because it was much too heavy and clumsy to jump out the window. The little tailor called the huntsmen to see the prisoner with their own eyes, while the hero went to the king, who had to keep his promise this time, whether he liked it or not. So he gave the tailor his daughter and half the kingdom. If he had known that he had been dealing with a mere tailor and not a hero from the wars, the entire affair would have caused him even more grief than it did. As it was, the wedding was celebrated with great splendor but little joy, and a king was made out of a tailor.

After some time had passed, the young queen heard her husband talking in his sleep one night. "Boy, finish that jerkin and mend the trousers fast, or else I'll give you a whack on your head with my yardstick!"

Now she knew the young lord was of humble origins, and the next morning she went to her father to complain and begged him to help her get rid of this husband who was nothing but a tailor. The king comforted her and said, "Leave the door of your bedroom open tonight. My servants shall be waiting outside, and when he's asleep, they'll go inside, tie him up, and take him aboard a ship that will carry him out into the wide world."

The king's daughter was content with this plan. But the king's armor-bearer had overheard everything, and since he was kindly disposed toward the young king, he told him all about the plot.

"I'm going to have to throttle their plans," said the little tailor.

That evening he went to bed with his wife at the usual time. When she thought he had fallen asleep, she got up, opened the door, and returned to the bed. The little tailor, who was only pretending to be asleep, began to cry out in a clear voice, "Boy, finish that jerkin and mend the trousers fast, or else I'll give you a whack on your head with my yardstick! I've slain seven with one blow, killed two giants, captured a unicorn, and trapped a wild boar. Do you think those fellows waiting outside my door could ever scare me?"

When the men heard the tailor talking like that, they were petrified and ran off as if the wild host of hell were after them, and none of them ever dared to do anything to him after this. Thus the tailor reigned as king and remained king for the rest of his life.

◆ 21 ◆

Cinderella

THE WIFE OF A RICH MAN FELL ILL, and as she felt her end approaching, she called her only daughter to her bedside and said, "Dear child, be good and pious. Then the dear Lord shall always assist you, and I shall look down from heaven and take care of you." She then closed her eyes and departed.

After her mother's death the maiden went every day to visit her grave and weep, and she remained good and pious. When winter came, snow covered the grave like a little white blanket, and by the time the sun had taken it off again in the spring, the rich man had a second wife, who brought along her two daughters. They had beautiful and fair features but nasty and wicked hearts. As a result a difficult time was ahead for the poor stepsister.

"Why should the stupid goose be allowed to sit in the parlor with us?" they said. "Whoever wants to eat bread must earn it. Out with this kitchen maid!"

They took away her beautiful clothes, dressed her in an old gray smock, and gave her wooden shoes.

"Just look at the proud princess and how decked out she is!" they exclaimed with laughter, and led her into the kitchen.

They expected her to work hard there from morning till night. She had to get up before dawn, carry the water into the house, make the fire, cook, and wash. Besides this, her sisters did everything imaginable to cause her grief and make her look ridiculous. For instance, they poured peas and lentils into the hearth ashes so she had to sit there and pick them out. In the evening, when she was exhausted from working, they took away her bed, and she had to lie next to the hearth in the ashes. This is why she always looked so dusty and dirty and why they all called her Cinderella.

One day it happened that her father was going to the fair and asked his two stepdaughters what he could bring them.

"Beautiful dresses," said one.

"Pearls and jewels," said the other.

"And you, Cinderella?" he asked. "What do you want?"

"Father," she said, "just break off the first twig that brushes against your hat on your way home and bring it to me."

So he bought beautiful dresses, pearls, and jewels for the two stepsisters, and as he was riding through some green bushes on his return journey, a hazel twig brushed against him and knocked off his hat. So he broke off that twig and took it with him. When he arrived home, he gave his stepdaughters what they had requested, and Cinderella received the twig from the hazel bush. She thanked him, went to her mother's grave, planted the twig on it, and wept so hard that the tears fell on the twig and watered it. Soon the twig grew and quickly became a beautiful tree. Three times every day Cinderella would go and sit beneath it and weep and pray, and each time, a little white bird would also come to the tree. Whenever Cinderella expressed a wish, the bird would throw her whatever she had requested.

In the meantime, the king had decided to sponsor a three-day festival, and all the beautiful young girls in the country were invited so that his son could choose a bride. When the two stepsisters learned that they too had been summoned to make an appearance, they were in good spirits and called Cinderella.

"Comb our hair, brush our shoes, and fasten our buckles!" they said. "We're going to the wedding at the king's castle."

Cinderella obeyed but wept, because she too would have liked to go to the ball with them, and so she asked her stepmother for permission to go.

"You, Cinderella!" she said. "You're all dusty and dirty, and yet you want to go to the wedding? How can you go dancing when you've got no clothes or shoes?"

When Cinderella kept pleading, her stepmother finally said, "I've emptied a bowlful of lentils into the ashes. If you can pick out all the lentils in two hours, you may have my permission to go."

The maiden went through the back door into the garden and cried out, "Oh, you tame pigeons, you turtledoves, and all you birds under heaven, come and help me pick

the good ones for the little pot,
the bad ones for your little crop."

Two white pigeons came flying to the kitchen window, followed by the turtledoves. Eventually, all the birds under heaven swooped down, swarmed into the kitchen, and settled around the ashes. The pigeons bobbed their heads and began to peck, peck, peck, peck, and all the other birds also began to peck, peck, peck, peck, and they put all the good lentils into the bowl. It did not take longer than an hour for the birds to finish the work, whereupon they flew away. Happy, because she thought she would now be allowed to go to the wedding, the maiden brought the bowl to her stepmother. But her stepmother said, "No, Cinderella. You don't have any clothes, nor do you know how to dance. Everyone would only laugh at you."

When Cinderella started crying, the stepmother said, "If you can pick two bowlfuls of lentils out of the ashes in one hour, I'll let you come along." But she thought, She'll never be able to do it.

Then the stepmother dumped two bowlfuls of lentils into the ashes, and the maiden went through the back door into the garden and cried out, "Oh, you tame pigeons, you turtledoves, and all you birds under heaven, come and help me pick

the good ones for the little pot,
the bad ones for your little crop."

Two white pigeons came flying to the kitchen window, followed by the turtledoves. Eventually, all the birds under heaven swooped down, swarmed into the kitchen, and settled around the ashes. The pigeons bobbed their heads and began to peck, peck, peck, peck, and all the other birds also began to peck, peck, peck, peck, and they put all the good lentils into the bowl. Before half an hour had passed, they finished their work and flew away. Happy, because she thought she would now be allowed to go to the wedding, the maiden carried the bowls to her stepmother. But her stepmother said, "Nothing can help you. I can't let you come with us because you don't have any clothes to wear and you don't know how to dance. We'd only be ashamed of you!"

Then she turned her back on Cinderella and hurried off with her two haughty daughters. When they had all departed, Cinderella went to her mother's grave beneath the hazel tree and cried out:

"Shake and wobble, little tree!
Let gold and silver fall all over me."

The bird responded by throwing her a gold and silver dress and silk slippers embroidered with silver. She hastily slipped into the dress and went to the wedding. She looked so beautiful in her golden dress that her sisters and stepmother did not recognize her and thought she must be a foreign princess. They never imagined it could be Cinderella; they thought she was sitting at home in the dirt picking lentils out of the ashes.

Now, the prince approached Cinderella, took her by the hand, and danced with her. Indeed, he would not dance with anyone else and would not let go of her hand. Whenever someone came and asked her to dance, he said, "She's my partner."

She danced well into the night, and when she wanted to go home, the prince said, "I'll go along and escort you," for he wanted to see whose daughter the beautiful maiden was. But she managed to slip away from him and got into her father's dovecote. Now the prince waited until her father came, and he told him that the unknown maiden had escaped into his dovecote. The old man thought, Could that be Cinderella? And he had an ax and pick brought to him so he could chop it down. However, no one was inside, and when they went into the house, Cinderella was lying in the ashes in her dirty clothes, and a dim little oil lamp was burning on the mantel of the chimney. Cinderella had swiftly jumped out the back of the dovecote and run to the hazel tree. There she had taken off the beautiful clothes and laid them on the grave. After the bird had taken them away, she had made her way into the kitchen, where she had seated herself in the gray ashes wearing her gray smock.

The next day when the festival had begun again and her parents and sisters had departed, Cinderella went to the hazel tree and cried out:

"Shake and wobble, little tree!
Let gold and silver fall all over me."

The bird responded by throwing her a dress that was even more splendid than the one before. And when she appeared at the wedding in this dress, everyone was amazed by her beauty. The prince had been waiting for her, and when she came, he took her hand right away and danced with no one but her. When others went up to her and asked her to dance, he said, "She's my partner."

When evening came and she wished to leave, the prince followed her, wanting to see which house she went into, but she ran away from him and disappeared into the garden behind the house. There she went to a beautiful tall tree covered with the most wonderful pears, and she climbed up into the branches as nimbly as a squirrel. The prince did not know where she had gone, so he waited until her father came and said, "The unknown maiden has slipped away from me, and I think she climbed the pear tree."

The father thought, Can that be Cinderella? And he had an ax brought to him and chopped the tree down, but there was no one in it. When they went into the kitchen, Cinderella was lying in the ashes as usual, for she had jumped down on the other side of the tree, brought the beautiful clothes back to the bird, and put on her gray smock.

On the third day, when her parents and sisters had departed, Cinderella went to her mother's grave again and cried out to the tree:

"Shake and wobble, little tree!
Let gold and silver fall all over me."

The bird responded by throwing her a dress that was more magnificent and radiant than all the others she had received, and the slippers were pure gold. When she appeared at the wedding in this dress, the people were so astounded they did not know what to say. The prince danced with no one but her, and whenever someone asked her to dance, he said, "She's my partner."

When it was evening and Cinderella wished to leave, the prince wanted to escort her, but she slipped away from him so swiftly that he could not follow her. However, the prince had prepared for this with a trick: he had all the stairs coated with pitch, and when Cinderella went running down the stairs, her left slipper got stuck there. After the prince picked it up, he saw it was small and dainty and made of pure gold.

Next morning he carried it to Cinderella's father and said, "No one else shall be my wife but the maiden whose foot fits this golden shoe."

The two sisters were glad to hear this because they had beautiful feet. The oldest took the shoe into a room to try it on, and her mother stood by her side. However, the shoe was too small for her, and she could not get her big toe into it. So her mother handed her a knife and said, "Cut your toe off. Once you become queen, you won't have to walk anymore."

The maiden cut her toe off, forced her foot into the shoe, swallowed the pain, and went out to the prince. He took her on his horse as his bride and rode off. But they had to pass the grave where the two pigeons were sitting on the hazel tree, and they cried out:

"Looky, look, look
at the shoe that she took.
There's blood all over, and her foot's too small.
She's not the bride you met at the ball."

He looked down at her foot and saw the blood oozing out. So he turned his horse around, brought the false bride home again, and said that she was definitely not the right one and the other sister should try on the shoe. Then the second sister went into a room and was fortunate enough to get all her toes in, but her heel was too large. So her mother handed her a knife and said, "Cut off a piece of your heel. Once you become queen, you won't have to walk anymore."

The maiden cut off a piece of her heel, forced her foot into the shoe, swallowed the pain, and went out to the prince. He took her on his horse as his bride, and rode off with her. As they passed the hazel tree the two pigeons were sitting there, and they cried out:

"Looky, look, look
at the shoe that she took.
There's blood all over, and her foot's too small.
She's not the bride you met at the ball."

He looked down at her foot and saw the blood oozing out of the shoe and staining her white stockings all red. Then he turned his horse around and brought the false bride home again.

"She isn't the right one either," he said. "Don't you have any other daughters?"

"No," said the man. "There's only little Cinderella, my dead wife's daughter, who's deformed, but she can't possibly be the bride."

The prince told him to send the girl to him, but the mother

responded, "Oh, she's much too dirty and really shouldn't be seen."

However, the prince demanded to see her, and Cinderella had to be called. First she washed her hands and face until they were clean, and then she went and curtsied before the prince, who handed her the golden shoe. She sat down on a stool, took her foot out of the heavy wooden shoe, and put it into the slipper that fit her perfectly. After she stood up and the prince looked her straight in the face, he recognized the beautiful maiden who had danced with him.

"This is my true bride!" he exclaimed.

The stepmother and the two sisters were horrified and turned pale with rage. However, the prince took Cinderella on his horse and rode away with her. As they passed the hazel tree the two white pigeons cried out:

"Looky, look, look
at the shoe that she took.
Her foot's just right, and there's no blood at all.
She's truly the bride you met at the ball."

After the pigeons had made this known, they both came flying down and landed on Cinderella's shoulders, one on the right, the other on the left, and there they stayed.

On the day that the wedding with the prince was to take place, the two false sisters came to ingratiate themselves and to share in Cinderella's good fortune. When the bridal couple set out for the church, the oldest sister was on the right, the younger on the left. Suddenly the pigeons pecked out one eye from each of them. And as they came back from the church later on the oldest was on the left and the youngest on the right, and the pigeons pecked out the other eye from each sister. Thus they were punished with blindness for the rest of their lives due to their wickedness and malice.

◈ 22 ◈

The Riddle

ONCE UPON A TIME there was a prince who was overcome by a desire to travel about the world, and the only person he took with him was his faithful servant. One day he found himself in a great forest when evening came. He had not found a place to spend the night and did not know what to do. Then he noticed a maiden going toward a small cottage, and when he came closer, he saw that she was young and beautiful. So he spoke to her and said, "Do you think, dear girl, that my servant and I could spend the night in the cottage?"

"Why, yes," said the maiden with a sad voice. "You certainly can, but I wouldn't advise it. Don't go in."

"Why not?" asked the prince.

The maiden sighed and said, "My stepmother practices evil arts and is not well-disposed toward strangers."

He realized then that he had come to the house of a witch. However, it was dark and he could not continue, and since he was fearless, he decided to go in. The old woman was sitting in an easy chair by the fire and looked at the strangers with her red eyes.

"Good evening!" she snarled, and then she pretended to be quite friendly. "Have a seat and rest yourselves!"

She was cooking something in a little pot on the fire, and she stoked the coals. The daughter had warned the two men to be careful not to drink or eat anything, for the old woman brewed deadly potions. The two men slept peacefully until early in the morning. When they were getting ready to depart and the prince was seated on his horse, the old woman said, "Wait a minute! I want to offer you a parting drink."

While she went to fetch it, the prince rode off, and the servant, who was still trying to strap his saddle on tight, was the only one there when the evil witch came back with the drink.

"Bring this to your master," she said, but at that moment the glass broke, the poison splattered on the horse, and it was so lethal that the animal fell down dead on the spot. The servant ran after his master and told him what had happened, but he did not want to abandon his saddle and so went back to fetch it. When he came to the dead horse, a raven was already sitting there and eating it.

"Who knows if we'll be able to find anything better to eat today?" said the servant, and so he killed the raven and took it with him.

They went on traveling the whole day in the forest but could not find their way out. At nightfall they came upon an inn and went inside. The servant gave the raven to the innkeeper and told him to prepare it for their supper. However, what they had stumbled on was a den of murderers, and when it was dark, twelve murderers arrived and wanted to kill and rob them. But before getting down to their work, they sat down at the table, and the innkeeper and the witch joined them. They all ate out of the same bowl of soup filled with the chopped meat of the raven. No sooner did they swallow a few bites than they fell down dead, for the raven had been infected by the poisoned horsemeat. Now there was nobody left in the big house except the innkeeper's daughter, who was honest and had not taken any part in the wicked deeds of the murders. She opened all the doors in the inn and showed the prince the vast treasures the murderers had accumulated. However, he wanted none of it and told her that she could keep it all, and he rode off with his servant.

After they had traveled about for a long time, they came to a city inhabited by a beautiful but haughty princess. She had proclaimed that she would wed any man who could give her a riddle she could not solve, but a man who offered a riddle that she was able to solve would have his head chopped off. She was allowed three days to think about the riddle, but she was so smart that she always solved it before the end of the time. In fact, nine men had already lost their lives by the time the prince arrived. Nevertheless, he was so bedazzled by her great beauty that he was willing to risk his life, and he appeared before her and posed his riddle.

"Can you guess this?" he asked. "One slew nobody and yet slew twelve."

The princess did not know what that could mean, and she thought and thought but could not come up with the answer. She consulted her riddle books, but there was nothing in them about this. In short, her wisdom had reached its limits, and she was at a loss as to what to do. So, on the first night, she ordered her maid to sneak into the prince's bedroom and listen to his dreams, for she thought he might talk in his sleep and reveal the riddle. But the clever servant took his master's place in the bed, and when the maid came in, he ripped off the cloak she had wrapped herself in and sent her running with a good beating. On the second night, the princess sent her chambermaid, to see if she might succeed better in eavesdropping, but again the servant took her cloak away and sent her running with a good beating. Now, on the third night, the prince thought he would be safe and lay down in his own bed. However, this time the princess herself came. She was wearing a misty gray cloak and sat down beside him. When she thought he was sleeping and dreaming, she spoke to him and hoped he would answer in his dreams as many do. But he was awake and understood and heard everything quite perfectly.

"One slew nobody," she said. "What does that mean?"

"A raven that ate a dead poisoned horse and died of it," he said.

Then she asked again, "And yet slew twelve. What does that mean?"

"Those are the twelve murderers who ate the raven and died of it."

When she knew the answer to the riddle, she wanted to sneak away, but he held her cloak so tightly, she had to leave it behind her. The next morning the princess announced she had solved the riddle and ordered the twelve judges to come. Then she explained the riddle in front of them, but the young prince asked for a hearing and declared, "She crept into my room during the night and questioned me all about the riddle. Otherwise she never would have solved it."

"Bring us proof!" the judges said.

Then the prince's servant brought in the three cloaks, and when the judges saw the misty gray one that the princess usually wore, they said, "Have the cloak embroidered with gold and silver, for it will be your wedding cloak."

◈ 23 ◈

The Mouse, the Bird, and the Sausage

ONCE UPON A TIME a mouse, a bird, and a sausage came together and set up house. For a long time they lived together in peace and happiness, and they managed to increase their possessions by a considerable amount. The bird's job was to fly into the forest every day and bring back wood. The mouse had to carry water, light the fire, and set the table, while the sausage did the cooking.

Yet, those who lead the good life are always looking for ways to make it even better. And, one day, as the bird was flying about, he met another bird and boasted about how wonderful his life was. But the other bird called him a poor sap because he had to do all the hard work, while his companions just enjoyed themselves at home. Indeed, after the mouse started the fire and carried the water into the house, she generally went to her little room and rested until she was called to set the table. The sausage always stayed by the pot and kept an eye on the cooking, and right before mealtime he usually slid through the stew or vegetables to make sure everything was salted and seasoned properly. And that was all he did. When the bird came home and laid down his load, they would sit down at the table, and after finishing the meal they would sleep soundly until the next morning. Such was their glorious life.

However, the bird had been disturbed by what the other bird had said, and next day he refused to fly into the forest. He told his companions that he had been their slave long enough, and that they must have taken him for a fool. He demanded that they try another arrangement. The mouse and the sausage argued against this, but the bird would not be denied, and he insisted that they try a new way. So they drew lots, and it fell upon the sausage to get the wood from then on, while the mouse became cook, and the bird was to fetch water.

What happened?

After the sausage went to fetch the wood, the bird started the fire, and the mouse put the kettle on the stove. Then they waited for the sausage to return with the wood for the next day. However, the sausage was gone so long that the other two had an uneasy feeling, and the bird flew out a little way to meet him. Not far from their home, however, he encountered a dog, and he learned that this dog had considered the sausage free game and had grabbed him and swallowed him down. The bird was furious and accused the dog of highway robbery, but it was of no use, for the dog maintained he had found forged letters on the sausage, and therefore the sausage had had to pay for this with his life.

Now the bird sadly picked up the wood and carried it back home. He told the mouse what he had seen and heard, and they were very distressed. Nevertheless, they agreed to do the best they could and stay together. Meanwhile, the bird set the table, and the mouse prepared the meal. She intended to put the finishing touches on it by seasoning it and sliding through the vegetables the way the sausage used to do, but before she even reached the middle, she got stuck and had to pay for it with her life.

When the bird came to serve the meal, there was no cook. He became so upset that he scattered wood all over the place, calling and searching for the mouse. But his cook was no longer to be found. Due to the bird's distraction the wood soon caught fire, and the house went up in flames. When the bird rushed to fetch some water, however, the bucket slipped and fell into the well, dragging the bird along. Since he could not get himself out, he was left to drown.

◈ 24 ◈

Mother Holle

A WIDOW HAD TWO DAUGHTERS, one who was beautiful and industrious, the other ugly and lazy. But she was fonder of the ugly and lazy one because she was her own daughter. The other had to do all the housework and carry out the ashes like a cinderella. Every day the poor maiden had to sit near a well by the road and spin and spin until her fingers bled.

Now, one day it happened that the reel became quite bloody, and when the maiden leaned over the well to rinse it, it slipped out of her hand and fell to the bottom. She burst into tears, ran to her step-mother, and told her about the accident. But the stepmother gave her a terrible scolding and was very cruel. "If you've let the reel fall in," she said, "then you'd better get it out again."

The maiden went back to the well but did not know where to begin. She was so distraught that she jumped into the well to fetch the reel, but she lost consciousness. When she awoke and regained her senses, she was in a beautiful meadow where the sun was shining and thousands of flowers were growing. She walked across this meadow, and soon she came to a baker's oven full of bread, but the bread was yelling, "Take me out! Take me out, or else I'll burn. I've been baking long enough!"

She went up to the oven and took out all the loaves one by one with the baker's peel. After that she moved on and came to a tree full of apples.

"Shake me! Shake me!" the tree exclaimed. "My apples are all ripe."

She shook the tree till the apples fell like raindrops, and she kept shaking until they had all come down. After she had gathered them and stacked them in a pile, she moved on. At last she came to a small cottage where an old woman was looking out of a window. She had such big teeth that the maiden was scared and wanted to run away. But the old woman cried after her, "Why are you afraid, my dear child? Stay with me, and if you do all the housework properly, everything will turn out well for you. Only you must make my bed nicely and carefully and give it a good shaking so the feathers fly. Then it will snow on earth, for I am Mother Holle."*

Since the old woman had spoken so kindly to her, the maiden plucked up her courage and agreed to enter her service. She took care of everything to the old woman's satisfaction and always shook the bed so hard that the feathers flew about like snowflakes. In return, the woman treated her well: she never said an unkind word to the maiden, and she gave her roasted or boiled meat every day. After the maiden had spent a long time with Mother Holle, she became sad. At first she did not know what was bothering her, but finally she realized she was homesick. Even though everything was a thousand times better there than at home, she still had a desire to return. At last she said to Mother Holle, "I've got a tremendous

*Whenever it snowed in olden days, people in Hessia used to say Mother Holle is making her bed.

longing to return home, and even though everything is wonderful down here, I've got to return to my people."

"I'm pleased that you want to return home," Mother Holle responded, "and since you've served me so faithfully, I myself shall bring you up there again."

She took the maiden by the hand and led her to a large door. When it was opened and the maiden was standing right beneath the doorway, an enormous shower of gold came pouring down, and all the gold stuck to her so that she became completely covered with it.

"I want you to have this because you've been so industrious," said Mother Holle, and she also gave her back the reel that had fallen into the well. Suddenly the door closed, and the maiden found herself back up on earth, not far from her mother's house. When she entered the yard, the cock was sitting on the well and crowed:

"*Cock-a-doodle-doo!*
My golden maiden, what's new with you?"

She went inside to her mother, and since she was covered with so much gold, her mother and sister gave her a warm welcome. Then she told them all about what had happened to her, and when her mother heard how she had obtained so much wealth, she wanted to arrange it so her ugly and lazy daughter could have the same good fortune. Therefore, her daughter had to sit near the well and spin, and she made the reel bloody by sticking her fingers into a thornbush and pricking them. After that she threw the reel down into the well and jumped in after it. Just like her sister, she reached the beautiful meadow and walked along the same path. When she came to the oven, the bread cried out again, "Take me out! Take me out, or else I'll burn! I've been baking long enough!"

But the lazy maiden answered, "I've no desire to get myself dirty!"

She moved on, and soon she came to the apple tree that cried out, "Shake me! Shake me! My apples are all ripe."

However, the lazy maiden replied, "Are you serious? One of the apples could fall and hit me on my head."

Thus she went on, and when she came to Mother Holle's cottage, she was not afraid because she had already heard of the old woman's big teeth, and she hired herself out to her right away. On the first day she made an effort to work hard and obey Mother Holle when the old woman told her what to do, for the thought of gold was on her mind. On the second day she started loafing, and on the third day she loafed even more. Indeed, she did not want to get out of bed in the morning, nor did she make Mother Holle's bed as she should have, and she certainly did not shake it hard so the feathers flew. Soon Mother Holle became tired of this and dismissed the maiden from her service. The lazy maiden was quite happy to go and expected that now the shower of gold would come. Mother Holle led her to the door, but as the maiden was standing beneath the doorway, a big kettle of pitch came pouring down over her instead of gold.

"That's a reward for your services," Mother Holle said, and shut the door. The lazy maiden went home covered with pitch, and when the cock on the well saw her, it crowed:

"*Cock-a-doodle-doo!*
My dirty maiden, what's new with you?"

The pitch did not come off the maiden and remained on her as long as she lived.

❖ 25 ❖

The Seven Ravens

THERE ONCE WAS A MAN who had seven sons, and no matter how much he wished for a little daughter, his wish remained unfulfilled. Then one day his wife gave him hope of another child, and when the baby was born, it was indeed a girl. Their joy was great, but the child was sickly and small, and because she was so weak, she had to be baptized at home. The father sent one of the boys to run quickly to the well for some baptismal water. The other six ran along with him, and since each of them scrambled to be the first to draw the water, the pitcher fell into the well. There they stood, not knowing what to do, nor did any of them dare go home. When they failed to return, their father grew impatient and said, "Those wicked boys must have forgotten what I sent them to do! They're probably playing games again." He was afraid that his daughter might die without being baptized, and in his anger he exclaimed "I wish those boys would all be turned into ravens!"

No sooner had he uttered those words than he heard a whirring over his head, and when he looked up, he saw seven ravens, black as coal, flying up and away. It was too late for the parents to revoke the curse, and even though they were sad about the loss of their seven sons, they were comforted to a certain extent by their dear little daughter, who grew stronger and more beautiful with each day that passed. For a long time she was unaware that she had brothers, because her parents took great care not to mention them. But one day she overheard some people talking about her and saying that though she was indeed beautiful, she was actually the one who had caused the misfortune that had struck her seven brothers. Upon hearing this she was greatly distressed. She went to her father and mother and asked whether she had brothers and what had happened to them. Her parents could no longer keep the secret from her. However, they said the will of heaven had been responsible for her brothers' fate and not her own birth. Nonetheless, their fate weighed heavily on the maiden's conscience, and she believed it was up to her to rescue them. From then on she had no peace of mind, and finally she secretly set out into the wide world to find some trace of her brothers and free them, no matter what it might cost. The only things she took with her were a little ring as a memento to remind her of her parents, a loaf of bread to still her hunger, a jug of water to quench her thirst, and a little stool to rest on when she became tired.

She set out, walking straight ahead, and went far, far away until she reached the end of the world. She came to the sun, but it was too hot and terrible, and it ate little children. So she turned away from there as quickly as she could and ran to the moon, but it was too cold, not to mention gruesome and wicked. When it saw the girl, it said, "I smell something! I smell human flesh!" Immediately she scampered away and went to the stars, which were friendly and kind to her. Each one was sitting on its own little chair, but the morning star stood up, handed her the drumstick of a chicken, and said, "If you don't have this drumstick, you won't be able to open the glass mountain, and that's where you'll find your brothers."

The girl took the drumstick, wrapped it carefully in a piece of cloth, and continued traveling until she reached the glass mountain. The gate was locked, but she was prepared to take out the drumstick. Yet, when she began unfolding the cloth, she found it was empty. Indeed, she had lost the gift of the good, kind stars. What was she to do now? She wanted to rescue her brothers but did not have a key to the glass mountain. So the good sister took a knife, cut off a little finger, stuck it in the gate, and was fortunate enough to unlock it. After she entered, a little dwarf came toward her and said, "What are you looking for, my child?"

"I'm looking for my brothers, the seven ravens," she replied.

"The lord ravens are not at home," the dwarf said. "But, if you wish to wait here until they return, come right in."

Then the dwarf brought in the ravens' meal on seven little plates, along with seven little cups, and their sister ate a tiny morsel from each one of the plates and took a little sip from each one of the cups. When she came to the last cup, she took the ring that she had been carrying with her and dropped it into the cup.

All at once there was a whirring and fluttering noise in the air, and the dwarf said, "Now the lord ravens will soon be home."

When they arrived, they wanted to eat and drink and went straight to their plates and cups. Then each one in his turn cried out, "Who's been eating from my plate? Who's been drinking from my cup? It was a human mouth."

And when the seventh brother got to the bottom of his cup, a little ring rolled out. He looked at it and recognized it as the ring that belonged to his parents.

"God grant us that our little sister may be here. Then we'd be saved!" he said.

The maiden was standing behind the door, and when she heard that, she came out, and all the ravens regained their human form. They hugged and kissed each other and went happily home.

◈ 26 ◈

Little Red Cap

ONCE UPON A TIME there was a sweet little maiden. Whoever laid eyes upon her could not help but love her. But it was her grandmother who loved her most. She could never give the child enough. One time she made her a present, a small, red velvet cap, and since it was so becoming and the maiden insisted on always wearing it, she was called Little Red Cap.

One day her mother said to her, "Come, Little Red Cap, take this piece of cake and bottle of wine and bring them to your grandmother. She's sick and weak, and this will strengthen her. Get an early start, before it becomes hot, and when you're out in the woods, be nice and good and don't stray from the path, otherwise you'll fall and break the glass, and your grandmother will get nothing. And when you enter her room, don't forget to say good morning, and don't go peeping in all the corners."

"I'll do just as you say," Little Red Cap promised her mother. Well, the grandmother lived out in the forest, half an hour from the village, and as soon as Little Red Cap entered the forest, she encountered the wolf. However, Little Red Cap did not know what a wicked sort of an animal he was and was not afraid of him.

"Good day, Little Red Cap," he said.

"Thank you kindly, wolf."

"Where are you going so early, Little Red Cap?"

"To Grandmother's."

"What are you carrying under your apron?"

"Cake and wine. My grandmother's sick and weak, and yesterday we baked this so it will help her get well."

"Where does your grandmother live, Little Red Cap?"

"Another quarter of an hour from here in the forest. Her house is under the three big oak trees. You can tell it by the hazel bushes," said Little Red Cap.

The wolf thought to himself, This tender young thing is a juicy morsel. She'll taste even better than the old woman. You've got to be real crafty if you want to catch them both. Then he walked next to Little Red Cap, and after a while he said, "Little Red Cap, just look at the beautiful flowers that are growing all around you! Why don't you look around? I believe you haven't even noticed how lovely the birds are singing. You march along as if you were going straight to school, and yet it's so delightful out here in the woods!"

Little Red Cap looked around and saw how the rays of the sun were dancing through the trees back and forth and how the woods were full of beautiful flowers. So she thought to herself, If I bring Grandmother a bunch of fresh flowers, she'd certainly like that. It's still early, and I'll arrive on time.

So she ran off the path and plunged into the woods to look for flowers. And each time she plucked one, she thought she saw another even prettier flower and ran after it, going deeper and deeper into the forest. But the wolf went straight to the grandmother's house and knocked at the door.

"Who's out there?"

"Little Red Cap. I've brought you some cake and wine. Open up."

"Just lift the latch," the grandmother called. "I'm too weak and can't get up."

The wolf lifted the latch, and the door sprang open. Then he went straight to the grandmother's bed without saying a word and gobbled her up. Next he put on her clothes and her nightcap, lay down in her bed, and drew the curtains.

Meanwhile, Little Red Cap had been running around and looking for flowers, and only when she had as many as she could carry did she remember her grandmother and continue on the way to her house again. She was puzzled when she found the door open, and as she entered the room, it seemed so strange inside that she thought, Oh, my God, how frightened I feel today, and usually I like to be at Grandmother's. She called out, "Good morning!" But she received no answer. Next she went to the bed and drew back the curtains. There lay her grandmother with her cap pulled down over her face giving her a strange appearance.

"Oh, Grandmother, what big ears you have!"

"The better to hear you with."

"Oh, Grandmother, what big hands you have!"

"The better to grab you with."

"Oh, Grandmother, what a terribly big mouth you have!"

"The better to eat you with!"

No sooner did the wolf say that than he jumped out of bed and gobbled up poor Little Red Cap. After the wolf had satisfied his desires, he lay down in bed again, fell asleep, and began to snore very loudly. The huntsman happened to be passing by the house and thought to himself, The way the old woman's snoring, you'd better see if anything's wrong. He went into the room, and when he came to the bed, he saw the wolf lying in it.

"So I've found you at last, you old sinner," said the huntsman. "I've been looking for you for a long time."

He took aim with his gun, and then it occurred to him that the wolf could have eaten the grandmother and that she could still be saved. So he did not shoot but took some scissors and started cutting open the sleeping wolf's belly. After he made a couple of cuts, he saw the little red cap shining forth, and after he made a few more cuts, the girl jumped out and exclaimed, "Oh, how frightened I was! It was so dark in the wolf's body."

Soon the grandmother came out. She was alive but could hardly breathe. Little Red Cap quickly fetched some large stones, and they filled the wolf's body with them. When he awoke and tried to run away, the stones were too heavy so he fell down at once and died.

All three were quite delighted. The huntsman skinned the fur from the wolf and went home with it. The grandmother ate the cake and drank the wine that Little Red Cap had brought, and soon she regained her health. Meanwhile, Little Red Cap thought to herself, Never again will you stray from the path by yourself and go into the forest when your mother has forbidden it.

There is also another tale about how Little Red Cap returned to her grandmother one day to bring some baked goods. Another wolf spoke to her and tried to entice her to leave the path, but this time Little Red Cap was on her guard. She went straight ahead and told her grandmother that she had seen the wolf, that he had wished her good day, but that he had had such a mean look in his eyes that "he would have eaten me up if we hadn't been on the open road."

"Come," said the grandmother. "We'll lock the door so he can't get in."

Soon after, the wolf knocked and cried out, "Open up, Grandmother. It's Little Red Cap, and I've brought you some baked goods."

But they kept quiet and did not open the door. So Grayhead circled the house several times and finally jumped on the roof. He wanted to wait till evening when Little Red Cap would go home. He intended to sneak after her and eat her up in the darkness. But the grandmother realized what he had in mind. In front of the house was a big stone trough, and she said to the child, "Fetch the bucket, Little Red Cap. I cooked sausages yesterday. Get the water they were boiled in and pour it into the trough."

Little Red Cap kept carrying the water until she had filled the big, big trough. Then the smell of sausages reached the nose of the wolf.

He sniffed and looked down. Finally, he stretched his neck so far that he could no longer keep his balance on the roof. He began to slip and fell right into the big trough and drowned. Then Little Red Cap went merrily on her way home, and no one harmed her.

◈ 27 ◈

The Bremen Town Musicians

A MAN HAD A DONKEY who had diligently carried sacks of grain to the mill for many years. However, the donkey's strength was reaching its end, and he was less and less fit for the work. His master thought it was time to dispense with him and save on food, but the donkey got wind of what was in store for him. So he ran away and set out for Bremen, where he thought he could become a town musician. After traveling some distance he came across a hunting dog lying on the roadside and panting as if he had run himself ragged.

"Why are you panting so hard, you old hound dog?" asked the donkey.

"Ah," the dog said, "because I'm old and getting weaker every day. Now I can't even hunt anymore, and my master wanted to kill me. Naturally, I cleared out, but how am I going to earn a living now?"

"You know what," said the donkey, "I'm going to Bremen to become a town musician, and you can come with me and also join the town band. I'll play the lute, and you, the drums."

The dog agreed, and they continued on their way. Soon after, they encountered a cat sitting on the roadside, making a long and sorry face.

"Well, what's gone wrong with you, old whiskers?" asked the donkey.

"How can I be cheerful when my neck's in danger?" the cat replied. "My mistress wanted to drown me because I'm getting on in years. Moreover, my teeth are dull, and I'd rather sit behind the stove and spin than chase after mice. Anyway, I managed to escape, but now I don't know what to do or where to go."

"Why don't you come along with us to Bremen? You know a great deal about night serenades, and you can become a town musician."

The cat thought that was a good idea and went along. Then the three fugitives passed a farmyard where a rooster was perched on the gate and crowing with all his might.

"Your crowing gives me the chills," said the donkey. "Why are you screaming like this?"

"I've predicted good weather for today," said the rooster, "because it's Our Lady's Day, when she washes the Christ Child's shirts and sets them out to dry. Still, my mistress has no mercy. Tomorrow's Sunday, and guests are coming. So she told the cook to cut off my head tonight because she wants to eat me in the soup tomorrow. Now you know why I'm screaming my lungs out, while there's still time to scream."

"That's foolish, redhead!" said the donkey. "You'd be smarter if you'd come along with us. We're off to Bremen where there are better things than death. You've got a good voice, and if we make music together, it's sure to be a good thing."

The rooster liked the proposal, and all four of them continued the journey together. However, they could not reach the town of Bremen in one day, and by evening they came to a forest, where they decided to spend the night. The donkey and the dog lay down under a big tree, while the cat and rooster climbed up and settled down in the branches. To be on the safe side, the rooster flew to the top. Before he went to sleep, he looked around in all directions, and it seemed to him he saw a light burning in the distance. He called to his companions and told them there must be a house nearby, since he could see something shining.

"Well, this place is not all that comfortable, so let's get moving," said the donkey.

The dog thought some bones and meat would be just right for him, and they all set out toward the light. Soon it began to grow brighter, and it got even more so once they reached a brightly lit robber's den. Since the donkey was the tallest, he went up to the window and looked inside.

"What do you see, gray steed?" the rooster asked.

"What do I see?" replied the donkey. "I see a table covered with wonderful food and drinks and some robbers sitting there and enjoying themselves."

"That would be just the thing for us!" said the rooster.

"You're right!" said the donkey. "If only we could get in!"

Then the animals discussed what they would have to do to drive

• 115 •

the robbers away. Finally they hit upon a plan. The donkey was to stand upright and place his forefeet on the windowsill. The dog was to jump on the donkey's back, and the cat was to climb upon the dog. When that was done, the rooster was to fly up and perch on the cat's head. After they put their plan into action, the signal was given, and they all started to make music together: the donkey brayed, the dog barked, the cat meowed, and the rooster crowed. Then they crashed into the room, shattering the window. Startled by the horrible cries, the robbers were convinced that a ghost had burst into the room, and they fled in great fright into the forest. Then the four companions sat down at the table, delightedly gathered up the leftovers, and ate as if there were no tomorrow.

When the four minstrels were finished, they put out the light and looked for a place to sleep, each according to his nature and custom. The donkey lay down on the dung heap in the yard, the dog behind the door, the cat on the hearth near the warm ashes, and the rooster on the beam of the roof. Since they were tired from their long journey, they soon fell asleep.

When it was past midnight and the robbers saw from the distance that there was no light in the house and everything seemed peaceful, the leader of the band said, "We shouldn't have let ourselves be scared out of our wits."

He ordered one of the robbers to return and check out the house. When he found everything quiet, the robber went into the kitchen to light a candle and mistook the cat's glowing fiery eyes for live coals. So he held a match to them to light a fire, but the cat did not appreciate the joke. He jumped into the robber's face, spitting and scratching, and the robber was so terribly frightened that he ran out the back door. However, the dog was lying there and bit him in the leg. When the robber raced across the yard, he passed the dung heap, and here the donkey gave him a solid kick with his hind foot. All this noise woke the rooster from his sleep, and he became lively again and crowed *"Cock-a-doodle-doo!"* from his beam.

The robber ran back to the leader as fast as he could and said, "There's a gruesome witch in the house! She spat on me and scratched my face with her long claws. At the door there's a man with a knife, and he stabbed my leg. In the yard there's a black monster who beat me with a wooden club. And on top of the roof the judge was sitting and screaming 'Bring me the rascal!' I got out of there as fast as I could!"

Since that time the robbers have never dared return to the house, but the four Bremen Town musicians liked the place so much that they stayed on forever.

And the last person who told this tale has still got warm lips.

◆ 28 ◆

The Singing Bone

ONCE UPON A TIME there was a country in great distress because a wild boar was devastating the farmers' fields, killing cattle, and ripping people apart with its tusks. The king promised a large reward to anyone who could rid the country of this plague. However, the beast was so big and so strong that no one dared go near the forest in which it dwelled. At last the king proclaimed that whoever caught or killed the wild boar would receive his only daughter for a wife.

Now, there were two brothers, sons of a poor man, who were living in that country, and they declared themselves willing to take on the dangerous challenge. The older brother, a cunning and smart fellow, was doing it out of pride, while the younger, innocent and naive, was doing it out of the goodness of his heart.

"You must enter the forest from opposite sides," said the king. "That way you'll be more sure of finding the beast."

So the older entered from the west and the younger from the east. After the younger had walked for a while, a little dwarf with a black spear approached him and said, "I'm giving you this spear because you have a good and pure heart. With this you can attack the wild boar, and you won't have to worry about his harming you."

He thanked the dwarf, set the spear on his shoulder, and continued walking without fear. Shortly after, he caught sight of the beast, and when it charged him, he stuck out the spear, and in its blind fury the boar ran into it with such force that its heart was cut in two. The young man swung the monster over his shoulder and headed home with the intention of bringing the boar to the king.

When he came out at the other side of the forest, he saw a house where people were dancing, drinking, and having a good time. His older brother had gone there thinking that the boar was not about to run away, and he had also wanted to pump himself up with courage first by having a few drinks. When he saw his younger brother coming out of the forest and carrying his prize, his jealous and wicked heart gave him no peace.

"Come inside, dear brother," he called to him. "Take a rest and refresh yourself with a glass of wine."

Since the younger brother did not suspect anything evil, he went inside and told him about the good dwarf who had given him a spear so he could kill the boar. The older brother kept him there till evening, and then they departed together. In the darkness they came to a bridge that spanned a brook, and the older brother let the younger go ahead of him, and when the younger was halfway across, his brother gave him such a hard blow from behind that he fell down dead. After the older brother buried him under the bridge, he took the boar and brought it to the king, pretending he was the one who had killed it. So the king gave him his daughter for his wife. When the younger brother never returned, the older said, "The boar probably ripped him apart." And everyone believed him.

However, nothing remains hidden from God, and this evil deed was bound to come to light.

After many years had passed, a shepherd was driving his flock across the bridge and saw a little bone, as white as snow, lying beneath it. He thought it would make a good mouthpiece for his horn, so he climbed down, picked it up, and carved a mouthpiece out of it. When he blew on it for the first time, the shepherd was startled to find that the little bone began to sing on its own accord:

"Oh, shepherd, shepherd, don't you know
you're blowing on my bone!
My brother killed me years ago,
buried me by the brook that flows,
carried off the dead wild boar,
and married the king's fine daughter."

"What a remarkable horn!" said the shepherd. "It sings by itself! I've got to take it to the king."

When he went to the king, the little horn began to sing its song again. The king understood it full well and had the ground under the bridge dug up. After the entire skeleton of the murdered man was revealed, the wicked brother could not deny the deed, and he was sewn up in a sack and drowned. However, the bones of his murdered brother were laid to rest in a beautiful grave in the churchyard.

◆ 29 ◆

The Devil With the Three Golden Hairs

ONCE UPON A TIME there was a poor woman who gave birth to a little son, and since he was born with a caul, it was prophesied he would marry the king's daughter by the time he was fourteen. Soon after, the king happened to come to the village, but no one knew that he was the king. When he asked the people about the latest news, they answered, "Just recently a child was born with a caul. Now fortune will shine on him in all his endeavors. Indeed, it's been prophesied that he'll marry the king's daughter by the time he's fourteen."

Since the king had an evil heart and was disturbed by the prophecy, he went to the boy's parents and pretended to be friendly.

"I know that you're very poor people," he said. "So let me have your child, and I'll take good care of him."

At first they refused, but when the stranger offered them a great deal of gold for him, they thought, Since he's fortune's favorite, it's bound to turn out well for him. Therefore, they finally agreed and gave the child to the stranger.

The king laid him in a box and rode away with him until he came to a deep river. Then he threw the box into the water and thought, Well, now I've rid my daughter of an undesirable suitor. But the box did not sink. Instead, it floated like a little boat, and not a single drop of water got into it. The box drifted to within two miles of the king's capital city, where it was blocked from going any further by a mill dam. Fortunately, the miller's apprentice was standing on the bank and saw it. Thinking he had found a great treasure, he used a hook to pull the box ashore. However, when he opened it, he discovered a lovely-looking boy who was alive and well. So he took the boy to the miller and his wife because they did not have any children. Indeed, they were delighted and said, "God has blessed us with this gift."

They took good care of the foundling and made sure that he was raised with all the best virtues. Now, one day the king happened to get caught in a thunderstorm and arrived at the mill. There he asked the miller and his wife whether the big boy was their son.

"No," they answered. "He's a foundling. Fourteen years ago he floated down to the mill dam, and our apprentice fished him out of the water."

The king realized that it was no one else but fortune's favorite, whom he had thrown into the water.

"My good people," he said, "would it be possible for the young boy to carry a letter to the queen? I'll give him two gold coins as a reward."

"As Your Majesty commands," they answered and told the young boy to get ready. Then the king wrote a letter to the queen, which said, "As soon as the boy arrives with this letter, he's to be killed and buried. All this is to be done before my return."

The boy set out with this letter but lost his way, and at night he came to a great forest. When he saw a small light in the darkness, he began walking toward it and soon reached a little cottage. Upon entering, he discovered an old woman sitting all alone by the fire. She was startled by the sight of him and asked, "Where did you come from and where are you going?"

"I'm coming from the mill," he answered, "and I'm on my way to deliver a letter to the queen. But since I've lost my way, I'd like to spend the night here."

"You poor boy," said the woman. "You've stumbled on a robbers' den. When they come home, they'll kill you."

"I don't care if they come," the young boy said. "I'm not afraid. Besides, I'm too tired to go any further."

He stretched himself out on a bench and fell asleep. Soon after, the robbers arrived and angrily asked who the strange boy was that was lying there.

"Oh," said the old woman, "he's just an innocent child who's lost his way in the forest, and I've taken him in out of pity. He's carrying a letter to the queen."

The robbers opened the letter and read it, and they discovered that the boy was to be killed immediately upon arrival. The hard-hearted robbers felt sorry for him, and the leader of the band tore up the letter and wrote another one, which said that the boy was to wed the king's daughter immediately upon arrival. They let him sleep peacefully on the bench until morning, and when he awoke, they showed him the right path out of the forest.

Once the queen received the letter and read it, she did as it said: she prepared a splendid wedding feast, and the king's daughter was married to fortune's favorite. Since the boy was handsome and friendly, she was quite happy and content to live with him. After some time passed, the king returned to the castle and saw that the prophecy had been fulfilled and that fortune's favorite had married his daughter.

"How did it happen?" he asked. "I gave entirely different orders in my letter."

The queen handed him the letter and told him to see what it said for himself. The king read the letter and realized right away that it had been switched for the one he wrote. He asked the young boy what had happened to the letter he had been entrusted to carry and why he had delivered another instead.

"I know nothing about it," he answered. "It must have been switched while I was asleep in the forest."

"Well, you're not going to get things as easily as you think!" said the king in a rage. "Whoever wants to have my daughter must first travel to hell and fetch three golden hairs from the devil's head. If you bring me what I want, you may keep my daughter."

This way the king hoped to get rid of him forever, but fortune's favorite answered, "You can count on me to fetch the golden hairs. I'm not afraid of the devil."

He then took his leave and began the journey. His way led him to a big city, where the watchman at the gate asked him what kind of trade he practiced and what he knew.

"I know everything," fortune's favorite said.

"Then you can do us a favor," the watchman responded, "and tell us why the fountain at our marketplace, which used to gush with wine, has run dry and doesn't even provide us with water anymore."

"Just wait until I return," he answered, "and you shall learn the reason why."

He continued on his way, and when he came to another city, the watchman at the gate again asked him what trade he practiced and what he knew.

"I know everything," he said.

"Then you can do us a favor and tell us why a tree in our city that used to bear golden apples doesn't produce even leaves anymore."

"Just wait until I return," he answered, "and you shall learn the reason why."

He went further and came to a big river that he had to cross. The ferryman asked him what kind of trade he practiced and what he knew.

"I know everything," he said.

"Then you can do me a favor," said the ferryman, "and tell me why I must take people back and forth without relief."

"Just wait until I return," he answered, "and you shall learn the reason why."

When fortune's favorite reached the other side of the river, he found the entrance to hell. It was dark and sooty inside, and the devil was not at home. However, his grandmother was sitting in a large easy chair.

"What do you want?" she asked him, but she did not look very wicked.

"I'd like to have three golden hairs from the devil's head," he replied, "or else I won't be able to keep my wife."

"That's a lot to ask," she said. "If the devil comes home and finds you, it will cost you your neck. But, since I feel sorry for you, I'll see if I can help."

She changed him into an ant and said, "Crawl into the folds of my skirt. You'll be safe there."

"All right," he answered. "That's fine, but there are still three things I'd like to know: Why has a fountain that used to gush with wine become dry and why doesn't it produce even water now? Why has a tree that used to bear golden apples no longer bear even leaves anymore? And, why must a ferryman take people back and forth without relief?"

"Those are difficult questions," she replied. "But keep still and quiet, and pay attention to what the devil says when I pull out the three golden hairs."

At nightfall the devil came home. No sooner did he enter the house than he noticed the air was not pure.

"I smell, I smell the flesh of a man," he said. "Something's wrong here."

Then he looked in all the nooks and crannies and searched around but could not find anything. The grandmother scolded him. "I've just swept," she said, "and put everything in order. Now you're messing it all up again. You're always smelling the flesh of men. Just sit down and eat your supper!"

After he had something to eat and drink, he was tired and laid his head in his grandmother's lap. Then he told her to pick the lice from his head for a while. Soon after, he fell asleep and began to snore and wheeze. Now the old woman grabbed hold of a golden hair, ripped it out, and put it down beside her.

"Ouch!" screamed the devil. "What are you doing to me?"

"I had a bad dream," the grandmother said, "and grabbed hold of your hair."

"What did you dream?" the devil asked.

"I dreamed there was a fountain at the marketplace that used to gush with wine, and it ran dry. It even stopped providing water. Why do you think that happened?"

"Ha!" the devil replied. "If they only knew! There's a toad sitting underneath a stone in the fountain. If they kill it, the wine will flow again."

The grandmother began lousing him again until he fell asleep and snored so loudly that the windows trembled. Then she tore out a second hair.

"*Hey!* What are you doing?" the devil screamed angrily.

"I didn't mean it," she said. "I did it in a dream."

"What did you dream this time?" he asked.

"I dreamed that in a kingdom there was an apple tree that used to bear golden apples, and now it can't produce even leaves. Why do you think that happened?"

"Ha!" the devil replied. "If they only knew! There's a mouse gnawing at the roots. When they kill the mouse, the tree will bear golden apples again. If it continues to gnaw much longer, the tree will wither completely away. Now leave me alone with your dreams! If you disturb me in my sleep one more time, I'll give you a good hard slap!"

The grandmother spoke softly to him and loused him again until he fell asleep and began snoring. Then she grabbed hold of the third golden hair and tore it out. The devil jumped up, screamed, and was about to teach her a lesson, but she calmed him down again and said,

"What can you do against dreams?"

"What did you dream?" he asked and was curious in spite of himself.

"I dreamed of a ferryman who complained that he had to take people back and forth without relief. Why do you think he's got to do this?"

"Ha! The fool!" the devil replied. "He just has to put the pole into the hand of someone who wants to get across, and this person will have to do the ferrying, and the ferryman will be free."

Since the grandmother had now torn out the three golden hairs and the three questions had been answered, she let the old snake rest peacefully and sleep until daybreak. Thereupon the devil departed, and the old woman took the ant from the fold in her skirt and restored fortune's favorite to his human form.

"Here are the three golden hairs," she said. "You undoubtedly heard what the devil said to your three questions."

"Yes," he answered. "I heard everything, and I'll certainly remember it all."

"Then you have what you need," she said, "and now you can move on."

He thanked the old woman for helping him out of his predicament and left hell in a happy mood, for he had achieved what he had set out to do. When he came to the ferryman, he was obliged to keep his promise.

"Take me across first," said fortune's favorite, "and I'll tell you how you can be relieved of your work."

When he was on the other side, he gave him the devil's advice. "When someone comes and wants to be taken across, just put the pole in his hands."

Then fortune's favorite moved on, and when he came to the city where the barren tree stood, the watchman was also expecting his answer. So fortune's favorite told him what he had heard from the devil. "Kill the mouse that's been gnawing on the roots, then the tree will bear apples again."

The watchman thanked him and rewarded him with two donkeys laden with gold. Next fortune's favorite went to the city where the fountain had run dry and told the watchman what the devil had said. "There's a toad in the fountain sitting underneath a stone. You must find it and kill it. Then the fountain will gush with plenty of wine again."

The watchman thanked him and also gave him two donkeys laden with gold. Finally, fortune's favorite returned home to his wife, who was very happy to see him again and to hear how successful he had been. He brought the king what he had demanded, the three golden hairs, and when the king saw the four donkeys laden with gold, he was very pleased and said, "Now all the conditions have been fulfilled, and you may keep my daughter. But, my dear son-in-law, tell me, where did you get all this gold? It's such a great treasure!"

"I found it on the ground and picked it up after I crossed a river," he replied. "The bank is completely covered with gold instead of sand."

"Can I also get some?" asked the king, who was very greedy.

"As much as you like," he answered. "There's a ferryman at the river. Just let him take you across, and you'll be able to fill your sacks to the brim."

The greedy king set out as fast as he could, and when he came to the river, he signaled the ferryman to take him across. The ferryman came and told him to get into the boat, and when they reached the other side, the ferryman put the pole into his hand and ran away. From then on the king was compelled to ferry people back and forth as punishment for his sins.

"Is he still ferrying?"

"Why, of course. Do you think someone's about to take the pole away from him?"

◈ 30 ◈

The Louse and the Flea

A LOUSE AND A FLEA KEPT HOUSE TOGETHER and were brewing beer in an eggshell when the louse fell in and was scalded. Then the flea began to scream as loud as he could, and the little door to the room asked, "Why are you screaming, flea?"

"Because louse has been scalded."

Then the door began to creak, and a little broom in the corner asked, "Why are you creaking, door?"

"Why shouldn't I creak?"

Louse has just got scalded.
Flea is weeping."

Then the broom began to sweep in a frenzy, and when a little cart came driving by, it asked, "Why are you sweeping, broom?"
"Why shouldn't I sweep?

Louse has just got scalded.
Flea is weeping.
Door is creaking."

"Well, then I'm going to race around," said the cart, and it began racing around furiously, and the dung heap, which it passed, asked, "Why are you racing around, cart?"
"Why shouldn't I race around?

Louse has just got scalded.
Flea is weeping.
Door is creaking.
Broom is sweeping."

"Then I'm going to burn with fury," said the dung heap, and it began to burn in bright flames. Then a little tree nearby asked, "Why are you burning, dung heap?"
"Why shouldn't I burn?

Louse has just got scalded.
Flea is weeping.
Door is creaking.
Broom is sweeping.
Cart is racing."

"Well, then I'm going to shake myself," said the tree, and it shook itself so hard that all its leaves began to fall. Then a maiden with a water jug came by and asked, "Tree, why are you shaking?"
"Why shouldn't I shake?

Louse has just got scalded.
Flea is weeping.
Door is creaking.
Broom is sweeping.
Cart is racing.
Dung heap is burning."

"Well, then I'm going to break my water jug," said the maiden, and as she was breaking it, the spring from which the water came asked, "Maiden, why are you breaking the water jug?"

"Why shouldn't I break it?

Louse has just got scalded.
Flea is weeping.
Door is creaking.
Broom is sweeping.
Cart is racing.
Dung heap is burning.
Tree is shaking."

"Goodness gracious!" said the spring. "Then I'm going to flow," and it began to flow so violently that they were all drowned in the water—the maiden, the tree, the dung heap, the cart, the door, the flea, and the louse, every last one of them.

◈ 31 ◈

The Maiden Without Hands

A MILLER HAD BEEN FALLING little by little into poverty, and soon he had nothing left but his mill and a large apple tree behind it. One day, as he was on his way to chop wood in the forest, he met an old man whom he had never seen before.

"There's no reason you have to torture yourself by cutting wood," the old man said. "I'll make you rich if you promise to give me what's behind your mill."

What else can that be but my apple tree, thought the miller, and he gave the stranger his promise in writing.

"In three years I'll come and fetch what's mine," the stranger said with a snide laugh, and he went away.

When the miller returned home, his wife went out to meet him and said, "Tell me, miller, how did all this wealth suddenly get into our house? All at once I've discovered our chests and boxes are full.

Nobody's brought anything, and I don't know how it's all happened."

"It's from a stranger I met in the forest," he said. "He promised me great wealth if I agreed in writing to give him what's behind our mill. We can certainly spare the large apple tree."

"Oh, husband!" his wife exclaimed in dread. "That was the devil! He didn't mean the apple tree but our daughter, who was behind the mill sweeping out the yard."

The miller's daughter was a beautiful and pious maiden who went through the next three years in fear of God and without sin. When the time was up and the day came for the devil to fetch her, she washed herself clean and drew a circle around her with chalk. The devil appeared quite early, but he could not get near her, and he said angrily to the miller, "I want you to take all the water away from her so she can't wash herself anymore. Otherwise, I have no power over her."

Since the miller was afraid of the devil, he did as he was told. The next morning the devil came again, but she wept on her hands and made them completely clean. Once more he could not get near her and said furiously to the miller, "Chop off her hands. Otherwise, I can't touch her."

The miller was horrified and replied, "How can I chop off the hands of my own child!"

But the devil threatened him and said, "If you don't do it, you're mine, and I'll come and get you myself!"

The father was so scared of him that he promised to obey. He went to his daughter and said, "My child, if I don't chop off both your hands, the devil will take me away, and in my fear I promised I'd do it. Please help me out of my dilemma and forgive me for the injury I'm causing you."

"Dear Father," she answered, "do what you want with me. I'm your child."

Then she extended both her hands and let him chop them off. The devil came a third time, but she had wept so long and so much on the stumps that they too were all clean. Then he had to abandon his game and lost all claim to her.

Now the miller said to his daughter, "I've become so wealthy because of you that I shall see to it you'll live in splendor for the rest of your life."

But she answered, "No, I cannot stay here. I'm going away and shall depend on the kindness of people to provide me with whatever I need."

Then she had her maimed arms bound to her back, and at dawn she set out on her way and walked the entire day until it became dark. She was right outside a royal garden, and by the glimmer of the moon she could see trees full of beautiful fruit. She could not enter the garden, though because it was surrounded by water. Since she had traveled the entire day without eating, she was very hungry. Oh, if only I could get in! she thought. I must eat some of the fruit or else I'll perish! Then she fell to her knees, called out to the Lord, and prayed. Suddenly an angel appeared who closed one of the locks in the stream so that the moat became dry and she could walk through it. Now she went into the garden accompanied by the angel. She caught sight of a beautiful tree full of pears, but the pears had all been counted. Nonetheless, she approached the tree and ate one of the pears with her mouth to satisfy her hunger, but only this one. The gardener was watching her, but since the angel was standing there, he was afraid, especially since he thought the maiden was a spirit. He kept still and did not dare to cry out or speak to her. After she had eaten the pear, and her hunger was stilled, she went and hid in the bushes.

The next morning the king who owned the garden came and counted the pears. When he saw one was missing, he asked the gardener what had happened to it, for the pear was not lying under the tree and had somehow vanished.

"Last night a spirit appeared," answered the gardener. "It had no hands and ate one of the pears with its mouth."

"How did the spirit get over the water?" asked the king. "And where did it go after it ate the pear?"

"Someone wearing a garment as white as snow came down from heaven, closed the lock, and dammed up the water so the spirit could walk through the moat. And, since it must have been an angel, I was afraid to ask any questions or to cry out. After the spirit had eaten the pear, it just went away."

"If it's as you say," said the king, "I shall spend the night with you and keep watch."

When it became dark, the king went into the garden and brought a priest with him to talk to the spirit. All three sat down beneath the tree and kept watch. At midnight the maiden came out of the bushes, walked over to the tree, and once again ate one of the pears with her mouth, while the angel in white stood next to her. The priest stepped forward and said to the maiden, "Have you come from heaven or from earth? Are you a spirit or a human being?"

"I'm not a spirit, but a poor creature forsaken by everyone except God."

"You may be forsaken by the whole world, but I shall not forsake you," said the king.

He took her with him to his royal palace, and since she was so beautiful and good, he loved her with all his heart, had silver hands made for her, and took her for his wife.

After a year had passed, the king had to go to war, and he placed the young queen under the care of his mother and said, "If she has a child, I want you to protect her and take good care of her, and write me right away."

Soon after, the young queen gave birth to a fine-looking boy. The king's mother wrote to him immediately to announce the joyful news. However, on the way the messenger stopped to rest near a brook, and since he was exhausted from the long journey, he fell asleep. Then the devil appeared. He was still trying to harm the pious queen, and so he exchanged the letter for another one that said that the queen had given birth to a changeling. When the king read the letter, he was horrified and quite distressed, but he wrote his mother that she should protect the queen and take care of her until his return. The messenger started back with the letter, but he stopped to rest at the same spot and fell asleep. Once again the devil came and put a different letter in his pocket that said that they should kill the queen and her child. The old mother was tremendously disturbed when she received the letter and could not believe it. She wrote the king again but received the same answer because the devil kept replacing the messenger's letters with false letters each time. The last letter ordered the king's mother to keep the tongue and eyes of the queen as proof that she had done his bidding.

But the old woman wept at the thought of shedding such innocent blood. During the night she had a doe fetched and cut out its tongue and eyes and put them away. Then she said to the queen, "I can't let you be killed as the king commands. However, you can't stay here any longer. Go out into the wide world with your child and never come back."

She tied the child to the queen's back, and the poor woman went off with tears in her eyes. When she came to a great wild forest, she fell down on her knees and prayed to God. The Lord's angel appeared before her and led her to a small cottage with a little sign saying "Free Lodging for Everyone." A maiden wearing a snow white garment came out of the cottage and said, "Welcome, Your Highness," and took her inside. She untied the little boy from her back and offered him her breast so he could have something to drink. Then she laid him down in a beautifully made bed.

"How did you know that I'm a queen?" asked the poor woman.

"I'm an angel sent by God to take care of you and your child," replied the maiden in white.

So the queen stayed seven years in the cottage and was well cared for. By the grace of God and through her own piety her hands that had been chopped off grew back again.

When the king finally returned from the wars, the first thing he wanted to do was to see his wife and child. However, his old mother began to weep and said, "You wicked man, why did you write and order me to kill two innocent souls?" She showed him the two letters that the devil had forged and resumed talking. "I did as you ordered," and she displayed the tongue and eyes.

At the sight of them the king burst into tears and wept bitterly over his poor wife and little son. His old mother was aroused and took pity on him.

"Console yourself," she said. "She's still alive. I secretly had a doe killed and kept its tongue and eyes as proof. Then I took the child and tied him to your wife's back and ordered her to go out into the wide world, and she had to promise me never to return here because you were so angry with her."

"I shall go as far as the sky is blue, without eating or drinking, until I find my dear wife and child," the king said. "That is, unless they have been killed or have died of hunger in the meantime."

The king wandered for about seven years and searched every rocky cliff and cave he came across. When he did not find her, he thought she had perished. During this time he neither ate nor drank, but God kept him alive. Eventually, he came to a great forest, where he discovered the little cottage with the sign "Free Lodging for Everyone." Then the maiden in white came out, took him by the hand, and led him inside.

"Welcome, Your Majesty," she said, and asked him where he came from.

"I've been wandering about for almost seven years looking for my wife and child, but I can't find them."

The angel offered him food and drink, but he refused and said he only wanted to rest awhile. So he lay down to sleep and covered his face with a handkerchief. Then the angel went into the room where the queen was sitting with her son, whom she was accustomed to calling Sorrowful, and said, "Go into the next room with your child. Your husband has come."

So the queen went to the room where he was lying, and the handkerchief fell from his face.

"Sorrowful," she said, "pick up your father's handkerchief and put it over his face again."

The child picked the handkerchief up and put it over his face. The king heard all this in his sleep and took pleasure in making the handkerchief drop on the floor again. The boy became impatient and said, "Dear Mother, how can I cover my father's face when I have no father on earth. I've learned to pray to 'our Father that art in heaven,' and you told me that my father was in heaven and that he was our good Lord. How am I supposed to recognize this wild man? He's not my father."

When the king heard this, he sat up and asked her who she was.

"I'm your wife," she replied, "and this is your son, Sorrowful."

When the king saw that she had real hands, he said, "My wife had silver hands."

"Our merciful Lord let my natural hands grow again," she answered.

The angel went back into the sitting room, fetched the silver hands, and showed them to him. Now he knew for certain that it was his dear wife and dear son, and he kissed them and was happy.

"A heavy load has been taken off my mind," he said.

After the Lord's angel ate one more meal with them, they went home to be with the king's old mother. There was rejoicing everywhere, and the king and queen had a second wedding and lived happily ever after.

◈ 32 ◈

Clever Hans

"WHERE ARE YOU GOING, Hans?" his mother asked.

"To Gretel's," Hans replied.

"Take care, Hans."

"Don't worry. Good-bye, Mother."

Hans arrived at Gretel's place.

"Good day, Gretel."

"Good day, Hans. Have you brought me anything nice?"

"Didn't bring anything. Want something from you."

Gretel gave him a needle.

"Good-bye, Gretel," Hans said.

"Good-bye, Hans."

Hans took the needle, stuck it in the hay wagon, and walked home behind the wagon.

"Good evening, Mother."

"Good evening, Hans. Where have you been?"

"At Gretel's."

"What did you bring her?"

"Didn't bring her a thing. Got something."

"What did Gretel give you?"

"Got a needle."

"Where'd you put the needle, Hans?"

"Stuck it in a hay wagon."

"That was stupid of you, Hans. You should have stuck it in your sleeve."

"Doesn't matter. I'll do better next time."

"Where are you going, Hans?"

"To Gretel's, Mother."

"Take care, Hans."

"Don't worry. Good-bye, Mother."

Hans arrived at Gretel's place.

"Good day, Gretel."

"Good day, Hans. Have you brought me anything nice?"

"Didn't bring anything. Want something from you."

Gretel gave Hans a knife.

"Good-bye, Gretel."

"Good-bye, Hans."

Hans took the knife, stuck it in his sleeve, and went home.

"Good evening, Mother."

"Good evening, Hans. Where have you been?"

"At Gretel's."

"What did you bring her?"

"Didn't bring her a thing. Got something."

"What did Gretel give you?"

"Got a knife."

"Where'd you put the knife, Hans?"

"Stuck it in my sleeve."

"That was stupid of you, Hans. You should have put it in your pocket."

"Doesn't matter. I'll do better next time."

"Where are you going, Hans?"

"To Gretel's, Mother."

"Take care, Hans."

"Don't worry. Good-bye, Mother."

Hans arrived at Gretel's place.

"Good day, Gretel."

"Good day, Hans. Have you brought me anything nice?"

"Didn't bring anything. Want something from you."

Gretel gave Hans a kid goat.

"Good-bye, Gretel."

"Good-bye, Hans."

Hans took the goat, tied its legs together, and stuck it in his pocket. By the time he got home, the goat had suffocated.

"Good evening, Mother."

"Good evening, Hans. Where have you been?"

"At Gretel's."

"What did you bring her?"

"Didn't bring a thing. Got something."

"What did Gretel give you?"

"Got a goat."

"Where'd you put the goat, Hans?"

"Stuck it in my pocket."

"That was stupid of you, Hans. You should have tied the goat to a rope."

"Doesn't matter. I'll do better next time."

"Where are you going, Hans?"

"To Gretel's, Mother."

"Take care, Hans."

"Don't worry. Good-bye, Mother."

"Good-bye, Hans."

Hans arrived at Gretel's place.

"Good day, Gretel."

"Good day, Hans. Have you brought me anything nice?"

"Didn't bring anything. Want something from you."

Gretel gave Hans a piece of bacon.

Hans took the bacon, tied it to a rope, and dragged it along behind him. The dogs came and ate the bacon. By the time Hans arrived home, he had the rope in his hand but nothing attached to it anymore.

"Good evening, Mother."

"Good evening, Hans. Where have you been?"

"At Gretel's."

"What did you bring her?"

"Didn't bring her a thing. Got something."

"What did Gretel give you?"

"Got a piece of bacon."

"What have you done with the bacon, Hans?"

"Tied it to a rope. Dragged it home. Dogs got it."

"That was stupid of you, Hans. You should have carried the bacon on your head."

"Doesn't matter. I'll do better next time."

"Where are you going, Hans?"

"To Gretel's, Mother."

"Take care, Hans."

"Don't worry. Good-bye, Mother."

"Good-bye, Hans."

Hans arrived at Gretel's place.

"Good day, Gretel."

"Good day, Hans. Have you brought me anything nice?"

"Didn't bring anything. Want something from you."

Gretel gave Hans a calf.

"Good-bye, Gretel."

"Good-bye, Hans."

Hans took the calf, set it on his head, and the calf kicked him in his face.

"Good evening, Mother."

"Good evening, Hans. Where have you been?"

"At Gretel's."

"What did you bring her?"

"Didn't bring her a thing. Got something."

"What did Gretel give you?"

"Got a calf."

"What have you done with the calf?"

"Put it on my head. Kicked me in my face."

"That was stupid of you, Hans. You should have led the calf to the stable and put it in the stall."

"Doesn't matter. I'll do better next time."

"Where are you going, Hans?"

"To Gretel's, Mother."

"Take care, Hans."

"Don't worry. Good-bye, Mother."

"Good-bye, Hans."

Hans arrived at Gretel's place.

"Good day, Gretel."

"Good day, Hans. Have you brought me anything nice?"

"Didn't bring anything. Want something from you."

"I'll come along with you," Gretel said.

Hans took Gretel, put a rope around her, led her into the stable, tied her to a stall, and threw her some grass. Then he went to his mother.

"Good evening, Mother."

"Good evening, Hans. Where have you been?"

"At Gretel's."

"What did you bring her?"

"Didn't bring her a thing."

"What did Gretel give you?"

"Got nothing. She came along."

"Where have you left Gretel?"

"Led her by a rope and tied her up in the stall and threw her some grass."

"That was stupid of you, Hans. You should have thrown friendly looks at her with the eyes."

Hans went into the stable, cut out the eyes of all the cows and sheep, and threw them in Gretel's face. Then Gretel got angry, tore herself loose, and ran away. That was how Hans lost his bride.

◈ 33 ◈

The Three Languages

THERE WAS ONCE AN OLD COUNT who lived in Switzerland, and he had an only son, who was quite stupid and could not learn anything.

"Listen, my son," the father said, "I can't get anything to sink into your head, no matter how much I try. So I'm sending you away from here and placing you under the care of a famous master. Let's see what he can do with you."

The young man was sent to a strange city and stayed with the master for a whole year. At the end of this time he came home, and his father asked, "Well, my son, what have you learned?"

"Father," he responded, "I've learned to understand the barking of dogs."

"May God have mercy on us!" the father exclaimed. "Is that all you've learned? Well, now I'm going to send you to a master in another city."

The young man was taken there and stayed one year with this master as well. When he came back home, his father asked again, "My son, what have you learned?"

"Father," he responded, "I've learned to understand the language of birds."

The father became infuriated and said, "You're hopeless! Why, you've wasted all this valuable time and have learned nothing! And you're not even ashamed to appear before my eyes! Well, I'm going to send you to a third master, but if you don't learn anything this time, I'm no longer going to be your father."

The son spent a whole year with the third master too, and when he returned home, the father asked, "My son, what have you learned?"

"Dear Father," he responded, "I've learned to understand the croaking of frogs."

Now the father was so infuriated that he jumped up, summoned his men, and said, "This creature is no longer my son. I'm expelling him and want you to take him out into the forest and kill him."

The count's men took him into the forest, but they felt so sorry for the son that they could not bring themselves to kill him and let him go. Then they cut out the eyes and tongue of a deer to provide the old man with proof of their deed.

Meanwhile, the young man wandered about, and after some time he came to a castle, where he asked for a night's lodging.

"All right," said the lord of the castle, "—if you're prepared to spend the night in the old tower. You may go there, but let me warn you that you'll be risking your life. The tower is full of wild dogs that bark and howl continually, and at certain times they must be given a human being, whom they devour right away."

The entire region had been enduring great sorrow and suffering because of this, and yet, nobody could do anything about it. However, the young man was fearless and said, "I shall go down and face the barking dogs. Just give me something that I can throw to them. They won't harm me."

Since he insisted, they gave him some food for the wild beasts and brought him down to the tower. When he entered, the dogs did not bark but wagged their tails in a friendly way and gathered around him. They ate what he set before them and did not touch a hair of his head. The next morning, to everyone's astonishment, he reappeared alive and well and said to the lord of the castle, "The dogs have spoken to me in their language and revealed to me why they've been dwelling here and causing terror in your country. They're under a curse and are compelled to protect a great treasure lying under the tower. They'll never find peace until the treasure is dug up, and they've told me how this can be done.''

All those who heard this rejoiced, and the lord of the castle said he would adopt him as his son if he could accomplish this task successfully. The young count went back down to the tower, and since he knew what was to be done, he completed it and brought up a chest filled with gold. From then on the wild dogs no longer howled, nor were they ever seen again, and the land was freed of this plague.

After a while the young man decided to go to Rome, and along the way he passed a swamp where some frogs were sitting and croaking. He stopped and listened, and when he heard what they were saying, he grew very pensive and sad. At last, when he arrived in Rome, he learned that the pope had just died, and the cardinals could not agree on a successor. Eventually, they resolved to wait for a divine miracle to reveal the person they should elect. At the very moment that they came to this decision the young count happened to enter the church, and two white doves swooped down to his shoulders and rested on them. The cardinals recognized this as a sign from God and asked him on the spot whether he wanted to be pope. At first he was undecided and did not know if he was worthy enough, but the doves persuaded him to do it, and finally he consented. He was annointed and consecrated, and thus the prophecy that he had heard from the frogs along the way was fulfilled. Indeed, it had been this very prophecy that had upset him, for he had not expected to become the holy pope. After that he had to sing mass and did not know a single word of it, but the two doves were still sitting on his shoulders and whispered the words in his ear.

◈ 34 ◈

Clever Else

THERE ONCE WAS A MAN who had a daughter called Clever Else. When she had grown up, her father said, "It's time for her to get married."

"I agree," said her mother. "If only someone would come along and take her."

At last someone named Hans came from far away, and he began courting her. However, he set one condition: Clever Else had to prove she was really smart.

"Oh," said her father, "she's as bright as the newborn day."

"Oh," said her mother, "she can see the wind coming down the road and hear flies cough."

"Fine and good," said Hans. "But if she isn't really smart, I'm not going to take her."

When they were sitting at the table and had finished their meal, the mother said, "Else, go down to the cellar and fetch some beer."

Clever Else took the pitcher from the wall, went down to the cellar, and along the way played with the lid by flapping it to pass the time. When she got down there, she took a stool and put it in front of the keg so she would not have to stoop, for she was afraid of hurting her back or causing herself some unexpected injury. Then she set the pitcher in front of her and turned the tap. While the beer was running, she kept her eyes busy by looking up at the wall, where she gazed around for some time. At last she caught sight of a pickax hanging directly above her. The masons had left it hanging there by mistake. Suddenly Clever Else began to weep, and she said, "If I get Hans and we have a child and he grows up and we send him to the cellar to draw some beer, the pickax will fall on his head and kill him."

Then she just sat there and wept and bawled with all her might on account of the impending disaster. Upstairs the others waited for the beer, but Clever Else did not return. Then the mother said to the maid, "You'd better go down to the cellar and see what's keeping Else."

The maid went and found her sitting in front of the keg and bawling with all her might.

"Else, why are you crying?" asked the maid.

"Why shouldn't I cry? If I get Hans and we have a child and he grows up and we send him to draw some beer, there's a good chance that the pickax will fall on his head and kill him."

"What a clever Else we've got!" said the maid, who sat down next to her and also began to weep about the disaster.

After a while, when the maid did not return and the others upstairs were getting thirsty for the beer, the father said to the servant, "You'd better go down to the cellar and see what's keeping Else and the maid."

The servant went downstairs and found Else and the maid sitting together and weeping.

"Why are you crying?" he asked.

"Oh," said Else, "why shouldn't I cry? If I get Hans and we have a child and he grows up and we send him to draw beer, the pickax will fall on his head and kill him."

"What a clever Else we've got!" said the servant, who sat down next to her and also began to howl loudly.

Upstairs the others waited for the servant, but when he did not appear, the husband said to his wife, "You'd better go down to the cellar and see what's keeping Else."

The wife went down and found all three wailing and wanted to know the reason. So Else told her that her future child would probably be killed by the pickax when he grew up and was sent to draw some beer, for the pickax would fall down.

"What a clever Else we've got!" her mother said, and she sat down next to her and began weeping.

Now, the husband waited upstairs awhile longer, but when his wife did not return and he grew thirstier and thirstier, he said, "I'd better go down to the cellar myself and see what's keeping Else."

When he reached the cellar and saw them all sitting together and weeping, he learned that Else's future child was the cause of it, for he might be killed by the pickax if he were under it drawing beer at the exact same time that the ax fell. Then he exclaimed, "What a clever Else we've got!" And he sat down and wept too.

The bridegroom continued to sit alone upstairs for a long time. But when it seemed that nobody would return, he thought, They're probably waiting for me to come downstairs. I'd better go down and see what they're up to.

When he got there and saw the five of them screaming and moaning quite pitifully, he asked, "Has there been an accident of some kind?"

"Oh, dear Hans," Else said, "if we get married and have a child, and he grows up and we happen to send him here to draw beer, then the pickax that's been left behind up there could fall on his head and split his skull in two! Don't you think that's reason enough to cry?"

"Well," said Hans, "I certainly don't need more brains than that for my household. Since you're such a clever Else, I'll have you for my wife." So he took her by the hand, led her upstairs, and married her.

One day, after Hans had been living with Else for some time, he said, "Wife, I'm going to go to work and earn some money, and I want you to go into the field and cut the wheat so we can have some bread.''

"Yes, my dear Hans, I'll do that.''

When Hans had gone away, she cooked some good porridge and took it with her into the field. When she got there, she said to herself, "What should I do first, cut the wheat or sleep? I think I'll sleep first.'' So she lay down in the wheatfield and fell asleep.

Meanwhile, Hans had been back at home for some time, and when Else did not appear, he said, "What a clever Else I've got! She's so industrious that she doesn't even come home to eat.''

But when evening came and she still did not appear, Hans went out to see what she had cut. However, nothing was cut, and she was lying asleep in the wheatfield. Hans hurried back home and fetched a net with bells used for catching birds. He hung it over Else while she continued sleeping. After that he ran home, locked the front door, and sat down on a chair to work.

Finally, when it was already quite dark, Clever Else awoke. As she stood up she heard jingling all around her, and the little bells rang at each step she took. Then she became frightened and so confused that she did not know whether she was really Clever Else.

"Is it me, or isn't it me?'' she asked.

Since she did not know what to answer, she just stood there in doubt for a while. Finally, she thought, I'll go home and ask whether it's me or not. They'll surely know.

She ran to the front door, but it was locked. Then she knocked at the window and called out, "Hans, is Else inside?''

"Yes,'' answered Hans. "She's here.''

That made her frightened, and she said, "Oh, God, then I'm not me,'' and she went to another house, but when the people heard the bells, they did not want to open the door. Since there was no place for her to go, Clever Else ran out of the village, and nobody has ever seen her again.

◈ 35 ◈

The Tailor in Heaven

ONE FINE DAY it happened that the good Lord decided to go for a walk in the heavenly garden. He took all the apostles and saints with him, and nobody was left in heaven except Saint Peter. The Lord ordered him not to let a soul enter during his absence. So Saint Peter stood at the gate and kept watch. Soon someone knocked, and Saint Peter asked who was there and what he wanted.

"I'm a poor honest tailor," a slick voice answered, "and I'd like to come in."

"Sure, you're honest!" said Saint Peter. "About as honest as a thief on the gallows. Your light fingers have stolen many pieces of cloth from people, and I'm certainly not going to let you enter heaven. The Lord has forbidden me to let anyone in while he's out."

"Have mercy," the tailor cried out. "They were just scraps of cloth that fell from the tables by themselves. They weren't stolen, and they're not even worth talking about. Look, I'm limping. I've got blisters all over my feet from walking here, and I can't possibly turn back. Let me in, and I'll do all the dirty work. I'll carry the babies, wash their diapers, clean the benches they play on, and mend their tattered clothes."

Saint Peter let himself be moved by pity and opened heaven's gate just wide enough for the lame tailor to slip his lean body through. He was ordered to sit down in a corner behind the door and to keep absolutely still so the Lord would not notice him upon his return and get angry. The tailor obeyed, but once when Saint Peter stepped out the door, the tailor got up, full of curiosity, and explored all the nooks and crannies of heaven, inspecting everything he saw. Finally, he came to a place where there were many beautiful and exquisite chairs, and in the middle was an armchair made of solid gold and studded with glistening jewels. It was much taller than the other chairs, and a golden footstool stood in front of it. This was the

Lord's armchair, and he sat in it when he was at home. It was from this seat that he could see everything that happened on earth. The tailor stood still and looked at the chair for a good long time, for it appealed to him more than anything else he had seen. Finally, his curiosity got the better of him, and he climbed up and sat down in the chair. Then he could see everything that was happening on earth, and he noticed an ugly woman washing some clothes at a brook. When she secretly put two veils aside, the tailor became so infuriated by the sight that he grabbed the golden footstool and hurled it down from heaven at the old thief on earth. Upon realizing that he could not retrieve the footstool, the tailor slipped quietly out of the armchair, took his place behind the door again, and pretended he had not been stirring up trouble.

When the Lord and Master returned with his heavenly retinue, he did not notice the tailor behind the door. But when he sat down in his armchair, he did indeed remark that his footstool was missing. He asked Saint Peter what had happened to it, but Saint Peter did not know. Then the Lord asked him whether he had let anyone in.

"I don't know of anyone who's been here," Saint Peter replied, "except a lame tailor who's still sitting behind the door."

Then the Lord had the tailor appear before him and asked him whether he had taken the footstool and what he had done with it.

"Oh, Lord," the tailor answered joyfully. "I threw it in anger at an old woman on earth because she was stealing two veils while washing clothes."

"How ridiculous you are!" exclaimed the Lord. "If I were to judge as you do, what do you think would have happened to you by now? I would no longer have any chairs, benches, armchairs, or even fire tongs, because I'd have thrown them all at sinners. It's clear that you can't stay here any longer. I want you to leave through heaven's gate. Then you may go wherever you will. Nobody shall dole out punishment but me, the Lord your God."

Saint Peter had to lead the tailor through heaven's gate, and since the tailor's shoes were torn and his feet were covered with blisters, the tailor took a stick in his hand for a cane and walked to Waitawhile, where the good soldiers sit and make merry.

◈ 36 ◈

The Magic Table, the Golden Donkey,
and the Club in the Sack

IN DAYS OF OLD there was a tailor who had three sons and only one
goat. Since they all lived on the goat's milk, she had to be fed well
and be taken out each day to graze somewhere. The sons took turns
doing this, and one day the oldest son led her to the churchyard,
where the finest grass was growing. He let her graze there and run
about. In the evening, when it was time to go home, he asked her,
"Goat, have you had enough?"

The goat answered:

"Oh, my, I'm stuffed!
Enough's enough.
Meh! Meh!"

"Then let's head for home," said the boy. He took her by the
rope, led her back to the barn, and tied her up.

"Well," said the old tailor, "did the goat have a proper feeding?"

"Oh," answered the son, "she's really stuffed. I can tell she's
had more than enough."

But the father wanted to make sure of everything himself. So he
went down to the barn, patted the precious creature, and asked,
"Goat, have you had enough?"

The goat replied:

"How can I have eaten enough
when the ground was dry and horribly rough
and the leaves and grass were much too tough?
Meh! Meh!"

"What's this I hear!" the tailor exclaimed, and he ran upstairs to
his son. "You liar!" he yelled. "You said the goat had enough to
eat, and yet you let her starve!" And in his rage he grabbed his

yardstick from the wall, gave his son a good beating, and drove him out of the house.

The next day it was the second son's turn, and he chose a place near the garden hedge where only the very best grass was growing, and the goat combed it clean. In the evening, when the son wanted to go home, he asked, "Goat, have you had enough?"

The goat answered:

"Oh, my, I'm stuffed!
Enough's enough.
Meh! Meh!"

"Then let's head for home," said the boy, and he pulled her home and tied her up in the barn.

"Well," said the old tailor, "did the goat have a proper feeding?"

"Oh," answered the son, "she's really stuffed. I can tell she's had more than enough."

Since the tailor did not trust his son, he went down to the barn and asked, "Goat, have you had enough?"

The goat replied:

"How can I have eaten enough
when the ground was dry and horribly rough
and the leaves and grass were much too tough?
Meh! Meh!"

"The godless scoundrel!" the tailor screamed. "How could he let such a good creature starve?" And he ran out, grabbed his yardstick, and beat his second son out of the house.

Now it was the third son's turn, and he wanted to do a good job. He looked for bushes with the finest leaves and let the goat eat them. In the evening, when he wanted to go home, he asked, "Goat, have you had enough?"

The goat answered:

"Oh, my, I'm stuffed!
Enough's enough.
Meh! Meh!"

"Then let's head for home," said the boy. He led her into the barn and tied her up.

"Well," said the old tailor, "did the goat have a proper feeding?"

"Oh," answered the son, "she's really stuffed. I can tell she's had more than enough."

Since the tailor did not trust him, he went downstairs and asked, "Goat, have you had enough?"

The wicked animal replied:

"How can I have eaten enough
when the ground was dry and horribly rough
and the leaves and grass were much too tough?
Meh! Meh!"

"Oh, you pack of liars!" the tailor exclaimed. "One as devious and unreliable as the next! You're not going to make a fool of me anymore!" And in his rage he lost control of himself, ran upstairs, and gave his third son such a terrible beating with his yardstick that the boy ran out of the house.

Now the old tailor was alone with his goat. The next morning he went down into the barn, petted the goat, and said, "Come, my dear little goat, I myself shall take you out to graze."

He took her by the rope and led her to green hedges, clusters of yarrow, and to other things that goats like to eat.

"This time you can eat to your heart's content," he said to her, and let her graze until evening. Then he said, "Goat, have you had enough?"

The goat answered:

"Oh, my, I'm stuffed!
Enough's enough.
Meh! Meh!"

"Then let's head for home," said the tailor, and he led her into the barn and tied her up. Just as he was about to leave, he turned around once more and said, "Now you've really had enough for once!"

But the goat was just as ornery to him as usual and cried out:

"How can I have eaten enough
when the ground was dry and horribly rough
and the leaves and grass were much too tough?
Meh! Meh!"

When the tailor heard that, he was stunned, and he realized he had driven his sons away without cause.

"Just you wait!" he exclaimed. "You ungrateful creature! Sending you away would be much too mild a punishment for you. I'm going to brand you so you'll never be able to show your face among honest tailors anymore."

He ran upstairs in great haste, fetched his razor, lathered the goat's head, and shaved it as smooth as the palm of his hand. And, since he thought the yardstick would be too good for her, he got out his whip and gave her such a thrashing that she leapt high in the air and dashed away.

When the tailor was all alone in his house, he fell into a great depression and wished his sons were there again. But no one knew where they had gone. Meanwhile, his oldest son had been taken on as an apprentice with a carpenter. He worked hard and learned diligently, and when the time came for him to depart and begin his travels as a journeyman, the master gave him a little table that did not appear to be anything special and was made out of ordinary wood. However, it had one good quality. Whenever one put it down and said, "Table, be covered," it would immediately be covered by a clean tablecloth, and on it would be a plate with a fork and a knife, and dishes with roasted and stewed meat, as much as there was room for on the table, and a large glass of sparkling red wine to tickle one's throat. The young journeyman thought, That's enough to keep you going for the rest of your life! Naturally, his spirits were high as he set out on his travels in the world. He did not care whether an inn was good or bad or whether he would find something to eat there or not. If he had no desire to stop at an inn, he just went into a field, a forest, or a meadow, wherever he liked. Then he took the little table off his back, set it down before him, and said, "Be covered!" In seconds everything his heart desired was there.

At length he decided to return to his father in the hope that his father's anger might have subsided and that he might be glad to see him with the magic table. Now, it happened that on his way home he stopped at an inn, which was filled with guests. They greeted him warmly and invited him to sit down and eat with them; otherwise, he would have trouble getting something to eat so late.

"No," the carpenter said, "I don't want to take away your last few morsels. Instead, I'd prefer you to be my guests."

They all laughed and thought he was joking with them, but he set up his little table in the middle of the room and said, "Table, be covered!"

Within seconds the table was covered with much better food than the innkeeper could have produced, and the guests inhaled the lovely aroma with their nostrils.

"Help yourselves, dear friends," said the carpenter, and when the guests realized he meant it, they did not have to be asked twice. They drew up their seats, pulled out their knives, and plunged in bravely. What astonished them was that a new dish appeared by itself as soon as one dish became empty. The innkeeper stood in a corner and watched everything without knowing what to say, but he thought, I could certainly use a cook like that in my business.

The carpenter and his companions enjoyed themselves until late into the night. Finally, they went to sleep, and the young journeyman put his magic table against the wall and went to bed too. The innkeeper's thoughts, however, left him no peace, and he recalled that there was an old table in the storage room that looked just like the magic one. He went and got it and then switched it quietly with the magic table. The next morning the carpenter paid for the lodging and packed the table on his back without realizing that he had the wrong one. He set out on his way and at noon came to his father, who welcomed him with great joy.

"Well, my dear son, what have you learned?" he asked him.

"Father, I've become a carpenter."

"That's a good trade," replied the old man, "but what have you brought back with you from your travels?"

"Father, the best thing I've brought back is this table."

The tailor examined it from all sides and said, "I can't say that you've made a masterpiece. It's just a shabby old table."

"But it's a magic table," answered his son. "When I put it down and tell it to be covered, the most delicious dishes appear at once, and wine as well. It will warm your heart with joy. Just invite all our relatives and friends. I'll provide them with good refreshments and a fine meal. My table will give them more than enough to eat."

When the company was assembled, he set the table in the middle of the parlor and said, "Table, be covered!" But the table did not move an inch. It remained just as bare as any ordinary table that cannot understand speech. The poor journeyman now realized that his table had been switched, and he was ashamed at having to appear like a liar. His relatives laughed at him, but they were forced to return home without having anything to eat or drink. His father got out his sewing material again and resumed working, while the son found a job with a master.

The second son had gone to a miller to serve an apprenticeship. When his years were up, the master said, "Since you've done such a good job, I'm going to give you a special kind of donkey. He doesn't draw carts, nor does he carry sacks."

"Well, what's he good for?" asked the young journeyman.

"He spits gold," the miller replied. "If you set him on a piece of cloth and say 'Bricklebrit,' the good animal will spit out gold pieces from the front and behind."

"That's a wonderful thing," said the journeyman, who thanked his master and went out into the world. Whenever he needed money, he only had to say "Bricklebrit" to his donkey, and it would rain gold pieces, which he picked off the ground. Wherever he went, only the best was good enough for him, and the more expensive the better, for his purse was always full. After he had traveled about in the world for some time, he thought, You really ought to seek out your father. If you return to him with the gold donkey, he's bound to forget his anger and give you a nice welcome.

It so happened that he stopped at the same inn in which his brother's magic table had been switched. He led his donkey by the bridle, and the innkeeper wanted to take the animal from him and tie it up, but the young journeyman said, "Don't bother yourself. I'll lead my gray steed into the stable myself and tie him up because I must know where he is."

The innkeeper found this strange and thought that whoever had to take care of his donkey himself did not have much money to spend. But when the stranger reached into his pocket, took out two gold coins, and told him to buy something very good for him, the innkeeper's eyes opened wide. He promptly ran and brought out the best food he could find. After the meal the guest asked the innkeeper what he owed him, and the innkeeper, who had no scruples about chalking up double the amount, charged him another couple of gold pieces. The journeyman reached into his pocket, but his gold had just run out.

"Wait a minute, innkeeper," he said. "I just want to go and fetch some gold."

As he left he took the tablecloth with him, and the innkeeper did not know what to make of that. Since he was curious, he sneaked after him, and when the guest bolted the stable door, the innkeeper peeped through a knothole. The stranger spread the tablecloth out under the donkey and said "Bricklebrit," and instantly the animal began to spit so much gold from the front and the rear that it was like a good rainfall.

"The devil take me!" said the innkeeper. "What a way to mint ducats! I wouldn't mind having a money purse like that!"

The guest paid his bill and went to sleep, but the innkeeper crept into the stable, led the money-maker away, and tied up another donkey in its place. Early the next morning the journeyman departed with a donkey that he thought was his gold donkey. At noon he arrived at his father's house, and the father was delighted to see his son again and gave him a nice welcome.

"What have you made of yourself, my son?" asked the old man.

"A miller, dear Father," he replied.

"What have you brought back with you from your travels?"

"Nothing but a donkey."

"There are plenty of donkeys here," the father said. "I really would have preferred a good goat."

"Yes," responded the son, "but this is not an ordinary donkey. It's a gold donkey. If I say 'Bricklebrit,' the good animal spits out enough gold to cover a piece of cloth. Just call our relatives together, and I'll make them all rich people."

"I like that idea," said the tailor. "Then I won't have to torture myself anymore with this sewing."

He himself ran off to gather the relatives together. As soon as they were all assembled, the miller told them to make room. Then he spread his piece of cloth on the floor and brought the donkey into the parlor.

"Now, pay attention," he said, and cried out "Bricklebrit!" But what fell were not gold pieces, and it was quite clear that the animal knew nothing about the art of making gold, for there are very few donkeys who become so accomplished. The poor miller made a long face. He realized that he had been cheated and apologized to his relatives, who went home as poor as they had come. As for the old man, there was nothing left to do but resume tailoring, and the son hired himself out to a miller.

The third brother had become an apprentice to a turner, and since this is a craft that demands great skill, his apprenticeship had lasted the longest. During this time he had received a letter from his brothers in which they told him about their terrible experiences with the innkeeper who had stolen their magical gifts on the last night before they were to arrive home. When he finished his apprenticeship as turner and was about to set out on his travels, his master gave him a sack because he had done such a good job.

"There's a club in the sack," said the master.

"I can carry the sack on my back, and it may come in handy, but what can I do with the club? It will only make the sack heavy."

"I'll tell you," responded the master. "If someone threatens to harm you, you just have to say, 'Club, come out of the sack,' and the club will jump out at the people and dance on their backs so spiritedly that they won't be able to move a bone in their body for a week. And the club won't let up until you say 'Club, get back in the sack.' "

The journeyman thanked him, swung the sack over his shoulder, and if anyone came too close to him and threatened him, he would say, "Club, come out of the sack," and the club would immediately jump out and dust off the fellow's coat or jacket without waiting for him to take it off, and then it would finish off all the others, one by one. And that would all happen so quickly that it would be over before one had any time to think.

It was evening when the young turner arrived at the inn where his two brothers had been cheated. He put his knapsack down on the table in front of him and began to tell stories about the remarkable things he had seen in the world.

"Yes," he said, "some people come across such things as a magic table, a gold donkey, and the like. These are wonderful things and not to be laughed at, but they're nothing compared to the treasure I've acquired. And I've got it right here in my sack."

The innkeeper pricked up his ears. What in the world could that be? he thought. Perhaps the sack is filled with jewels. There's no reason why they shouldn't be mine as well, for all good things come in threes.

When it was bedtime, the guest stretched himself out on the bench and put his sack underneath his head as a pillow. When the innkeeper thought the guest was sound asleep, he went over to him and cautiously tugged and pulled at the sack to see if he could quietly replace it with another. But the turner had been waiting for this moment, and just as the innkeeper was about to make a final hearty tug, he cried out, "Club, come out of the sack!"

Immediately the club jumped out of the sack and beat the innkeeper all over his body until the seams of his clothes burst. The innkeeper screamed for mercy, but the louder he screamed the harder the club beat in rhythm on his back until the innkeeper eventually fell to the ground exhausted. Then the turner said, "If you don't give me the magic table and the gold donkey, the dance will soon begin again."

"Oh, no!" the innkeeper exclaimed. "I'll gladly return everything to you. Just have that cursed hobgoblin crawl back into the sack!"

"Mercy shall prevail over justice this time," said the journeyman, "but you'd better watch your step in the future." Then he cried out, "Club, get back in the sack!"

The next morning the turner took the magic table and the gold donkey and continued his journey home to his father. The tailor was delighted to see him again and asked him what he had learned in foreign countries.

"Dear Father," he replied, "I've become a turner."

"That's a craft that demands a lot of skill," said the father. "What have you brought back with you from your travels?"

"A precious thing, dear Father," he replied. "A club in a sack."

"What!" exclaimed the father. "A club! That's not worth the trouble! You can chop off a club from any old tree."

"But not this kind, dear Father. If I say, 'Club, come out of the sack,' the club will come out and start dancing vigorously on anyone who threatens me, and the club won't stop until the person is lying on the ground and begging for mercy. You see, this club helped me get back the magic table and the gold donkey that the thieving innkeeper stole from my brothers. Now, I want you to invite both of them and all our relatives, for I'm going to provide them with food and drink and fill their pockets with gold as well."

Although the old tailor did not entirely believe him, he gathered all the relatives together. The turner spread out a piece of cloth in the parlor, led the gold donkey inside, and said to his brother, "Now, dear brother, speak to him."

The miller said "Bricklebrit," and within seconds there were gold pieces pouring onto the cloth as though there had been a sudden thunderstorm. Moreover, the donkey did not stop until they all had more than they could carry. (I can tell from the look on your face that you would have liked to have been there too.) Then the turner fetched the table and said, "Now, dear brother, speak to it."

No sooner did the carpenter say "Table, be covered," than it was covered and offered an abundance of the finest dishes. Never in his life had the old tailor enjoyed such a meal as the one held in his house that day. All the relatives stayed late into the night, and they were merry and happy. The tailor locked up his needle and thread and his yardstick and flat iron in a cupboard and lived with his sons in joy and splendor.

But what ever happened to the goat that was to blame for the tailor's driving out his three sons? Let me tell you.

She was so ashamed of her bald head that she ran to a foxhole and crawled inside. When the fox came home, a pair of eyes glared at him out of the darkness. He became so frightened that he ran away. When he encountered the bear, he looked so upset that the bear said, "What's the matter, brother fox? Why are you making such a face?"

"Oh," answered Red Fox, "a gruesome beast is sitting in my cave, and he glared at me with fiery eyes!"

"Well, we'll soon get rid of him," said the bear, and he went to the cave and looked inside. But when he saw the fiery eyes, he too was struck by fear. He wanted nothing to do with the gruesome beast and took off. Soon he met the bee, and when the bee noticed that the bear was looking very pale, she said, "Bear, you look so miserable. What's happened to your good spirits?"

"It's easy for you to talk," the bear responded, "but there's a gruesome beast with glaring eyes in Red Fox's house, and we can't drive him out."

"I feel sorry for you, bear," said the bee. "You and the fox barely acknowledge me when you see me because I'm such a poor weak creature. Still, I think I can help you."

She flew into the foxhole, landed on the goat's smooth-shaven head, and stung her so hard that the goat jumped up screaming *"Meh! Meh!"* and ran like mad out into the world. And to this day nobody knows what has become of her.

◈ 37 ◈

Thumbling

THERE WAS ONCE A POOR FARMER who was sitting by the hearth one evening and poking the fire, while his wife was spinning nearby.

"How sad that we have no children!" he said. "It's so quiet here, and other homes are full of noise and life."

"Yes," his wife responded with a sigh. "If only we had a child, just one, even if it were tiny and no bigger than my thumb, I'd be quite satisfied. We'd surely love him with all our hearts."

Now it happened that the wife fell sick, and after seven months she gave birth to a child that was indeed perfect in every way but no bigger than a thumb.

"It's just as we wished," they said, "and he shall be dear to our hearts."

Because of his size they named him Thumbling. Although they fed him a great deal, the child did not grow any bigger but stayed exactly as he was at birth. Still, he had an intelligent look and soon revealed himself to be a clever and nimble fellow who succeeded in all his endeavors.

One day the farmer was getting ready to chop wood in the forest, and he said to himself, "If only there were someone who could drive the wagon into the forest after me."

"Oh, Father," cried Thumbling, "I'll take care of the wagon. You can count on me. It'll be in the forest whenever you want it."

The man laughed and said, "How're you going to manage that? You're much too small to handle the reins."

"That's not important," Thumbling said. "I just need Mother to hitch the horse, and I'll sit down in his ear and tell him which way to go."

"Well," answered the father. "Let's try it once."

When the time came, the mother hitched up the horse and put Thumbling in his ear. Then the little fellow shouted commands. "Giddyap! Whoa! Giddyap!" Everything went quite well, as if a master were at the reins, and the wagon drove the right way toward the forest. As it took a turn and the little fellow cried out "Giddyap! Giddyap!" two strangers happened to come along.

"My word!" said one of them. "What's that? There goes a wagon without a driver, and yet, I hear a voice calling to the horse."

"There's something strange going on here," said the other. "Let's follow the wagon and see where it stops."

The wagon drove right into the forest up to the spot where the wood was being chopped. When Thumbling saw his father, he called out to him, "You see, Father, here I am with the wagon! Now just get me down."

The father grabbed the horse with his left hand, and with his right he took his little son out of its ear. Then Thumbling plopped himself sprightly on a piece of straw. When the two men caught sight of him, they were so amazed that they could not open their mouths. One of the men took the other aside and said, "Listen, that little fellow could make our fortune if we exhibit him in the big city for money. Let's buy him."

They went to the farmer and said, "Sell us the little man, and we'll see to it that he's treated well."

"No," answered the father, "he's the apple of my eye, and I wouldn't sell him for all the gold in the world."

But when Thumbling heard the offer, he crawled up the pleat of his father's coat, stood up on his shoulder, and whispered into his ear, "Father, don't you worry. Just give me away. I'll manage to get back soon."

So the father gave him to the two men for a tidy sum of money.

"Where do you want to sit?" they asked Thumbling.

"Oh, set me on the brim of your hat. Then I'll be able to walk back and forth and look at the countryside without any danger of falling off."

They did as he requested, and after Thumbling took leave of his father, they set out on their way. They walked until dusk, and just then the little fellow said, "Put me down. It's urgent."

"Just stay up there," said the man on whose head he was sitting. "I don't mind. I'm used to the birds dropping something on me every now and then."

"No," said Thumbling. "I know what's proper. Hurry up and put me down!"

The man took off his hat and set the little fellow on a field by the wayside. Then Thumbling jumped and crawled among the clods scattered here and there on the ground. Suddenly he slipped into a mousehole, which was what he had been looking for.

"Good-bye, gentlemen!" he cried out, laughing at them. "Just go home without me."

They ran over to the spot and stuck sticks into the mousehole, but their efforts were in vain. Thumbling kept retreating farther and farther into the hole. When it became pitch dark outside, the two men had to head back home, full of rage but with empty purses.

When Thumbling saw they were gone, he crawled out of the underground passage and said, "It's so dangerous walking in the field after dark. You can easily break a neck or a leg." Fortunately, he stumbled upon an empty snail shell. "Thank goodness," he said. "I can spend the night here in safety." After he got inside and was about to go to sleep, he heard two men walking by and talking.

"How are we going to manage to get the rich pastor's money and silver?" one of them asked.

"I can tell you how," said Thumbling, interrupting them.

"What was that?" the other thief said in horror. "I heard a voice!"

The two men remained standing there and listened. Then Thumbling spoke again. "Take me with you, and I'll help you."

"Where are you, then?"

"Just look on the ground and pay attention to where the voice is coming from," he answered.

After a while the thieves found him and lifted him up in the air.

"You little tyke," they said. "How are you going to help us?"

"Look," he answered, "I'll crawl between the iron bars into the pastor's room, and I'll hand you whatever you want."

"All right," they said. "Let's see what you can do."

When they got to the pastor's house, Thumbling crawled into the room and immediately cried out with all his might, "Do you want to have everything that's here?"

The thieves were alarmed and said, "Speak softly so nobody wakes up."

But Thumbling pretended not to understand and screamed once more, "What do you want? Do you want everything that's here?"

The maid, who was sleeping in the room next-door, heard the voices. She sat up in bed and listened. But the thieves had retreated some distance out of fright. Gradually they regained their courage and thought, The little fellow is just teasing us. So they came back and whispered to him, "Now, be serious and hand us something."

Once again Thumbling screamed as loud as he could, "Sure, I'll give you all you want! Just reach in here with your hands!"

The maid was still listening and heard everything quite clearly. She jumped out of bed and stumbled into the room through the door. The thieves rushed away and ran as if a wild huntsman were after them. Since the maid could not see a thing, she went to light a candle. When she returned with it, Thumbling had left without being seen and headed into the barn. The maid searched the entire place, but after finding nothing, she went back to bed and thought she had only been seeing and hearing things in her dreams.

In the meantime, Thumbling climbed about in the hay and found himself a nice place to sleep. He intended to rest there until daybreak and then return home to his parents. However, life did not turn out the way he expected! Indeed, there is a great deal of sorrow and misery in this world! When the day dawned, the maid got out of bed to feed the cows. Her first round was in the barn where she picked up an armful of hay, and it was that very hay in which Thumbling was lying asleep. Indeed, he was sleeping so soundly that he did not notice a thing, nor did he wake up until he was in the jaws of a cow that picked him up with the hay.

"Oh, God!" he exclaimed. "How did I get into this churning mill?"

But soon he realized where he was, and he had to be careful not to get caught between the cow's teeth or else he would be crushed. Soon he slipped down into the cow's stomach with the hay.

"Hey, they forgot to put windows in this room!" he said. "No sunshine possible here, and it seems they won't be bringing candles."

He was not very pleased with the accommodations, and the worst of it was that the fresh hay kept coming through the door, and the space became cramped. At last his fright became so great that he cried out as loud as he could, "No more fodder! No more fodder!"

The maid was milking the cow when she heard the voice without seeing anybody. She recognized it as the same voice she had heard during the night and became so frightened that she slipped off her stool and spilled the milk. She ran in haste to her master and exclaimed, "Oh, God, Pastor! The cow just talked!"

"You're crazy," responded the parson, but he decided to go into the barn himself to check on the matter. No sooner did he set foot in the barn than Thumbling cried out once again, "No more fodder! No more fodder!"

Now even the parson became frightened, and he concluded that an evil spirit had got into the cow and ordered it to be killed. So the cow was slaughtered, and the stomach where Thumbling was stuck was thrown on the dung heap. Thumbling had great difficulty working his way through, but he managed to find a way out for himself. However, just as he was about to stick out his head, another misfortune occurred: a hungry wolf came running by and swallowed the whole stomach with one gulp. Yet, Thumbling did not lose courage. Perhaps, he thought, the wolf will listen to reason. So he called to him from his belly, "Dear wolf, I happen to know where you can find a wonderful meal."

"Tell me where," said the wolf.

"It's in such and such a house. You have to crawl through the drain, and then you'll find all the cake, bacon, and sausages you want to eat."

Thumbling gave him an exact description of his father's house, and the wolf did not have to be told twice. When night came, he squeezed his way through the drain into the pantry and ate to his heart's content. When he had eaten his fill, he wanted to go back outside. However, he had become so fat that he could not return the same way. Thumbling had counted on this and began making a racket in the wolf's belly. Indeed, he threw a fit and yelled as loud as he could.

"Will you be quiet!" said the wolf. "You're waking everyone up."

"So what!" said the little fellow. "You've had your fill. Now I want to have some fun too." And he kept screaming with all his might.

At last his father and mother woke up, ran to the pantry, and looked through a crack in the door. When they saw the wolf in there, they ran back. The man fetched an ax, and the woman, a scythe.

"Stay behind me," said the man as they approached the pantry. "If my blow doesn't kill him right away, then swing your scythe and cut his body to pieces."

When Thumbling heard his father's voice, he cried out, "Dear Father, I'm in here! I'm stuck in the wolf's body."

"Thank God!" said his father, full of joy. "Our dear son has come back to us." And he told his wife to put down the scythe so Thumbling would not be hurt. Then he lifted his arm and gave the wolf such a blow on his head that he fell down dead. He and his wife fetched a pair of scissors and a knife, cut the wolf's body open, and pulled the little fellow out.

"Oh," said the father, "we've been worried to death about you!"

"Yes, Father, I've traveled about the world a great deal. Thank God that I can breathe fresh air again!"

"Where in heaven's name have you been?"

"Oh, Father, I was in a mousehole, a cow's stomach, and a wolf's belly. Now I'm going to stay with you."

"And we shall never sell you again for all the riches in the world," said his parents. They hugged and kissed their dear Thumbling. Then they gave him something to eat and drink and had some new clothes made for him because his old ones had been spoiled during his journey.

◈ 38 ◈

The Wedding of Mrs. Fox

FIRST TALE

ONCE UPON A TIME there was an old fox with nine tails who believed his wife was unfaithful to him and wanted to put her to the test. So he stretched himself out under the bench, kept perfectly still, and pretended to be dead as a doornail. Mrs. Fox went up to her room and shut herself in, while her maid, Miss Cat, went to the hearth and started cooking. When it became known that the old fox had died, suitors began to present themselves. Now, the maid heard someone outside knocking at the door, and when she went and opened it, there was a young fox, who said:

"What are you doing now, Miss Cat?
Are you wide awake or asleep on the mat?"

She answered:

"I'm not asleep. I'm wide awake.
What do you think, for goodness sake!
I'm using butter to brew warm beer.
You can be my guest if you stay right here."

"No, thank you, Miss Cat," said the fox. "But tell me, what's Mrs. Fox doing?"

"She's sitting in her room
and weeping in her gloom.
Her eyes are now quite red,
for old Mr. Fox is dead."

"Be so kind as to tell her, Miss Cat, that a young fox is here who would very much like to court her."
"Very well, my young man."

The cat went up the stairs, *trip-trap*,
and knocked upon the door, *tap-tap*.
"Mrs. Fox, are you in there?"
"Oh, yes, Kitty Cat, yes, my dear."
"Well, a suitor's here to see you."
"What's he like? I want a clue.

"Does he have nine beautiful tails like my late Mr. Fox?"
"Oh, no," answered Miss Cat. "He has only one."
"Then he's not for me."
Miss Cat went downstairs and sent the suitor away. Soon there again was a knock at the door, and there was another fox outside who wanted to court Mrs. Fox. Since he had only two tails, he fared no better than the first one. After that, others came, each with one tail more than the previous one, and they were all rejected. At last a fox came who had nine tails like old Mr. Fox. When the widow heard that, she spoke joyfully to the maid:

"It's time to open the gate and the door,
and sweep Mr. Fox out over the floor."

However, just as the wedding was being held, old Mr. Fox stirred from under the bench, rose up, and gave the whole crowd a good beating. Then he drove everyone, including Mrs. Fox, out of the house.

SECOND TALE

AFTER OLD MR. FOX HAD DIED, the wolf came courting. When he knocked at the door, the cat who was Mrs. Fox's maid opened it, and she was greeted by the wolf, who said:

"Good day, Mrs. Cat of Sweeping-Pit.
Are you all alone with your bright wit?
I'm sure you're making something tasty right now."

The cat answered:

"I'm crumbling bread into my milk right here.
Be my guest and pull up a chair."

"No, thank you, Mrs. Cat," the wolf replied. "Is Mrs. Fox at home?"
The cat said:

"She's sitting in her room
and is weeping in her gloom.
Many are the tears she's shed,
for old Mr. Fox is dead."

The wolf answered:

"If she wants another husband who's very fair,
tell her that I'm right down here."
The cat ran up without a sound
and let her tail just swish around
until she reached the parlor door,
where with five golden rings she knocked.
"Mrs. Fox, are you there?" she called and knocked once more.
"If you want another husband who's very fair,
I can tell you that he's right down there."

Mrs. Fox asked, "Is the gentleman wearing red trousers, and does he have a pointed mouth?"
"No," said the cat.

"Then he's not for me."

After the wolf was turned down, he was followed by a dog, a stag, a hare, a bear, a lion, and all the animals of the forest, one after the other. However, they all lacked one of the distinguished qualities of old Mr. Fox, and each time, the cat had to send the suitor away. Finally, a young fox appeared, and Mrs. Fox asked, "Is the gentleman wearing red trousers, and does he have a pointed mouth?"

"Yes," said the cat. "That he does."

"Then let him come up," said Mrs. Fox, and she ordered the maid to prepare the wedding feast.

"It's time to open the windows
and make sure that old Mr. Fox now goes.
Indeed, he brought back many mice,
but he ate them all alone
and never did he offer me one."

Then young Mr. Fox was married to Mrs. Fox. Afterward there was dancing and rejoicing, and if they have not stopped dancing, then they are still at it even now.

◈ 39 ◈

The Elves

FIRST TALE

THERE WAS ONCE A SHOEMAKER who, through no fault of his own, had become so poor that he had only enough leather left for a single pair of shoes. That evening he cut out the shoes, which he planned to work on the next morning, and since he had a clear conscience, he lay down quietly in his bed, commended himself to God, and fell asleep. In the morning, after he had said his prayers and was about to sit down to do his work, he saw the two shoes standing all finished on his workbench. He was so astounded by this that he did not know what to say. He took the shoes in his hand to examine them more closely and saw that the shoes were perfect. Not a single bad stitch could be found, and it was as if the shoes were intended to be masterpieces.

Shortly after, a customer entered the shop, and he liked the shoes so much he paid more than the usual price for them. The money enabled the shoemaker to purchase leather for two pairs of shoes. In the evening he cut them out and planned to begin work on them with renewed vigor the next morning. However, it was not necessary, for the shoes were already finished by the time he awoke. Once again he found customers for them, and they gave him enough money to purchase leather for four pairs of shoes. The following morning he found the four pairs of shoes already made, and so it went: whatever he cut out in the evening was finished by morning, and soon he had a decent income again and eventually became a well-to-do man.

Now one evening, not long before Christmas, it happened that the man had been cutting leather, and just before he went to bed, he said to his wife, "What would you think about staying up tonight? If we do that, we might be able to see who's been lending us such a helping hand."

His wife agreed and lit a candle. Then they hid themselves behind some clothes that were hanging in the corner of the room and watched closely. When it was midnight, two cute little naked elves scampered into the room, sat down at the shoemaker's workbench, took all the work that had been cut out, and began to stitch, sew, and hammer so skillfully and nimbly with their little fingers that the amazed shoemaker could not take his eyes off them. Indeed, they did not stop until everything was done and the shoes were left standing on the workbench. Then they quickly ran away.

The next morning the wife said, "The little men have made us rich. We ought to show them that we're grateful for their help. Do you know what? Since they run around without any clothes on and must be freezing, I'm going to sew some shirts, coats, jackets, and trousers for them. I'll also knit a pair of stockings for each, and you can make them both a pair of shoes."

"That's fine with me," the husband said.

In the evening, after they had finished everything, they put the gifts on the workbench, instead of the cut-out leather, and hid themselves in order to see how the elves would react. At midnight the elves came scampering into the room and wanted to get right down to work, but they found the nice little clothes instead of the cut-out leather. At first they were puzzled, but then they were tremendously pleased. They put the clothes on quickly, smoothed them down, and said:

"Now we look so fine and dandy,
no more need to work and be so handy!"

Then they skipped, danced, and jumped over chairs and benches. Finally, they danced right out the door and were never seen again. But the shoemaker continued to be prosperous until the end of his life and succeeded in all his endeavors.

SECOND TALE

ONCE UPON A TIME there was a poor servant girl who was industrious and neat. She swept the house every day and dumped the dirt on a large pile outside the door. One morning, when she was about to start work again, she found a letter on the pile, and since she could not read, she put the broom in the corner and took the letter to her employers. It was an invitation from the elves, who asked the girl to be godmother for one of their children at a christening. The maiden did not know what to do, but her employers finally persuaded her that it would not be wise to refuse the invitation, and she accepted.

Three elves came and led her to a hollow mountain where the little folk lived. Everything there was tiny and indescribably dainty and splendid. The mother was lying on a black ebony bed with pearl knobs. The covers were embroidered with gold. The cradle was ivory. The bathtub was made of gold. After the maiden performed her duties as godmother, she wanted to go back home, but the elves implored her earnestly to spend three days with them. She remained and had a pleasant and joyful time. The little folk did all they could to please her. Finally, when she insisted it was time for her to leave, they filled her pockets with gold and led her back out the mountain.

When she arrived home, she wanted to resume her work, so she took the broom that was standing in the corner and began sweeping. At that moment some strange people came out of the house and asked her who she was and what she was doing there. Indeed, she had not been gone for three days, as she had thought, but she had spent seven years in the mountains with the little folk. In the meantime, her former employers had died.

THE ELVES HAD STOLEN a mother's child from the cradle and had replaced the baby with a changeling who had a fat head and glaring eyes and would do nothing but eat and drink. In her distress the mother went to her neighbor and asked for advice. The neighbor told her to carry the changeling into the kitchen, put him down on the hearth, start a fire, and boil water in two eggshells. That would make the changeling laugh, and when he laughed, he would lose his power. The woman did everything the neighbor said, and when she put the eggshells filled with water on the fire, the blockhead said:

> "Now I'm as old
> as the Westerwald,
> and in all my life I've never seen
> eggshells cooked as these have been."

And the changeling began to laugh. As soon as he laughed, a bunch of elves appeared. They had brought the right child with them and put him down on the hearth and took the changeling away.

◈ 40 ◈

The Robber Bridegroom

ONCE UPON A TIME there was a miller who had a beautiful daughter, and when she was grown-up, he wanted to see her well provided for and well married. If the right suitor comes along and asks to marry her, he thought, I shall give her to him.

It was not long before a suitor appeared who seemed to be very rich, and since the miller found nothing wrong with him, he promised him his daughter. The maiden, however, did not love him the way a bride-to-be should love her bridegroom, nor did she trust him. Whenever she looked at him or thought about him, her heart shuddered with dread.

One day he said to her, "You're my bride-to-be, and yet, you've never visited me."

"I don't know where your house is," the maiden replied.

"My house is out in the dark forest," said the bridegroom.

She tried to make excuses and told him she would not be able to find the way. But the bridegroom said, "Next Sunday I want you to come out and visit me. I've already invited the guests, and I shall spread ashes on the ground so you can find the way."

When Sunday arrived and the maiden was supposed to set out on her way, she became very anxious but could not explain to herself why she felt so. She filled both her pockets with peas and lentils to mark the path. At the entrance to the forest, she found that ashes had been spread, and she followed them while throwing peas right and left on the ground with each step she took. She walked nearly the whole day until she came to the middle of the forest. There she saw a solitary house, but she did not like the look of it because it was so dark and dreary. She went inside and found nobody at home. The place was deadly silent. Then suddenly a voice cried out:

"Turn back, turn back, young bride.
The den belongs to murderers,
Who'll soon be at your side!"

The maiden looked up and saw that the voice came from a bird in a cage hanging on the wall. Once again it cried out:

"Turn back, turn back, young bride.
The den belongs to murderers,
Who'll soon be at your side!"

The beautiful bride moved from one room to the next and explored the entire house, but it was completely empty. Not a soul could be found. Finally, she went down into the cellar, where she encountered a very, very old woman, whose head was constantly bobbing.

"Could you tell me whether my bridegroom lives here?" asked the bride.

"Oh, you poor child," the old woman answered. "Do you realize where you are? This is a murderer's den! You think you're a bride soon to be celebrating your wedding, but the only marriage you'll celebrate will be with death. Just look! They ordered me to put this big kettle of water on the fire to boil. When they have you in their power, they'll chop you to pieces without mercy. Then they'll cook you and eat you, because they're cannibals. If I don't take pity on you and save you, you'll be lost forever."

The old woman then led her behind a large barrel, where nobody could see her.

"Be still as a mouse," she said. "Don't budge or move! Otherwise, it will be all over for you. Tonight when the robbers are asleep, we'll escape. I've been waiting a long time for this chance."

No sooner was the maiden hidden than the godless crew came home, dragging another maiden with them. They were drunk and paid no attention to her screams and pleas. They gave her wine to drink, three full glasses, one white, one red, and one yellow, and soon her heart burst in two. Then they tore off her fine clothes, put her on a table, chopped her beautiful body to pieces, and sprinkled the pieces with salt. Behind the barrel, the poor bride shook and trembled, for she now realized what kind of fate the robbers had been planning for her. One of them noticed a ring on the murdered maiden's little finger, and since he could not slip it off easily, he took a hatchet and chopped the finger off. But the finger sprang into the air and over the barrel and fell right into the bride's lap. The robber took a candle and went looking for it, but he could not find it. Then another robber said, "Have you already looked behind the barrel?"

Now the old woman called out, "Come and eat! You can look for it tomorrow. The finger's not going to run away from you."

"The old woman's right," the robbers said, and they stopped looking and sat down to eat. The old woman put a sleeping potion into their wine, and soon they lay down in the cellar, fell asleep, and began snoring. When the bride heard that, she came out from behind the barrel and had to step over the sleeping bodies lying in rows on the ground. She feared she might wake them up, but she got safely through with the help of God. The old woman went upstairs with her and opened the door, and the two of them scampered out of the murderers' den as fast as they could. The wind had blown away the ashes, but the peas and lentils had sprouted and unfurled, pointing the way in the moonlight. They walked the whole night, and by morning they had reached the mill. Then the maiden told her father everything that had happened.

When the day of the wedding celebration came, the bridegroom appeared, as did all the relatives and friends that the miller had invited. As they were all sitting at the table, each person was asked to tell a story. The bride, though, remained still and did not utter a word. Finally, the bridegroom said, "Well, my dear, can't you think of anything? Tell us a good story."

"All right," she said. "I'll tell you a dream: I was walking alone through the forest and finally came to a house. There wasn't a soul to be found in the place except for a bird in a cage on the wall that cried out:

'Turn back, turn back, young bride.
The den belongs to murderers,
Who'll soon be at your side!'

Then the bird repeated the warning.

(My dear, it was only a dream.)

"After that I went through all the rooms, and they were empty, but there was something about them that gave me an erie feeling. Finally, I went downstairs into the cellar, where I found a very, very old woman, who was bobbing her head. I asked her, 'Does my bridegroom live in this house?' 'Oh, you poor child,' she responded, 'you've stumbled on a murderers' den. Your bridegroom lives here, but he wants to chop you up and kill you, and then he wants to cook you and eat you.'

(My dear, it was only a dream.)

"The old woman hid me behind a large barrel, and no sooner was I hidden than the robbers returned home, dragging a maiden with them. They gave her all sorts of wine to drink, white, red, and yellow, and her heart burst in two.

(My dear, it was only a dream.)

"One of the robbers saw that a gold ring was still on her finger, and since he had trouble pulling it off, he took a hatchet and chopped it off. The finger sprang into the air, over the barrel, and right into my lap. And here's the finger with the ring!"

With these words she produced the finger and showed it to all those present.

The robber, who had turned white as a ghost while hearing her story, jumped up and attempted to flee. However, the guests seized him and turned him over to the magistrate. Then he and his whole band were executed for their shameful crimes.

◈ 41 ◈

Herr Korbes

ONCE UPON A TIME there were a hen and a rooster who wanted to take a trip together. The rooster built a beautiful carriage that had four red wheels, and then he hitched four mice to it. The hen climbed into the carriage along with the rooster, and they drove off together. Soon they came across a cat who asked, "Where are you going?"

"We're going to see Herr Korbes today.
We're off without delay."

"Take me with you," said the cat.

"Gladly," answered the rooster. "Sit in the back so you won't fall off in front.

Be sure you take good care,
for I've got clean red wheels down there.
Roll on, you wheels, high ho!
Squeak, squeak, you mice, high ho!
We're going to see Herr Korbes today.
We're off without delay."

Soon a millstone came, then an egg, a duck, a pin, and finally a sewing needle, who all got into the carriage and rode along. However, when they arrived at Herr Korbes's house, he was not there. The mice pulled the carriage into the barn. The hen and the rooster flew up on a perch. The cat settled down by the hearth. The duck took a place by the well sweep. The egg wrapped itself in a towel. The pin stuck itself in a chair cushion. The sewing needle jumped on the bed right into the pillow. And the millstone set itself down above the door.

When Herr Korbes came home, he went to the hearth to make a fire, but the cat threw ashes right into his face. He ran quickly into the kitchen to wash the ashes off, but the duck splashed water in his face. As he tried to dry himself with the towel the egg rolled toward him and broke open, so his eyes became glued shut. Now he wanted to rest and sit down in the chair, but the pin stuck him. In his rage he ran and threw himself down on his bed, but the sewing needle stuck him as his head hit the pillow. He let out a scream and was so furious that he decided to run out into the wide world. However, just as he got through the front door, the millstone jumped down and killed him.

Herr Korbes must have been a very wicked man.

◈ 42 ◈

The Godfather

A POOR MAN HAD SO MANY CHILDREN that he had already asked everyone in the world to be godfather, and when he had yet another child, there was nobody left to ask. He did not know what to do, and in his distress he lay down, fell asleep, and had a dream showing him that he should go outside the town gate and ask the first person he met to be godfather. When he awoke, he decided to undertake what the dream had shown. He went out in front of the gate and asked the first man he met to be godfather. The stranger gave him a little bottle of water and said, "This water has miraculous powers. You can cure the sick with it, but you must keep your eye on Death. If he's standing at the head of the sick person, then give the patient some of the water, and he'll get well. However, if Death is standing at the patient's feet, there is nothing that can be done, and the patient must die."

From then on the man could always predict whether a sick person could be saved or not. He became famous because of his skill and earned a great deal of money. One day he was summoned to the king's child, and when he entered the room, he saw Death standing by the child's head and cured him with the water. The same thing happened a second time. But the third time, Death was standing at the foot of the bed, and the child had to die.

Once, the man decided to visit the godfather and tell him how well he had been doing with the water. When he entered the house, though, he noticed there were some very strange things happening. On the first landing he encountered a shovel and a broom having a terrible argument that led to blows.

"Where does the godfather live?" he asked them.

"One flight up," answered the broom.

When he came to the second landing, he saw a bunch of dead fingers lying there.

"Where does the godfather live?" he asked.

"One flight up," replied one of the fingers.

On the third landing there was a pile of skulls who told him to go up one flight. On the fourth landing he saw some fish sizzling in a pan over a fire. They were frying themselves and also told him, "One flight up." After he had climbed to the fifth floor, he came to a door of a room and looked through the keyhole. There he saw the godfather, who had a pair of long horns. When he opened the door and went inside, the godfather quickly jumped into bed and covered himself.

"Godfather, you certainly have a strange household!" the man said. "When I came to the first landing, a broom and shovel were quarreling so violently that they gave each other terrible blows."

"How can you be so simpleminded!" said the godfather. "That was the kitchen boy and the maid just talking to each other."

"On the second landing I saw dead fingers lying about."

"My goodness, how foolish you are! Those were salsify roots."

"On the third landing there were skulls lying about."

"You stupid man, those were cabbage heads."

"On the fourth landing I saw fish frying themselves."

Just as he said that, the fish came in and served themselves on a platter.

"And when I came to the fifth landing, I looked through the keyhole, and I saw you, godfather, and you had such long, long horns."

"Now, that's just not true!"

The man became frightened and ran away.

Indeed, there is no telling what the godfather might have done to him if he had stayed.

◈ 43 ◈

Mother Trudy

ONCE UPON A TIME there was a little girl who was stubborn and curious, and whenever her parents told her to do something, she would not obey them. Well, how could things possibly go well for her?

One day she said to her parents, "I've heard so much about Mother Trudy that I'd like to see her someday. People say that there are unusual things about her house, and there are also strange things inside. All that's made me very curious."

However, her parents gave her strict instructions not to go near the house.

"Mother Trudy is an evil woman," they said. "She does wicked things, and if you go to her, you'll no longer be our child."

But the girl did not pay any attention to her parents' instructions and went to Mother Trudy's house all the same. When she got there, Mother Trudy asked, "Why are you so pale?"

"Oh," she answered, trembling all over, "I'm so terrified by what I've just seen."

"What have you seen?"

"I saw a black man on your stairs."

"That was a charcoal burner."

"Then I saw a green man."

"That was a huntsman."

"After that I saw a bloodred man."

"That was a butcher."

"Oh, Mother Trudy, I was so petrified. I looked through the window and didn't see you, but I saw the devil with a fiery head."

"Oho!" she said. "Then you've seen the witch in her proper dress. I've been wanting you here and waiting for a long time. Now you shall provide me with light!"

Then she changed the girl into a block of wood and threw it into the fire. And when the wood was blazing, she sat down next to it, warmed herself, and said, "That really does give off a bright light."

◆ 44 ◆

Godfather Death

A POOR MAN HAD TWELVE CHILDREN and had to work day and night just to feed them. When the thirteenth was born, the man was in such great distress that he did not know what to do. So he just ran out onto the large highway, having decided to ask the first man he met to be godfather. The first man he encountered was the good Lord, who already knew what was on his mind, and he said to him, "Poor man, I feel sorry for you. I shall hold your child at the christening, and I shall take care of him and see that he's happy on earth."

"Who are you?" asked the man.

"I am your dear Lord."

"Then I don't want you to be godfather," said the man. "You give to the rich and let the poor go hungry."

The man said that because he did not know how wisely God distributes wealth and poverty. Thus he turned away from God and moved on. Then the devil came up to him and said, "What are you looking for? If you make me your child's godfather, I'll give him plenty of gold and all the pleasures of the world as well."

"Who are you?" asked the man.

"I'm the devil."

"Then I don't want you to be godfather," the man said. "You deceive people and lead them astray."

He continued on his way, and soon spindle-legged Death came toward him and said, "Take me as godfather."

"Who are you?" the man asked.

"I'm Death, and I make all people equal."

"You're just the right one," said the man. "You take the rich and poor alike without making distinctions. I want you to be my child's godfather."

"I shall make your child rich and famous," Death answered. "Indeed, whoever has me for a friend shall never know need."

"Next Sunday is the christening," said the man. "Make sure you're there on time."

Death appeared as he had promised, and he made for a very proper godfather.

When the boy was old enough, his godfather appeared one day and told him to come along with him. He led him into the forest, showed him an herb that grew there, and said, "Now you shall receive your christening gift. I'm going to make you into a famous doctor. Whenever you are summoned to a sick person, I shall appear on each occasion. If I stand at the head of the patient, you can firmly declare that you'll make him well again. Then give him some of the herb, and he'll recover. However, if I stand at the feet of the patient, he's mine, and you must say there's nothing you can do, and no doctor in the world can save him. But beware that you don't use the herb against my will or you shall be in for trouble!"

It did not take long for the young man to become the most famous doctor in the whole world. His reputation was such that people said, "He only has to look at a sick person, and he can tell the condition and whether the person will get well or must die." People came from far and wide to seek his help in curing the sick, and they gave him so much money that he was soon a rich man.

Now it happened that the king fell ill. The doctor was summoned and was supposed to determine whether recovery was possible. When he approached the bed, Death was standing at the feet of the king. So he knew no cure was possible.

If only I could outwit Death just once! thought the doctor. Of course, he'll hold it against me, but since I'm his godson, perhaps he'll let it pass. It's worth a try. So he took the sick man and turned him the other way around so that Death stood at his head. Then he gave him some of the herb, and the king began recovering and became well again. But Death went to the doctor, pointed his finger at him, and threatened him with angry and sinister looks.

"Well, you've pulled the wool over my eyes. I'll forgive you this once because you're my godson. But if you try it again, you'll be risking your own neck. I myself shall come and take you away!"

Soon thereafter, the king's daughter fell seriously ill. She was his only child, and he wept day and night until he could no longer see out of his eyes. Then he issued a proclamation that whoever saved his daughter from death would become her husband and inherit the crown. When the doctor approached her bed, he saw Death at her feet. He should have recalled his godfather's warning, but he was swayed by the great beauty of the princess and the happiness he envisioned having as her husband, so he threw caution to the winds. Death gave him angry looks, raised his hand, and threatened him with his withered fist, but the doctor refused to take notice. Instead he lifted the sick maiden, put her head where the feet had been, and gave her the herb. Immediately her cheeks flushed red, and life could be seen stirring in her once more.

When Death found himself cheated out of his claim a second time, he strode up to the doctor and said, "It's all over for you! Now it's your turn to die."

He grabbed the doctor so hard with his icy hand that the young man could not resist. Then he led him down into an underground cave. There the doctor saw thousands and thousands of candles burning in countless rows, some large, some medium, others small. With every moment some went out and others flared up again, so that the little flames seemed to be constantly changing and popping up and down.

"You see," said Death, "these candles are the lights of people's lives. The large ones belong to the children, the medium ones to married couples in their best years, the small ones to old people. But often children and young people can have small candles too."

"Show me my life candle," the doctor said, for he thought it would still be quite large.

Death pointed to a tiny stub that was just about to go out and said, "There it is. You see it?"

"Oh, dear godfather," the doctor was struck by horror, "light a new one for me! Please do me this favor so I can enjoy my life and become king and marry the beautiful princess."

"I can't," replied Death. "First one candle must go out before a new one can be lit."

"Then put the old one on top of a new candle so it will continue to burn after it goes out," the doctor pleaded.

Death pretended that he wanted to fulfill his wish. He reached for a large new candle, but since he really wanted revenge, he purposely made a mistake in transferring the stub, and it went out. All at once the doctor fell to the ground and had indeed fallen into the hands of Death.

◈ 45 ◈

Thumbling's Travels

A TAILOR HAD A SON who turned out to be small, not much bigger than a thumb. He was, therefore, called Thumbling. However, he had plenty of courage and said to his father, "I intend to go out into the world, and I shall do it."

"That's right, my son," said the old man, who took a long darning needle, held it over a candle, and made a knob of sealing wax on it. "Now you've got a sword to take with you on the way."

The little tailor wanted to eat one more meal with his family and hopped into the kitchen to see what his mother was cooking for the last time. She had just finished, and the dish stood on the hearth.

"Mother," he said, "what's there to eat today?"

"See for yourself," said his mother. So Thumbling jumped onto the hearth and looked inside the dish. However, he stuck his neck out too far, and the steam from the food caught hold of him and carried him up and out the chimney. For a while he rode around in the air on the steam, until he finally sank to the ground. Now the little tailor was out in the wide world. He traveled about and began working for a master tailor as an apprentice, but the food was not good enough for him.

"Mistress," he said to the master's wife, "if you don't give us something better to eat, I'm going to leave tomorrow morning, and I'll write with chalk on your door, 'Too much potatoes, too little meat! Bye, bye, potato king!' "

"What more do you want, grasshopper?" the master's wife asked, and she grew so angry that she grabbed a rag and tried to hit him. However, my little tailor crawled nimbly under the thimble, peeped out from under, and stuck his tongue out at her. She lifted the thimble and was about to grab him when Thumbling hopped into the rag. As the master's wife tried to untangle the rag and find him, he disappeared into a crack in the table.

"Ho, ho, mistress!" he called out and raised his head. When she went to hit him, he jumped down into the drawer. At length she caught him and kicked him out of the house.

The little tailor traveled on and came to a forest. There he met a band of robbers who planned to steal the king's treasure. When they saw the little tailor, they thought, A little fellow like that can crawl through a keyhole and serve us as a picklock.

"Hey, you!" one of the robbers called. "Yes, you giant Goliath! Do you want to come with us to the treasure chamber? We want you to crawl in and throw out the money."

Thumbling thought about it awhile, and at last he said yes and went with them to the treasure chamber. He examined the door from top to bottom to see if there was a crack. It did not take long for him to discover one wide enough to slip through. He wanted to go through right then and there, but one of the guards standing before the door noticed him and said to the other, "Just look at that ugly spider crawling there! I'm going to stamp it to death."

"Leave the poor creature alone," said the other. "It's never done a thing to harm you."

So Thumbling made it safely through the crack into the treasure chamber, opened the window under which the robbers were standing, and threw down to them one taler after another. Just as the little tailor was right in the middle of his work, he heard the king coming to inspect the treasure chamber. Hastily Thumbling crawled into a hiding place. When the king noticed that many hard coins were missing, he could not figure out how they might have been stolen, since the locks and bolts were in good condition and everything seemed to be well-protected. As he left the chamber, he said to the two guards, "Be on the alert! Somebody's after the money."

When Thumbling resumed his work, the guards heard the money

inside moving and jingling, *clink-clank, clink-clank.* They quickly ran inside and tried to grab the thief. However, the little tailor had heard them coming and was much swifter than they were. He jumped into a corner and covered himself with a taler so that nothing could be seen of him. Then he began to tease the guards.

"Here I am!"

The guards ran over, but when they got to the spot, he was already in another place beneath a taler and called out, "Hey, here I am!"

The guards rushed quickly to the next spot, but Thumbling was long since in a third corner and called out, "Hey, here I am!"

So he made fools of them and drove them all around the treasure chamber until they were exhausted and went away. Then, little by little, he proceeded to toss all the talers out the window. As he threw the last one with all his might, he nimbly hopped on it himself and flew with it out the window. The robbers congratulated him with great words of praise.

"You're a tremendous hero!" they said. "Do you want to be our captain?"

Thumbling thanked them but said that he wanted to see the world first. Then they divided the loot, and the little tailor asked for only a kreuzer because he could not carry any more than that.

Once again he buckled his sword around his waist; he said farewell to the robbers and began traveling. He worked as an apprentice for several masters, but he did not find the work to his taste. Finally, he hired himself out as a servant in an inn. However, the maids could not stand him because he saw everything they did on the sly without their being able to see him. Moreover, he told the innkeeper what they stole off the plates and took from the cellar to fill their own pockets.

"Just wait!" the maids said. "We'll pay you back!"

Indeed, they arranged to play a mean trick on him. Sometime later, when one of the maids was mowing in the garden and saw Thumbling running around in the grass and climbing up and down the plants, she quickly mowed him up with the grass, wrapped everything in a large cloth, and secretly threw it to the cows. Among the cows was a big black one that swallowed Thumbling down without hurting him. Yet, he did not like it down there, for it was very dark, and there was no light. When the cow was being milked, he cried out:

"Strip, strap, strull,
how soon will the bucket be full?"

But because of the noise from the milking, no one could understand what he said. Afterward the master of the house entered the barn and said, "Tomorrow that cow shall be slaughtered."

Thumbling became frightened, and he shouted loud and clear, "Let me out first! I'm sitting inside!"

The master heard the voice quite well, but he did not know where it came from.

"Where are you?" he asked.

"In the black one," Thumbling answered, but the master did not realize what that was supposed to mean and went away.

The next morning the cow was slaughtered, and fortunately Thumbling was not struck by anything during the chopping and slicing. However, he got mixed in with the sausage meat. When the butcher arrived and began his work, he cried out with all his might, "Don't chop too deep! Don't chop too deep! I'm stuck down here!"

Not a soul heard his voice because the noise of the chopping knives was too great. Now poor Thumbling was really in trouble, but where there's a will there's a way. Indeed, he jumped so nimbly between the chopping knives that none touched him, and he got away with his skin intact. Still, he could not find his way out of the meat entirely and was stuffed into a blood sausage with bits of bacon. The space there was rather cramped. Besides that he was hung up in a chimney to be smoked, and time hung very heavy on his hands. Finally, during winter he was taken down because the sausage was to be served to a guest. When the innkeeper's wife began cutting the sausage into slices, he took care not to stick his head too far out, otherwise it would have been cut off. At last he saw a chance to escape, cleared a way for himself, and jumped out.

Since things had gone so badly for him at that house, the little tailor did not want to stay any longer and resumed his travels. But his freedom did not last long. He crossed paths with a fox in an open field, and because the fox was lost in thought, he just snapped Thumbling up.

"Hey, Mr. Fox!" the little tailor exclaimed. "It's me you've got stuck in your throat! Let me go!"

"You're right," the fox replied. "There's practically nothing to eat on you, and I should let you go, but only if you promise me all the chickens in your father's barnyard."

"With all my heart!" said Thumbling. "You shall have every single chicken. I swear it!"

The fox let him go and even carried him back home. When the father saw his dear son again, he gladly gave the fox all the chickens he had.

"To make up for it, I've brought you a tidy sum of money," said Thumbling, and he handed his father the kreuzer that he had earned during his travels.

"But why did the fox get all those poor little chickens to eat?"
"Oh, you fool, don't you think that your father would care more for his child than for all the chickens in his barnyard?"

◈ 46 ◈

Fichter's Bird

ONCE UPON A TIME there was a sorcerer who used to assume the guise of a poor man and go begging from house to house to catch beautiful girls. No one knew where he took them, since none of the girls ever returned.

One day he appeared at the door of a man who had three beautiful daughters. He looked like a poor, weak beggar and carried a basket on his back as though to collect handouts in it. He begged for some food, and when the oldest daughter came out to hand him a piece of bread, he had only to touch her, and that compelled her to jump into his basket. Then he rushed away with great strides and carried her to his house in the middle of a dark forest. Everything was splendid inside the house, and he gave her whatever she desired.

"My darling," he said, "I'm sure you'll like it here, for there's everything your heart desires."

After a few days had gone by, he said, "I must go on a journey and leave you alone for a short time. Here are the keys to the house. You may go wherever you want and look at everything except one room, which this small key here opens. If you disobey me, you shall be punished by death." He also gave her an egg and said, "I'm giving you this egg for safekeeping. You're to carry it wherever you go. If you lose it, then something awful will happen."

She took the keys and the egg and promised to take care of everything. When he was gone, she went all around the house and explored it from top to bottom. The rooms glistened with silver and gold, and she was convinced that she had never seen such great splendor. Finally, she came to the forbidden door. She wanted to walk past it, but curiosity got the better of her. She examined the key, which looked like all the others, stuck it into the lock, turned it a little, and the door sprang open. But, what did she see when she entered? There was a large bloody basin in the middle of the room, and it was filled with dead people who had been chopped to pieces. Next to the basin was a block of wood with a glistening ax on top of it. She was so horrified by this that she dropped the egg she had been holding in her hand, and it plopped into the basin. She took it out and wiped the blood off, but to no avail: the blood reappeared instantly. She wiped and scraped, but she could not get rid of the spot.

Not long after this, the sorcerer came back from his journey, and the first things he demanded from her were the keys and the egg. When she handed them to him, she was trembling, and he perceived right away, by the red spots on the egg, that she had been in the bloody chamber.

"Since you went into that chamber against my will," he said, "you shall go back in, against your will. This is the end of your life."

He threw her down, dragged her along by her hair, cut her head off on the block, and chopped her into pieces, so that her blood flowed on the floor. Then he tossed her into the basin with the others.

"Now I shall fetch the second daughter," said the sorcerer.

Once again he went to the house in the guise of a poor man and begged. When the second daughter brought him a piece of bread, he caught her as he had the first, just by touching her. Then he carried her away, and she fared no better than her sister, for she succumbed to her own curiosity. She opened the door to the bloody chamber, looked inside, and had to pay for this with her life when the sorcerer returned from his journey.

Now he went and fetched the third daughter, but she was smart and cunning. After he had given her the keys and the egg and had departed, she put the egg away in a safe place. Then she explored the house and eventually came to the forbidden chamber. But, oh, what did she see? Her two dear sisters lay there in the basin cruelly murdered and chopped to pieces. However, she set to work right away, gathered the pieces together, and arranged them in their proper order: head, body, arms, and legs. When nothing more was missing, the pieces began to move and join together. Both the maidens opened their eyes and were alive again. Then they all rejoiced, kissed, and hugged each other.

When the sorcerer returned, he demanded his keys and egg right away, and when he could not discover the least trace of blood, he said, "You've passed the test, and you shall be my bride."

But, he no longer had any power over her and had to do what she requested.

"All right," she answered. "But first I want you to carry a basket full of gold to my father and mother, and you're to carry it on your back by yourself. In the meantime I shall prepare for the wedding."

Then she ran to her sisters, whom she had hidden in a little chamber.

"The time has come when I can save you," she said. "The villain himself shall carry you back home. But as soon as you get there, you must send me help."

She put her two sisters into a basket and covered them completely with gold until nothing could be seen of them at all. Then she called the sorcerer to her and said, "Now take the basket away. But don't you dare stop and rest along the way! I'll be keeping an eye on you from my window."

The sorcerer lifted the basket onto his back and went on his way. The basket, however, was so heavy that sweat ran down his face. At one point he sat down and wanted to rest for a while, but one of the sisters called from the basket, "I can see through my window that you're resting. Get a move on at once!"

Whenever he stopped along the way, he heard a voice and had to keep moving. Although he had run out of breath and was groaning, he finally managed to bring the basket with the gold and the two maidens to their parents' house.

Back at his place, the bride was preparing the wedding feast and sent invitations to all the sorcerer's friends. Then she took a skull with grinning teeth, decorated it with jewels and a wreath of flowers, carried it up to the attic window, and set it down so it faced outward. When everything was ready, she dipped herself into a barrel of honey, cut open a bed, and rolled around in the feathers so she looked like a strange bird, and it was impossible to recognize her. Afterward she went out of the house, and on the way she met some of the wedding guests, who asked:

"Where are you coming from, oh, Fitcher's bird?"
"From Fitze Fitcher's house, haven't you heard?"
"And what may the young bride be doing there?"
"She's swept the whole house from top to bottom.
Just now she's looking out the attic window."

Finally, she met the bridegroom who was walking back slowly. He also asked:

"Where are you coming from, oh, Fitcher's bird?"
"From Fitze Fitcher's house, haven't you heard?"
"And what may the young bride be doing there?"
"She's swept the whole house from top to bottom.
Just now she's looking out the attic window."

The bridegroom looked up and saw the decorated skull. He thought it was his bride and nodded and greeted her in a friendly way. However, once he and his guests were all gathered inside the house, the bride's brother and relatives arrived. They had been sent to rescue her, and they locked all the doors of the house to prevent anyone from escaping. Then they set fire to the house, and the sorcerer and all his cronies were burned to death.

◈ 47 ◈

The Juniper Tree

ALL THIS TOOK PLACE A LONG TIME AGO, most likely some two thousand years ago. There was a rich man who had a beautiful and pious wife, and they loved each other very much. Though they did not have any children, they longed to have some. Day and night the wife prayed for a child, but still none came, and everything remained the same.

Now, in the front of the house there was a yard, and in the yard stood a juniper tree. One day during winter the wife was under the tree peeling an apple, and as she was peeling it, she cut her finger, and her blood dripped on the snow.

"Oh," said the wife, and she heaved a great sigh. While she looked at the blood before her, she became quite sad. "If only I had a child as red as blood and as white as snow!" Upon saying that, her mood changed, and she became very cheerful, for she felt something might come of it. Then she went home.

After a month the snow vanished. After two months everything turned green. After three months the flowers sprouted from the ground. After four months all the trees in the woods grew more solid, and the green branches became intertwined. The birds began to sing, and their song resounded throughout the forest as the blossoms fell from the trees. Soon the fifth month passed, and when the wife stood under the juniper tree, it smelled so sweetly that her heart leapt for joy. Indeed, she was so overcome by joy that she fell down on her knees. When the sixth month had passed, the fruit was large and firm, and she was quite still. In the seventh month she picked the juniper berries and ate them so avidly that she became sad and sick. After the eighth month passed, she called her husband to her and wept.

"If I die," she said, "bury me under the juniper tree."

After that she was quite content and relieved until the ninth month had passed. Then she had a child as white as snow and as red as blood. When she saw the baby, she was so delighted that she died.

Her husband buried her under the juniper tree, and he began weeping a great deal. After some time he felt much better, but he still wept every now and then. Eventually, he stopped, and after more time passed, he took another wife. With his second wife he had a daughter, while the child from the first wife was a little boy, who was as red as blood and as white as snow. Whenever the woman looked at her daughter, she felt great love for her, but whenever she looked at the little boy, her heart was cut to the quick. She could not forget that he would always stand in her way and prevent her daughter from inheriting everything, which was what the woman had in mind. Thus the devil took hold of her and influenced her feelings toward the boy until she became quite cruel toward him: she pushed him from one place to the next, slapped him here and cuffed him there, so that the poor child lived in constant fear. When he came home from school, he found no peace at all.

One time the woman went up to her room, and her little daughter followed her and said, "Mother, give me an apple."

"Yes, my child," said the woman, and she gave her a beautiful apple from the chest that had a large heavy lid with a big, sharp iron lock.

"Mother," said the little daughter, "shouldn't brother get one too?"

The woman was irritated by that remark, but she said, "Yes, as soon as he comes home from school." And, when she looked out of the window and saw he was coming, the devil seemed to take possession of her, and she snatched the apple away from her daughter.

"You shan't have one before your brother," she said and threw the apple into the chest and shut it.

The little boy came through the door, and the devil compelled her to be friendly to him and say, "Would you like to have an apple, my son?" Yet, she gave him a fierce look.

"Mother," said the little boy, "how ferocious you look! Yes, give me an apple."

Then she felt compelled to coax him.

"Come over here," she said as she lifted the lid. "Take out an apple for yourself."

And as the little boy leaned over the chest, the devil prompted her, and *crash!* She slammed the lid so hard that his head flew off and fell among the apples. Then she was struck by fear and thought, How am I going to get out of this? She went up to her room and straight to her dresser, where she took out a white kerchief from a drawer. She put the boy's head back on his neck and tied the neckerchief around it so nothing could be seen. Then she set him on a chair in front of the door and put the apple in his hand.

Some time later little Marlene came into the kitchen and went up to her mother, who was standing by the fire in front of a pot of hot water, which she was constantly stirring.

"Mother," said Marlene, "brother's sitting by the door and looks very pale. He's got an apple in his hand, and I asked him to give me the apple, but he didn't answer, and I became very scared."

"Go back to him," said the mother, "and if he doesn't answer you, give him a box on the ear."

Little Marlene returned to him and said, "Brother, give me the apple."

But he would not respond. So she gave him a box on the ear, and his head flew off. The little girl was so frightened that she began to cry and howl. Then she ran to her mother and said, "Oh, Mother, I've knocked my brother's head off!" And she wept and wept and could not be comforted.

"Marlene," said the mother. "What have you done! You're not to open your mouth about this. We don't want anyone to know, and besides there's nothing we can do about it now. So we'll make a stew out of him."

The mother took the little boy and chopped him into pieces. Next she put them into a pot and let them stew. But Marlene stood nearby and wept until all her tears fell into the pot, so it did not need any salt.

When the father came home, he sat down at the table and asked, "Where's my son?"

The mother served a huge portion of the stewed meat, and Marlene wept and could not stop.

"Where's my son?" the father asked again.

"Oh," said the mother, "he's gone off into the country to visit his mother's great uncle. He intends to stay there awhile."

"What's he going to do there? He didn't even say good-bye to me."

"Well, he wanted to go very badly and asked me if he could stay there six weeks. They'll take good care of him."

"Oh, that makes me sad," said the man. "It's not right. He

should have said good-bye to me.'' Then he began to eat and said, ''Marlene, what are you crying for? Your brother will come back soon.'' Without pausing he said, ''Oh, wife, the food tastes great! Give me some more!'' The more he ate, the more he wanted. ''Give me some more,'' he said. ''I'm not going to share this with you. Somehow I feel as if it were all mine.''

As he ate and ate he threw the bones under the table until he was all done. Mean-

while, Marlene went to her dresser and took out her best silk neckerchief from the bottom drawer, gathered all the bones from beneath the table, tied them up in her silk kerchief, and carried them outside the door. There she wept bitter tears and laid the bones beneath the juniper tree. As she put them there, she suddenly felt relieved and stopped crying. Now the juniper tree began to move. The branches separated and came together again as though they were clapping their hands in joy. At the same time smoke came out of the tree, and in the middle of the smoke there was a flame that seemed to be burning. Then a beautiful bird flew out of the fire and began singing magnificently. He soared high in the air, and after he vanished, the juniper tree was as it was before. Yet, the silk kerchief was gone. Marlene was very happy and gay. It was as if her brother were still alive, and she went merrily back into the house, sat down at the table, and ate.

Meanwhile, the bird flew away, landed on a goldsmith's house, and began to sing:

"My mother, she killed me.
My father, he ate me.
My sister, Marlene, she made sure to see
my bones were all gathered together,
bound nicely in silk, as neat as can be,
and laid beneath the juniper tree.
Tweet, tweet! What a lovely bird I am!"

The goldsmith was sitting in his workshop making a golden chain. When he heard the bird singing on his roof, he thought it was very beautiful. Then he stood up, and as he walked across the threshold, he lost a slipper. Still, he kept on going, right into the middle of the street with only one sock and a slipper on. He was also wearing his apron, and in one of his hands he held the golden chain, in the other his tongs. The sun was shining brightly on the street as he walked, and then he stopped to get a look at the bird.

"Bird," he said, "how beautifully you sing! Sing me that song again."

"No," said the bird, "I never sing twice for nothing. Give me the golden chain, and I'll sing it for you again."

"All right," said the goldsmith. "Here's the golden chain. Now sing the song again."

The bird swooped down, took the golden chain in his right claw, went up to the goldsmith, and began singing:

"My mother, she killed me.
My father, he ate me.
My sister, Marlene, she made sure to see
my bones were all gathered together,

bound nicely in silk, as neat as can be,
and laid beneath the juniper tree.
Tweet, tweet! What a lovely bird I am!"

Then the bird flew off to a shoemaker, landed on his roof, and sang:

"My mother, she killed me.
My father, he ate me.
My sister, Marlene, she made sure to see
my bones were gathered together,
bound nicely in silk, as neat as can be,
and laid beneath the juniper tree.
Tweet, tweet! What a lovely bird I am!"

When the shoemaker heard the song, he ran to the door in his shirt sleeves and looked up at the roof, keeping his hand over his eyes to protect them from the bright sun.

"Bird," he said. "How beautifully you sing!" Then he called into the house, "Wife, come out here for a second! There's a bird up there. Just look. How beautifully he sings!" Then he called his daughter and her children, and the journeyman, apprentices, and maid. They all came running out into the street and looked at the bird and saw how beautiful he was. He had bright red and green feathers, and his neck appeared to glisten like pure gold, while his eyes sparkled in his head like stars.

"Bird," said the shoemaker, "now sing me that song again."

"No," said the bird. "I never sing twice for nothing. You'll have to give me a present."

"Wife," said the man, "go into the shop. There's a pair of red shoes on the top shelf. Get them for me."

His wife went and fetched the shoes.

"There," said the man. "Now sing the song again."

The bird swooped down, took the shoes in his left claw, flew back up on the roof, and sang:

"My mother, she killed me.
My father, he ate me.
My sister, Marlene, she made sure to see
my bones were all gathered together,
bound nicely in silk, as neat as can be,
and laid beneath the juniper tree.
Tweet, tweet! What a lovely bird I am!"

When the bird finished the song, he flew away. He had the chain in his right claw and the shoes in his left, and he flew far away to a mill. The mill went *clickety-clack, clickety-clack, clickety-clack.* The miller had twenty men sitting in the mill, and they were hewing a stone. Their chisels went *click-clack, click-clack, click-clack.* And the mill kept going *clickety-clack, clickety-clack, clickety-clack.* The bird swooped down and landed on a linden tree outside the mill and sang:

   "My mother, she killed me."

Then one of the men stopped working.

   "My father, he ate me."

Then two more stopped and listened.

   "My sister, Marlene, she made sure to see."

Then four more stopped.

   "My bones were all gathered together,
   bound nicely in silk, as neat as can be."

Now only eight kept chiseling.

   "And laid beneath . . ."

Now only five.

   ". . . the juniper tree."

Now only one.

   "*Tweet, tweet!* What a lovely bird I am!"

Then the last one also stopped and listened to the final words.
   "Bird, how beautifully you sing! Let me hear that too. Sing your song again for me."
   "No," said the bird. "I never sing twice for nothing. Give me the millstone, and I'll sing the song again."
   "I would if I could," he said. "But the millstone doesn't belong to me alone."

"If he sings again," said the others, "he can have it."

Then the bird swooped down, and all twenty of the miller's men took beams to lift the stone. "Heave-ho! Heave-ho! Heave-ho!" Then the bird stuck his neck through the hole, put the stone on like a collar, flew back to the tree, and sang:

"My mother, she killed me.
My father, he ate me.
My sister, Marlene, she made sure to see
my bones were all gathered together,
bound nicely in silk, as neat as can be,
and laid beneath the juniper tree.
Tweet, tweet! What a lovely bird I am!"

When the bird finished his song, he spread his wings, and in his right claw he had the chain, in his left the shoes, and around his neck the millstone. Then he flew away to his father's house.

The father, mother, and Marlene were sitting at the table in the parlor, and the father said, "Oh, how happy I am! I just feel so wonderful!"

"Not me," said the mother. "I feel scared as if a storm were about to erupt."

Meanwhile, Marlene just sat there and kept weeping. Then the bird flew up, and when he landed on the roof, the father said, "Oh, I'm in such good spirits. The sun's shining so brightly outside, and I feel as though I were going to see an old friend again."

"Not me," said his wife. "I'm so frightened that my teeth are chattering. I feel as if fire were running through my veins."

She tore open her bodice, while Marlene sat in a corner and kept weeping. She had her handkerchief in front of her eyes and wept until it was completely soaked with her tears. The bird swooped down on the juniper tree, where he perched on a branch and began singing:

"My mother, she killed me."

The mother stopped her ears, shut her eyes, and tried not to see or hear anything, but there was a roaring in her ears like a turbulent storm, and her eyes burned and flashed like lightning.

"My father, he ate me."

"Oh, Mother," said the man, "listen to that beautiful bird singing so gloriously! The sun's so warm, and it smells like cinnamon."

"My sister, Marlene, made sure to see."

Then Marlene laid her head on her knees and wept and wept, but the man said, "I'm going outside. I must see the bird close up."

"Oh, don't go!" said the wife. "I feel as if the whole house were shaking and about to go up in flames!"

Nevertheless, the man went out and looked at the bird.

"My bones were all gathered together,
bound nicely in silk, as neat as can be,
and laid beneath the juniper tree.
Tweet, tweet! What a lovely bird I am!"

After ending his song, the bird dropped the golden chain, and it fell around the man's neck just right, so that it fit him perfectly. Then he went inside and said "Just look how lovely that bird is! He gave me this beautiful golden chain, and he's as beautiful as well!"

But the woman was petrified and fell to the floor. Her cap slipped off her head, and the bird sang again:

"My mother, she killed me."

"Oh, I wish I were a thousand feet beneath the earth so I wouldn't have to hear this!"

"My father, he ate me."

Then the woman fell down again as if she were dead.

"My sister, Marlene, she made sure to see."

"Oh," said Marlene, "I want to go outside too and see if the bird will give me something." Then she went out.

"My bones were all gathered together,
bound nicely in silk, as neat as can be."

Then the bird threw her the shoes.

"And laid them beneath the juniper tree.
Tweet, tweet! What a lovely bird I am!"

Marlene felt gay and happy. She put on the new red shoes and danced and skipped back into the house.

"Oh," she said, "I was so sad when I went out, and now I feel so cheerful. That certainly is a splendid bird. He gave me a pair of red shoes as a gift."

"Not me," said the wife, who jumped up, and her hair flared up like red-hot flames. "I feel as if the world were coming to an end. Maybe I'd feel better if I went outside."

As she went out the door, *crash!* the bird threw the millstone down on her head, and she was crushed to death. The father and Marlene heard the crash and went outside. Smoke, flames, and fire were rising from the spot, and when it was over, the little brother was standing there. He took his father and Marlene by the hand, and all three were very happy. Then they went into the house, sat down at the table, and ate.

◈ 48 ◈

Old Sultan

A FARMER HAD A FAITHFUL DOG NAMED SULTAN, and when the dog had grown old and lost all his teeth, he could no longer grip things tightly. One day, as the farmer was standing by the front door with his wife, he said, "I'm going to shoot old Sultan tomorrow. He's no longer of any use to us."

His wife felt sorry for the faithful creature, and she replied, "Couldn't we just keep him on and feed him? After all, he's served us so many years and has been loyal to us."

"My God!" the husband exclaimed. "Don't you have any sense? He doesn't have a tooth left in his head, and there's not a thief who'd be afraid of him. It's time for him to go. He served us well, but he was also fed well in return."

The poor dog was basking nearby in the sun and overheard

everything that was said. He was sad that the next day was to be his last. But he had a good friend, the wolf, and in the evening he sneaked out into the forest to see him and whine about his impending fate.

"Listen, cousin," said the wolf. "Keep your spirits up. You can depend on me to help you out of your dilemma. In fact, I've already thought of something. Early tomorrow morning your master will be going out with his wife to make hay, and they'll take their little child with them because nobody will be staying at home. They generally lay the child behind the hedge in the shade while they work. Now, I want you to lie down next to the child as if you wanted to guard him. I'll come out of the forest and steal the child. Then you've got to take to your heels as if you wanted to get the child away from me. I'll let him drop, and you bring him back to his parents, who'll believe that you rescued him. Then they'll be too grateful to think of harming you. On the contrary, they'll be completely indebted to you and give you anything you want."

The dog liked the scheme, and he carried it out just as planned. When the wolf stole the child and began carrying him through the fields, the father screamed, and when old Sultan brought the child back, he was happy and patted the dog.

"Nobody's going to touch a hair on your head," he said. "You can stay here and eat your fill for as long as you live." Then he turned to his wife and said, "Go home right away and cook some bread mush. He won't need to chew that. Also, bring the pillow from my bed. I want to give him that as a gift to lie on."

From then on old Sultan had it good, and he could not have wished for a better life. Soon after, the wolf visited him and was glad to learn that everything succeeded so well.

"Now, cousin," he said, "I hope you'll wink an eye when I steal a fat sheep from your master every now and then. Times are getting hard for all of us."

"Don't count on that," the dog answered. "I intend to stay faithful to my master, and I can't let you do it."

The wolf did not believe that the dog meant what he said. So during the night he crept into the yard to steal a sheep. However, the farmer, who had learned about the wolf's plan from the faithful Sultan, was waiting for him and gave him a good thrashing with a flail. The wolf was forced to scamper away, but he cried out at the dog, "Just wait, you traitor! You'll pay for this!"

The next morning the wolf sent the boar as his second to challenge the dog to meet him out in the forest and settle their affair. Old Sultan could find no one who would be his second except for a three-legged cat. And, when they went out together, the poor cat limped and had to hold his tail erect because of the pain he was suffering. The wolf and his second were already at the spot. When they saw the opponent coming, they thought he was carrying a saber with him because they mistook the cat's erect tail for a saber. Moreover, on seeing the cat limping on three legs, they thought he was picking up stones to throw at them. The wolf and the boar became so frightened that the boar crept into some bushes and the wolf jumped up a tree. When the dog and cat arrived at the spot, they were puzzled to find no one there. However, the wild boar had not been able to conceal himself completely in the bushes. One of his ears was showing, and as the cat was looking cautiously about, the boar twitched his ear. The cat thought a mouse might be stirring in the bushes and jumped on it. She took a good hard bite, and the boar leapt with a loud cry and ran away.

"The guilty one's sitting up there in the tree!" he screamed.

The dog and the cat looked up and saw the wolf, who was so ashamed he had shown such cowardice that he accepted the dog's offer of peace.

◈ 49 ◈

The Six Swans

ONCE THERE WAS A KING who was hunting in a vast forest, and he began chasing a deer so intensely that none of his men could follow him. When evening drew near, he stopped, looked around him, and realized he was lost. He searched for a way out of the forest but was unable to find one. Then he caught sight of an old woman, nodding her head back and forth and heading toward him. She was, however, a witch.

"Dear woman," he said to her, "can you show me the way out of the forest?"

"Oh, yes, Your Majesty," she answered. "I certainly can, but on one condition, and if you don't fulfill it, you'll never find your way out of the forest, and you will starve to death."

"What kind of condition?" asked the king.

"I have a daughter," said the old woman, "who is as beautiful as any maiden in the world. Indeed, she is worthy to be your wife, and if you make her your queen, I'll show you the way out of the forest."

The king was so tremendously frightened that he consented, and the old woman led him to her little hut, where her daughter was sitting by the fire. The maiden greeted the king as though she had been expecting him, and he observed that she was very beautiful. Nevertheless, he did not like her, and he could not look at her without secretly shuddering. After he had lifted the maiden onto his horse, the old woman showed him the way, and once the king reached the royal palace again, the wedding was celebrated.

The king had already been married before this, and he had seven children by his first wife, six boys and a girl, whom he loved more than anything in the world. Since he now feared that the stepmother might not treat them well and might even harm them, he brought them to a solitary castle in the middle of a forest. It lay so well concealed and the way to it was so hard to find that he himself would not have found it if a wise woman had not given him a ball of yarn with magic powers. When he threw the ball before him, the yarn unwound itself and showed him the way.

Now, the king went out to visit his dear children so often that the queen began to notice his absences. Since she was curious and wanted to know what he was doing out in the forest all alone, she gave his servants a great deal of money, and they revealed the secret. They also told her about the ball of yarn that alone could show the way. For a while she had no peace of mind, but she finally discovered where the king kept the ball. Then she made small white silk shirts, and she used the witchcraft that she had learned from her mother to sew a magic spell into them.

One day when the king had gone hunting, she took the little shirts, went out into the forest, and let the ball of yarn show her the way. When the children saw someone coming in the distance, they thought their dear father was coming to see them and ran joyfully out to greet him. But she threw a shirt over each one of them, and as soon as they were touched by the shirts, they were turned into swans and flew away over the forest. The queen went home delighted with herself, thinking that she was rid of her stepchildren. However, the girl had not run outside with her brothers, and the queen knew nothing about the girl.

The following day the king went to visit his children, but he found only the girl.

"Where are your brothers?" the king asked.

"Oh, dear Father," she answered, "they've gone away and left me alone." And she told him how, from her window, she had seen her brothers turn into swans, and how they had flown away over the forest. Then she showed him the feathers that they had dropped in the yard and left for her to gather.

The king mourned for his sons but had no idea that the queen had done this evil deed. Yet, he did fear that his daughter might also be stolen from him, and he wanted to take her with him. However, she was afraid of the stepmother and begged the king to allow her to spend one last night in the forest castle. I can't stay here any longer, the poor girl thought. I shall go and search for my brothers.

When night came, she fled the castle and went straight into the forest. She walked the whole night long and the entire next day without stopping, until she became so exhausted that she could go no farther. Then she saw a hut, and after entering it, she found a room with six small beds. Since she was afraid to lie down in any of the beds, she crawled underneath one and lay down on the hard floor, intending to spend the night there. However, just when the sun was about to set, she heard a rustling sound and saw six swans come flying through the window. They landed on the floor and blew at each other until all their feathers were blown off. After that their swan skins slipped off like shirts. The maiden observed all this, and when she recognized her brothers, she rejoiced and crawled out from under the bed. Her brothers were delighted to see their little sister, but their joy was short-lived.

"You can't stay here," they said to her. "This is a robbers' den. When they come home and find you here, they'll kill you."

"Can't you protect me?" asked their sister.

"No," they replied. "You see, we can take off our swan skins for only a quarter of an hour every evening. During this time we assume our human form, but after that we're changed back into swans."

Their sister wept and asked, "Can't you be set free?"

"We don't think so," they said. "The conditions are too hard. You'd have to go six years without speaking to anyone or laughing, and during this time you'd have to sew six little shirts for us made of asters. If just one single word were to fall from your lips, then all your work would be for naught."

Nevertheless, the maiden decided to set her brothers free, even if it might cost her her life. She left the hut, went into the middle of the forest, climbed a tree, and spent the night there. The next morning she got down, gathered asters, and began to sew. She could not talk to anyone, nor did she have a desire to laugh: she just sat there and concentrated on her work.

After she had spent a long time there, the king of the country happened to go hunting in the forest, and his huntsmen came to the tree where the maiden was perched. They called to her and said, "Who are you?"

She did not answer.

"Come down to us," they said. "We won't harm you."

She merely shook her head. When they continued to bother her with questions, she threw them her golden necklace and thought that would satisfy them. Yet, they persisted. Then she threw them her girdle, and when this did not work either, she threw down her garters and little by little everything that she had on and could do without until she had nothing left but her little shift. Still the huntsmen did not let themselves be deterred by all this. They climbed the tree, carried her down, and led her to the king, who asked, "Who are you, and what were you doing in that tree?"

She did not answer. He tried questioning her in all the languages he knew, but she remained as silent as a fish. Eventually, her beauty moved the king's heart, and he fell deeply in love with her. He covered her with his cloak, lifted her onto his horse, and brought her to his castle. There he had her dressed in rich garments, and her beautiful features were as radiant as the day is bright. Still, it was impossible to get her to utter a single word. He had her sit next to him at the table, and her modest ways and her polite manners pleased him so much that he said, "This maiden is the one I shall marry and no other woman in the world except her."

Within a few days he married her, but the king had an evil mother, who was dissatisfied with this marriage and spoke ill of the young queen.

"That wench! Why won't she speak?" she said. "Where does she come from? She's not worthy of a king."

A year later, when the queen gave birth to her first child, the old woman took the child away from her and smeared the queen's mouth with blood while she was asleep. Then the old woman went to the king and accused the young queen of being a cannibal. The king refused to believe this and would not tolerate anyone harming his wife. Meanwhile, the queen continued to sit and sew the shirts, and did not pay attention to anything else.

The next time, she gave birth to another handsome boy, and her wicked mother-in-law tried the same deception, but the king could not bring himself to believe the charges brought against his wife.

"She's too pious and good," he said. "She'd never do anything like that. If she could talk, she could defend herself, and her innocence would come to light.''

However, when the old woman stole the third newborn baby and accused the queen, who did not say one word in her own defense, the king could do nothing but hand her over to a court, which condemned her to death by fire.

The day came for the sentence to be carried out, but it was also the last day of the six years during which she had not been allowed to speak or laugh. Indeed, this meant that she had set her brothers free from the power of the magic spell. The six shirts were finished except for the left sleeve of the last shirt. When the queen was led to the stake, she carried the shirts over her arm, and as she stood on the stack of wood and the fire was about to be lit, she looked up and saw the six swans come flying through the air. Now she knew that her rescue was near at hand, and her heart jumped for joy. The swans swooped down and landed close by so that she could throw the shirts over them. As soon as the shirts touched them, the swan skins fell off, and her brothers stood before her in the flesh. They looked handsome and vigorous. Only the youngest was missing his left arm, and he had a swan's wing on his shoulder instead. They embraced and kissed each other, and the queen went up to the king, who was quite stunned by all this.

''Dearest husband,'' she said. ''Now I may speak and tell you that I'm innocent and was unjustly accused.''

She told him how the old woman had been deceiving him and had taken away her three children and hidden them. Then, to the king's great joy, the children were brought to him, and as a punishment the wicked mother-in-law was tied to the stake and burned to ashes. Thereafter, the king and queen, along with her six brothers, lived for many years in peace and happiness.

◈ 50 ◈

Brier Rose

IN TIMES OF OLD there lived a king and queen, and every day they said, "Oh, if only we had a child!" Yet, they never had one.

Then one day, as the queen went out bathing, a frog happened to crawl ashore and say to her, "Your wish shall be fulfilled. Before the year is out, you shall give birth to a daughter."

The frog's prediction came true, and the queen gave birth to a girl who was so beautiful that the king was overjoyed and decided to hold a great feast. Not only did he invite his relatives, friends, and acquaintances, but also the wise women, in the hope that they would be generous and kind to his daughter. There were thirteen wise women in his kingdom, but he had only twelve golden plates from which they could eat. Therefore, one of them had to remain home.

The feast was celebrated with tremendous splendor, and when it drew to a close, the wise women bestowed their miraculous gifts upon the child. One gave her virtue, another beauty, the third wealth, and so on, until they had given her nearly everything one could possibly wish for in the world. When eleven of them had offered their gifts, the thirteenth suddenly entered the hall. She wanted to get revenge for not having been invited, and without greeting anyone or looking around, she cried out with a loud voice, "In her fifteenth year the princess shall prick herself with a spindle and fall down dead!"

That was all she said. Then she turned around and left the hall. Everyone was horrified, but the twelfth wise woman stepped forward. She still had her wish to make, and although she could not undo the evil spell, she could nevertheless soften it.

"The princess shall not die," she said. "Instead, she shall fall into a deep sleep for one hundred years."

Since the king wanted to guard his dear child against such a catastrophe, he issued an order that all spindles in his kingdom were to be burned. Meanwhile, the gifts of the wise women fulfilled their promise in every way: the girl was so beautiful, polite, kind, and sensible that whoever encountered her could not help but adore her.

Now, on the day she turned fifteen, it happened that the king and queen were not at home, and she was left completely alone in the palace. So she wandered all over the place and explored as many rooms and chambers as she pleased. She eventually came to an old tower, climbed its narrow winding staircase, and came to a small door. A rusty key was stuck in the lock, and when she turned it, the door sprang open, and she saw an old woman in a little room sitting with a spindle and busily spinning flax.

"Good day, old granny," said the princess. "What are you doing there?"

"I'm spinning," said the old woman, and she nodded her head.

"What's the thing that's bobbing about in such a funny way?" asked the maiden, who took the spindle and wanted to spin too, but just as she touched the spindle, the magic spell began working, and she pricked her finger with it.

The very moment she felt the prick, she fell down on the bed that was standing there, and she was overcome by a deep sleep. This sleep soon spread throughout the entire palace. The king and queen had just returned home, and when they entered the hall, they fell asleep, as did all the people of their court. They were followed by the horses in the stable, the dogs in the courtyard, the pigeons on the roof, and the flies on the wall. Even the fire flickering in the hearth became quiet and fell asleep. The roast stopped sizzling, and the cook, who was just about to pull the kitchen boy's hair because he had done something wrong, let him go and fell asleep. Finally, the wind died down so that not a single leaf stirred on the trees outside the castle.

Soon a brier hedge began to grow all around the castle, and it grew higher each year. Eventually, it surrounded and covered the entire castle, so that it was no longer visible. Not even the flag on the roof could be seen. The princess became known by the name Beautiful Sleeping Brier Rose, and a tale about her began circulating throughout the country. From time to time princes came and tried to break through the hedge and get to the castle. However, this was impossible because the thorns clung together tightly as though they had hands, and the young men got stuck there. Indeed, they could not pry themselves loose and died miserable deaths.

After many, many years had gone by, a prince came to this country once more and heard an old man talking about the brier hedge. Supposedly there was a castle standing behind the hedge, and in the castle was a remarkably beautiful princess named Brier Rose, who had been sleeping for a hundred years, along with the king and queen and their entire court. The old man also knew from his grandfather that many princes had come and had tried to break through the brier hedge, but they had got stuck and had died wretched deaths.

"I am not afraid," said the young prince. "I intend to go and see the beautiful Brier Rose."

The good old man tried as best he could to dissuade him, but the prince would not heed his words.

Now the hundred years had just ended, and the day on which Brier Rose was to wake up again had arrived. When the prince approached the brier hedge, he found nothing but beautiful flowers that opened of their own accord, let him through, and then closed again like a hedge. In the castle courtyard he saw the horses and the spotted hunting dogs lying asleep. The pigeons were perched on the roof and had tucked their heads beneath their wings. When he entered the palace, the flies were sleeping on the wall, the cook in the kitchen was still holding his hand as if he wanted to grab the kitchen boy, and the maid was sitting in front of the black chicken that she was about to pluck. As the prince continued walking, he saw the entire court lying asleep in the hall with the king and queen by the throne. Then he moved on, and everything was so quiet that he could hear himself breathe.

Finally, he came to the tower and opened the door to the small room in which Brier Rose was asleep. There she lay, and her beauty was so marvelous that he could not take his eyes off her. Then he leaned over and gave her a kiss, and when his lips touched hers, Brier Rose opened her eyes, woke up, and looked at him fondly. After that they went downstairs together, and the king and queen woke up along with the entire court, and they all looked at each other in amazement. Soon the horses in the courtyard stood up and shook themselves. The hunting dogs jumped around and wagged their tails. The pigeons on the roof lifted their heads from under their wings, looked around, and flew off into the fields. The flies on the wall continued crawling. The fire in the kitchen flared up, flickered, and cooked the meat. The roast began to sizzle again, and the cook gave the kitchen boy such a box on the ear that he let out a cry, while the maid finished plucking the chicken.

The wedding of the prince with Brier Rose was celebrated in great splendor, and they lived happily to the end of their days.

◈ 51 ◈

Foundling

ONCE UPON A TIME a forester went out hunting in the forest, and as
he entered it, he heard some cries like those of a small child. He
followed the sounds and eventually came to a big tree where he saw
a little child sitting on the top. The child's mother had fallen asleep
with him under the tree, and a hawk had seen the child in her lap. So
it had swooped down, carried the child away with its beak, and set
him down on top of the tree. The forester climbed the tree and
brought the child down, and he thought, You ought to take him
home with you and raise him with your little Lena.

So he took the boy home, and the two children grew up together.
However, the boy who had been found on top of the tree was called
Foundling because he had been carried off by a bird. Foundling and
Lena were very fond of each other. In fact, they loved each other so
much that they became sad if they were not constantly within sight
of each other.

Now the forester had an old cook, and one evening she took two
buckets and began fetching water. But she did not go to the well
simply one time but many times. When Lena saw this, she asked,
"Tell me, old Sanna, why are you fetching so much water?"

"If you promise to keep quiet, I'll let you in on my secret."

Lena of course replied that she would not tell a soul. Then the
cook said, "Early tomorrow morning, when the forester goes out
hunting, I'm going to heat some water over the fire, and when it's
boiling, I'm going to throw Foundling in and cook him."

Early the next morning the forester got up to go out hunting, and
when he had gone, the children were still in bed. Then Lena said to
Foundling, "If you won't forsake me, I won't forsake you."

"Never ever," said Foundling.

"Well then, I'm going to tell you something," said Lena. "Last
night old Sanna was fetching many buckets of water into the house,
and I asked her why she was doing that. She said that if I wouldn't

tell a soul, she'd let me in on her secret. I promised her not to tell a living soul. Then she said that early this morning, when my father goes out hunting, she would boil a kettle full of water, throw you in, and cook you. So let's get up quickly, dress ourselves, and go away together."

Then the two children got up, dressed themselves quickly, and went away. When the water in the kettle began to boil, the cook went into the bedroom to get Foundling and throw him into the kettle. But as she entered the room and went over to the beds, she saw that the two children were gone and became greatly alarmed.

"What shall I say when the forester comes home and sees that the children are gone?" she said. "I'd better send some people after them to get them back."

The cook sent three servants to run after them and bring them back. But the children were sitting at the edge of the forest and saw the three servants coming from afar.

"If you won't forsake me, I won't forsake you," said Lena.

"Never ever," said Foundling.

"Then change yourself into a rosebush, and I'll be the rose on it," said Lena.

When the three servants reached the edge of the forest, they saw nothing but a rosebush with a little rose on it. The children were nowhere to be seen.

"There's nothing doing here," they said, and they went home, where they told the cook they had seen nothing but a rosebush with a rose on it. Then the cook scolded them. "You blockheads! You should have cut the rosebush in two, plucked the rose, and brought it back with you. Now go quickly and do it!"

So they had to set out once more and look for the children. But when the children saw them coming from afar, Lena said, "If you won't forsake me, I won't forsake you."

"Never ever," said Foundling.

"Then change yourself into a church, and I'll be the chandelier hanging in it," Lena said.

When the three servants arrived at the spot, there was nothing but a church and a chandelier inside it.

"What's there to do here? Let's go home."

When they got home, the cook asked whether they had found anything. They said no. They had found nothing but a church with a chandelier inside.

"You fools!" the cook scolded. "Why didn't you destroy the church and bring back the chandelier?"

This time the old cook herself set out on foot and pursued the children with the three servants. But the children saw the three servants coming from afar and also the cook, who was waddling behind them.

"Foundling," said Lena. "If you won't forsake me, I won't forsake you."

"Never ever," said Foundling.

"Then change yourself into a pond," said Lena, "and I'll be the duck swimming on it."

When the cook arrived and saw the pond, she lay down beside it and began to drink it up. However, the duck quickly swam over, grabbed her head in its beak, and dragged her into the water. The old witch was thus drowned, and the children went home together. They were very happy, and if they have not died, they are still alive.

◈ 52 ◈

King Thrushbeard

A KING HAD A DAUGHTER whose beauty was beyond comparison, but she was so proud and haughty that no suitor was good enough for her. Indeed, she rejected one after the other and ridiculed them as well. Once her father held a great feast and invited all the marriageable young men from far and wide to attend. They were all lined up according to their rank and class: first came the kings, then the dukes, princes, counts, and barons, and finally the gentry. The king's daughter was conducted down the line, and she found fault with each one of the suitors there. One was too fat for her. "That wine barrel!" she said. Another was too tall. "Tall and thin, he looks like a pin!" The third was too short. "Short and fat, he's built like a vat!" The fourth was too pale. "He resembles death!" The fifth was too red. "What a rooster!" The sixth did not stand straight enough. "Green wood, dried behind the stove!"

There was not a single man whom she did not criticize, but she made the most fun of a good king who stood at the head of the line and had a chin that was a bit crooked.

"My goodness!" she exclaimed, and laughed. "He's got a chin like a thrush's beak!" From then on, everyone called him Thrushbeard.

When her father saw that she did nothing but ridicule people, and that she scorned all the suitors who were gathered there, he was furious and swore that she would have to marry the very first beggar who came to his door. A few days later a minstrel came and began singing beneath the windows to earn some money. When the king heard him, he said, "Have him come up here."

The minstrel, who was dressed in dirty, tattered clothes, entered the hall and sang in front of the king and his daughter. When he was finished, he asked for a modest reward.

"Your singing has pleased me so much," the king said, "that I shall give you my daughter for your wife."

The king's daughter was horrified, but the king said, "I swore I'd give you to the very first beggar who came along, and I intend to keep my word."

All her objections were to no avail. The minister was fetched, and she was compelled to wed the minstrel. When that was done, the king said, "It's not fitting for you to stay in my palace any longer since you're now a beggar woman. I want you to depart with your husband."

The beggar took her by the hand, and she had to go with him on foot. When they came to a huge forest, she asked:

"Tell me, who might the owner of this forest be?"
"King Thrushbeard owns the forest and all you can see.
If you had taken him, it would belong to you."
"Alas, poor me! What can I do?
I should have wed King Thrushbeard. If only I knew!"

Soon they crossed a meadow, and she asked again:

"Tell me, who might the owner of this meadow be?"
"King Thrushbeard owns the meadow and all you can see.
If you had taken him, it would belong to you."
"Alas, poor me! What can I do?
I should have wed King Thrushbeard. If only I knew!"

Then they came to a large city, and she asked once more:

"Tell me, who might the owner of this city be?"
"King Thrushbeard owns the city and all you can see.
If you had taken him, it would belong to you."
"Alas, poor me! What can I do?
I should have wed King Thrushbeard. If only I knew!"

"I'm not at all pleased by this," said the minstrel. "Why are you always wishing for another husband? Do you think I'm not good enough for you?"

Finally, they came to a tiny cottage, and she said:

"Oh, Lord! What a wretched tiny house!
It's not even fit for a mouse."

The minstrel answered, "This house is mine and yours, and we shall live here together."

She had to stoop to get through the low doorway.

"Where are the servants?" the king's daughter asked.

"What servants?" answered the beggar. "You must do everything yourself if you want something done. Now, make a fire at once and put the water on so you can cook me my meal. I'm very tired."

However, the king's daughter knew nothing about making a fire or cooking, and the beggar had to lend a hand himself if he wanted anything done in a tolerable fashion. After they had eaten their meager meal, they went to bed. But the next morning he got her up very early because she had to take care of the house. For a few days they lived like this and managed as best they could. When they had consumed all their provisions, the man said, "Wife, we can't go on this way any longer. We've used everything up, and we're not earning a thing. You've got to weave baskets."

He went out to cut some willows and brought them home, but the rough willows bruised her tender hands.

"I see that won't work," said the man. "Let's try spinning. Perhaps you'll be better at that."

She sat down at the spinning wheel and tried to spin, but the hard thread soon cut her soft fingers, and blood began to flow.

"See now," said the man. "You're not fit for any kind of work. I made a bad bargain when I got you. But let's see how things go if I start a business with pots and earthenware. You're to sit in the marketplace and sell the wares."

Oh, she thought, if some people from my father's kingdom come to the marketplace and see me selling wares, they'll surely make fun of me!

But there was no way to avoid it. She had to obey her husband if she did not want to die of hunger. The first time everything went well. People gladly bought her wares because she was beautiful, and they paid what she asked. Indeed, many gave her money and did not even bother to take the pots with them. So the couple lived off their earnings as long as they lasted. Then her husband bought a lot of new earthenware. His wife sat down with it at a corner in the marketplace, set her wares around her, and offered them for sale. Suddenly, a drunken hussar came galloping along and rode right over the pots so that they were all smashed to pieces. She began to weep and was paralyzed with fear.

"Oh, what's going to happen to me!" she exclaimed. "What will my husband say?"

She ran home and told him about the accident, and he responded by saying, "In heaven's name, who would ever sit down at a corner in the marketplace with earthenware? Now stop your weeping. I see full well that you're not fit for proper work. I've already been to the king's castle and have asked whether they could use a kitchen maid, and they've promised me to take you on. In return you'll get free meals.''

Now the king's daughter became a kitchen maid and had to assist the cook and do the lowest kind of work. She sewed two little jars inside her pockets and carried home the leftovers so they could have some food to live on. One day it happened that the king's oldest son was celebrating his wedding, and the poor woman went upstairs, stood outside the door of the large hall, and wanted to look inside. When the candles were lit, each guest entered, one more exquisitely dressed than the next, and everything was full of splendor. With a sad heart she thought about her fate and cursed her pride and arrogance for bringing about her humiliation and great poverty. Sometimes the servants threw her pieces of the delicious dishes they were carrying in and out of the hall, and she could also smell the aroma of the food. She put the pieces into her pockets and intended to carry them home.

Suddenly the king's son entered. He was dressed in velvet and silk and had a golden chain around his neck. And, when he saw the beautiful woman standing in the doorway, he grabbed her by the hand and wanted to dance with her, but she refused. Indeed, she was horrified because she saw it was King Thrushbeard, who had courted her and whom she had rejected with scorn. Although she struggled, it was to no avail, for he pulled her into the hall. Then the string that held her pockets together broke, and the jars fell out, causing the soup to spill and the scraps of food to scatter on the floor. When the people saw that, they laughed a good deal and poked fun at her. She was so ashamed that she wished she were a thousand fathoms under the earth. She ran out the door and tried to escape, but a man caught up with her on the stairs and brought her back. When she looked at him, she saw it was King Thrushbeard again, and he said to her in a friendly way, ''Don't be afraid. I and the minstrel who lived with you in the wretched cottage are one and the same person. I disguised myself out of love for you, and I was also the hussar who rode over your pots and smashed them to pieces. I did all that to humble your proud spirit and to punish you for the insolent way you behaved toward me.''

Then she shed bitter tears and said, ''I've done a great wrong and don't deserve to be your wife.''

However, he said, ''Console yourself. The bad days are over. Now we shall celebrate our wedding.''

The chambermaids came and dressed her in splendid clothes, and her father came along with his entire court, and they wished her happiness in her marriage with King Thrushbeard. Then the real rejoicing began, and I wish that you and I had been there too.

❖ 53 ❖

Snow White

ONCE UPON A TIME, in the middle of winter, when snowflakes were falling like feathers from the sky, a queen was sitting and sewing at a window with a black ebony frame. And as she was sewing and looking out the window, she pricked her finger with the needle, and three drops of blood fell on the snow. The red looked so beautiful on the white snow that she thought to herself, If only I had a child as white as snow, as red as blood, and as black as the wood of the window frame!

Soon after she gave birth to a little daughter who was as white as snow, as red as blood, and her hair as black as ebony. Accordingly, the child was called Snow White, and right after she was born, the queen died. When a year had passed, the king married another woman, who was beautiful but proud and haughty, and she could not tolerate anyone else who might rival her beauty. She had a magic mirror and often she stood in front of it, looked at herself, and said:

"Mirror, mirror, on the wall,
who in this realm is the fairest of all?"

Then the mirror would answer:

"You, my queen, are the fairest of all."

That reply would make her content, for she knew the mirror always told the truth.

In the meantime, Snow White grew up and became more and

more beautiful. By the time she was seven years old, she was as beautiful as the day is clear and more beautiful than the queen herself. One day when the queen asked her mirror:

"Mirror, mirror, on the wall,
who in this realm is the fairest of all?"

The mirror answered:

"You, my queen, may have a beauty quite rare,
but Snow White is a thousand times more fair."

The queen shuddered and became yellow and green with envy. From that hour on, her hate for the girl was so great that her heart throbbed and turned in her breast each time she saw Snow White. Like weeds, the envy and arrogance grew so dense in her heart that she no longer had any peace, day or night. Finally, she summoned a huntsman and said, "Take the child out into the forest. I never want to lay eyes on her again. You are to kill her and to bring me back her lungs and liver as proof of your deed."

The huntsman obeyed and led Snow White out into the forest, but when he drew his hunting knife and was about to stab Snow White's innocent heart, she began to weep and said, "Oh, dear huntsman, spare my life, and I'll run into the wild forest and never come home again."

Since she was so beautiful, the huntsman took pity on her and said, "You're free to go, my poor child!" Then he thought, The wild beasts will soon eat you up. Nevertheless, he felt as if a great weight had been lifted off his mind, because he did not have to kill her. Just then a young boar came dashing by, and the huntsman stabbed it to death. He took out the lungs and liver and brought them to the queen as proof that the child was dead. The cook was ordered to boil them in salt, and the wicked woman ate them and thought that she had eaten Snow White's lungs and liver.

Meanwhile, the poor child was all alone in the huge forest. When she looked at all the leaves on the trees, she was petrified and did not know what to do. Then she began to run, and she ran over sharp stones and through thornbushes. Wild beasts darted by her at times, but they did not harm her. She ran as long as her legs could carry her, and it was almost evening when she saw a little cottage and went inside to rest. Everything was tiny in the cottage and indescribably dainty and neat. There was a little table with a white tablecloth, and on it were seven little plates. Each plate had a tiny spoon next to it, and there were also seven tiny knives and forks and seven tiny cups. In a row against the wall stood seven little beds covered with sheets as white as snow. Since she was so hungry and thirsty, Snow White ate some vegetables and bread from each of the little plates and had a drop of wine to drink out of each of the tiny cups, for she did not want to take everything from just one place. After that she was tired and began trying out the beds, but none of them suited her at first: one was too long, another too short, but at last, she found that the seventh one was just right. So she stayed in that bed, said her prayers, and fell asleep.

When it was completely dark outside, the owners of the cottage returned. They were seven dwarfs who searched in the mountains for minerals with their picks and shovels. They lit their seven little candles, and when it became light in the house, they saw that someone had been there, for none of their things was in the exact same spot in which it had been left.

"Who's been sitting in my chair?" said the first dwarf.

"Who's been eating off my plate?" said the second.

"Who's been eating my bread?" said the third.

"Who's been eating my vegetables?" said the fourth.

"Who's been using my fork?" said the fifth.

"Who's been cutting with my knife?" said the sixth.

"Who's been drinking from my cup?" said the seventh.

Then the first dwarf looked around and noticed that his bed had been wrinkled and said, "Who's been sleeping in my bed?"

The others ran over to their beds and cried out, "Someone's been sleeping in my bed too!"

But when the seventh dwarf looked at his bed, he saw Snow White lying there asleep. So he called the others over to him, and when they came, they were so astounded that they fetched their seven little candles to allow more light to shine on Snow White.

"Oh, my Lord! Oh, my Lord!" they exclaimed. "What a beautiful child!"

They were so delirious with joy that they did not wake her up. Instead, they let her sleep in the bed, while the seventh dwarf spent an hour in each one of his companions' beds until the night had passed. In the morning Snow White awoke, and when she saw the seven dwarfs, she was frightened. But they were friendly and asked, "What's your name?"

"My name's Snow White," she replied.

"What's brought you to our house?" the dwarfs continued.

She told them how her stepmother had ordered her to be killed, how the huntsman had spared her life, and how she had run all day until she had eventually discovered their cottage.

Then the dwarfs said, "If you'll keep house for us, cook, make the beds, wash, sew, and knit, and if you'll keep everything neat and orderly, you can stay with us, and we'll provide you with everything you need."

"Yes," agreed Snow White, "with all my heart."

So she stayed with them and kept their house in order. In the morning they went to the mountains to search for minerals and gold. In the evening they returned, and their dinner had to be ready. During the day Snow White was alone, and the good dwarfs made sure to caution her.

"Beware of your stepmother," they said. "She'll soon know that you're here. Don't let anybody in!"

Since the queen believed she had eaten Snow White's liver and lungs, she was totally convinced that she was again the most beautiful woman in the realm. And when she went to her mirror, she said:

"Mirror, mirror, on the wall,
who in this realm is the fairest of all?"

The mirror answered:

"You, my queen, may have a beauty quite rare,
but beyond the mountains, where the seven dwarfs dwell,
Snow White is thriving, and this I must tell:
Within this realm she's still a thousand times more fair."

The queen was horrified, for she knew that the mirror never lied, which meant that the huntsman had deceived her and Snow White was still alive. Once more she began plotting ways to kill her. As long as Snow White was the fairest in the realm, the queen's envy would leave her no peace. Finally, she thought up a plan. She painted her face and dressed as an old peddler woman so that nobody could recognize her. Then she crossed the seven mountains in this disguise and arrived at the cottage of the seven dwarfs, where she knocked at the door and cried out, "Pretty wares for sale! Pretty wares!"

Snow White looked out of the window and called out, "Good day, dear woman, what do you have for sale?"

"Nice and pretty things! Staylaces in all kinds of colors!" she replied and took out a lace woven from silk of many different colors.

I can certainly let this honest woman inside, Snow White thought. She unbolted the door and bought the pretty lace.

"My goodness, child! What a sight you are!" said the old woman. "Come, I'll lace you up properly for once."

Snow White did not suspect anything, so she stood in front of the old woman and let herself be laced with the new staylace. However, the old woman laced her so quickly and so tightly that Snow White lost her breath and fell down as if dead.

"Well, you used to be the fairest in the realm, but not now!" the old woman said and rushed off.

Not long after, at dinnertime, the dwarfs came home, and when they saw their dear Snow White lying on the ground, they were horrified. She neither stirred nor moved and seemed to be dead. They lifted her up, and when they saw that she was laced too tightly, they cut the staylace in two. At once she began to breathe a little, and after a while she had fully revived. When the dwarfs heard what had happened, they said, "The old peddler woman was none other than the wicked queen! Beware, don't let anyone in when we're not with you!"

When the evil woman returned home, she went to her mirror and asked:

"Mirror, mirror, on the wall,
who in this realm is the fairest of all?"

Then the mirror answered as usual:

> "You, my queen, may have a beauty quite rare,
> but beyond the mountains, where the seven dwarfs dwell,
> Snow White is thriving, and this I must tell:
> Within this realm she's still a thousand times more fair."

When the queen heard that, she was so upset that all her blood rushed to her heart, for she realized that Snow White had recovered. "This time I'm going to think of something that will destroy her," she said, and by using all the witchcraft at her command, she made a poison comb. Then she again disguised herself as an old woman and crossed the seven mountains to the cottage of the seven dwarfs, where she knocked at the door and cried out, "Pretty wares for sale! Pretty wares!"

Snow White looked out the window and said, "Go away! I'm not allowed to let anyone in."

"But surely you're allowed to look," said the old woman, and she took out the poison comb and held it up in the air. The comb pleased the girl so much that she let herself be carried away and opened the door. After they agreed on the price, the old woman said, "Now I'll give your hair a proper combing for once."

Poor Snow White did not give this a second thought and let the old woman do as she wished. But no sooner did the comb touch her hair than the poison began to take effect, and the maiden fell to the ground and lay there unconscious.

"You paragon of beauty!" said the wicked woman. "Now you're finished!" And she went away.

Fortunately, it was nearly evening, the time when the seven dwarfs began heading home. And, when they arrived and saw Snow White lying on the ground as if she were dead, they immediately suspected the stepmother and began looking around. As soon as they found the poison comb, they took it out, and Snow White instantly regained consciousness. She told them what had happened, and they warned her again to be on her guard and not to open the door for anyone.

In the meantime, the queen returned home, went to the mirror, and said:

> "Mirror, mirror, on the wall,
> who in this realm is the fairest of all?"

Then the mirror answered as before:

"You, my queen, may have a beauty quite rare,
but beyond the mountains, where the seven dwarfs dwell,
Snow White is thriving, and this I must tell:
Within this realm she's still a thousand times more fair."

When she heard the mirror's words, she trembled and shook with rage.

"Snow White shall die!" she exclaimed. "Even if it costs me my own life!"

Then she went into a secret and solitary chamber where no one else ever went. Once inside she made a deadly poisonous apple. On the outside it looked beautiful—white with red cheeks. Anyone who saw it would be enticed, but whoever took a bite was bound to die. When the apple was ready, the queen painted her face and dressed herself up as a peasant woman and crossed the seven mountains to the cottage of the seven dwarfs. When she knocked at the door, Snow White stuck her head out of the window and said, "I'm not allowed to let anyone inside. The seven dwarfs have forbidden me."

"That's all right with me," answered the peasant woman. "I'll surely get rid of my apples in time. But let me give you one as a gift."

"No," said Snow White. "I'm not allowed to take anything."

"Are you afraid that it might be poisoned?" said the old woman. "Look, I'll cut the apple in two. You eat the red part, and I'll eat the white."

However, the apple had been made with such cunning that only the red part was poisoned. Snow White was eager to eat the beautiful apple, and when she saw the peasant woman eating her half, she could no longer resist, stretched out her hand, and took the poisoned half. No sooner did she take a bite than she fell to the ground dead. The queen stared at her with a cruel look, then burst out laughing and said, "White as snow, red as blood, black as ebony! This time the dwarfs won't be able to bring you back to life!"

When she got home, she asked the mirror:

"Mirror, mirror, on the wall,
who in this realm is the fairest of all?"

Then the mirror finally answered, "You, my queen, are now the fairest of all." So her jealous heart was satisfied as much as a jealous heart can be satisfied.

When the dwarfs came home that evening, they found Snow White lying on the ground. There was no breath coming from her lips, and she was dead. They lifted her up and looked to see if they could find something poisonous. They unlaced her, combed her hair, washed her with water and wine, but it was to no avail. The dear child was dead and remained dead. They laid her on a bier, and all seven of them sat down beside it and mourned over her. They wept for three whole days, and then they intended to bury her, but she looked so alive and still had such pretty red cheeks that they said, "We can't possibly bury her in the dingy ground."

Instead, they made a transparent glass coffin so that she could be seen from all sides. Then they put her in it, wrote her name on it in gold letters, and added that she was a princess. They carried the coffin to the top of the mountain, and from then on one of them always stayed beside it and guarded it. Some animals came also and wept for Snow White. There was an owl, then a raven, and finally a dove. Snow White lay in the coffin for many, many years and did not decay. Indeed, she seemed to be sleeping, for she was still as white as snow, as red as blood, and her hair as black as ebony.

Now it happened that a prince came to the forest one day, and when he arrived at the dwarfs' cottage, he decided to spend the night. Then he went to the mountain and saw the coffin with beautiful Snow White inside. After he read what was written on the coffin in gold letters, he said to the dwarfs, "Let me have the coffin, and I'll pay you whatever you want."

But the dwarfs answered, "We won't give it up for all the gold in the world."

"Then give it to me as a gift," he said, "for I can't go on living without being able to see Snow White. I'll honor her and cherish her as my dearly beloved."

Since he spoke with such fervor, the good dwarfs took pity on him and gave him the coffin. The prince ordered his servants to carry the coffin on their shoulders, but they stumbled over some shrubs, and the jolt caused the poisoned piece of apple that Snow White had bitten off to be released from her throat. It was not long before she opened her eyes, lifted up the lid of the coffin, sat up, and was alive again.

"Oh, Lord! Where am I?" she exclaimed.

The prince rejoiced and said, "You're with me," and he told her what had happened. Then he added, "I love you more than anything else in the world. Come with me to my father's castle. I want you to be my wife."

Snow White felt that he was sincere, so she went with him, and their wedding was celebrated with great pomp and splendor.

Now, Snow White's stepmother had also been invited to the

wedding celebration, and after she had dressed herself in beautiful clothes, she went to the mirror and said:

"Mirror, mirror, on the wall,
who in this realm is the fairest of all?"

The mirror answered:

"You, my queen, may have a beauty quite rare,
but Snow White is a thousand times more fair."

The evil woman uttered a loud curse and became so terribly afraid that she did not know what to do. At first she did not want to go to the wedding celebration. But, she could not calm herself until she saw the young queen. When she entered the hall, she recognized Snow White. The evil queen was so petrified with fright that she could not budge. Iron slippers had already been heated over a fire, and they were brought over to her with tongs. Finally, she had to put on the red-hot slippers and dance until she fell down dead.

◈ 54 ◈

The Knapsack, the Hat, and the Horn

ONCE UPON A TIME there were three brothers who found themselves getting poorer and poorer. Eventually their plight became so great that they had nothing to eat and were starving.

"We can't go on like this," they said. "We'd better go out into the world and see if we can change our luck."

So they set out and traveled quite some distance. Their way took them over fields of green grass, but they did not encounter much luck. Then one day they reached a large forest, and in the middle of the forest there was a mountain. When they came closer, they saw that the mountain was all silver.

"Now that I've found the good luck that I was searching for," said the oldest, "I don't want anything more."

He took as much of the silver as he could carry, turned around, and went back home. But the others said, "We expect much more from our luck than mere silver."

Indeed, they did not touch any of the silver and continued on their way. After they had traveled a few more days, they came to a mountain that was all gold. The second brother stopped, pondered the situation, and was undecided.

"What should I do?" he asked. "Should I take enough gold to last me the rest of my life, or should I continue on my way?"

Finally, he decided to fill his pockets with as much gold as they could hold, said farewell to his brother, and went home. But the third brother said, "Silver and gold mean nothing to me. I won't give up on my luck. Maybe I'll come across something better."

He went on, and after three days he came to a forest that was so much greater than the others that it appeared to be endless. Since he had found nothing to eat or drink, he was at the point of collapsing and decided to climb a tree to find out whether he could see the end of the forest. However, there were nothing but treetops as far as his eyes could see. Tormented by hunger, he climbed down the tree and said to himself, "If only I could get something to fill my stomach once more!" When he reached the bottom of the tree, he was amazed to find a table spread with food, and his nose picked up the aroma.

"This time," he said, "my wish has been granted in the nick of time!"

Without asking who had brought the food and who had cooked it, he approached the table and ate heartily until he had satisfied his hunger. When he was finished, he thought, It would be a shame to leave this fine tablecloth out here in the forest where it might be ruined. So he folded it neatly and put it into his knapsack. Then he moved on, and in the evening when he grew hungry again, he decided to test his little tablecloth. After spreading it out on the ground, he said, "I wish you were covered again with good food." No sooner did he utter his wish than the tablecloth was covered with the most delicious kinds of food. "Now I realize in what kitchen the cooking's been done for me," he said. "You're more precious to me than mountains of silver and gold."

Indeed, he knew that he had a magic tablecloth. But the tablecloth was not enough to get him to return home and settle down. On the contrary, he wanted to continue traveling about the world and to keep trying his luck. One evening, as he was going through a lonely forest, he met a charcoal burner covered with black soot. The charcoal burner was preparing a meal of baked potatoes on a fire.

"Good evening, blackbird," said the traveler. "How are things in this lonely place?"

"One day's just like the next," responded the charcoal burner, "and every night, potatoes. Would you like to have some? You can be my guest."

"No thanks," answered the traveler. "I don't want to take away your meal. You weren't counting on a guest, but if you'll put up with me, I'd like to invite you to a meal."

"Who's going to prepare it for you?" said the charcoal burner. "You apparently don't have anything with you, and there's nobody within miles of here who could bring you something."

"Despite that, you shall have the most delicious meal you've ever tasted," he answered. Then the traveler took the tablecloth from his knapsack, spread it on the ground, and said, "Table, be covered!"

All at once there were boiled and roasted meats, and they were as hot as if they had just come out of the kitchen. The charcoal burner gaped, but he did not have to be asked twice to help himself to the food. Indeed, he shoveled bigger and bigger pieces of meat into his black mouth. When they had eaten their fill, the charcoal burner grinned and said, "Listen, your tablecloth has won my approval. Something like that would be perfect for me in this forest, where nobody ever cooks anything for me. Let me propose an exchange: there's an old soldier's knapsack hanging in the corner. It's clearly a plain old thing, but it has miraculous powers. Since I no longer need it, I'll let you have it in exchange for the tablecloth."

"First I must know what kind of miraculous powers they are," responded the traveler.

"Let me tell you," answered the charcoal burner. "If you tap it with your hand, a corporal will appear with six men armed from head to foot, and whatever you command, they will carry it out."

"As far as I'm concerned, it's a deal," said the traveler. "Let's exchange."

He gave the charcoal burner the tablecloth, took the knapsack off the hook, slung it over his shoulder, and said good-bye. When he had gone a short distance, he decided to test the knapsack's miraculous powers and tapped it. All at once seven stalwart soldiers appeared, and the corporal said, "What does my lord and master desire?"

"I want you to march back to the charcoal burner on the double and demand my magic tablecloth from him."

They did an about-face to the left, and before he knew it, they were back with the tablecloth, which they had taken from the charcoal burner without much trouble. Now the traveler ordered them to retire, and he continued his journey hoping that his luck would shine even brighter. At sundown he came across another charcoal burner who was preparing dinner by a fire.

"Would you care to join me?" asked the sooty fellow. "Potatoes with salt, but no grease. If you want some, just sit down by my side."

"No thanks," he said. "This time you shall be my guest." And he spread his tablecloth on the ground. A moment later it was covered with the most delicious dishes. They ate and drank together and were in good spirits. After the meal the charcoal burner said, "Up there on the shelf there's an old worn-out hat that has strange powers. As soon as someone puts it on and turns it around on his head, cannons will begin firing just as if twelve in a row went off at the same time. There's nothing that can withstand them, for they can demolish anything in sight. The hat is of no use to me, and I'd gladly exchange it for your tablecloth."

"It's a deal," the traveler answered. He took the hat, put it on, and left the tablecloth behind. Yet, no sooner had he gone a short distance than he tapped his knapsack, and his soldiers fetched the tablecloth for him once again. "One thing follows the next," he thought. "I feel as if my luck hasn't run out yet." And his intuition did not deceive him.

After he had traveled another day, he came across a third charcoal burner who invited him to eat a meal of potatoes without grease, just like the others. Once more the traveler invited the charcoal burner to join him in a meal set by his magic tablecloth, and the charcoal burner enjoyed the food so much that he offered him a horn in exchange for the tablecloth. This horn had very different powers from those of the hat. As soon as it was blown, first the walls and fortifications would be turned to rubble, and then cities and villages would be leveled. Of course, the traveler did not hesitate to give up the magic tablecloth for the horn, but later on he sent his team of soldiers to demand it back. At length he had accumulated all three things, the knapsack, the hat, and the horn.

"Now, I'm a made man," he said, "and it's time to return home and see how my brothers are doing."

By the time he returned home, his brothers had built a beautiful house with their silver and gold and were leading a carefree life. Yet, when he entered their house, his brothers refused to recognize him as their brother because he was wearing a tattered coat, a shabby hat on his head, and a battered knapsack on his back. Instead, they ridiculed him and said, "You're an impostor! Our brother scorned silver and gold to follow his lucky star. When he returns here, it won't be as a beggar but as a mighty king in full splendor and riding in a carriage."

Upon saying that, they drove him out of the house, but he became so enraged that he tapped his knapsack and kept tapping it until one hundred and fifty men stood before him in a row. He ordered them to surround his brothers' house, and two of them were to take hazel switches and whip his insolent brothers until they knew who he was. There was a tremendous uproar, and people ran to help the two brothers in their predicament, but they could do nothing against the soldiers. Eventually, the king got wind of this, and in his anger he ordered a captain to take a company of soldiers and to drive the

· 225 ·

troublemaker from the city. But the man with the knapsack responded by assembling a huge troop of soldiers who forced the captain and his men to retreat with bloody noses.

"I'll bring this vagabond under control yet!" the king said.

The following day the king sent an even larger company against him, but it managed to accomplish even less than the other one. The man with the knapsack called up even more soldiers to oppose the king's men, and since he wanted to end everything quickly, he turned his hat around on his head a few times. Then the heavy artillery came into play, and the king's men were devastated and forced to flee.

"I'm not going to make peace," he said, "until the king gives me his daughter for my wife and I rule the entire kingdom in his name."

The king was informed of this declaration, and he said to his daughter, "Necessity is a tough nut to crack. There's nothing I can do but give in to his demand. If I am to have peace and keep the crown on my head, I must give you away."

So the marriage was celebrated, but the king's daughter was disturbed because her husband was a commoner who wore a shabby hat and an old knapsack on his back. She wanted very much to get rid of him and was constantly thinking of ways to do it. Then the thought occurred to her, Could it be that his miraculous powers are in the knapsack? So she feigned affection for him and caressed him, and when his heart softened, she said, "If only you would take off that wretched knapsack! It's so unbecoming that it makes me ashamed of you."

"My dear girl," he answered, "this knapsack is my greatest treasure. As long as I have it, I don't have to fear anything in the world." And he revealed to her the miraculous powers with which the knapsack was endowed. Then she embraced him as if she wanted to kiss him, but she nimbly lifted the knapsack from his shoulders and ran away with it. As soon as she was alone, she tapped it and commanded the soldiers to seize their former master and escort him out of the royal palace. They obeyed her, and the devious woman ordered more men to follow him and chase him right out of the country. He would certainly have been lost had he not been wearing his hat, and no sooner were his hands free than he turned the hat a few times. Within seconds cannons began to thunder and demolish everything in sight. The king's daughter herself had to go and beg for mercy. Since she pleaded so passionately and promised to change her ways for the better, he let himself be persuaded and granted her peace.

After that she pretended to be friendly and behaved as if she loved him. It did not take long before she succeeded in deceiving him, so he confided to her that, even if someone got hold of his knapsack, that person could do nothing against him as long as he had the old hat. Once she knew that secret, she waited until he fell asleep. Then she took the hat away from him and had him thrown out on the street.

He still had the horn, however, and his rage was so great that he blew it with all his might. All at once everything collapsed—the walls, the fortifications, the cities, and the villages—and the king and his daughter were crushed to death. If he had not stopped blowing at that point, everything would have been devastated, and not a single stone would have remained standing on top of another.

After that nobody dared to oppose him, and he made himself king of the entire country.

◈ 55 ◈

Rumpelstiltskin

ONCE UPON A TIME there was a miller who was poor, but he had a beautiful daughter. Now it happened that he was talking with the king one time, and in order to make himself seem important, he said to the king, "I have a daughter who can spin straw into gold."

"That is an art that pleases me!" the king replied. "If your daughter is as talented as you say, then bring her to my castle tomorrow, and I'll put her to a test."

When the maiden was brought to him, he led her into a room that was filled with straw. There he gave her a spinning wheel and spindle and said, "Now get to work! If you don't spin this straw into gold by morning, then you must die." Then he locked the door himself, and she remained inside all alone.

The miller's poor daughter sat there feeling close to her wits' end, for she knew nothing about spinning straw into gold, and her fear grew greater and greater. When she began to weep, the door suddenly opened, and a little man entered.

"Good evening, mistress miller, why are you weeping so?"

"Qh," answered the maiden, "I'm supposed to spin straw into gold, and I don't know how."

The little man then asked, "What will you give me if I spin it for you?"

"My necklace," the maiden said.

The little man took the necklace and sat down at the wheel, and *whizz, whizz, whizz*, three times round, the spool was full. Then he inserted another one, and *whizz, whizz, whizz*, the second was full. And so it went until morning, when all the straw was spun, and all the spools were filled with gold. The king appeared right at sunrise, and when he saw the gold, he was surprised and pleased, but his heart grew even greedier. He locked the miller's daughter in another room that was even larger than the first and ordered her to spin all the straw into gold if she valued her life. The maiden did not know what to do and began to weep. Once again the door opened, and the little man appeared and asked, "What will you give me if I spin the straw into gold for you?"

"The ring from my finger," answered the maiden.

The little man took the ring, began to work away at the wheel again, and by morning he had spun all the straw into shining gold. The king was extremely pleased by the sight, but his lust for gold was still not satisfied. So he had the miller's daughter brought into an even larger room filled with straw and said to her, "You must spin all this into gold tonight. If you succeed, you shall become my wife." To himself he thought, Even though she's just a miller's daughter, I'll never find a richer woman anywhere in the world.

When the maiden was alone, the little man came again for a third time and asked, "What will you give me if I spin the straw into gold once more?"

"I have nothing left to give," answered the maiden.

"Then promise me your first child when you become queen."

Who knows whether it will ever come to that? thought the miller's daughter. And since she knew of no other way out of her predicament, she promised the little man what he had demanded. In return the little man spun the straw into gold once again. When the king came in the morning and found everything as he had wished, he married her, and the beautiful miller's daughter became a queen.

After a year she gave birth to a beautiful child. The little man had disappeared from her mind, but now he suddenly appeared in her room and said, "Now give me what you promised."

The queen was horrified and offered the little man all the treasures of the kingdom if he would let her keep her child, but the little man replied, "No, something living is more important to me than all the treasures in the world."

Then the queen began to grieve and weep so much that the little man felt sorry for her. "I'll give you three days' time," he said. "If you can guess my name by the third day, you shall keep your child."

The queen spent the entire night trying to recall all the names she had ever heard. She also sent a messenger out into the country to inquire high and low what other names there were. On the following day, when the little man appeared, she began with Kaspar, Melchior, Balzer, and then repeated all the names she knew, one after the other. But to all of them, the little man said, "That's not my name."

The second day she had her servants ask around in the neighboring area what names people used, and she came up with the most unusual and strangest names when the little man appeared.

"Is your name Ribsofbeef or Muttonchops or Lacedleg?"

But he always replied, "That's not my name."

On the third day the messenger returned and reported, "I couldn't find a single new name, but as I was climbing a high mountain at the edge of the forest, where the fox and the hare say good night to each other, I saw a small cottage, and in front of the cottage was a fire, and around the fire danced a ridiculous little man who was hopping on one leg and screeching:

'Today I'll brew, tomorrow I'll bake.
Soon I'll have the queen's namesake.
Oh, how hard it is to play my game,
for Rumpelstiltskin is my name!' "

You can imagine how happy the queen was when she heard the name. And as soon as the little man entered and asked "What's my name, Your Highness?" she responded first by guessing.

"Is your name Kunz?"

"No."

"Is your name Heinz?"

"No."

"Can your name be Rumpelstiltskin?"

"The devil told you! The devil told you!" the little man screamed, and he stamped so ferociously with his right foot that his leg went deep into the ground up to his waist. Then he grabbed the other foot angrily with both hands and ripped himself in two.

❖ 56 ❖

Sweetheart Roland

ONCE UPON A TIME there was a woman who was a real witch, and she had two daughters, one ugly and evil, whom she loved because she was her own daughter, and the other beautiful and good, whom she hated because she was her stepdaughter. At one time the stepdaughter had a beautiful apron that the other daughter liked and coveted so much out of envy that she told her mother she wanted the apron and had to have it.

"Be quiet, my child," said the old woman. "You shall have it soon. Your stepsister has long since 'deserved to die, and tonight, when she's asleep, I'll come and chop off her head. Just make sure that you lie on the far side of the bed, and push her toward the front."

That would have been the end of the poor maiden had she not been standing in a corner and listening to everything. That day she was not allowed to go outside at all, and when bedtime came, the witch's daughter climbed into bed first so she could lie down on the far side. But after she fell asleep, the other sister pushed her gently toward the front and took her place on the far side, next to the wall. During the night the old woman crept into the room. She held an ax in her right hand and with her left hand felt around to see if someone was actually lying up front. Then she gripped the ax with both hands and began chopping until she chopped off her own child's head.

When she left the room, the maiden stood up and went to her sweetheart, whose name was Roland, and knocked at his door. When he came outside, she said to him, "Listen, dearest Roland, we must flee in haste. My stepmother tried to kill me, but she killed her own daughter instead. When the sun rises and she sees what she's done, we'll be lost."

"Before we go, you'd better take her magic wand first," said Roland. "Otherwise, we won't be able to escape if she comes after us."

The maiden fetched the magic wand, and she also took her dead sister's head and let three drops of blood drip on the floor, one in front of the bed, one in the kitchen, and one on the stairs. Then she hurried away with her sweetheart.

Now, when the witch got up the next morning, she called her daughter and wanted to give her the apron, but she did not come.

"Where are you?" she cried out.

"Here I am! On the stairs sweeping," answered one of the drops of blood.

The old woman went out but saw no one on the stairs and called out once again.

"Where are you?"

"Here I am! In the kitchen warming myself," the second drop of blood replied.

The old woman went into the kitchen, but she found no one there and called once again.

"Where are you?"

"Here I am! In bed sleeping," the third drop of blood cried.

The old woman went into the room and approached the bed. Yet, what did she see but her own daughter swimming in blood! And it was the witch herself who had chopped off her head.

The old woman became furious and rushed to the window. Since she could see quite far into the world, she spotted her stepdaughter fleeing with her sweetheart Roland.

"That won't help you!" she exclaimed. "Even though you've had a head start, you'll never escape me!" She put on her seven-league boots, in which she covered an hour's walk in one step, and it did not take her long before she had overtaken them. However, when the maiden saw the old woman coming, she used the magic wand to turn her sweetheart Roland into a lake and herself into a duck that swam in the middle of the lake. The witch stood on the shore, threw bread crumbs into the water, and tried her best to lure the duck to shore. But the duck would not let itself be enticed, and by nightfall the old woman had to turn back without having accomplished anything.

Meanwhile, the maiden and her sweetheart resumed their natural forms and continued walking the whole night through until daybreak. Then the maiden changed herself into a beautiful flower growing in the middle of a brier hedge, and her sweetheart was changed into a fiddler. Shortly after, the witch came striding along and said to the fiddler, "Dear fiddler, may I pluck the beautiful flower?"

"Of course," he answered, "and I'll play a tune while you're doing it."

Since she knew who the flower was, she quickly crawled into the hedge to pluck it. However, he began to play a tune, and willy-nilly she was compelled to dance because it was a magic melody. The faster he played, the more violent were the jumps she was forced to make, and the thorns tore the clothes from her body and scratched her so that blood flowed from her wounds. Since the fiddler did not let up, she had to keep dancing until she fell to the ground dead.

Once they were free, Roland said, "Now I'll go to my father and arrange for the wedding."

"In the meantime, I'll stay here and wait for you," said the maiden. "Just to make sure that nobody recognizes me, I'll turn myself into a red stone."

Roland departed, and the maiden lay in the field as a red stone and waited for her sweetheart. However, when Roland returned home, he was ensnared by another woman, who made him forget the maiden. Meanwhile, the poor maiden stayed in the field a long time, but when he failed to come back, she grew sad, turned herself into a flower, and thought, Someone will surely come along and trample me.

It so happened that a shepherd was tending his sheep on the field and saw the flower. Since it was so beautiful, he plucked the flower, took it with him, and tucked it away in a chest. From that time on, amazing things began to happen in the shepherd's cottage. When he got up in the morning, all the work would already be done: the room would be swept clean, the table and benches would be dusted, the fire in the hearth would be made, and water would be inside. At noon when he came home, the table would be set and a good meal would be served. He could not figure out how all this was happening, for he never saw a living soul, and his cottage was too small for anyone to hide in. Of course, he liked the good service, but eventually he became frightened and went to a wise woman to ask for her advice.

"There's magic behind all this," the wise woman said. "You must get up very early some morning and keep a lookout for anything that moves in the room. Then, if you see something, no matter what it is, quickly throw a white cloth over it. That will hold the magic in check."

The shepherd did as she told him, and on the following morning, right at daybreak, he saw the chest open and the flower come out. In the wink of an eye he ran over and threw the white cloth over the flower, and suddenly the transformation came to an end: a beautiful maiden stood before him, and she confessed that she had been the flower and had kept house for him. Then she told him about her adventures, and since he took a liking to her, he asked her to marry him. However, she answered no, because she wanted to remain true to her sweetheart Roland, even though he had forsaken her. Still, she promised the shepherd that she would remain there and continue to keep house for him.

Now the time had come for Roland to celebrate his wedding. According to the old custom of that country, a proclamation was issued, and all the girls were to gather together at the wedding and sing in honor of the bridal pair. When the faithful maiden heard about this, she grew so sad that she thought her heart would burst. She did not want to go to the wedding, but the other girls came and took her with them. Whenever her turn came to sing, she would step back, but finally she was the only one left and was obliged to sing a song. As she began to sing and her voice reached Roland's ears, he jumped up and exclaimed, ''I know that voice! That's my true bride. I don't want anyone else.''

Everything that he had forgotten and everything that had vanished from his mind suddenly filled his heart again. So the faithful maiden married her sweetheart Roland. Her sorrows came to an end just as her joy began to flourish.

◆ 57 ◆

The Golden Bird

IN DAYS OF OLD there was a king who had a beautiful pleasure garden behind his castle, and in this garden there was a tree that bore golden apples. After the apples became ripe, they were counted, but on the very next morning one was missing. This was reported to the king, and he ordered the tree to be guarded every night.

Now, the king had three sons, and at nightfall he sent the oldest to the garden. When midnight came, however, he could not prevent himself from sleeping, and the next morning another apple was missing. The following night the second son had to keep watch, but he did not fare any better. When the clock struck twelve, he fell asleep, and in the morning another apple was missing. Then it was the third son's turn to keep watch. He was also ready, but the king did not trust him and thought he would do even worse than his brothers. Finally, he gave him permission, and the young prince lay down under the tree, kept watch, and fought off sleep. When the clock struck twelve, there was a rustling above him, and in the moonlight he saw a bird flying through the air. The bird's feathers were made of pure gold and glistened as it descended onto the tree. When the bird pecked off an apple, the young prince shot an arrow at it. The bird flew off, but the arrow clipped one of the golden feathers, and it dropped to the ground. The young prince picked up the feather, brought it to the king the next morning, and told him what had happened during the night. The king assembled his councillors and everyone declared that a feather like this was worth more than the entire kingdom.

"If the feather is so precious," the king announced, "then one alone won't do for me. I must have, and intend to have, the whole bird."

So the oldest son set out; he believed he would certainly find the bird because he was so clever. After he had gone a short way, he saw a fox sitting at the edge of a forest, took aim with his gun, and was about to fire when the fox cried out, "Don't shoot! I'll give you some good advice if you hold your fire. You're on the right way to the golden bird, and tonight you'll come to a village where you'll see two inns facing each other. One will be brightly lit with a great deal of merrymaking inside. Be sure you keep away from that place. Instead, you should go into the other inn, even though it looks dismal."

How can such a foolish beast give sensible advice? thought the prince, and he pulled the trigger. However, his shot missed the fox, who stretched out his tail and dashed quickly into the forest. Then the prince continued his journey, and by evening he arrived at the village where the two inns were standing: in one of them there was singing and dancing, while the other appeared rather dismal and shabby.

I'd certainly be a fool, he thought, if I were to stay at that dismal-looking inn instead of staying at this fine one here. So he went into the cheerful inn, lived to the hilt like a king, and forgot the bird, his father, and all the good lessons he had ever learned.

After some time had passed, it became clear that the oldest son would not return. Therefore, the second son set out to look for the golden bird. Like the oldest son, he too met the fox, who gave him good advice that he did not heed. He came to the two inns and saw his brother at the window of the inn in which there were sounds of carousing. When his brother called out to him, he could not resist; he went inside and began living only to satisfy his lust.

Some more time passed, and now the youngest prince wanted to set out and try his luck. But his father would not let him.

"It's no use," the king said. "He'll have less of a chance of finding the golden bird than his brothers. And, if he has a mishap, he won't know how to fend for himself. He's not the smartest person in the world."

However, the prince kept insisting, and the king finally gave him permission to set out. Once again the fox was sitting at the edge of the forest, pleaded for his life, and gave good advice. Since the young prince was good-natured, he said, "Don't worry, little fox, I won't harm you."

"You won't regret it," answered the fox. "Now climb on my tail, and I'll help you get there more quickly."

No sooner did the prince sit down on the fox's tail than the fox began to run. And he went up hill and down dale so swiftly that the wind whistled through the prince's hair. When they came to the village, the prince got off the tail, followed the fox's good advice, and, without looking around, entered the shabbier inn. After spending a pleasant night there, he went out to the field the next morning and found the fox already sitting on the ground.

"I'm going to tell you what else you've got to do," said the fox. "If you go straight ahead, you'll eventually come to a castle. In front of this castle there's a whole troop of soldiers lying on the ground, but don't pay any attention to them, for they'll all be snoring and sleeping. Go right through the middle of their ranks and straight into the castle. Next, you're to go through all the rooms until you come to a chamber where the golden bird is hanging in a wooden cage. Nearby you'll also find a golden cage hanging just for decoration. But be careful not to take the bird out of its plain cage and put it into the splendid one. Otherwise, you'll be in for trouble."

Upon saying these words, the fox stretched out his tail again, and the prince sat down on it. The fox raced up hill and down dale so swiftly that the wind whistled through the prince's hair. When the prince arrived at the castle, he found everything just as the fox had said it would be. Upon entering the last room, he saw the golden bird sitting in its wooden cage and also a golden cage beside it. The three golden apples were lying about the room as well. The prince thought it would be ridiculous to leave the beautiful bird in the plain, ugly cage. So he opened the door, grabbed hold of the bird, and put it into the golden cage. At that very moment the bird uttered a piercing cry that caused the soldiers to wake up; they rushed inside and took him off to prison. The next morning he was brought before the court, and after he confessed to everything, he was sentenced to death. However, the king said he would spare his life under one condition: the prince had to promise to bring him the golden horse that ran faster than the wind; if he did, he would receive the golden bird as his reward.

The prince set out, but he sighed and grew sad, for he did not know where to find the golden horse. Suddenly, he saw his old friend the fox again, sitting by the roadside.

"You see," said the fox, "all this happened because you didn't listen to me. However, keep your spirits up. I'm here to assist you, and I'll tell you how to get the golden horse. First, you must go straight ahead until you come to a castle where the horse is standing in the stable. There will be grooms lying on the ground in front of the stable, but they'll be snoring and sleeping, and you'll be able to lead the golden horse out of its stall with ease. But make sure you put the plain wooden and leather saddle on the horse and not the golden one that's hanging nearby. Otherwise, you'll be in for trouble."

Then the fox stretched out its tail, and the prince sat down on it. The fox raced up hill and down dale so swiftly that the wind whistled through the prince's hair. Shortly after, everything happened as the fox said it would. The prince entered the stable where the golden horse was standing. However, when he was about to put the saddle on the horse, he thought, I'd be putting this beautiful horse to shame if I didn't give it the fine saddle that it deserves! Yet, no sooner did the golden saddle touch the horse than it began to neigh loudly, which caused the grooms to wake up; they seized the prince and threw him into prison. The next morning he was sentenced to death by the court. However, the king promised to spare his life and grant him the golden horse, as well, if the prince would fetch him the beautiful princess from the golden castle.

Now, the prince set out with a heavy heart, but fortunately for him he soon encountered the faithful fox.

"I really should leave you to your bad luck," said the fox, "but I feel sorry for you and want to help you out of your difficulty. This path leads directly to the golden castle. You'll arrive there in the evening, and at night, when everything's quiet, the beautiful princess will go to the bathhouse to bathe herself. When she goes there, you're to run up to her and give her a kiss. Then she'll follow you, and you can take her with you. But don't allow her to take leave of her parents. Otherwise, you'll be in for trouble."

The fox stretched out his tail, and the prince sat down on it. The fox raced up hill and down dale so swiftly that the wind whistled through the prince's hair. When he arrived at the golden castle, it was just as the fox had said it would be. The prince waited until midnight, when everyone lay in a deep sleep and the beautiful maiden went to the bathhouse. Then he ran up to her and gave her a kiss. She said she would gladly go with him, but she implored him with tears to let her say farewell to her parents. At first he resisted her pleas, but when she kept on weeping and fell at his feet, he finally gave in. But no sooner did the maiden approach her father's bed than he and everyone else in the castle woke up, and the prince was seized and put in prison. The next morning the king said to him, "Your life is worth nothing, and you'll be pardoned only if you take away the mountain that's lying in front of my window and blocking my view. If you successfully perform this task within eight days, you shall have my daughter as reward."

The prince began to dig and shovel without stopping, but when he saw how little he had accomplished after seven days, that all his work amounted to nothing, he gave up all hope and became very depressed. However, on the evening of the seventh day, the fox appeared and said, "You don't deserve my assistance, but just go and get some sleep. I'll do the job for you."

The next morning, when the prince awoke and looked out the window, the mountain had vanished. His heart filled with joy, and he rushed to the king and reported that he had completed his task. Whether the king liked it or not, he had to keep his word and give him his daughter.

The prince and the king's daughter now set out together, and it did not take long before the faithful fox joined them.

"Nothing could be better than what you have now," said the fox, "but the golden horse goes along with the princess from the golden castle."

"How am I to get it?" asked the prince.

"I'll tell you," answered the fox. "First you must bring the beautiful maiden to the king who sent you to the golden castle. There will be enormous rejoicing, and they'll gladly give you the golden horse. When they lead it out, mount it right away and shake hands with everyone and say good-bye. Make sure that the beautiful maiden is the last person, and when you have clasped her hand, swing her up to you in one motion and gallop away. Nobody can possibly catch you, for the horse runs faster than the wind."

Everything went as planned, and the prince carried off the beautiful maiden on the golden horse. The fox followed them, and then he said to the prince, "Now I'll help you get the golden bird. As you begin approaching the castle where the golden bird's being kept, let the maiden get down from the horse, and I'll look after her. Then ride the golden horse into the castle courtyard. There will be great rejoicing at the sight of the golden horse, and they'll carry out the golden bird. As soon as you have the cage in your hand, race away and fetch the princess."

After this plan had also been successfully carried out and the prince was about to ride home with his treasures, the fox said, "Now I want you to reward me for my help."

"What would you like?" asked the prince.

"When we come to the forest, I want you to shoot me dead and cut off my head and paws."

"What kind of gratitude is that?" said the prince. "I can't possibly do what you wish."

"If you won't do it, I'll have to leave you. But before I depart, I want to give you one last piece of advice. Beware of two things: don't buy flesh that's bound for the gallows, and don't sit on the edge of a well." Upon saying that, the fox ran into the forest.

What a strange animal! the prince thought. He's got all kinds of weird notions. Who would want to buy flesh bound for the gallows? And I've never had any desire to sit on the edge of a well.

He continued his journey with the beautiful maiden, and his way led again through the village where his two brothers had remained. Upon noticing that there was a great commotion and uproar, he asked what was going on and was told that two men were about to be hanged. When he came closer to the scene, he saw that the men were his brothers, who had committed all sorts of terrible acts and had squandered all their possessions. He asked whether they could be pardoned in some way.

"If you're willing to buy their freedom," the people answered. "But why would you want to waste your money on such evil criminals and set them free?"

However, he did not think twice about it and purchased their freedom. When they were released, he continued the journey in the company of his brothers. After some time they came to the forest where they had first met the fox, and since it was cool and lovely there and the sun was very hot, the two brothers said, "Let's go over to the well and rest awhile. We could also eat and drink."

He agreed, and during their conversation he forgot the fox's warning and sat down on the edge of the well, not suspecting anything evil. But the two brothers pushed him backward into the well, took the maiden, the horse, and the bird, and went home to their father.

"Not only have we brought you the golden bird," they said to the king, "but we've also got the golden horse and the maiden from the golden castle."

There was a great celebration, but the horse refused to eat, the bird did not sing, and the maiden sat and wept.

Meanwhile, the youngest brother managed to survive. Fortunately, the well had been dry, and he fell on soft moss without harming himself. For a while he could not get out, but his faithful fox stood by his side even then and helped him out of his dilemma. He jumped down the well and scolded the prince for not listening to his advice.

"But I won't abandon you," the fox said. "You'll soon see the light of day."

The fox told him to grab his tail and hold it tightly. Then he pulled him up to the top.

"You're still not completely out of danger," the fox said. "Your brothers were not positive that you had died. So they've ordered that the forest be surrounded by guards who are to shoot you on sight."

Along the way the prince came across a poor man, with whom he exchanged clothes. That was how the prince succeeded in reaching the king's court without being recognized. However, the bird began to sing, the horse began to eat, and the beautiful maiden stopped weeping. The king was astonished and asked, "What does all this mean?"

"I don't know," said the beautiful maiden, "but I was sad, and now I'm very cheerful. I feel as if my true bridegroom had come."

She told the king what had happened, even though the two older brothers had threatened to kill her if she revealed anything. The king ordered everyone in the castle to gather around him, and the young prince appeared also, as a poor man in rags. But the princess recognized him at once and embraced him. The godless brothers were seized and executed, while the youngest married the beautiful princess and was designated heir to the king.

But what happened to the poor fox? Well, many years later the prince went walking through the forest again and encountered the fox, who said, "Now you have everything you desired, but there's been no end to my misfortune, even though it's been within your power to free me."

Once again the fox implored him to shoot him dead and cut off his head and paws. This time the prince did it, and no sooner was it done than the fox turned into none other than the brother of the beautiful princess, who was finally released from a magic spell that had been cast over him. Now nothing more was missing from their happiness as long as they lived.

◈ 58 ◈

The Dog and the Sparrow

THERE ONCE WAS A SHEEPDOG whose master was cruel and let him starve. When he could no longer stand it, he departed sadly. Along the road he met a sparrow who said, "Brother dog, why are you so sad?"

"I'm hungry and have nothing to eat," the dog answered.

"Dear brother," responded the sparrow, "come with me to the city, and I'll see that you get plenty to eat."

So they went into the city together, and when they came to a butcher shop, the sparrow said to the dog, "Stay here. I'm going to peck off a piece of meat, and it will drop down for you."

The bird flew to a counter and looked around to make sure that nobody had noticed him. Then he pecked, pulled, and tugged until a piece of meat lying near the edge of the counter slipped down to the ground. The dog grabbed it at once, ran into a corner, and devoured it.

"Now come with me to another shop," said the sparrow. "I'll get you one more piece so you'll be full."

When the dog had eaten the second piece, the sparrow asked, "Brother dog, have you had enough?"

"Yes, I've had enough meat," he answered. "But I still haven't had any bread."

"You'll get that too," said the sparrow. "Just come along with me."

So he led him to a baker's shop and pecked at some rolls until they tumbled down, and when the dog desired even more, the sparrow led him to another shop and fetched more bread for him. After that had been consumed, the sparrow said, "Brother dog, have you had enough now?"

"Yes," he answered. "Let's take a little walk outside the city."

Then the two of them went strolling down the highway, but the weather was so warm that, after they had gone a little way, the dog said, "I'm tired and would very much like to sleep."

"All right, just go to sleep," answered the sparrow. "In the meantime I'll sit down on a branch."

The dog lay down on the road and fell soundly asleep. While he lay there and slept, a wagoner came along with his wagon loaded with two barrels of wine and drawn by three horses. The sparrow realized that the wagon was heading straight down the lane in which the dog was lying and that it was not going to swerve.

"Wagoner, don't do that, or I'll make you a poor man!" the sparrow cried out.

"You won't make me poor!" the wagoner bellowed as he whipped the horses and drove the wagon over the dog, killing him with the wheels.

"You've run over my brother dog and killed him! That will cost you your wagon and horses!" exclaimed the sparrow.

"Don't make me laugh! My horses and wagon!" said the wagoner. "You can't do anything to harm me."

He drove on, but the sparrow crawled under the canvas and pecked at one of the bungholes of a barrel until a bung came out. Then all the wine ran out without the wagoner noticing it. Only after he turned around at one point did he realize that the wagon was dripping. So he examined the barrels and found that one was empty.

"Oh, poor me!" the wagoner cried out.

"Not poor enough yet," said the sparrow, and he flew down onto the head of one of the horses and pecked its eyes out. When the wagoner saw that, he pulled out his ax and tried to hit the sparrow with it. But the bird flew into the air, and the wagoner instead struck his horse on the head and it fell down dead.

"Oh, poor me!" the wagoner cried out.

"Not poor enough yet," said the sparrow, and when the wagoner drove away with two horses, the sparrow crawled under the canvas again and pecked out the bung of the second barrel so that all the wine flowed out. When the wagoner became aware of that, he cried out once more, "Oh, poor me!"

But the sparrow answered, "Not poor enough yet." He flew down and landed on the head of the second horse and pecked its eyes out. The wagoner ran over and took out his ax, but the sparrow flew up into the air and thus caused the wagoner to strike his second horse dead.

"Oh, poor me!"

"Not poor enough yet," said the sparrow, who landed on the head of the third horse and pecked its eyes out. The wagoner swung his ax at the sparrow in rage without bothering ·to look around. However, he missed the bird and struck his third horse dead.

"Oh, poor me!" he cried out.

"Not poor enough yet," answered the sparrow. "Now I'm going to make you poor at your own home." And he flew off.

The wagoner had to leave the wagon standing there and walked home highly annoyed and furious. "Oh," he said to his wife, "you can't imagine the bad luck I've had! The wine ran out, and all three horses are dead."

"Oh, husband!" she answered. "A wicked bird has flown into our house! It's brought all the birds in the whole world together, and they've descended on our wheat in the loft and are eating it up."

The wagoner climbed up to the loft, and there he saw thousands of birds on the floor eating the wheat, and the sparrow was sitting in the middle.

"Oh, poor me!" the wagoner cried out.

"Not poor enough yet," answered the sparrow. "Wagoner, it's going to cost you your life!" And the sparrow flew off.

With all his property gone, the wagoner now went downstairs and sat by the stove, feeling angry and bitter. Then the sparrow landed outside his window and called out, "Wagoner, it's going to cost you your life."

The wagoner grabbed his ax and threw it at the sparrow. But it missed the bird and merely broke the windowpane in two. The sparrow hopped inside the house, sat down on the stove, and called out, "Wagoner, it's going to cost you your life!"

Now the wagoner was furious and blind with rage. He chopped the stove in two and continued to chop all the furniture—the mirror, the benches, the table—and finally the walls of the house, all in an effort to hit the sparrow, who flew from spot to spot. At last the wagoner caught the bird with his hand.

"Do you want me to kill it?" his wife asked.

"No!" he yelled. "That would be too merciful. I want it to die a more cruel death. I'm going to swallow it."

Then he took the bird and swallowed him whole. However, the sparrow began to flutter inside his body and fluttered back up again into the man's mouth. Once there he stuck out his head and cried, "Wagoner, it's going to cost you your life!"

The wagoner handed the ax to his wife and said, "Wife, kill the bird in my mouth!"

His wife swung the ax, but she missed and hit the wagoner right on the head, and he fell down dead. But the sparrow flew up and away.

◆ 59 ◆

Freddy and Katy

ONCE THERE WAS A MAN NAMED FREDDY and a woman named Katy who got married and began living together in wedlock. One day Freddy said, "I'm going to the field, Katy. When I return, I want some roast meat on the table to take care of my hunger and a cool drink for my thirst."

"Just run along, Freddy," Katy answered. "Just go. I'll have everything ready the way you want it."

When noontime drew near, she got a sausage from the chimney, put it in a frying pan, added butter, and set it on the fire. The sausage began to fry and sizzle, and while Katy was standing there and holding the handle of the pan, she began thinking, and it occurred to her, You could go down into the cellar and draw the beer before the sausage is done. She fixed the pan so it would not tip, took a tankard, and went down into the cellar, where she began to draw the beer. As the beer was flowing into the tankard and Katy was gazing at it, she suddenly recalled, Hey, the dog's upstairs, and since he's not tied up, he could get the sausage from the pan. Oh, it's a lucky thing I thought of that!

She ran up the cellar stairs in a jiffy, but her spitz had already grabbed the sausage with his jaws and was dragging it along the ground. Still, Katy was quick to act: she ran after him and chased him a long way over the fields, but the dog was faster and clasped the sausage tightly as he dashed off with it beyond her reach.

"What's gone is gone," said Katy, who turned back home. Since she was tired from running, she walked very slowly and cooled herself off. In the meantime, the beer continued to flow from the keg, for Katy had forgotten to shut the tap. When the tankard became full and there was no more room in it, the beer flowed over onto the cellar floor until the whole keg was empty. As soon as Katy reached the top of the stairs, she saw the accident and cried out, "Heavens! How are you going to keep Freddy from noticing it?"

She thought for a while until she finally remembered a sack with fine wheat flour that was still up in the loft. It had been bought at the last fair, and she thought it would be a good idea to fetch it and sprinkle it over the beer. "Yes," she said, "a stitch in time saves nine." She climbed up to the loft, brought down the sack and threw it right on the tankard full of beer, causing it to topple. Now even Freddy's drink swam about in the cellar. "That's quite all right," said Katy. "They all belong in the same boat together." Then she scattered the flour all over the cellar. When she was finished, she was tremendously pleased with her work and said, "How clean and neat everything looks here!"

At noon Freddy came home and said, "Well, wife, what have you made for me?"

"Oh, Freddy," she answered, "I wanted to fry a sausage for you, but while I was drawing the beer in the cellar, the dog came and made off with the pan. Then, while I was chasing the dog, the beer ran over, and as I went to dry up the beer with the wheat flour, I knocked over the tankard. But don't get upset, the cellar is all dry again."

"Katy, Katy!" he said. "You shouldn't have done that! Just think! You let the sausage be carried off, you let the beer run out of the keg, and on top of it, you squandered our fine flour!"

"Well, Freddy, I didn't know that. You should have told me."

If that's the way your wife is, Freddy thought, then you'd better take precautions. Now, Freddy had saved up a nice sum in talers that he finally changed into gold, and he went to Katy and said, "Look, these here are yellow chips, and I'm going to put them into a pot and bury them in the stable under the cow's manger. Make sure you keep away from them, or I'll teach you a lesson!"

"Don't worry, Freddy," she said. "I promise not to touch them."

Soon after, while Freddy was away, some peddlers came to the village selling clay pots and bowls, and they asked the young woman whether she wanted to trade with them.

"Oh, you're so kind," she said. "I don't have any money and can't buy anything. But if you can use yellow chips, I'll make a trade with you."

"Yellow chips? Why not? But we'd like to have a look first."

"Well, just go into the barn and dig under the cow's manger and you'll find the yellow chips. I'm not allowed to go there."

The scoundrels went there, dug up the ground, and found pure gold. Then they put it into their pack and ran off, leaving the pots and bowls behind in the house. Katy thought she should make use of her new kitchenware, but since there was already so much of it in the kitchen, she knocked the bottoms out of all the new pots and hung them as ornaments on the fence poles all around the house. When Freddy came and saw the new ornaments, he asked, "Katy, what have you done?"

"Well, Freddy, I bought them with the yellow chips that were buried under the cow's manger. I didn't go near them myself. I made the peddlers dig them up."

"Oh, wife!" said Freddy. "What have you done? They weren't yellow chips. They were pure gold, our entire fortune! You shouldn't have done that."

"Well, Freddy," she said. "I didn't know that. You should have told me before."

Katy stood there awhile and tried to think of something. Finally, she said, "Listen, Freddy, we can get the gold back. Let's run after the thieves."

"All right," said Freddy. "Let's try it, but take some butter and cheese so that we have something to eat along the way."

"Yes, Freddy, I'll take some along."

They set out on foot, and since Freddy was faster, Katy trailed after him. It's to my advantage, she thought. If we turn back, then I'll have a head start. Now she came to a hill where there were deep wagon ruts on both sides of the road. "Just look!" said Katy. "They've trampled and torn apart the poor earth, so that it's all beaten up! It will never get well again as long as it lives." Out of the kindness of her heart, she took out the butter and smeared the ruts on the right and left so they would not be hurt so much by the wheels. While she was performing this charitable work and was bending over, a cheese rolled out of her pocket and down the hill.

"I've already climbed up the hill once," said Katy, "and I'm not going down again. Let some other cheese run down and fetch it back."

So she took another cheese and rolled it down the hill. However, this cheese did not come back either, so she sent a third one after it and thought, Perhaps they don't like to walk alone and are waiting for company. When all three of them failed to return, she said, "I'm not sure what all this means, but it's possible that the third one didn't find the way and has gone astray. I'll just send a fourth to call them all back."

The fourth did not do the job any better than the third. Then Katy became so annoyed that she threw the fifth and sixth down the hill too, and they were the last she had. For a while she stood and waited for them to come back, but when they did not return, she said, "Oh, you're just the right ones to send in search of death because you really drag your feet. Do you think I'm going to wait for you any longer? I'm moving on, and you can catch up with me. You've got younger legs than mine."

Katy went on and found Freddy, who had stopped to wait for her because he wanted something to eat.

"Now let's have some of the food you brought along."

She handed him the dry bread.

"Where's the butter and cheese?" her husband asked.

"Oh, Freddy," said Katy, "I smeared the ruts with the butter, and the cheese will soon be here. One got away from me, and so I sent the others after it."

"You shouldn't have done that, Katy," said Freddy. "Just think! You smeared the butter on the road, and you let the cheese roll down the hill!"

"Well, Freddy, you should have told me."

They ate the dry bread together, and Freddy said, "Katy, did you lock up the house before you left?"

"No, Freddy, you should have told me before."

"Well, then go home and lock it up before we continue on our way. Also, bring something else to eat with you. I'll wait for you here."

As Katy began walking back, she began thinking, Freddy obviously wants something else to eat. Since he doesn't like butter and cheese, I'll bring him some dried pears in a handkerchief and a jug full of vinegar to drink.

When she was about to leave the house again, she bolted the upper half of the door and took the lower half off the hinges. Then she carried it on her back because she thought the house would be safer if she kept the door with her. Then she took her time walking back since she thought to herself, Freddy will have all the more time to rest himself.

Once she reached her husband again, Katy said, "There, Freddy, now you have the house door, and you'll be able to keep the house safe yourself."

"Oh, God!" he said. "What a clever wife I've got! She takes off the lower half of the door so that anyone can walk in, and she bolts the upper half. Now it's too late to go home again, but since you brought the door here, you'll carry it the rest of the way yourself."

"I don't mind carrying the door, Freddy, but the dried pears and the jug of vinegar are too heavy for me. I'll hang them on the door and let the door carry them."

Now they went into the forest to look for the thieves, but they did not find them. When it finally became dark, they climbed up into a tree to spend the night. No sooner were they sitting up high than some men came along who tend to carry off things that do not want to be carried away and who tend to find things before they are lost. They camped out right beneath the tree in which Freddy and Katy were sitting. They made a fire and began to divide their loot. Freddy climbed down the other side of the tree and gathered some stones, after which he climbed back. He wanted to throw the stones at the thieves to kill them. However, he missed, and the thieves cried out, "Soon it will be morning, and the wind's knocking down the pinecones."

Katy was still carrying the door on her back, and since it was so heavy and weighing her down, she thought the dried pears were to blame and said, "Freddy, I've got to throw the dried pears down."

"No, Katy, not now," he answered. "They could give us away."

"Oh, Freddy, I've got to! They're too heavy for me."

"Well then, do it, for all I care!"

She rolled the pears down between the branches, and the thieves said, "Here come some bird droppings."

Shortly afterward, since the door was still very heavy on her back, Katy said, "Oh, Freddy, I've got to pour out the vinegar."

"No, Katy, you mustn't do that. It could give us away."

"Oh, Freddy, I've got to! It's too heavy for me."

"Well then, do it, for all I care!"

So she poured out the vinegar, and it splattered all over the thieves.

"The dew's already falling," the men said to one another.

Finally, Katy thought, Could it be the door that's been weighing me down? And she said, "Freddy, I've got to throw the door down."

"No, Katy, that could give us away."

"Oh, Freddy, I've got to. It's too heavy for me."

"No, Katy, hold on to it tight."

"Oh, Freddy, I'm going to let it drop."

"All right!" Freddy answered irritably. "Let it drop for all I care!"

Then the door fell down with a great crash, and the thieves below cried out, "The devil's coming down the tree!"

They cleared out and left everything behind. Early the next morning, when Freddy and Katy came down the tree, they found all their gold again and carried it home.

When they were home once more, Freddy said, "Katy, you've got to be industrious and work hard now."

"Yes, Freddy, of course I will. I'll go into the field and cut down the fruit."

When Katy went into the field, she said to herself, "Should I eat before I cut, or should I sleep before I cut. I think I'll eat!" So Katy ate and became tired from eating. When she started to cut some fruit, she began daydreaming and cut all her clothes to pieces—her apron, her dress, and her blouse. Upon snapping out of her dream, she stood there half naked and said to herself, "Is that me, or is it someone else? Oh, that's not me!"

Meanwhile, it was already night, and Katy ran into the village and knocked on her husband's window.

"Freddy!" she called out.

"What is it?"

"I'd like to know if Katy's inside."

"Yes, yes," answered Freddy. "She's probably lying down asleep."

"Good," she said. "Then I'm clearly at home already," and she ran off.

Outside the village Katy came across some thieves who were planning a theft. She went up to them and said, "I want to help you steal."

The thieves thought she knew her way around the region and agreed to let her join them. Then Katy went in front of the houses and called out, "Folks, do you have anything you want stolen?"

This won't do! thought the thieves, and they wished they could get rid of Katy.

"There's a turnip patch owned by the parson outside the village," they said to her. "We want you to go there and pull up some of the turnips for us."

Katy went to the patch and began to pull up some turnips, but she was so lazy that she remained in a crouched position. Soon a man came by, stopped, watched her, and thought the devil was tearing up all the turnips in the patch. So he ran to the parson in the village and said, "Parson, the devil's in your turnip patch, and he's tearing up all your turnips."

"Oh, God!" exclaimed the parson. "I've got a lame foot and can't run out to banish him."

"I'll carry you on my back," said the man, and he carried him out to the field. When they got to the turnip patch, Katy straightened herself up.

"Oh, it's really the devil!" the parson cried, and they both rushed off. Indeed, since his fright was so great, the parson was able to run faster with his lame foot than the man who had carried him with his two sound legs.

◆ 60 ◆

The Two Brothers

ONCE UPON A TIME there were two brothers, one rich and the other poor. The rich brother was a goldsmith and evil-hearted. The poor brother earned a living by making brooms and was kind and honest. He had two sons who were twins, and they looked so much alike that they seemed like two peas in a pod. Every now and then the twins went to their rich uncle's house and were given the leftovers to eat.

One day the poor man happened to be in the forest gathering brushwood when he saw a bird pure as gold and more beautiful than any bird he had ever seen. So he picked up a little stone, threw it at the bird, and was lucky enough to hit it. However, only a single golden feather dropped to the ground, and the bird flew off. The man took the feather and brought it to his brother, who examined it and said, "It's pure gold," and he gave him a lot of money for it.

The next day the poor man climbed a birch tree to cut a few branches. Just then the same bird flew out, and after the man searched awhile, he found a nest with an egg in it. The egg was made of gold, and he took it home with him. Afterward he showed it to his brother, who once again said, "It's pure gold," and he gave him what it was worth. Finally, the goldsmith said, "I'd like to have the bird itself."

The poor man went into the forest for a third time and saw the golden bird perched on a tree. He took a stone, knocked the bird down, and brought it to his brother, who gave him a huge amount of gold for it.

Now I'll be able to take care of things, the poor man thought, and went home with a happy feeling.

The goldsmith was clever and cunning and knew exactly what kind of bird it was. He called his wife and said, "Roast this golden bird for me, and make sure that none of it gets lost! I want to eat it all by myself."

Indeed, the bird was not an ordinary creature. It possessed a miraculous power, and whoever ate its heart and liver would find a gold piece under his pillow every morning. The goldsmith's wife prepared the bird, put it on a spit, and let it roast. Now it happened that, while the bird was roasting over the fire, the wife had to leave the kitchen to take care of something else. Just then the two sons of the poor broom-maker ran in, stopped in front of the spit, and turned it a few times. When two little pieces dropped from the bird into the pan, one of the boys said, "Let's eat the two little pieces. I'm so hungry, and nobody's bound to notice it."

So they ate the two pieces, but the wife returned and saw that they had eaten something.

"What did you eat?" she asked.

"A couple of pieces that fell out of the bird," they answered.

"That must have been the heart and liver," the wife said, and she was horrified. She quickly slaughtered a cock, took out its heart and liver, and put them in the golden bird so her husband would not miss them and get angry. When the golden bird was done, she carried it to the goldsmith, who consumed it all by himself and left nothing over. However, when he reached under his pillow the next morning expecting to find a gold piece, there was nothing there out of the ordinary.

In the meantime, the two boys did not realize how fortunate they had been. When they got up the next morning, something fell on the floor making a tingling sound. Upon looking to see what made the sound, they found two gold pieces, which they brought to their father. He was amazed and said, "How can that have happened?"

When they found another two the following morning and continued to find two every morning thereafter, the father went to his brother and told him the strange story. The goldsmith knew immediately how everything had happened and that the children had eaten the heart and liver of the golden bird. Since he was envious and hard-hearted, he sought revenge and said to the father, "Your children are in league with the devil. Don't take the gold, and don't let them stay in your house any longer. The devil's got them in his power and can also bring about your own ruin."

The father was afraid of the devil, and even though it was painful for him, he led the twins out into the forest and with a sad heart left them there. The two boys wandered around the forest and searched for the way back home, but they repeatedly lost their way and could not find it. Finally, they encountered a huntsman, who asked, "Where do you come from?"

"We're the poor broom-maker's sons," they answered and then

told him that their father no longer wanted them in his house because every morning there was a gold piece under each one of their pillows.

"Well," said the huntsman, "that's really nothing terrible as long as you remain good and upright and don't become lazy."

The kind man took a liking to the boys, and since he did not have any sons himself, he took them home with him and said, "I shall be your father and bring you up."

So they learned all about hunting from him, and he saved the gold pieces that they found every morning when they got up, in case they might need them in the future. One day, when they were finally grown-up, their foster father took them into the forest and said, "Today you're to be tested in shooting to determine whether I can release you from your apprenticeship and pronounce you full-fledged huntsmen."

They went with him to the raised blind and waited for a long time, but no game appeared. Then the huntsman looked above him, and when he saw some wild geese flying by in a triangle formation, he said to one of the brothers, "Now shoot one from each corner."

He did it and passed the test. Soon after, more geese came flying by in the number two formation. The huntsman told the other brother likewise to shoot one goose from each corner, and he also passed the test. Now the foster father said, "You have completed your apprenticeship, and I pronounce you both full-fledged huntsmen."

At that point the two brothers went into the forest together, took counsel with each other, and decided on a plan of action. When they sat down in the evening to eat, they said to their foster father, "We're not going to touch the food or take a single bite until you grant us one request."

"What is your request?" he asked.

"Since we're now full-fledged huntsmen," they replied, "we must also prove ourselves. So we want your permission to leave and travel about the world."

"You speak like real huntsmen," said the old man joyfully. "Your desire is my very own wish. Set out on your journey; everything will go well for you."

In a merry mood, they then ate and drank together. When the appointed day for their departure arrived, their foster father gave each of them a good gun and a dog and had each of them take as many of the saved-up gold pieces as he desired. Then the old man accompanied them part of the way, and when they were about to take their leave, he gave them a shiny knife and said, "If ever you should separate, stick this knife into a tree at the crossroad. Then if one of you comes back, he can see how his absent brother is doing, for the side of the blade facing the direction he took will rust if he's dying but will stay bright as long as he's alive.''

The two brothers continued on their way and came to a huge forest that was impossible to cross in one day. So they spent the night there and ate what they had in their hunting pouches. On the second day they went onward but still did not reach the end. Now they had nothing more to eat, and one of them said, ''We must shoot something, or we'll starve.''

He loaded his gun and looked around. When he saw an old hare running by, he took aim, but the hare cried out:

"Dear huntsman, if you let me live,
two of my young to you I'll give."

Then the hare jumped into the bushes and brought back two young ones. The little creatures were so frisky and charming that the huntsmen did not have the heart to kill them. So they kept them, and the little hares followed at their heels. Soon after, a fox came slinking by, and they were about to shoot it when the fox cried out:

"Dear huntsman, if you let me live,
two of my young to you I'll give."

He also brought two young ones, and the huntsmen had no desire to kill the little foxes. They gave them to the hares for company, and the animals continued to follow the huntsmen. Soon a wolf came out of the thicket, and just as the huntsmen took aim at him, he cried out:

"Dear huntsman, if you let me live,
two of my young to you I'll give."

The huntsmen added the two young wolves to the other animals, and they all followed the two young men. Then a bear came, and he had no desire to have his days of wandering ended, so he cried out:

"Dear huntsman, if you let me live,
two of my young to you I'll give."

Two young bears joined the other animals, and now there were eight of them. Finally, who should come along shaking his mane but the lion! And he also cried out:

"Dear huntsman, if you let me live,
two of my young to you I'll give."

He too fetched two of his young ones, and now the huntsmen had two lions, two bears, two wolves, two foxes, and two hares who followed and served them. Meanwhile, however, the brothers were still starving, and they said to the foxes, "Listen, you tricky creatures, get us something to eat. After all, we know you're crafty and cunning."

"There's a village not far from here," they answered. "In the past we were able to get many a chicken there. We'll show you the way."

The brothers went to the village, bought themselves something to eat, and had their animals fed. Then they continued on their way. But the foxes were very familiar with the region and knew exactly where the chicken yards were, so they could guide the huntsmen to the right spots. For a while they traveled about, but they could not find employment that would allow them all to remain together. Eventually, the brothers said, "There's no other way. We'll have to separate."

They divided the animals so that each had a lion, a bear, a wolf, a fox, and a hare. Then they said farewell, took a vow of brotherly love unto death, and stuck the knife that their foster father had given them into a tree. Then one went to the east, the other to the west.

Soon the younger brother arrived with his animals in a city that was completely draped in black crepe. He went into an inn and asked the innkeeper whether he could put up his animals there. The innkeeper gave him a stable that had a hole in the wall. The hare crawled through it and fetched himself a head of cabbage; the fox fetched a hen, and after he had eaten the hen, he went and got a cock as well. However, the wolf, the bear, and the lion were too big to slip through the hole. So the innkeeper took them to a meadow where a cow was grazing, and there they could eat their fill. After the huntsman had taken care of his animals, he asked the innkeeper why the city was draped in black crepe.

"Because our king's only daughter shall perish tomorrow," said the innkeeper.

"Is she that sick?" asked the huntsman.

"No," the innkeeper replied. "She's hale and hearty, but she must die nonetheless."

"But why?" asked the huntsman.

"Outside the city there's a dragon living on a high mountain," said the innkeeper. "Every year he demands that he be given a pure virgin or he'll lay waste to the entire country. Now all the maidens have been given to him, and there's no one left but the king's daughter. Despite that, the dragon shows no mercy. She must be delivered to him, and that's to be done tomorrow.''

"Why doesn't someone slay the dragon?" asked the huntsman.

"Ah," responded the innkeeper. "Many, many knights have tried, but they've all forfeited their lives. The king's promised to give his daughter's hand in marriage to the man who slays the dragon, and this man would also inherit the kingdom after the king's death."

The huntsman said nothing more, but the next morning he took his animals and climbed the dragon's mountain with them. At the top was a small church, and there were three full goblets on the altar with a piece of paper next to them that said, "Whoever drinks these goblets shall become the strongest man on earth and shall be able to wield the sword that lies buried at the threshold of the door." The huntsman did not drink the goblets but went outside and searched for the sword in the ground, which he was not able to move. Then he went back inside, drank the goblets, and was now strong enough to pull out the sword and wield it with ease. When the hour came for the maiden to be delivered to the dragon, the king, the marshal, and the entire court accompanied her. From afar she could see the huntsman standing on top of the dragon's mountain. She thought it was the dragon standing there and waiting for her, and she did not want to go. But finally she had to begin the painful journey; the whole kingdom would have been lost otherwise. The king and his court returned home in full mourning, but the king's marshal was assigned to stay there and watch everything from a distance.

When the king's daughter reached the top of the mountain, it was not the dragon standing there but the young huntsman, who comforted her and told her he wanted to save her. He led her into the church and locked her inside. Shortly after, with a great roar the seven-headed dragon descended on the spot. When he caught sight of the huntsman, he was astounded, and he said, "What do you think you're doing on this mountain?"

"I've come to fight you," replied the huntsman.

"Many a knight has lost his life here," declared the dragon. "I'll soon finish you off as well!" Then flames shot from his seven jaws.

The flames were intended to set fire to the dry grass, and the dragon hoped to smother the huntsman with the fire and smoke, but the huntsman's animals came running to his aid and stamped the fire out. The dragon then attacked the huntsman, but the man swung his sword so swiftly that it sang in the air and cut off three of the dragon's heads. Now the dragon was really furious: he rose up, began shooting flames directly at the huntsman, and got set to dive down at him. However, the huntsman once again lashed out with his sword and cut off three more heads. The monster sank to the ground and was exhausted. Nevertheless, he tried to charge the huntsman again, but the young man used his last bit of strength to cut off the dragon's tail. Then, since the huntsman could not continue fighting, he called his animals, who tore the dragon to pieces. When the battle was over, the huntsman opened the church and found the princess lying on the ground. She had fainted from fear and fright during the combat. So he carried her outside, where she regained consciousness and opened her eyes. When he showed her the dragon's devastated body and told her she was now free, the princess was overjoyed and said, "Now you shall be my very dear husband, for my father promised my hand in marriage to the man who could slay the dragon."

The princess then took off her coral necklace and divided it among the animals as little collars to reward them, and the lion received the golden clasp to the necklace. However, her handkerchief with her name embroidered on it went to the huntsman, who proceeded to cut out the tongues of the seven dragon's heads, wrap them in the handkerchief, and put them away carefully.

When that was done, he felt so tired and exhausted from the fire and battle that he said to the maiden, "We're both so tired and exhausted, perhaps it would be best if we slept awhile."

The princess agreed, and they lay down on the ground. Then the huntsman said to the lion, "I want you to keep watch so that no one surprises us in our sleep."

When the huntsman and the princess fell asleep, the lion lay down beside them to keep watch, but he too was tired from the battle. So he called the bear and said, "Lie down beside me. I've got to sleep a little. If anything happens, wake me up."

The bear lay down next to the lion, but he too was tired. So he called the wolf and said, "Lie down beside me. I've got to sleep a little. If anything happens, wake me up."

The wolf lay down next to the bear, but he too was tired. So he called the fox and said, "Lie down beside me. I've got to sleep a little. If anything happens, wake me up."

The fox lay down beside the wolf, but he too was tired. So he called the hare and said, "Lie down beside me. I've got to sleep a little. If anything happens, wake me up."

The hare lay down next to the wolf, but he too was tired. However, there was no one left whom he could call on to help him, and soon he fell asleep. Once that happened, they were all asleep and sleeping soundly, the princess, the huntsman, the lion, the bear, the wolf, the fox, and the hare.

Meanwhile, the marshal, who had been assigned the task of watching everything from a distance, did not see the dragon fly off. So, when everything was calm on the mountain, he summoned his courage and climbed the mountain, where he found the dragon lying on the ground and torn to pieces. Not far from there were the king's daughter and the huntsman with his animals. They were all sound asleep, and since the marshal was a wicked and godless man, he took his sword and cut off the huntsman's head. Next he lifted the maiden in his arms and carried her down the mountain. When she awoke, she was petrified, but the marshal said, "I've got you in my power, so you'd better say that it was I who slew the dragon."

"I can't do that," she replied. "It was a huntsman with his animals. They were the ones who did it."

Then the marshal drew out his sword and threatened to kill her if she did not obey him. Thus he forced her to promise that she would do as he commanded. Afterward he brought her to the king, who was overcome by joy upon seeing his dear daughter alive again when he had thought she had already been torn to pieces by the dragon.

"I've slain the dragon and saved the maiden and the whole kingdom," said the marshal. "Therefore I claim your daughter for my wife as you promised."

"Is what he says true?" the king asked the maiden.

"Oh, yes," she answered. "It must probably be true, but I insist that the wedding be held in a year and a day and not before." Indeed, she hoped to hear from her dear huntsman by then.

Meanwhile, the animals were still lying asleep beside their dead master on the dragon's mountain. Then a bumble bee came and landed on the hare's nose, but the hare brushed it aside with his paw. The bumble bee came a second time, but the hare brushed it aside again and continued to sleep. Finally, it came a third time and stung him on the nose, so that he woke up. As soon as the hare was awake, he woke the fox, and the fox woke the wolf, who woke the bear, and the bear woke the lion. And when the lion saw that the maiden was gone and his master was dead, he began roaring dreadfully loud and cried out, "Who did that? Bear, why didn't you wake me?"

The bear asked the wolf, "Why didn't you wake me?"

And the wolf asked the fox, "Why didn't you wake me?"

The fox asked the hare, "Why didn't you wake me?"

The poor hare was the only one who did not know what to answer, and the guilt fell on his shoulders. They wanted to pounce on him, but he pleaded with them and said, "Don't kill me! I'll bring our master back to life. I know a mountain where a root grows that cures and heals all kinds of sicknesses and wounds. You only have to stick the root in the sick person's mouth. But it takes two hundred hours to get to the mountain."

"Well, you've got to dash there and back and fetch the root within twenty-four hours," declared the lion.

The hare raced away, and within twenty-four hours he was back with the root. The lion put the huntsman's head back in position, and the hare stuck the root in his mouth. All at once, everything functioned together again: his heart beat, and life returned to him. When the huntsman awoke, he was distressed not to find the maiden by his side. She must have gone away while I was asleep to get rid of me, he thought.

In his great haste the lion had put his master's head on backward. However, the huntsman was so preoccupied by his sad thoughts about the king's daughter that he did not notice it. Only at noon, when he wanted to eat something, did he realize that his head was on backward. He was at a loss to understand how that had happened, and he asked the animals. The lion told him that they had all been so tired that they had fallen asleep and that upon awakening they had found him dead with his head cut off. The hare had then fetched the root of life, but the lion in his haste had held his head the wrong way. After saying all that, the lion wanted to correct his mistake. So he tore off the head of the huntsman, turned it around, and the hare healed him again with the root.

The huntsman nevertheless remained in a gloomy mood. He traveled about the world and made his animals dance before crowds of people. After a year had passed, he happened to return to the same city where he had rescued the king's daughter from the dragon, and this time the city was draped completely in crimson.

"What does all that mean?" he asked the innkeeper. "A year ago the city was draped in black. What's the meaning of the crimson?"

"A year ago the princess was supposed to have been delivered to the dragon," answered the innkeeper. "But the marshal fought and slew the dragon. Tomorrow his wedding with the princess will be celebrated. That's why the city, in its mourning, was draped in black then, and that's why the city, in its joy, is draped in crimson today."

At noon on the next day, when the wedding was to take place, the huntsman said to the innkeeper, "Do you think, innkeeper, that it might be possible for me to eat bread from the king's table right here at your place?''

''Well,'' said the innkeeper, ''I'd be willing to bet a hundred gold pieces that you can't possibly do that.''

The huntsman accepted the wager and put up a pouch with one hundred gold pieces to match the innkeeper's money. Then he called the hare and said, ''Go there, my speedster, and fetch me some of the bread fit for a king.''

Now, the little hare was the weakest of the animals, and it was impossible for him to pass his task on to any of the others: he had to perform it by himself. My God, he thought, if I amble down the street by myself, the butchers' dogs will soon be after me! And it happened just as he thought it would. The dogs chased after him and wanted to tear his good fur to shreds. However, you should have seen the hare run! He sped to the castle and took refuge in the sentry box without the guard noticing him. When the dogs came and tried to get him out, the soldier would take no nonsense from them and hit them with the butt of his rifle, so they ran away yelping and howling. When the hare saw the coast was clear, he ran into the palace and straight to the king's daughter. Then he sat down under her chair and scratched her foot.

''Get out of here!'' she said, for she thought it was her dog. The hare scratched her foot a second time, and she repeated ''Get out of here!'' for she thought it was her dog. But the hare did not let himself be deterred and scratched a third time. Then she looked down and recognized the hare by his coral collar. So she picked him up, carried him into her chamber, and said, ''My dear hare, what do you want?''

''My master, the dragon-slayer, is here,'' he answered, ''and he's sent me to fetch some bread fit for a king.''

The princess was filled with joy. She summoned the baker and ordered him to bring her a loaf of bread fit for a king.

''But the baker must also carry it for me,'' said the hare. ''Otherwise, the butchers' dogs will hurt me.''

The baker carried the bread up to the door of the inn for the hare. Then the hare stood up on his hind legs, took the loaf of bread in his front paws, and brought it to his master.

''You see, innkeeper,'' the huntsman said, ''the hundred gold pieces are mine.''

The innkeeper was astonished, but the huntsman continued to speak. ''Well, innkeeper, I've got the bread, but now I want some of the king's roast as well.''

"I'd like to see that," said the innkeeper, but he did not want to bet anymore.

The huntsman called the fox and said, "Little fox, go there and fetch me a roast fit for a king."

The red fox knew the shortcuts better than the hare, and he went through holes and around corners without the dogs catching sight of him. Once at the castle he sat under the chair of the princess and scratched her foot. When she looked down, she recognized the fox by his coral collar, carried him into her chamber, and said, "My dear fox, what do you want?"

"My master, the dragon-slayer, is here," he answered, "and he's sent me to ask for a roast fit for a king."

She summoned the cook and ordered him to prepare a roast fit for a king and to carry it for the fox up to the door of the inn. There the fox took the dish from him, wagged his tail to brush off the flies that had settled on the roast, and brought it to his master.

"You see, innkeeper," said the huntsman, "bread and meat are here, but now I want to have some vegetables fit for a king." So he called the wolf and said, "Dear wolf, go straight to the castle and fetch me some vegetables fit for a king."

So the wolf went straight to the castle, for he was afraid of no one, and when he reached the princess, he tugged at her dress from behind so that she had to turn around. She recognized him by his coral collar, took him into her chamber, and said, "My dear wolf, what do you want?"

"My master, the dragon-slayer, is here," he answered, "and he's sent me to ask for some vegetables fit for a king."

She summoned the cook, who had to prepare some vegetables fit for a king, and she ordered him to carry them for the wolf to the door of the inn. There the wolf took the dish and brought it to his master.

"You see, innkeeper, now I've got bread, meat, and vegetables, but I also want some sweets fit for a king." So he called the bear and said, "Dear bear, since you're fond of licking sweet things, go and fetch me sweets fit for a king."

So the bear trotted off to the castle, and everyone cleared out of his way. When he reached the sentry box, the guards barred his way with their guns and did not want to let him enter the royal castle. But he stood up on his hind legs and slapped the guards left and right, forcing them to fall apart. Then he went straight to the king's daughter, stood behind her, and growled softly. She looked behind her, recognized the bear, and told him to go with her into her chamber.

"My dear bear," she said, "what do you want?"

"My master, the dragon-slayer, is here," he answered, "and I'm to ask for some sweets fit for a king."

She summoned the confectioner and ordered him to make sweets fit for a king and to carry them up to the door for the bear. There the bear licked the sugarplums that had rolled off, stood on his hind legs, and brought them to his master.

"You see, innkeeper," said the huntsman, "now I've got bread, meat, vegetables, and sweets, but I also want to drink wine fit for a king." So he called his lion and said, "Dear lion, since you like to indulge yourself and get tipsy, go and fetch me some wine fit for a king."

When the lion strode down the street, the people fled from him, and when he came to the guards, they wanted to bar his way, but he only had to let out a roar, and they all dashed away. The lion then went to the royal chamber and knocked on the door with his tail. The king's daughter came out and would have been petrified had she not recognized him by the golden clasp of her necklace. She invited him inside and said, "My dear lion, what do you want?"

"My master, the dragon-slayer, is here, and I'm to ask for some wine fit for a king."

She summoned the cupbearer and ordered him to give the lion some wine fit for a king.

"I want to go with him to make sure that I get the right kind," said the lion.

He went downstairs with the cupbearer, and when they were below, the cupbearer was about to draw some ordinary wine that the king's servants usually drank when the lion said, "Stop! I want to taste the wine first." He drew half a measure for himself and drank it down. "No," he said, "that's not the right kind."

The cupbearer glared at him and was cross. Then he went on and was about to offer him wine from another barrel reserved for the king's marshal.

"Stop!" said the lion. "I want to taste the wine first." He drew half a measure for himself and drank it down. "It's better than the first, but it's still not the right kind."

Now the cupbearer got angry and said, "How can a stupid beast understand anything about wine?"

But the lion gave him such a blow behind the ears that he fell hard on the ground. When he got up, he did not utter a word but led the lion into a special small cellar where the king's wine was kept solely for his private use. The lion drew half a measure for himself, tasted the wine, and said, "That's the right kind," and he ordered the cupbearer to fill six bottles with the wine. Then they climbed back upstairs, and when the lion left the cellar and stepped outside, he began to stagger back and forth. Since he was a bit drunk, the cupbearer had to carry the wine up to the door for him. There the lion took the basket in his mouth and carried it to his master.

"You see, innkeeper," the huntsman said, "I've got bread, meat, vegetables, sweets, and wine fit for a king, and now I want to dine with my animals."

He sat down at the table, ate and drank, and shared his meal with the hare, the fox, the wolf, the bear, and the lion. The huntsman was in good spirits, for he realized that the king's daughter was fond of him. After the meal was over, he said, "Innkeeper, now that I've eaten and drunk just like a king, I'm going to the king's palace, where I shall marry his daughter."

"How are you going to do that?" asked the innkeeper. "She already has a bridegroom, and the wedding's to be celebrated today."

The huntsman took out the handkerchief that the king's daughter had given him on the dragon's mountain, and it still contained the seven tongues of the monster.

"All I need," he said, "is what I'm holding here in my hand."

The innkeeper looked at the handkerchief and said, "Even if I believe everything else, I can't believe this, and I'm willing to stake my house and everything I own on it."

Then the huntsman took out a pouch with a thousand gold pieces in it, put the pouch on the table, and said, "I'll match your house and property with this."

Meanwhile, the king and his daughter were sitting at the royal table, and the king asked her, "What did all those wild animals want who came to you and kept running in and out of my castle?"

"I'm not allowed to say," she answered. "But you'd do well to send for the master of those animals."

The king sent a servant to the inn and had the stranger invited to the palace. The servant arrived just as the huntsman concluded the bet with the innkeeper.

"You see, innkeeper," said the huntsman, "the king's sent a servant to invite me to the palace, but I refuse to go the way I am." Then he turned to the servant and said, "Please be so kind as to tell the king to send me royal garments, a coach with six horses, and servants to attend me."

When the king heard the answer, he said to his daughter, "What should I do?"

"You'd do well to honor his request and send for him," she said.

So the king sent royal garments, a coach with six horses, and servants to attend him. When the huntsman saw them coming, he said, "You see, innkeeper, my request has been honored," and he dressed himself in the royal garments, took the handkerchief with the seven tongues of the dragon, and drove to the palace. When the king saw him coming, he said to his daughter, "How shall I receive him?"

"You'd do well to go and meet him," she answered.

The king went to meet him and led him up to the palace, while the animals followed behind. The king showed the young huntsman to a place next to him and his daughter. The seat on the other side was taken by the marshal, who did not recognize the huntsman. Just then the seven heads of the dragon were carried out for display, and the king said, "Since the marshal cut off the seven heads of the dragon, I shall give him my daughter to be his wife today."

Then the huntsman stood up, opened the seven jaws, and said, "Where are the seven tongues of the dragon?"

Upon hearing that, the marshal was so frightened that he turned pale and did not know what to reply. Finally, he said, "Dragons have no tongues."

"Liars should have no tongues," said the huntsman. "But the dragon's tongues can prove who the real dragon-slayer is."

Then he unwrapped the handkerchief to reveal the seven tongues. When he stuck each tongue back into the mouth where it belonged, each fit perfectly. Next he took the handkerchief, on which the name of the king's daughter had been embroidered, showed it to the maiden and asked her to point out which man she had given it to.

"To the man who slew the dragon," she replied.

Then he called his animals, took off their coral collars and the golden clasp from the lion, and asked the maiden to tell to whom they belonged.

"The necklace and the golden clasp were mine," she answered, "but I divided the necklace among the animals who had helped in slaying the dragon."

Then the huntsman said, "After I was weary from the fight, I lay down to rest and sleep, and the marshal came and cut off my head. Then he carried off the king's daughter and pretended it was he who had slain the dragon. To prove that he's been lying, I have brought the tongues, the handkerchief, and the necklace." And then he told how his animals had healed him through a miraculous root and how he had traveled around for a year and had finally come back to the spot where he learned about the treachery of the marshal, thanks to the innkeeper's story.

"Is it true that this man slew the dragon?" the king asked his daughter.

"Yes," she replied, "it's true. Now I may reveal the marshal's shameful crime, for it has been exposed without my speaking about it. You see, the marshal made me take a vow of silence, and that's why I had insisted upon waiting a year and a day before celebrating the wedding."

The king summoned twelve councillors and ordered them to pronounce judgment on the marshal, and they sentenced him to be torn apart by four oxen. Thus the marshal was executed and the king gave his daughter to the huntsman and named him viceroy over the entire kingdom. The wedding was celebrated with great rejoicing, and the young king sent for his father and foster father and overwhelmed them with fine gifts. Nor did he forget the innkeeper. He too was sent for, and the young king said, "You see, innkeeper, I've married the king's daughter, and your house and property are mine."

"Yes," he said, "by right everything is yours."

But the young king said, "No, it is by mercy that I shall act. You shall keep your house and property. Moreover, I want you to retain the one thousand gold pieces as a gift."

Now, the young king and young queen were in good spirits and had a happy life together. He often went out hunting, since that gave him pleasure, and his faithful animals always accompanied him. Nearby was a forest, however, that was said to be enchanted. Whoever entered did not return very easily. But the young king had a great desire to go hunting in it, and he kept bothering the old king until he obtained permission to go there. So he rode out with a large retinue, and when he came to the forest, he saw a doe as white as snow and said to his men, "Wait here until I return. I want to hunt that beautiful doe."

He rode into the forest in pursuit of the doe, and only his animals followed him. His men stopped and waited until evening, but he did not come back. So they rode home and said to the young queen, "The young king went hunting after a beautiful white doe in the enchanted forest and did not return."

Upon hearing this she became very worried about him. Meanwhile, he had kept riding after the beautiful doe, never managing to overtake it. Each time he thought he had the doe within his aim, the animal would dart away and run off into the distance, until finally it vanished altogether. When the huntsman realized that he had gone deep into the forest, he took out his horn and blew it. There was no response, however, for his men could not hear it. After night began to fall, he saw that he could not get home that day. So, intending to spend the night there, he dismounted and built a fire near a tree. While he was sitting by the fire and his animals were lying beside him, he thought he heard a human voice. He looked around but did not see anyone. Soon after, he heard a groan that sounded as though it were coming from above. When he looked up, he saw an old woman sitting in the tree moaning and groaning.

"*Oooh! Oooh!* I'm freezing," she cried.

"Climb down," he said, "and warm yourself if you're freezing."

"No, your animals will bite me," she replied.

"They won't harm you, granny," he answered. "Just come down."

However, she was a witch and said, "I'm going to throw down a switch from the tree. If you hit them on their backs with it, they won't hurt me."

Then she threw the switch to him, and when he hit them with it, they immediately lay still and were turned to stone. When the witch was safe from the animals, she jumped down, touched him with a switch, and he was turned to stone. Whereupon she laughed and then dragged him and the animals to a pit where there were already many more such stones.

When the young king did not come back at all, the young queen's worries and fears increased. Now, it happened that just at this time the other brother, who had gone to the east when the twins had separated, came to this kingdom. He had been looking for employment and had found none. Therefore, he had been traveling about and having his animals dance in front of crowds of people. Eventually, it occurred to him to take a look at the knife they had stuck into the tree upon their separation to see how his brother was doing. When he got there, his brother's side of the knife was half rusty and half bright. At once he became alarmed and thought, My brother must have met with a great misfortune. But perhaps I can still save him, for half the knife is bright.

He went half off to the west with his animals, and when he arrived at the city gate, the guards approached him and asked whether they should announce his arrival to his wife, for the young queen had been upset for several days about his absence and had been afraid that he had been killed in the enchanted forest. The guards, of course, believed that he was none other than the young king himself because he resembled him so much and also had the wild animals following him. The brother realized that they had mistaken him for his brother and thought, It's perhaps best that I pretend to be him. Then I'll be able to rescue him more easily.

So he let himself be conducted by the guards into the palace and was jubilantly received. The young queen thought for sure he was her husband and asked him why he had stayed away so long.

"I lost my way in the forest and could not find the way back any sooner," he said.

In the evening he was taken to the royal bed, but he placed a double-edged sword between himself and the young queen. She did not know what to make of it, but she did not dare to ask.

He remained there a few days and inquired into everything concerning the enchanted forest. Finally, he said, "I must go hunting there once more."

The king and the young queen tried to talk him out of it, but he insisted and set out with a large retinue. When he reached the forest, he went through everything his brother had. He saw a white doe and said to his men, "Stay here and wait until I return." He rode into the forest, and his animals followed after him. But he could not overtake the doe and went so deep into the forest that he had to spend the night there. After he had built a fire, he heard a groan above him.

"*Oooh! Oooh!* I'm freezing!"

He looked up and saw the same witch sitting in the tree.

"If you're freezing, climb down, granny," he said, "and warm yourself."

"No, your animals will bite me," she replied.

"They won't harm you," he said.

"I'm going to throw down a switch from the tree to you," she said. "If you hit them with it, they won't hurt me."

When the huntsman heard that, he did not trust the old woman and said, "I won't hit my animals. Either you come down, or I'll come get you!"

"Do you really think you can do something?" she cried. "There's no way you can harm me!"

But he answered, "If you don't come down, I'll shoot you down."

"Go ahead and shoot," she said. "I'm not afraid of your bullets."

So he took aim and fired at her, but the witch was protected against lead bullets, and she let out a shrill laugh. "You'll never hit me!" she exclaimed.

But the huntsman knew just what to do: he took off three silver buttons from his jacket and loaded his gun with them, for her witchcraft was powerless against them. When he now pulled the trigger, she fell from the tree with a scream. Then he put his foot on her and said, "You old witch, if you don't tell me right away where my brother is, I'll pick you up with both my hands and throw you into the fire.''

Since she was terribly frightened, she begged for mercy and said, ''He's been turned to stone along with his animals, and they're lying in a pit.''

He forced her to go with him, and there he threatened her by saying, ''You old monkey, now you'd better restore life to my brother and all the other creatures that are lying there, or I'll throw you into the fire!''

She took a switch and touched the stones, and his brother and the animals came back to life again, and many others as well, such as merchants, artisans, and shepherds, who arose, thanked the huntsman for their release, and went home. Meanwhile, when the twin brothers saw each other again, they kissed each other, and their hearts were full of joy. Then they grabbed the witch, tied her up, and put her into the fire. After she had been burned, the forest opened up all by itself and became bright and clear, so that one could see the royal castle, which was about a three-hour walk from there.

Now the two brothers headed toward home together and along the way told each other about their adventures. When the younger one said that he was viceroy for the whole kingdom, the other said, ''I realized that right away. When I came into the city, I was mistaken for you and shown every royal honor. The young queen thought I was her husband, and I had to sleep in your bed.''

When the other heard that, he became so jealous that he drew his sword and cut off his brother's head. However, when he saw his brother lying there dead and his red blood flowing, he was overcome by remorse.

''My brother rescued me!'' he exclaimed. ''And in return I've killed him!''

He uttered cries of grief, and then his hare came and offered to fetch the root of life. The hare dashed off and returned at just the right time. The dead brother was brought back to life and did not even notice his wound. When they continued on their journey, the younger brother said, ''You look like me. You're dressed in royal garments like me, and your animals are like mine. Let's enter from opposite gates and go to the king's chamber at the same time from opposite directions.''

So they took separate paths, and simultaneously the guards came from opposite gates to the old king and announced that the young king had returned with his animals from the hunt.

"It's not possible," the king said. "The gates are an hour's walk apart."

Just then, however, the two brothers arrived at the palace courtyard from two sides and came upstairs.

"Tell me," the king said to his daughter, "which one is your husband. They look exactly alike, and I can't tell them apart."

The young queen was very upset and could not tell them apart either. Finally, she remembered the necklace that she had given the animals. She searched and found the golden clasp on the lion, and then she exclaimed happily, "The man whom this lion follows is my husband!"

Then the young king laughed and said, "Yes, you've found the right one."

Now they all sat down at the table and ate and drank, and they were in a merry mood. That night, when the young king went to bed, his wife asked him, "Why did you always place a double-edged sword in our bed these last few nights? I thought you might want to slay me."

Then he realized how faithful his brother had been.

◈ 61 ◈

Little Farmer

THERE ONCE WAS A VILLAGE where all the farmers were rich except one who was poor, and he was called Little Farmer. He did not even have a cow, much less the money to buy one. Since he and his wife wanted to own one, he said to her one day, "Listen, I have a good idea. We'll ask our cousin the carpenter to make us a calf out of wood and then paint it brown so that it will look like all the other cows. In time it's bound to get big and become a cow."

His wife liked the idea, and their cousin the carpenter took his plane and saw and built a perfect-looking calf. Then he painted it brown and lowered its head to make it seem that the calf was eating. When the cows were driven out to pasture the next morning, Little Farmer called the cowherd to him and said, "Look, I've got a little calf here, but it's still quite small and needs to be carried."

"All right," said the cowherd, and he lifted it in his arms and carried it to the pasture. There he put it down on the grass, and the little calf just stayed at the same spot as if it were eating.

"It'll soon be running around by itself," the cowherd said. "Just look at how it won't stop eating!"

In the evening, when he wanted to drive the herd back home, he said to the calf, "If you can stand there and eat your fill, then you can also walk back on your own four legs. I don't feel like carrying you in my arms again."

Meanwhile, Little Farmer stood in front of his door waiting for his little calf. When the cowherd drove the cows through the village and the little calf was missing, he asked where it was.

"It's still standing and eating in the pasture," said the cowherd. "It didn't want to stop and come with me."

"My God!" said Little Farmer. "I've got to have my calf back."

Then they went back to the meadow together, but someone had stolen the calf, and it was gone.

"It must have gone astray," said the cowherd.

"Don't give me that story!" said Little Farmer, and he took the cowherd to the mayor, who decided that the cowherd was negligent and ordered him to give Little Farmer a cow to replace the missing calf.

Now Little Farmer and his wife had the cow that they had longed for in the past. They were exceedingly happy, but they had no fodder and could not give it anything to eat. They soon had to slaughter it and salted the meat so it would keep. Then Little Farmer took the cowhide to the city, where he intended to sell it and buy a new calf with the profit. On the way he passed a mill where a raven was sitting with broken wings. Out of pity for the bird, he picked it up and wrapped it in the hide. Just then the weather became bad, and a storm arose with wind and rain. Since he could not continue on his way, he stopped at the mill where he requested lodging. The miller's wife was alone at the house and said to Little Farmer, "Lie down on the straw over there," and she gave him bread and cheese. Little Farmer ate the food and lay down with the cowhide next to him. Now the miller's wife thought, I'm sure he's asleep since he was so tired.

Soon the priest arrived, and the miller's wife welcomed him warmly. "My husband's away," she said. "So let's treat ourselves to a feast!"

Little Farmer's ears perked when he heard her talking about a feast. He was very disturbed that she had made him put up with bread and cheese. Then the miller's wife brought out four different things: a roast, a salad, a cake, and some wine. As they were about to sit down and eat there was a knock at the door.

"Oh, God! It's my husband," said the wife. She quickly hid the roast in the tile stove, the wine under the pillow, the salad on the bed, the cake under the bed, and the priest in the hallway cupboard. Then she let her husband in and said, "Thank God you're here again! That's some weather outside. You'd think that the world were coming to an end!"

The miller saw Little Farmer lying on the straw and asked, "What's that fellow doing there?"

"Ah," said his wife, "the poor fellow came here in the storm and rain and asked for shelter. So I gave him some bread and cheese and showed him to that place on the straw."

"Well, I've got no objections," said the husband, "but get me something to eat and be quick about it."

"There's nothing but bread and cheese," the wife said.

"I'll eat anything," answered her husband, "even if it's just bread and cheese." Then he glanced over at Little Farmer and called, "Come over here and eat a little more with me!"

Little Farmer did not have to be asked twice but got up and joined the miller in his meal. Afterward the miller noticed the cowhide wrapped around the raven lying on the floor, and he asked, "What have you got there?"

"I've got a fortune-teller that's wrapped up inside," answered Little Farmer.

"Can he predict my future?" asked the miller.

"Why not?" responded Little Farmer. "However, he only predicts four things, and the fifth he keeps to himself."

The miller was curious and said, "Let him predict my future."

So Little Farmer pressed the raven's head so that it cawed *"Krr! Krr!"*

"What did he say?" asked the miller.

"His first prediction is that there's wine under the pillow," Little Farmer answered.

"Good heavens!" exclaimed the miller, who went over and found the wine. "Go on," he said.

Little Farmer made the raven caw again and said, "His second prediction is that there's a roast in the tile stove."

"Good heavens!" exclaimed the miller, who went over and found the roast.

Little Farmer made the raven caw once more and said, "His third prediction is that there's salad on the bed."

"Good heavens!" exclaimed the miller, who went over and found the salad.

Finally, Little Farmer pressed the raven's head one more time so that it cawed, and he said, "His fourth prediction is that there's cake under the bed."

"Good heavens!" exclaimed the miller, who went over and found the cake.

Now the two of them sat down at the table, but the miller's wife was frightened to death. So she went to bed and took all the keys with her. The miller wanted to know the fifth prediction, but Little Farmer said, "First let's eat these four things in peace, for the fifth is something awful."

So they ate, and afterward they bargained over how much money the miller should pay Little Farmer for the fifth prediction. Finally, they agreed on three hundred talers, and Little Farmer pressed the raven's head one more time so that it cawed loudly.

"What did he say?" asked the miller.

"He said the devil's hiding in the hallway cupboard outside," replied Little Farmer.

"I want the devil out of there at once!" said the miller, and he unlocked the front door. The wife was forced to turn over the keys, and Little Farmer opened the cupboard. Then the priest ran out as fast he could, and the miller exclaimed, "It's true! I saw the black scoundrel with my own eyes!"

At dawn the next morning Little Farmer made off with his three hundred talers. When he returned home, his affairs began to show gradual improvement. He built himself a charming house, and the farmers said, "Little Farmer's surely been to that land where golden snow falls and where people take home money by the shovelful."

So Little Farmer was summoned by the mayor and ordered to reveal where he had gotten his wealth.

"I sold my cowhide in the city for three hundred talers," he said.

When the farmers heard that, they all wanted to take advantage of the opportunity. They ran home, slaughtered all their cows, and then skinned them in order to sell them in the city at a great profit.

"My maid must go first," the mayor declared.

However, when she got to the city, the merchant gave her only three talers for a cowhide, and when the rest of them came, he did not give them even that much.

"What am I supposed to do with all these cowhides?" he asked.

Now, the farmers were furious that Little Farmer had pulled the wool over their eyes, and they wanted revenge. So they went to the mayor and accused the farmer of fraud. The innocent Little Farmer was unanimously sentenced to death by a jury and was to be rolled into the water in a barrel full of holes. Little Farmer was led out to the water, and a priest was brought to read him the last rites. All the others had to leave, and when Little Farmer looked at the priest, he recognized the man who had been with the miller's wife.

"Since I set you free from the cupboard," he said, "you can set me free from the barrel."

Just at that moment the shepherd came by with his flock of sheep, and Little Farmer happened to know that for a long time this man had wanted to become mayor. Therefore, Little Farmer screamed with all his might, "No, I won't do it! Even if the whole world wants it, I won't do it!"

When the shepherd heard the screams, he went over and asked, "What's going on? What won't you do?"

"They want to make me mayor," said Little Farmer, "providing that I get into this barrel, but I won't do it."

"If that's all that it takes to become mayor," said the shepherd, "I'll get in right away."

"If you get in," said Little Farmer, "they'll make you mayor for sure."

The shepherd was happy to comply and got inside. Then Little Farmer slammed the lid down, took the shepherd's flock, and drove it away. Meanwhile, the priest went to the villagers and said he had read the last rites. They then went and rolled the barrel toward the water. When the barrel began to roll, the shepherd cried out, "I'll gladly be mayor!"

They believed it was no one else but Little Farmer screaming and said, "We believe you, but first we want you to look around down there." And they rolled the barrel into the water.

Then the farmers went home, and when they returned to the village, Little Farmer came along in good spirits, calmly driving a flock of sheep. The farmers were astonished and said, "Little Farmer, where are you coming from? Are you coming from the water?"

"Of course," he answered. "I sank deep down into the water until I reached the bottom. Then I kicked the lid off the barrel and crawled out. There were beautiful meadows with lots of sheep grazing on them. So I brought back a flock of them with me."

"Are there any more left?" the farmers asked.

"Oh, yes," said Little Farmer, "more than you could possibly use."

So the farmers decided to fetch some sheep too, each one a flock, and the mayor declared, "I'm going first!"

They all went down to the water together, and just then there happened to be in the sky the small flocks of clouds that are called little fleece. They were reflected in the water, and the farmers exclaimed, "We can already see the fleece of the sheep down below!"

The mayor pushed to the front and announced, "I'll dive down first and look around. If everything looks all right, I'll call you."

So he jumped into the water, and there was a big *splash!* It sounded as if he had yelled "Rush!" and the whole group of farmers plunged into the water after him. Thus the entire village was wiped out, and since Little Farmer was the sole survivor and heir, he became a rich man.

◈ 62 ◈

The Queen Bee

ONCE TWO PRINCES WENT FORTH in search of adventure, and after they fell into a wild, decadent way of life, they never returned home again. Their youngest brother, who was called Simpleton, went out to look for them, but when he finally found them, they ridiculed him for thinking that he, as naive as he was, could make his way in the world when they, who were much more clever, had not been able to succeed.

At length the three of them traveled together and came to an anthill. The two oldest wanted to smash it and watch the small ants crawl around in fright and carry away their eggs, but Simpleton said, "Leave the little creatures in peace. I won't let you disturb them."

They continued on their way and came to a lake where a great many ducks were swimming. The two brothers wanted to catch a few and roast them, but Simpleton would not let them.

"Leave the creatures in peace," he said. "I won't let you kill them."

Next they came to a beehive, and there was so much honey in the hive that it had dripped down the tree trunk. The two older brothers wanted to build a fire underneath it and suffocate the bees to get at the honey. However, Simpleton prevented them again and said, "Leave the creatures in peace. I won't let you burn them."

Finally, the three brothers came to a castle, and they saw nothing but stone horses standing in the stables. Not a living soul could be seen. They went through all the halls until they reached the end, where there was a door with three locks hanging on it. In the middle of the door there was a peephole through which one could look into the room. In there they saw a gray dwarf sitting at a table. They called to him once, then twice, but he did not hear them. Finally, they called a third time, and he got up, opened the locks, and came out. However, he did not say a word. Instead, he just led them to a richly spread table, and after they had something to eat and drink, he brought each one to his own bedroom.

The next morning the gray dwarf went to the oldest brother, beckoned to him, and conducted him to a stone tablet on which were inscribed three tasks that had to be performed if the castle was to be disenchanted. The first task involved gathering one thousand pearls that were lying in the moss of the forest. They belonged to the king's daughter and had to be collected from the moss before sundown. If one single pearl was missing, the seeker would be turned to stone.

The oldest brother went to the moss and searched the entire day, but when the day drew to a close, he had found only one hundred. Consequently, he was turned into stone as was ordained by the tablet. The next day the second brother undertook the adventure, but he did not fare much better than the oldest: he found only two hundred pearls and was turned into stone. Finally, it was Simpleton's turn to search for the pearls in the moss. However, because it was so difficult to find them and everything went so slowly, he sat down on a stone and began to weep. While he was sitting on the stone and weeping, the king of the ants whose life he had once saved came along with five thousand ants, and it did not take long before the little creatures had gathered the pearls together and stacked them in a pile.

Now, the second task was to fetch the key to the bedroom of the king's daughter from the lake. When Simpleton came to the lake, the ducks whose lives he had once saved came swimming toward him and then dived down to fetch the key from the depths.

Next came the third task, which was the hardest. The king had three daughters who lay asleep, and Simpleton had to pick out the youngest and the loveliest. However, they all looked exactly alike, and the only difference between them was that they each had eaten a different kind of sweet before falling asleep: the oldest had eaten a piece of sugar, the second a little syrup, the youngest a spoonful of honey. Just then the queen bee whom Simpleton had protected from the fire came along and tested the lips of all three princesses. At last she settled on the mouth of the princess who had eaten honey, and thus the prince was able to recognize the right daughter. Now the magic spell was broken, and everyone was set free from the deep sleep. All those who had been turned into stone regained their human form. Simpleton married the youngest and loveliest daughter and became king after her father's death, while his two brothers were married to the other two sisters.

◈ 63 ◈

The Three Feathers

ONCE UPON A TIME there was a king who had three sons. Two of them were bright and clever, but the third was just called Simpleton because he did not speak much and was naive. When the king became old and weak and began thinking about his end, he was uncertain about which of his sons should inherit his kingdom.

"I want you to go forth," he said to them, "and whoever brings me the finest carpet shall be king after my death."

To make sure that they would not quarrel among themselves, he led them outside the castle, blew three feathers into the air, and said, "You're to follow the flight of the feathers."

One feather flew to the east, the next to the west, and the third flew straight ahead but not very far, and soon it fell to the ground. So one brother went to the right, the other to the left, and the two of them made fun of Simpleton because he had to stay where the third feather had fallen.

Now Simpleton sat down and was sad. However, all at once he noticed there was a trapdoor next to the feather. He lifted it up, discovered some stairs, and went down. Then he came to another door, knocked, and heard a voice calling from inside:

"Maiden, maiden, green and small,
hop to it, hoptoad, and don't you fall.
Hoptoad's dog, hop back and forth,
and quickly see who's at the door."

The door opened, and there he saw a large fat toad surrounded by lots of little toads. The large toad asked him what he desired, and he answered, "I'd like to have the most beautiful and finest carpet."

Then the toad called one of the young ones and said:

"Maiden, maiden, green and small,
hop to it, hoptoad, and don't you fall.
Hoptoad's dog, hop lively, hop sprightly,
Fetch me the box as quick as can be."

The young toad fetched the box, and the fat toad opened it and gave Simpleton a carpet so beautiful and fine that nobody on earth could possibly have woven it. So he thanked her and climbed back up the stairs.

In the meantime, the two others, who considered their brother so stupid, did not think that he would find anything, let alone bring it back. "Why should we exert ourselves by searching?" they said, and they snatched some material from the first shepherd's wife they met and brought it home to the king. At the same time Simpleton also returned and brought his beautiful carpet. When the king saw it, he was astonished and said, "According to my decree the kingdom belongs to the youngest."

However, the two oldest would not leave their father in peace and declared it was impossible for Simpleton to become king since he had no understanding of anything. Therefore, they begged the king to set a new condition, and the father said, "Whoever brings me the most beautiful ring shall inherit the kingdom."

He led the three brothers outside, blew three feathers into the air, and beckoned them to follow the feathers. Once again the two oldest went to the east and the west, and Simpleton went straight ahead, where the feather flew and fell next to the trapdoor. He climbed down again to the fat toad and said to her that he needed the most beautiful ring in the world. The toad had the large box brought to her immediately, took out a ring, and gave it to him. The ring sparkled with precious gems and was so beautiful that no goldsmith on earth could possibly have made it.

In the meantime, the two oldest made fun of Simpleton for wanting to search for a golden ring. Again they did not exert themselves but just knocked the nails out of an old wagon ring and brought it to the king. However, when Simpleton displayed his golden ring, the father declared once more, "The kingdom belongs to him."

Nevertheless, the two oldest sons kept pestering the king until he set a third condition and proclaimed that whoever brought home the most beautiful woman would inherit the kingdom. He blew the three feathers into the air again, and they flew just as they had before.

Simpleton did not waste any time and went directly to the toad and said, "I'm to bring home the most beautiful woman in the world."

"My goodness!" answered the toad. "The most beautiful woman! I don't happen to have her right on hand, but you shall still get her nonetheless." Then the toad gave him a yellow turnip that had been hollowed out and had six little mice harnessed to it.

"What am I to do with that?" asked Simpleton quite sadly.

"Just put one of my little toads inside," answered the toad.

Then he chose one of the toads from the group at random and put her into the yellow shell. No sooner was the little toad inside than she turned into a remarkably beautiful maiden, the turnip into a coach, and the six mice into horses. Then he kissed her, drove off with the horses at a rapid pace, and brought her to the king. His brothers also returned, but they had not exerted themselves. Instead, they had taken the first good-looking peasant women they could find. When the king saw them, he said, "The kingdom belongs to my youngest son after my death."

Once again the two oldest sons made such a racket that it was deafening to the king's ears. "We'll never accept Simpleton as king!" They demanded that preference be shown to the one whose woman could jump through a hoop hanging in the middle of the hall, for they thought, Peasant women can do that easily. They're very strong, but the delicate maiden will jump to her death.

The old king relented on this occasion as well, and the two peasant women jumped through the hoop. However, they were so clumsy that they fell and broke their chubby arms and legs. Then Simpleton's beautiful maiden jumped through the hoop as gracefully as a deer, and all objections by the two oldest sons had to stop. So Simpleton received the crown and reigned wisely for a long time thereafter.

◈ 64 ◈

The Golden Goose

THERE WAS ONCE A MAN WHO HAD THREE SONS, and the youngest, who was called Simpleton, was constantly mocked, disdained, and slighted. Now, one day it happened that the oldest brother decided to go into the forest to chop wood, and before he went, his mother gave him a nice, fine pancake and a bottle of wine so that he would not have to suffer from hunger or thirst. When he reached the forest, he met a gray old dwarf, who wished him good day and said, "Give me a piece of the pancake from your pocket, and let me have a drink of wine. I'm very hungry and thirsty."

However, the clever son answered, "If I give you my pancake and my wine, then I won't have anything for myself. So get out of my way," and he left the dwarf standing there and went farther into the forest. When he began chopping down a tree, it did not take long for him to make a slip and cut himself in the arm. So he had to return home and have his arm bandaged. All this happened because of the gray dwarf.

Shortly thereafter, the second son went into the forest, and the mother gave him a pancake and a bottle of wine, just as she had given the oldest. The second son too met the gray old dwarf, who asked him for a piece of the pancake and a drink of wine. But the second son also spoke quite sensibly. "Whatever I give you, I'll be taking from myself. So get out of my way." Then he left the dwarf standing there and went farther into the forest. Soon his punishment came as well. After he had whacked a tree a few times, he struck himself in the leg. Consequently, he had to be carried home.

Then Simpleton said, "Father, let me go now and chop some wood."

"Your brothers hurt themselves doing that," said the father. "So I want you to steer clear of the woods, especially since you know nothing about chopping down trees."

However, Simpleton kept insisting until his father finally said,

"Go ahead. Perhaps you'll learn something after you've hurt yourself."

The mother gave him a pancake made out of water and ashes along with a bottle of sour beer. When he went into the forest, he too met the gray old dwarf, who greeted him and said, "Give me a piece of your pancake and a drink out of your bottle. I'm very hungry and thirsty."

"I have only a pancake made of ashes and some sour beer," answered Simpleton. "If that's all right with you, let's sit down and eat."

So they sat down, and when Simpleton took out his cake made of ashes, it turned out to be a fine pancake, and the sour beer was good wine. After they had eaten and drunk, the dwarf said, "Since you have such a good heart and gladly share what you have, I'm going to grant you some good luck. There's an old tree over there. Just go and chop it down, and you'll find something among the roots." Then the dwarf took leave of him.

Simpleton went over and chopped down the tree. When it fell, he saw a goose with feathers of pure gold lying among the roots. He lifted the goose up and carried it with him to an inn, where he intended to spend the night. Now, the innkeeper had three daughters, and when they saw the goose, they were curious to know what kind of strange bird it was. Moreover, they each wanted to have one of its golden feathers. The oldest thought, I'll surely find an opportunity to pluck one of its feathers.

At one point Simpleton went out, and she seized the goose by its wing, but her hand and fingers remained stuck to it. Soon afterward the second sister came and also intended to pluck a golden feather. However, no sooner did she touch her sister than she became stuck to her. Finally, the third sister came with the same intention, but the other two screamed, "Keep away! For heaven's sake, keep away!"

But she did not comprehend why she should keep away and thought, If they're there, I see no reason why I can't be. So she ran over, and when she touched her sister, she became stuck to her, and all three had to spend the night with the goose.

The next morning Simpleton took the goose in his arm, set out, and did not bother himself about the three sisters who were stuck to the goose. They were compelled to run after him constantly, left and right, wherever his legs took him. In the middle of a field they came across the parson, and when he saw the procession, he said, "Shame on you, you naughty girls! Is that the right way to behave?"

Upon saying that, he grabbed the youngest sister by the hand and attempted to pull her away, but when he touched her, he also got stuck and had to run along behind them. Shortly afterward the sexton came by and saw the parson trailing the three girls on their heels. In his amazement he called out, "Hey, Parson, where are you off to in such a hurry? Don't forget that we have a christening today!"

The sexton ran up to the parson, and as soon as he touched his sleeve, he became stuck like the others. Now the five of them had to trot after Simpleton, one stuck to the other, and they approached two farmers who were coming from the fields with their hoes. The parson called out to them to set them loose. However, as soon as they touched the sexton, they got stuck, and now there were seven of them trailing Simpleton and his goose.

After some time Simpleton came to a city ruled by a king who had a daughter that was so serious, she never laughed. Consequently, the king issued a decree that whoever could make her laugh would have her for his wife. When Simpleton heard that, he went before the king's daughter with his goose and its followers, and when she saw the seven people all attached to one another and running along, she burst out laughing, and it appeared as if she would never stop. So Simpleton demanded the princess as his bride, but the king had no desire to have him for a son-in-law and raised all kinds of objections. Eventually, he said that first Simpleton would have to produce a man capable of drinking the contents of a cellar full of wine before he could wed his daughter.

Now, Simpleton quickly remembered the gray dwarf, for he thought that he might help him. Therefore, he went out into the forest, right to the spot where he had chopped down the tree. There he saw a man with a sad face sitting and moping. Simpleton asked what was bothering him so much, and he answered, "I'm terribly thirsty and don't seem to be able to quench my thirst. I can't stand cold water, and just now I emptied a barrel of wine, but that was like a drop on a hot stone."

"Well, I can help you," said Simpleton. "Just come with me, and you'll be able to drink your fill."

He led him to the king's cellar, and the man rushed over to the large barrels and set to work: he drank so much that his sides began to hurt, but before the day was over, he had emptied the entire cellar. So once again Simpleton demanded his bride, but the king was perturbed that such a common fellow, whom everyone called Simpleton, was to have his daughter. Therefore, he set a new condition: now Simpleton had to produce a man who could eat a mountain of bread.

Simpleton immediately reacted by going directly into the forest. There, on the same spot as before, he saw a man sitting who was pulling in a belt around his waist. The man made an awful face and said, "I've eaten an oven full of coarse bread, but what good is that when I'm as hungry as a lion. My stomach's still empty, and I have to pull in my belt if I don't want to die of hunger."

Simpleton was glad to hear that and said, "Get up and come with me. You shall eat your fill."

He led him to the king's courtyard, where the king had gathered all the flour of the entire kingdom and had had it baked into a tremendous mountain. However, the man from the forest stepped up to it, began eating, and consumed the whole mountain in one day. Now for the third time, Simpleton claimed his bride, but the king found another way out and demanded a ship that could sail on land and water.

"As soon as you come sailing back in it," he said, "you shall have my daughter for your wife."

Simpleton went straight into the forest and encountered the gray old dwarf to whom he had given his cake.

"I've drunk and eaten for you," said the dwarf. "Now I'll also give you the ship. I'm doing all this because you treated me so kindly."

Then he gave him the ship, and when the king saw it, he could no longer prevent him from marrying his daughter. The wedding was celebrated, and after the king's death, Simpleton inherited the kingdom and lived happily ever after with his wife.

◈ 65 ◈

All Fur

ONCE UPON A TIME there was a king whose wife had golden hair and was so beautiful that her equal could not be found anywhere on earth. Now, it happened that she became sick, and when she felt she was about to die, she called the king to her and said, "If you desire to marry again after my death, I'd like you to take someone who is as beautiful as I am and who has golden hair like mine. Promise me that you will do this."

After the king had promised her that, she closed her eyes and died. For a long time the king could not be consoled and did not think about remarrying. Finally, his councillors said, "This cannot continue. The king must marry again so that we may have a queen."

Messengers were sent far and wide to search for a bride who might equal the beauty of the dead queen. Yet, they could not find anyone like her in the world, and even had they found such a woman, she certainly would not have had such golden hair. So the messengers returned with their mission unaccomplished.

Now, the king had a daughter who was just as beautiful as her dead mother, and she also had the same golden hair. When she was grown-up, the king looked at her one day and realized that her features were exactly the same as those of his dead wife. Suddenly he fell passionately in love with her and said to his councillors, "I'm going to marry my daughter, for she is the living image of my dead wife."

When the councillors heard that, they were horrified and said, "God has forbidden a father to marry his daughter. Nothing good can come from such a sin, and the kingdom will be brought to ruin."

When she heard of her father's decision, the daughter was even more horrified, but she still hoped to dissuade him from carrying out his plan. Therefore, she said to him, "Before I fulfill your wish, I must have three dresses, one as golden as the sun, one as silvery as the moon, and one as bright as the stars. Furthermore, I want a cloak made up of a thousand kinds of pelts and furs, and each animal in your kingdom must contribute a piece of its skin to it." She thought, He'll never be able to obtain all those furs, and by demanding this, I shall divert my father from his evil intentions.

The king, however, persisted, and the most skillful women in his realm were assembled to weave the three dresses, one as golden as the sun, one as silvery as the moon, and one as bright as the stars. His huntsmen had to catch all the animals in his entire kingdom and take a piece of their skin. Thus a cloak was made from a thousand kinds of fur. At last, when everything was finished, the king ordered the cloak to be brought and spread out before her. Then he announced, "The wedding will be tomorrow."

When the king's daughter saw that there was no hope whatsoever of changing her father's inclinations, she decided to run away. That night, while everyone was asleep, she got up and took three of her precious possessions: a golden ring, a tiny golden spinning wheel, and a little golden reel. She packed the dresses of the sun, the moon, and the stars into a nutshell, put on the cloak of all kinds of fur, and blackened her face and hands with soot. Then she commended herself to God and departed. She walked the whole night until she reached a great forest, and since she was tired, she climbed into a hollow tree and fell asleep.

When the sun rose, she continued to sleep and sleep until it became broad daylight. Meanwhile, it happened that the king who was the lord of this forest was out hunting in it, and when his dogs came to the tree, they started to sniff and run around it and bark.

"Go see what kind of beast has hidden itself there," the king said to his huntsmen.

The huntsmen obeyed the king's command, and when they returned to him, they said, "There's a strange animal lying in the hollow tree. We've never seen anything like it. Its skin is made up of a thousand different kinds of fur, and it's lying there asleep."

"See if you can catch it alive," said the king. "Then tie it to the wagon, and we'll take it with us."

When the huntsmen seized the maiden, she woke up in a fright and cried to them, "I'm just a poor girl, forsaken by my father and mother! Please have pity on me and take me with you."

"You'll be perfect for the kitchen, *All Fur*," they said. "Come with us, and you can sweep up the ashes there."

So they put her into the wagon and drove back to the royal castle. There they showed her to a little closet beneath the stairs that was never exposed to daylight.

"Well, you furry creature," they said, "you can live and sleep here."

Then she was sent to the kitchen, where she carried wood and water, kept the fires going, plucked the fowls, sorted the vegetables, swept up the ashes, and did all the dirty work. All Fur lived there for a long time in dire poverty. Ah, my beautiful princess, what shall become of you?

At one time a ball was being held in the castle, and All Fur asked the cook, "May I go upstairs and watch for a while? I'll just stand outside the door."

"Yes," said the cook. "Go ahead, but be back in half an hour. You've got to sweep up the ashes."

All Fur took her little oil lamp, went to her closet, took off her fur cloak, and washed the soot from her face and hands so that her full beauty came to light again. Then she opened the nut and took out the dress that shone like the sun. When that was done, she went upstairs to the ball, and everyone made way for her, for they had no idea who she was and believed that she was nothing less than a royal princess. The king approached her, offered her his hand, and led her forth to dance. In his heart he thought, Never in my life have my eyes beheld anyone so beautiful! When the dance was over, she curtsied, and as the king was looking around she disappeared, and nobody knew where she had gone. The guards who were standing in front of the castle were summoned and questioned, but no one had seen her.

In the meantime, the princess had run back to her closet and had undressed quickly. Then she blackened her face and hands, put on the fur cloak, and became All Fur once more. When she went back to the kitchen, she resumed her work and began sweeping up the ashes.

"Let that be until tomorrow," said the cook. "I want you to make a soup for the king. While you're doing that, I'm going upstairs to watch a little. You'd better not let a single hair drop into the soup or else you'll get nothing more to eat in the future!"

The cook went away, and All Fur made the soup for the king by brewing a bread soup as best she could. When she was finished, she fetched her golden ring from the closet and put it into the bowl in which she had prepared the soup. When the ball was over, the king ordered the soup to be brought to him, and as he ate it, he was convinced that he had never eaten a soup that had tasted as good. However, he found a ring lying at the bottom of the bowl when he had finished eating, and he could not imagine how it could have got there. He ordered the cook to appear before him, and the cook became terrified on learning that the king wanted to see him.

"You must have let a hair drop into the soup," he said to All Fur. "If that's true, you can expect a good beating!"

When he went before the king, he was asked who had made the soup.

"I did," answered the cook.

However, the king said, "That's not true, for it was much different from your usual soup and much better cooked."

"I must confess," responded the cook. "I didn't cook it. The furry creature did."

"Go and fetch her here," said the king.

When All Fur appeared, the king asked, "Who are you?"

"I'm just a poor girl that no longer has a mother or father."

"Why are you in my castle?" the king continued.

"I'm good for nothing but to have boots thrown at my head," she replied.

"Where did you get the ring that was in the soup?" he asked again.

"I don't know anything about the ring," she answered. So the king could not find out anything and had to send her away.

Some months later there was another ball, and like the previous time, All Fur asked the cook's permission to go and watch.

"Yes," he answered. "But come back in half an hour and cook the king the bread soup that he likes so much."

She ran to the little closet, washed herself quickly, took the dress as silvery as the moon out of the nut, and put it on. When she appeared upstairs, she looked like a royal princess. The king approached her again and was delighted to see her. Since the dance had just begun, they danced together, and when the dance was over, she again disappeared so quickly that the king was unable to see where she went. In the meantime, she returned to the little closet, made herself into the furry creature again, and returned to the kitchen to make the bread soup. While the cook was still upstairs, she fetched the tiny golden spinning wheel, put it into the bowl, and covered it with the soup. Then the soup was brought to the king, and he ate it and enjoyed it as much as he had the previous time. Afterward he summoned the cook, who again had to admit that All Fur had made the soup. Now All Fur had to appear before the king once more, but she merely repeated that she was good for nothing but to have boots thrown at her and that she knew nothing about the tiny golden spinning wheel.

When the king held a ball for the third time, everything happened just as it had before. To be sure, the cook now asserted, "Furry creature, I know you're a witch. You always put something in the soup to make it taste good and to make the king like it better than anything I can cook."

However, since she pleaded so intensely, he let her go upstairs at a given time. Thereupon she put on the dress as bright as the stars and entered the ballroom wearing it. Once again the king danced with the beautiful maiden and thought that she had never been more beautiful. While he danced with her, he put a golden ring on her finger without her noticing it. He had also ordered the dance to last a very long time, and when it was over, he tried to hold on to her hands, but she tore herself away and quickly ran into the crowd, vanishing from his sight. However, she had stayed upstairs too long, more than half an hour, and she could not take off her beautiful dress but had to throw her fur cloak over it. Moreover, she was in such a hurry, she could not make herself completely black, and one of her fingers was left white. Then All Fur ran into the kitchen and cooked the soup for the king. While the cook was away, she put the golden reel into the bowl. So, when the king found the reel at the bottom of the bowl, he summoned All Fur and saw the ring that he had put on her finger during the dance. Then he seized her hand and held it tight, and when she tried to free herself and run away, the fur cloak opened a bit, and the dress of bright stars was unveiled. The king grabbed the cloak and tore it off her. Suddenly her golden hair toppled down, and she stood there in all her splendor unable to conceal herself any longer. After she had wiped the soot and ashes from her face, she was more beautiful than anyone who had ever been glimpsed on earth.

"You shall be my dear bride," the king said, "and we shall never part from each other!"

Thereupon the wedding was celebrated, and they lived happily together until their death.

◈ 66 ◈

The Hare's Bride

THERE ONCE WAS A WOMAN who lived with her daughter, and near their dwelling they had a beautiful cabbage garden. During the winter, however, a little hare got into the garden and began eating up the cabbage. So the woman said to her daughter, "Go out into the garden and chase the hare away."

"*Shoo! Shoo!*" cried the maiden to the hare. "Stop eating all our cabbage!"

"Come here, maiden," said the hare. "Sit down on my tail and come with me to my little hut."

The maiden was unwilling, and the next day the hare again came and ate the cabbage.

"Go out into the garden," said the mother, "and chase the hare away."

"*Shoo! Shoo!*" cried the maiden. "Stop eating all our cabbage!"

"Come here, maiden," said the hare. "Sit down on my tail and come with me to my little hut."

The maiden was unwilling. On the third day the hare again came and ate the cabbage. The woman then said to her daughter, "Go out into the garden and chase the hare away."

"*Shoo! Shoo!* Stop eating all our cabbage!" cried the maiden.

"Come here, maiden," said the hare. "Sit down on my tail and come with me to my little hut."

The maiden sat down on the hare's tail, and the hare carried her far away to his hut and said, "Now, cook some green cabbage and millet. I'm going out to invite the wedding guests."

Then all the wedding guests gathered together. (Who were the wedding guests? Well, I can tell you what someone else told me: all the hares were there, the crow as parson to marry the couple, the fox as sexton, and the altar was under the rainbow.) However, the maiden was sad because she was so alone. Then the hare came back and said, "Open the door! Open the door! The wedding guests are all nice and merry."

The bride said nothing but wept. The hare went away and then came back again.

"Open the door! Open the door! The wedding guests are hungry."

Again the bride said nothing but wept, and the hare went away. Then he came and said, "Open the door! Open the door! The wedding guests are waiting."

The bride said nothing, and the hare went away. However, this time the maiden made a straw doll, dressed it in her clothes, gave it a big spoon, stood it in front of the kettle with the millet, and then went home to her mother.

Again the hare came and said, "Open the door! Open the door!"

Finally, he opened the door and smashed the doll on its head so that the cap fell off. When he realized that it was not his bride, the hare went off and was sad.

❖ 67 ❖

The Twelve Huntsmen

ONCE UPON A TIME there was a prince who was betrothed to a maiden and loved her very much. One day, as he was sitting with her and feeling very happy, he received news that his father was seriously ill and wanted to see him one more time before he died.

"I must go away now and leave you," he said to his beloved. "Please take this ring to remember me by. When I become king, I shall come back for you."

Then he rode away, and when he got home, he saw that his father was very sick and on the verge of death.

"Dearest son," the king said to him, "I wanted to see you one more time before my end. Promise me that you shall marry according to my will," and he named a certain king's daughter who was to become his wife.

So distressed was the son that he did not even stop to think about what he was doing and said, "Yes, dear Father, your will shall be done."

The king then closed his eyes and died. Some time later, when the son had been proclaimed king and the period of mourning had passed, he had to keep the promise that he had given his father. So he made it known that he wanted to wed the king's daughter, and soon she was promised to him. When his first bride heard about that, she grieved so much about his infidelity that she almost died. Then her father said to her, "My dear child, why are you so sad? Name your wish, and I shall grant it."

She thought for a moment and then said, "Dear Father, I would like to have eleven young women who all look like me in face, form, and stature."

"If it's possible," said the king, "your wish shall be fulfilled." And he ordered his men to search all over his whole kingdom for as long as was necessary until they found eleven young women who looked exactly like his daughter in face, form, and stature.

When the young women appeared before the princess, she ordered twelve hunting outfits made, one just like the next, and the eleven young women had to put on the outfits, while she herself put on the twelfth. She then took leave of her father and rode away with the eleven young women until they came to the court of her former bridegroom, whom she loved so dearly. There she asked whether he needed any huntsmen and whether he would like to take all twelve of them into his service. The king looked at her and did not recognize her. But since they were fine-looking fellows, he said, yes, he would gladly employ them. And so they became the king's twelve huntsmen.

Now, the king had a lion that was a remarkable animal, for he could detect anything hidden and secret. One evening he happened to come to the king and said, "You think you've got twelve huntsmen?"

"Yes," said the king. "Twelve huntsmen they are."

"You're wrong," said the lion. "They're twelve women."

"That's not true at all," answered the king. "How are you going to prove that?"

"Oh, just have some peas scattered in your antechamber," responded the lion. "You'll be able to tell right away. Men walk firmly when they walk over peas. Not a pea will move. But women trip and skid and glide their feet, and the peas will roll."

The king liked his advice very much and ordered peas to be scattered over the floor. However, one of the king's servants was kindly disposed to the huntsmen, and when he heard that they were going to be put to a test, he went to them and told them everything. "The lion wants to prove to the king that you're women," he said.

The king's daughter thanked him and afterward spoke to her young women. "Control yourselves when you walk over the peas. Just step on them firmly."

The next morning, when the king summoned the twelve huntsmen to him and they entered the antechamber where the peas were lying, they stepped so firmly on them and had such a strong and steady gait that not a single pea moved or rolled. After they departed, the king said to the lion, "You lied to me. They walk like men."

"They knew they were being put to a test," answered the lion. "So they controlled themselves when they walked. Now, if you have twelve spinning wheels brought into the antechamber, they'll go over to them and be delighted. No man would ever do that."

The king liked the advice, and he ordered that twelve spinning wheels be brought into the antechamber. However, the servant who sided with the huntsmen went to them and revealed the lion's plan. When they were alone, the princess said to the eleven young women, "Control yourselves and do not look at the spinning wheels when you enter the room."

The next morning, when the king summoned his twelve huntsmen, they came through the antechamber and did not even so much as glance at the spinning wheels. Once again the king said to the lion, "You lied to me. It's clear that they're men, for they didn't even glance at the spinning wheels."

"They knew they were being put to a test and thus controlled themselves," answered the lion.

However, the king did not believe him anymore. The twelve huntsmen became his steady companions whenever he went out hunting, and the longer they were with him, the fonder he grew of them. Now, it happened one day that news came of the king's betrothed, who was bound to arrive soon. When the true bride heard that, it was almost like a stab in her heart, and she was so hurt that she fell to the ground unconscious. The king, who thought that something had happened to his dear huntsman, ran over to help him and pulled off his glove. However, when he saw the ring that he had given to his first bride and looked at her face, he recognized her. His heart was moved so much that he gave her a kiss, and when she opened her eyes, he said, "You are mine, and I am yours. No one in the world can ever change that."

So the king sent a message to the other bride telling her to return to her own kingdom, for he already had a wife, and whoever finds his old key does not need a new one. Thereupon the wedding was celebrated, and the lion regained favor with the king, for he had really been telling the truth all along.

◈ 68 ◈

The Thief and His Master

JAN WANTED HIS SON TO LEARN A TRADE. Therefore, he went to church and prayed to the Lord to tell him what would be best for his son. The sexton was standing behind the altar and said, "Thieving, thieving."

So Jan went to his son and told him he had to learn how to be a thief because the Lord wanted it that way. He then set out with his son to look for a man who knew something about thieving. After they had traveled for a long time, they finally reached a great forest, where they found a little cottage with an old woman sitting inside.

"Do you happen to know a man who's good at thieving?" Jan asked.

"You can learn what you want here," said the woman. "My son's a master thief."

Then Jan talked with her son and asked him whether he was really good at thieving.

"Your son will be taught well," said the master thief. "Come back in a year, and if you can still recognize him, I won't take any money for my services. However, if you don't recognize him, you must give me two hundred talers."

The father went home again, and the son learned all kinds of witchcraft and thieving. When the year was over, the father set out by himself and began fretting because he did not know how he would be able to recognize his son. As he was walking along and fretting he encountered a little dwarf, who said, "Man, what are you worrying about? You look quite gloomy."

"Oh," Jan said, "I hired my son out as an apprentice to a master thief a year ago. He told me to return about now, and if I can't recognize my son, I must pay him two hundred talers. But if I recognize my son, I won't have to give him anything. Now I fear I won't be able to recognize him, and I don't know where I'll get the money to pay him."

Then the dwarf told him to take a crust of bread with him and stand beneath the chimney once he got there. "You'll see a basket up on the crossbeam, and a bird will peep out of it. That will be your son."

So Jan went there and threw a crust of black bread in front of the basket, and a bird came out and looked at it.

"Hello there, son, is that you?" said the father.

The son was glad to see his father, but the master thief said, "The devil must have given you the clue! How else could you have recognized your son?"

"Let's go, Father," said the boy.

Then the father and son set out for home. On the way a coach came driving by, and the son said, "I'm going to turn myself into a big greyhound. Then you can earn a lot of money by selling me."

A nobleman called from the coach, "Hey, my good fellow, do you want to sell your dog?"

"Yes," said the father.

"How much do you want for it?"

"Thirty talers."

"Well, man, that's certainly a lot, but since it's such a fine-looking dog, I'll pay."

The nobleman took the dog into his coach, but after they had driven along for a while, the dog jumped out of the coach window. Now he was no longer a greyhound and went back to his father.

They made their way home together, and on the following day there was a fair in the neighboring village. So the boy said to his father, "Now I'm going to turn myself into a fine-looking horse, and you'll sell me at the fair. But when you sell me, make sure that you take off the bridle so I can become a human being again."

The father took the horse to the fair, and the master thief came and bought the horse for a hundred talers. However, the father forgot to take off the bridle, and the master thief went home with the horse and put him in the stable. When the maid crossed the entrance to the stable, the horse cried out, "Take my bridle off! Take my bridle off!"

The maid stopped and listened. "My goodness! You can talk!"

She went and took the bridle off, and the horse became a sparrow and flew out the door. Then the master thief also became a sparrow and flew after him. They met and held a contest in midair, but the master lost and fell into the water, where he turned himself into a fish. The boy also turned himself into a fish, and they held another contest. Once again the master lost, and he turned himself into a rooster, while the boy changed himself into a fox and bit the master's head off. So the master died, and he has remained dead up to this very day.

◈ 69 ◈

Jorinda and Joringel

ONCE UPON A TIME there was an old castle in the middle of a great, dense forest. An old woman lived there all by herself, and she was a powerful sorceress. During the day she turned herself into a cat or a night owl, but in the evening she would return to her normal human form. She had the ability to lure game and birds, which she would slaughter and then cook or roast. If any man came within a hundred steps of the castle, she would cast a spell over him, so that he would not be able to move from the spot until she broke the spell. If an innocent maiden came within her magic circle, she would change her into a bird and stuff her into a wicker basket. Then she would carry the basket up to a room in her castle where she had well over seven thousand baskets with rare birds of this kind.

Now, once there was a maiden named Jorinda, who was more beautiful than any other maiden in the kingdom. She was betrothed to a handsome youth named Joringel. During the time before their marriage, they took great pleasure in being in each other's company.

One day they went for a walk in the forest so they could be alone and talk intimately with one another.

"Be careful," Joringel said, "that you don't go too close to the castle."

At dusk the sun shone brightly through the tree trunks and cast its light on the dark green of the forest. The turtledoves were singing mournfully in the old beech trees, and at times Jorinda wept. Then she sat down in the sunshine and sighed, and Joringel sighed too. They became very sad as if they were doomed to die, and when they looked around them, they became confused and did not know how to get home. The sun was still shining half above and half behind the mountains. When Joringel looked through the bushes and saw the wall of the old castle not very far away, he became so alarmed that he was nearly frightened to death, while Jorinda sang:

"Oh, my bird, with your ring of red,
sitting and singing your tale of woe!
You tell us now that the poor dove is dead.
You sing your tale of woe—*oh-oh, oh-oh!*"

Just then, as Joringel looked at Jorinda, she was turned into a nightingale singing *"oh-oh, oh-oh!"* A night owl with glowing eyes flew around her three times, and each time it cried, *"To-whoo! To-whoo! To-whoo!"*

Joringel could not budge. He stood there like a stone, unable to weep, to talk, or to move hand or foot. When the sun was about to set, the owl flew into a bush and then immediately returned as a haggard old woman, yellow and scrawny, with large red eyes and a crooked nose that almost touched her chin with its tip. She muttered something to herself, caught the nightingale, and carried it away in her hand. Joringel was still unable to speak, nor could he move from the spot. The nightingale was gone. Soon the woman came back and said with a muffled voice, "Greetings, Zachiel. When the moon shines into the basket, let him loose, Zachiel, just at the right moment."

Then Joringel was set free, and he fell on his knees before the woman and begged her to give Jorinda back to him, but she said he would never get her back again and went away. He shouted, he wept, he moaned, but it was all in vain. "Oh, no, what's to become of me?"

Joringel went off and eventually came to an unfamiliar village, where he tended sheep for a long time. He often went round and round the castle and always kept his distance. Finally, he dreamed one night that he had found a flower as red as blood, and in the middle of it was a pearl. He plucked the flower and went with it to the castle: everything that he touched with the flower was set free from the magic spell. He also dreamed that he managed to regain his Jorinda with the flower.

When he awoke the next morning, he began searching all over the mountains and valleys for the flower of his dream. He searched for nine days, and early on the ninth day he found a flower as red as blood. In its middle was a large dewdrop as big as the finest pearl.

He carried this flower day and night until he reached the castle. When he came to within a hundred steps of the castle, he was not spellbound but was able to get to the gate. Overjoyed by that, Joringel touched the gate with the flower, and it sprang open. So he entered, crossed the courtyard, and listened for the sound of birds. Finally, he heard them and went toward the room where the sorceress was feeding the birds in their seven thousand baskets. When she saw Joringel, she became angry, very angry. She began berating him and spitting poison and gall at him, but she could only come within two feet of him, and he paid no attention to her. Instead, he went and examined the baskets with the birds. Since there were hundreds of nightingales, he did not know how he would be able to find his Jorinda again. While he was examining the baskets, he noticed that the old woman had stealthily picked up one of the baskets and was heading toward the door. Quick as a flash he ran over and touched the basket with the flower and the old woman as well. Now she could no longer use her magic, and thus Jorinda appeared before him. She threw her arms around his neck and was just as beautiful as before. After Joringel had turned all the other birds into young women, he went home with his Jorinda, and they lived happily together for a long time.

◈ 70 ◈

The Three Sons of Fortune

A FATHER ONCE CALLED HIS THREE SONS to him and gave the first a rooster, the second a scythe, and the third a cat.

"I'm already quite old," he said, "and my death is near. So I want to provide for you before my end. I have no money, and what I'm giving you now does not seem to be worth much. But everything depends on whether you use these gifts intelligently. Just search for a country where such things are still unknown, and your fortune will be made."

After the father's death, the oldest son set out with his rooster, but wherever he went, the people already knew about roosters. As he approached the cities he saw roosters from afar perched on towers and turning with the wind. As he approached villages he heard several roosters crowing, and nobody found anything remarkable about his bird. It seemed as if the oldest son would not make his fortune with the rooster, but finally he landed on an island where the people knew nothing about roosters and did not even know how to regulate the time of their days. To be sure, they knew when it was morning and evening, but if they happened to wake during the night, then nobody knew how to determine what time it was.

"Just look at this noble creature!" he said. "It's got a ruby red crown on its head and wears spurs like a knight. It will crow three times during the night at set hours, and when it crows the last time, you'll know that the sun is about to rise. But, if it crows during broad daylight, you'd better prepare yourself for a certain change in the weather."

The people were extremely pleased by the rooster, and they did not sleep a wink the next night so that they could listen and enjoy the rooster, which crowed loudly and clearly at two, four, and six in the morning to announce the time. Then they asked him whether the rooster was for sale and how much he wanted for it.

"I want about as much gold as a donkey can carry," he answered.

"So little for such a precious bird!" they all exclaimed as if in a chorus, and they gladly gave him what he demanded.

When he returned home with his wealth, his brothers were astounded, and the second said, "Well, it's time for me to set out and see whether I can make as much of a profit with my scythe as you did with your rooster."

At first it did not seem he would, for everywhere he went he met farmers with scythes on their shoulders just as good as his. However, he eventually reached an island where the people knew nothing about scythes. When the grain was ripe there, they brought cannons to the fields and shot down the grain. That was a very uncertain way of doing things: some of the cannons would hit targets beyond the grain, while others would shoot off the ears instead of the stems. A great deal was destroyed in the process, and over and beyond that, the noise was unbearable. So the man went out to the fields and began to mow the grain so quietly and quickly that the people gaped in amazement. They were willing to give him anything he wanted for the scythe, and he received a horse loaded with as much gold as it could carry.

Now the third brother wanted to see if he could make something out of his cat, and he had the exact same experiences as his brothers. As long as he stayed on the mainland, he accomplished nothing:

there were cats everywhere. Indeed, there were so many that the newborn kittens were generally thrown into the water to drown. Therefore, he sailed to an island, and fortunately for him, it happened that nobody there had ever seen a cat before. In fact, the mice had multiplied so much that they had gained the upper hand. They could dance all over the tables and benches whether the master was home or not. The people complained a great deal about this plague, and even the king in his castle did not know what to do about it: there were mice squeaking in every corner and gnawing whatever they could lay hold of with their teeth.

Once the cat began to hunt them, she was soon able to clear out several rooms in the castle. So the people begged the king to buy this miraculous creature for the kingdom. The king gladly gave the third brother what he demanded, and that was a mule loaded with gold, and he returned home with the greatest treasure of all.

The cat continued to have a great time hunting mice in the royal castle, and she killed so many that it was impossible to count them. Finally, she became hot from all that work and got thirsty. So she stopped in her tracks, turned her head, and cried out, *"Meow! Meow!"*

Upon hearing these strange cries, the king and his entire court became so terrified that they all ran out of the castle in dread. When they were outside the castle, the king held a council meeting to determine what measures should be taken. At last it was decided to send a page to the cat to demand that she leave the castle or be removed by force. The councillors said, "Since we're accustomed to the mice, it would be better to be plagued by them than to surrender our lives to such a monster."

So the page went to the castle to ask the cat whether she would voluntarily evacuate the castle. But the cat, whose thirst had become even greater in the meantime, merely answered with *"Meow! Meow!"*

The page understood that to mean "Not at all! Not at all!" and he brought the reply to the king.

"Well," said the councillors. "She shall have to yield to force."

Cannons were brought before the castle, which was soon set on fire by a barrage of shots. When the fire reached the room where the cat was sitting, she jumped safely out of the window. However, the besiegers did not stop until the whole castle was leveled to the ground.

How Six Made Their Way in the World

ONCE UPON A TIME there was a man who had mastered all kinds of skills. He had fought in the war and had conducted himself correctly and courageously, but when the war was over, he was discharged and received three pennies for traveling expenses.

"Just you wait!" he said. "I won't put up with that. If I find the right people, I'll force the king to turn over all the treasures of his kingdom to me."

Full of rage, he went into the forest, and there he saw a man tearing up six trees as if they were blades of wheat. "Will you be my servant and travel with me?" he asked.

"Yes," the man answered. "But first I want to bring this little bundle of firewood home to my mother." He took one of the trees and wrapped it around the others, lifted the bundle onto his shoulders, and carried it away. Then he returned and went off with his master, who said, "We two shall certainly make our way anywhere in the world."

After they had walked for a while, they found a huntsman who was kneeling down and taking aim at something with his gun.

"Huntsman, what are you going to shoot?" the master asked him.

"There's a fly sitting on the branch of an oak tree two miles from here. I want to shoot out its left eye," he answered.

"Oh, come with me," said the man. "If we three stick together, we'll certainly make our way anywhere in the world."

The huntsman was willing and went with him. As they approached seven windmills they saw the sails rotating swiftly, even though there was no wind coming from any direction, nor was there a leaf stirring.

"What in the world can be driving those windmills? There's not a breeze around," the man said. He continued on with his servants for about two miles, and then they saw a man sitting on a tree. He was holding one nostril closed while blowing through the other.

"My goodness! What are you doing up there?" the man asked.

"Two miles from here are seven windmills," he said. "I'm blowing them so that they'll turn."

"Oh, come with me," said the man. "If we four stick together, we'll certainly make our way anywhere in the world."

So the blower got down from the tree and went along with them. After some time they saw a man standing on one leg, while the other was lying unbuckled on the ground next to him.

"You've made things comfortable for yourself," said the man. "Time for a rest, I suppose?"

"I'm a runner," he answered, "and I've unbuckled my leg so that I don't run too fast. When I run with two legs, I go faster than any bird can fly."

"Oh, come with me. If we five stick together, we certainly shall make our way anywhere in the world."

So he went along with them, and shortly thereafter they met a man who was wearing a cap that completely covered one of his ears.

"Where are your manners?" the master asked him. "You shouldn't drape your cap over one ear like that. You look like a dunce."

"It's got to be this way," said the man. "If I put on my cap straight, then a tremendous frost will come, and all the birds in the air will freeze and drop down dead to the ground."

"Oh, come with me," said the master. "If we six stick together, we'll certainly make our way anywhere in the world."

Now the six came to a city where the king had proclaimed that whoever ran a race against his daughter and won would become her husband. But whoever lost would have to pay for it with his head. Then the man appeared before the king and said, "I want to race but under the condition that one of my servants runs for me."

The king answered, "Then his life must also be placed at stake, and you and he will forfeit your lives if you lose."

When they agreed on the terms and everything was set, the master buckled on the runner's other leg and said to him, "Now show us how quick you are and help us win."

The runner and the king's daughter were both given jugs and set off running at the same time. Yet, within seconds after the king's daughter had run but a short stretch, the spectators could no longer see the runner, for he soared by them just like the wind. In a short time he arrived at the spring, filled the jug with water, and turned around. Halfway back, however, he was overcome by fatigue, put the jug on the ground, lay down, and fell asleep. For his pillow he had taken a dead horse's skull that had been lying on the ground so that he would not be too comfortable and would wake up in time to continue the race. In the meantime, the king's daughter, who was much better at running than ordinary people, had reached the spring and was hurrying back with her jug full of water. When she saw the runner lying asleep on the ground, she was delighted and said, "Now the enemy's been delivered into my hands." She emptied his jug and continued running. Everything would have been lost for the runner if the huntsman had not by chance been standing on the top of the castle and if he had not seen everything with his sharp eyes.

"I'll make sure that the king's daughter does not defeat us!" he said, and he loaded his gun and aimed so carefully that he shot the horse's skull out from under the runner's head without hurting him. The runner awoke, jumped up, and saw that his jug was empty and that the king's daughter was way ahead of him. However, he did not lose heart, but ran back to the spring with the jug, filled it anew with water, and managed to beat the king's daughter home with ten minutes to spare.

"You see," he said, "it was about time that I really started using my legs. I wouldn't exactly call that *running,* what I was doing before."

However, the king was vexed—and his daughter, even more so—that a common discharged soldier should win the race. Therefore, they consulted with each other, seeking a way to get rid of him and all his companions as well. Finally, the king said to her, "I've got an idea. Don't fret. They'll never show their faces around here again." Then he went to the six and said, "I want you to eat, drink, and be merry," and he led them to a room that had an iron floor. The doors were also made of iron, and the windows were lined with iron bars. In the room there was a table covered with delicious food, and the king said to them, "Go inside and enjoy yourselves."

When they were inside, the king had the door locked and bolted. Then he summoned the cook and commanded him to make a fire and keep it going under the room until the iron became burning hot. The cook did that, and it began to get hot in the room. The six, who were sitting at the table, felt very warm, but they thought this was due to the food. However, when the heat became greater and greater and they wanted to leave the room, they found the doors and windows locked. Now they realized that the king had devised something evil and meant to suffocate them.

"He won't succeed!" said the man with the cap. "I'm going to let a frost come that will put the fire to shame and send it crawling away."

So he put his cap on straight, and immediately there was a frost, causing all the heat to disappear and the food on the table to freeze.

After two hours had passed and the king thought they had all perished in the heat, he had the door opened and looked in himself to see how they were. Yet, when the door was opened, all six of them were well and vigorous. Indeed, they declared that it would be nice to get outside and warm themselves, for the food had frozen to the dishes because of the cold conditions in the room. The king stormed furiously down the stairs, scolded the cook, and asked him why he had not done what he had ordered. But the cook answered, "There's more than enough heat. Just look for yourself."

The king saw a tremendous fire blazing under the iron room and realized that he could not get the better of the six by doing something like that. So he tried to think of something new to get rid of the unwelcome guests. He summoned the master and said, "If you will accept gold and give up your claim to my daughter, you can take away as much gold as you like."

"That's fine with me, Your Majesty," he answered. "If you give me as much as my servant can carry, I won't claim your daughter."

The king was satisfied with that, and the master added, "In two weeks I shall return here to fetch the gold." Then he summoned all the tailors in the entire kingdom, and for two weeks they had to sit and sew a sack. When it was finished, the strong man, who could tear up trees, swung the sack over his shoulder and went to the king, who said, "Who's that powerful fellow carrying such a bundle of canvas on his shoulder? Why, it's as big as a house!" Suddenly he became horrified and thought, What a lot of gold he'll carry away! So the king ordered that a ton of gold be brought, and all of that took sixteen of his strongest men to carry, but the strong man grabbed it with one hand, put it into the sack and said, "Why don't you bring more right away? This will barely cover the bottom."

Gradually, the king had his whole treasure brought, and the strong man tossed it all into the sack, but it only became half full.

"Bring some more!" the strong man cried. "These few crumbs aren't enough to fill it."

So seventeen thousand wagons of gold from all over the kingdom had to be driven to the spot, and the strong man stuffed them all into the sack along with the oxen that were harnessed to the wagons.

"Since I don't have the time to inspect everything," he said, "I'll just take what comes until the sack's completely full."

When everything was in the sack, there was still room for a lot more, but the strong man said, "I think it's time to put an end to this. Sometimes one has to tie up a sack even if it's not quite full." Then he hoisted it onto his back and went away with his companions.

When the king saw one single man carrying away all the treasures of his kingdom, he was furious and ordered his cavalry to pursue the six and take the sack away from the strong man. Two of the king's regiments soon caught up with the six and called to them:

"You're our prisoners! Put down the sack with the gold, or else you'll be cut to pieces!"

"What did you say?" asked the blower. "We're your prisoners? Before that ever happens, all of you will soon be dancing around in the air." With that he held one nostril and blew through the other at the two regiments, sending them flying in every which direction, up into the blue and over hill and dale. Some were scattered this way, others that way, while a sergeant begged for mercy. Since he was a brave fellow, who had nine wounds and did not deserve to be humiliated, the blower let up a bit, and the sergeant came out of it without being harmed. Then the blower said to him, "Now go home to the king and tell him, all he has to do is send a few more regiments, and I'll blow them all sky high!"

When the king received the message, he said, "Let those fellows go. There's something extraordinary about them."

So the six brought their wealth back home, divided it among themselves, and lived happily until their death.

◈ 72 ◈

The Wolf and the Man

ONCE THE FOX WAS TELLING THE WOLF about the strength of human beings, and he maintained that no animal could defeat a man. Therefore, animals had to use cunning if they were to protect themselves against him.

"If only I could have a chance to see a man just once, then I'd go after him just the same!" answered the wolf.

"I can help you do that," said the fox. "Just come to me early tomorrow morning, and I'll show you one."

The wolf was right on time early the next day, and the fox brought him to the path that the huntsman took every day. First came an old discharged soldier.

"Is that a man?" asked the wolf.

"No," answered the fox. "That used to be one."

Next came a little boy who was on his way to school.

"Is that a man?"

"No, but he'll become one someday."

Finally, the huntsman came with a double-barreled gun on his back and a hunting knife at his side. Then the fox said to the wolf, "Look, here comes a man. You can go after him, but as for me, I'm going back to my den."

So the wolf went after the man, and when the huntsman saw him coming, he said, "It's a shame that I didn't load my gun with bullets." Still, he took aim and let the wolf have a load of buckshot in his face.

The wolf winced but did not let himself be frightened. Indeed, he kept charging so that the huntsman let him have a second load of buckshot. Yet, the wolf was able to bear the pain and sprang at the huntsman, who now drew out his shiny knife and gave him a few gashes left and right, causing the wolf to bleed all over and return howling to the fox.

"Well, brother wolf," said the fox, "did you manage to finish off the man?"

"Ah," answered the wolf. "I had no idea that the man was so strong. First he took a stick from his shoulder and blew into it. Then something flew into my face that tickled me in the most terrible way. After that he blew into the stick again, and something flew into my nose like lightning and hail. When I got very close, he drew a shiny rib from his body and began beating me so badly that I almost lost my life."

"You see what a braggart you are!" said the fox. "You always talk so big that your deeds can never match your words."

◈ 73 ◈

The Wolf and the Fox

THE WOLF HAD THE FOX LIVING WITH HIM, and since the wolf was stronger, the fox had to do whatever the wolf wanted. So the fox's greatest desire was to get rid of his master.

One day they both happened to be walking through the forest, and the wolf said, "Red Fox, get me something to eat, or else I'll eat you instead!"

"I know of a farmyard where there are two young lambs," the fox responded. "If you want, we can go and fetch one."

That was fine with the wolf, and off they went. The fox stole a little lamb, brought it to the wolf, and departed. Meanwhile, the wolf ate the lamb but was not satisfied. He wanted to have the other as well and went to fetch it. However, he was so clumsy while trying to get it that the lamb's mother heard him and made such a terrible noise by bleating and whining that the farmers came running. Upon discovering the wolf, they beat him mercilessly until he retreated, limping and howling, back home to the fox.

"That was some trap you led me into!" he said. "I wanted to get the other lamb, but the farmers caught me and beat me to a pulp."

"Why are you such a glutton?" replied the fox.

The following day they went out into the fields again, and once more the greedy wolf said, "Red Fox, get me something to eat, or else I'll eat you instead!"

"I know of a farmhouse where the wife will be baking pancakes tonight. Let's go there and get some."

They went to the farm, and the fox sneaked around the house, looking and sniffing about until he discovered where the dish was. Then he snatched six pancakes and brought them to the wolf.

"Now you've got plenty to eat," he said and went his way.

The wolf gulped down the pancakes in a jiffy and said, "They've only increased my appetite." So he went to the farmhouse and reached for the dish. However, it fell to the ground and made such a tremendous crash that the farmer's wife came out. When she saw the wolf, she called some people, who rushed to her side and beat the wolf so badly that he ran back to the fox in the forest with two lame legs and howled like mad. "That was some nasty trap you led me into!" he exclaimed. "The farmers caught me and tanned my hide."

However, the fox answered, "Why are you such a glutton?"

On the third day they were out in the fields again, and although the wolf could only limp with great difficulty, he said:

"Red Fox, get me something to eat, or else I'll eat you instead!"

"I know of a man who's been doing some slaughtering, and the salted meat is in a barrel in his cellar. Let's go and get it."

"This time I'm going to tag along with you," said the wolf. "Then you can help me if I can't get away."

"That's all right with me," said the fox, and he showed him all the shortcuts and ways that enabled them finally to get into the cellar. There they found plenty of meat, and immediately the wolf began gobbling it down. I've got some time before I have to stop, he thought.

The fox also enjoyed the meat, but he kept looking around, and he often ran to the hole through which they had come, to make sure that his body was still thin enough to slip through.

"My dear fox," said the wolf, "could you tell me why you're continuously running back and forth and jumping in and out of the cellar?"

"I just want to see if anybody's coming," the sly fox answered. "Just don't eat too much."

Right at that moment the farmer came. He had heard the fox jumping in and out of the cellar. When the fox saw him coming, he went right through the hole in one jump and landed outside. The wolf wanted to follow him, but he had eaten too much and was so fat that he could not get through. Consequently, he got stuck in the hole. Then the farmer came with a club and beat him to death, while the fox ran into the forest, glad to be rid of the old glutton.

◈ 74 ◈

The Fox and His Cousin

THE SHE-WOLF GAVE BIRTH TO A CUB and invited the fox to be
godfather. "In truth, he is a close relative of ours," she said. "He's
got a good head on his shoulders and is very clever. He can instruct
my son and help him get by in the world."

The fox appeared, made an honorable impression, and said, "My
dear cousin, whom I hold in such great esteem, thank you for the
honor that you have bestowed on me. You can rest assured that I
shall conduct myself in a way that will make you happy."

The fox enjoyed the meal during the christening feast, and he was
very merry. Afterward he said, "My dear cousin, it is our duty to
look after the child. You must have good food so that he'll grow big
and strong. I know a barn full of sheep where we can easily fetch a
good piece of meat."

The wolf liked the suggestion, and she went out with the fox
toward the barnyard. He pointed out the barn to her from the
distance and said, "You'll be able to creep in there unnoticed. In the
meantime, I'll look around on the other side to see whether I can
catch a chicken."

He did not move, however, but lay down, stretched out his legs,
and rested at the edge of the forest. The wolf crept into the barn but
came across a dog that made such a racket that the farmers came
running. They caught the wolf and poured burning lye over her coat.
Nevertheless, she managed to escape and dragged herself into the
forest. The fox was lying there and made sounds as if he were
moaning. "Ah!" he said, "dear wolf, I've had a terrible time of it!
The farmers attacked me and broke every limb of my body! If you
don't want me to waste away here and perish, you must carry me
away."

Although the wolf herself could barely move, she was greatly
worried about the fox. Therefore, she lifted him onto her back and

slowly carried the fox, who was perfectly sound and fit, toward her house. When they arrived, he cried out, "Farewell, dear cousin, I hope the roasting you got has done you some good!"

The fox laughed in her face and then ran off.

◈ 75 ◈

The Fox and the Cat

ONE DAY THE CAT HAPPENED TO MEET MR. FOX in the forest, and because she thought to herself, He is so clever, experienced, and greatly respected in the world, she spoke to him in a friendly way. "Good day, my dear Mr. Fox. How are things going with you? What's up? How are you managing in these hard times?"

The fox, consumed by his own arrogance, examined the cat from head to toe and pondered for some time whether he should deign to answer or not. Finally, he said, "Oh, you miserable whisker-licker, you spotted fool, you meager mouse-hunter, what nerve you have! How dare you ask how things are going with me? What have you ever learned? How many skills have you acquired?"

"I can do only one thing," responded the cat modestly.

"What's that?" asked the fox.

"When the dogs are chasing after me, I can save myself by scrambling up a tree."

"Is that all?" said the fox. "I've acquired over a hundred skills and have a bagful of tricks besides. You're so pitiful that you make me want to cry. But I'll take you with me and teach you how to get away from dogs."

Just at that moment a huntsman approached with four dogs. The cat sprang nimbly up a tree and sat down at the top, where the branches and leaves completely concealed her.

"Open your bag, Mr. Fox! Open your bag!" the cat called out to him, but the dogs had already pounced on him and held him tight.

"Oh, Mr. Fox," cried the cat, "you and your hundred skills don't seem to be working right now. If you had been able to climb up here like me, you wouldn't be doomed to die!"

◈ 76 ◈

The Pink Flower

THERE ONCE WAS A QUEEN whom the Lord had prevented from having children. Every morning she went into the garden and begged God in heaven to bestow a son or daughter on her. Eventually, an angel came down from heaven and said, "You may now rest content. You shall have a son who will have the power to wish for anything he wants in the world and have all his wishes granted."

The queen went to the king and told him the good news, and when the time came, she gave birth to a son, and the king's joy was great. Soon she began taking walks every day with her child in the animal park, and it was there that she bathed herself in a clear spring. Once, when the child was already somewhat older, she happened to fall asleep holding him on her lap. Then the old cook, who knew the child possessed magic wishing powers, came by and stole the boy away from her. Next the cook took a chicken, tore it apart, and let the blood drip on her apron and dress. Then he carried the child to a secret place, where a wet nurse was compelled to suckle him. Finally, he ran to the king and accused the queen of allowing her child to be stolen by wild animals. When the king saw the blood on her apron, he believed the cook and became so furious that he had a tall tower built that neither the rays of the sun nor the rays of the moon could penetrate. Then he ordered his wife to be walled up and imprisoned in this tower, where she was to sit for seven years without food or drink so she would perish. However, God sent her two angels. They came to her from heaven in the form of white doves and were commanded to fly to her twice a day and to bring her food until the seven years were over.

Meanwhile, the cook kept thinking, If the child has the power of wishing and I'm here, then he could easily bring about my end. So he left the castle and went to the boy, who was already big enough to talk.

"Wish yourself a beautiful castle with a garden and everything else that goes along with it," he said.

No sooner did the boy complete the wish than everything that he had wished for stood before him. After some time had passed, the cook said, "It's not good for you to be so alone, wish yourself a beautiful maiden to keep you company."

So the prince wished for a maiden, and all at once she stood before him and was more beautiful than any painter could have portrayed her. Now, the two of them played together and loved each other with all their hearts, and the old cook went hunting like a nobleman. However, it occurred to him that the prince might one day wish to be with his father, and this thought disturbed the cook a great deal. So he went out, took the maiden aside, and said, "Tonight, when the boy's asleep, go to his bed and plunge this knife into his heart and bring me his heart and tongue. If you refuse to do this, you will lose your own life."

Thereupon he went away, and when he returned the next day, she had not done it and said, "Why should I shed innocent blood when the boy has never harmed a living soul."

"If you continue to refuse, then it will cost you your own life," the cook declared again.

When he had gone away, she had a little fawn fetched and slaughtered. Then she took out its heart and tongue and put them on a plate. When she saw the old cook coming, she said to the boy, "Lie down in bed and pull the covers over you."

Then the villain entered and said, "Where's the boy's heart and tongue?"

The maiden handed him the plate, but the prince threw the covers off him and said, "You old sinner! Why did you want to kill me? Now I shall pronounce your sentence: You shall become a black poodle and wear a golden chain around your neck, and you shall eat burning coals until the flames come spewing from your throat."

Immediately after these words were said, the old man was turned into a poodle and had a golden chain around his neck. All the cooks of the castle were ordered to bring him live coals, which he ate until he spewed flames from his throat. The prince remained in the castle a little longer, but he continued to think about his mother and wonder whether she was still alive. Finally, he said to the maiden, "I want to return to my homeland. If you'll come with me, then I'll take good care of you."

"Ah," she answered. "It's a long way off, and what shall I do in a foreign country where nobody knows me?"

Since she did not really want to go and they did not want to be separated from each other, he made a wish that turned her into a beautiful pink flower and then he put her into his pocket. Then he went back to his homeland, and the poodle had to tag along after him. His first stop was the tower in which his mother was imprisoned. Since the tower was so high, he wished for a ladder that would reach the top. Thereupon he climbed the ladder, looked inside, and called out, "Dearest Mother, Your Royal Highness, are you still alive, or are you dead?"

"I've just eaten, and I'm content," she answered, for she thought that the angels had come.

"I'm your dear son that the wild animals supposedly stole from your lap," he said. "But I'm still alive and shall rescue you soon."

Now he climbed down, went to his father, and had himself announced as a huntsman from a foreign land seeking employment. The king answered that he was willing to employ him if he was a skillful huntsman and could procure game for him. However, there had never been deer or any other game in the entire region or even on its borders. Still, the huntsman promised to provide him with as much venison as he needed for the royal table. Then he ordered all the huntsmen to assemble and ride out into the forest with him. After they went outside, he ordered them to form a circle that was to remain open at one end, and he stepped into the middle of the circle and began wishing. Suddenly some two hundred or more deer came running into the circle, and the huntsmen shot them dead. Afterward the dead animals were loaded onto sixty farm wagons and driven back home to the king. After having gone many years without it, the king, for once, was able to deck his table with venison.

So delighted was the king by the game that he ordered the entire court to dine with him the following day, and he made a great banquet. When they were all gathered together, the king said to the huntsman, "Because you were so skillful, you shall sit next to me."

"My Lord and Majesty, I beg your pardon. I'm nothing but a common huntsman."

However, the king said, "You shall sit next to me," and insisted until the huntsman did as he was told.

While the huntsman was sitting there, he thought about his mother and wished that one of the king's high officials would ask after the queen, how she was doing in the tower and whether she was still alive or had perished. No sooner had he wished it than the marshal began to speak: "Your Majesty, we're sitting here and celebrating in joy, but how is the queen doing in the tower? Is she still alive or has she perished?"

"She let my dear son be torn to pieces by wild beasts," the king answered. "So I don't want to hear anything about her."

Then the huntsman stood up and said, "Most gracious Father, she's still alive, and I am her son. The wild beasts did not steal me. Rather it was the evil old cook who took me from her arms after she had fallen asleep. And it was he who sprinkled the blood of a chicken on her apron." He then took the dog with the golden chain and said, "This is the villain," and he ordered burning coals brought, which the dog was forced to eat in the presence of the entire court, so that flames spewed from his throat. After that the huntsman asked the king if he wanted to see the cook in his true form and then wished the dog back into the cook, who suddenly stood there in a white apron with a knife at his side. When the king saw him, he became furious and ordered him to be thrown into the deepest dungeon.

The huntsman resumed talking and said, "Father, do you also want to see the maiden who looked after me so tenderly and was supposed to murder me but refused, even though her own life was at stake?"

"Yes," the king answered. "I'd like to see her very much."

"Most gracious Father," said the son. "I'm going to show her to you in the form of a beautiful flower." And he reached into his pocket, pulled out the pink flower, and placed it on the royal table. The king had never seen a flower as beautiful as that. His son then said to him, "Now I'll show her to you in her true form," and he wished the flower to become a maiden. All at once she was there and was so beautiful that no painter could ever have made her look more beautiful.

Now the king sent two chambermaids and two servants to the tower to fetch the queen to the royal table. But, when she was led into the hall, she refused to eat anything at all and said, "Our most gracious and merciful Lord, who kept me alive in the tower, shall soon grant me salvation."

She lived three days more and then died in bliss. After she was buried, the two white doves that had brought her the food in the tower and who were really angels from heaven, followed her and perched on her grave. The old king had the cook torn into four parts, but his grief gnawed at his heart, and he died soon after. His son married the beautiful maiden whom he had brought home in his pocket in the form of a flower, and only God knows whether they are still living today.

◈ 77 ◈

Clever Gretel

THERE WAS ONCE A COOK NAMED GRETEL, who wore shoes with red heels, and when she went out in them, she whirled this way and that way and was as happy as a lark. "You really are quite pretty!" she would say to herself. And when she returned home, she would drink some wine out of sheer delight. Since the wine would whet her appetite, she would take the best things she was cooking and taste them until she was content. Then she would say, "The cook must know what the food tastes like!"

One day her master happened to say to her, "Gretel, tonight I'm having a guest for dinner. Prepare two chickens for me and make them as tasty as possible."

"I'll take care of it, sir," Gretel responded. So she killed two chickens, scalded them, plucked them, stuck them on a spit, and toward evening placed them over a fire to roast. The chickens began to turn brown and were almost ready, but the guest did not make his appearance. So Gretel called to her master, "If the guest doesn't come soon, I'll have to take the chickens off the fire. It would be a great shame if they weren't eaten now, while they're still at their juiciest."

"Then I'll run and fetch the guest myself," said the master.

When the master had left the house, Gretel laid the spit with the chickens to one side and thought, If I keep standing by the fire, I'll just sweat and get thirsty. Who knows when they'll come? Meanwhile, I'll hop down into the cellar and take a drink.

She ran downstairs, filled a jug with wine, and said, "May God bless it for you, Gretel!" and she took a healthy swig. "The wine flows nicely," she continued talking, "and it's not good to interrupt the flow." So she took another long swig. Then she went upstairs and placed the chickens back over the fire, basted them with butter, and merrily turned the spit. Since the roast chickens smelled so good, Gretel thought, Perhaps something's missing. I'd better taste

◆ 312 ◆

them to see how they are. She touched one of them with her finger and said, "Goodness! The chickens are really good! It's a crying shame not to eat them all at once!" She ran to the window to see if her master was on his way with the guest, but when she saw no one coming, she returned to the chickens and thought, That one wing is burning. I'd better eat it up.

So she cut it off, ate it, and enjoyed it. When she had finished, she thought, I'd better eat the other wing or else my master will notice that something's missing. After she had consumed the two wings, she returned to the window, looked for her master, but was unable to see him. Who knows, it suddenly occurred to her, Perhaps they've decided not to come and have stopped somewhere along the way. Then she said to herself, "Hey, Gretel, cheer up! You've already taken a nice chunk. Have another drink and eat it all up! When it's gone, there'll be no reason for you to feel guilty. Why should God's good gifts go to waste?"

Once again she ran down into the cellar, took a good honest drink, and then went back to eat up the chicken with relish. When the one chicken had been eaten and her master still had not returned, Gretel looked at the other bird and said, "Where one is, the other should be too. The two of them belong together: whatever's right for one is right for the other. I think if I have another drink, it won't do me any harm." Therefore she took another healthy swig and let the second chicken run to join the other.

Just as she was in the midst of enjoying her meal, her master came back and called, "Hurry, Gretel, the guest will soon be here!"

"Yes, sir, I'll get everything ready," answered Gretel.

Meanwhile, the master checked to see if the table was properly set and took out the large knife with which he wanted to carve the chickens and began sharpening it on the steps in the hallway. As he was doing that the guest came and knocked nicely and politely at the door. Gretel ran and looked to see who was there, and when she saw the guest, she put her finger to her lips and whispered, "Shhh, be quiet! Get out of here as quick as you can! If my master catches you, you'll be done for. It's true he invited you to dinner, but he really wants to cut off both your ears. Listen to him sharpening his knife!"

The guest heard the sharpening and hurried back down the steps as fast as he could. Gretel wasted no time and ran screaming to her master. "What kind of guest did you invite!" she cried.

"Goodness gracious, Gretel! Why do you ask? What do you mean?"

"Well," she said, "he snatched both chickens just as I was about to bring them to the table, and he's run away with them!"

"That's not at all a nice way to behave!" said her master, and he was disappointed by the loss of the fine chickens. "At least he could have left me one of them so I'd have something to eat."

He then shouted after the guest to stop running, but the guest pretended not to hear. So the master ran after him, with the knife still in his hand, and screamed, "Just one, just one!" merely meaning that the guest should at least leave him one of the chickens and not take both. But the guest thought that his host was after just one of his ears, and to make sure that he would reach home safely with both his ears, he ran as if someone had lit a fire under his feet.

◈ 78 ◈

The Old Man and His Grandson

ONCE UPON A TIME there was a very old man, so old that his eyes had grown dim, his ears were hard of hearing, and his knees trembled. When he sat at the table, he could barely hold his spoon, and often he spilled soup on the tablecloth, while some of it would also drip from his mouth. His son and daughter-in-law found this disgusting and eventually forced the old grandfather to sit in a corner behind the stove. They gave him his food in a clay bowl and very little at that. Whenever he would glance sadly in the direction of the table, tears would well up in his eyes.

One day his hands trembled so much that he could not even hold on to the bowl, and it fell to the ground and broke. The young woman scolded him, but he only sighed and did not respond. So for a few pennies she bought him a wooden bowl, and from then on he had to eat out of that. Some time later, as they were sitting there again, the small four-year-old grandson was piecing together some wooden planks on the ground.

"What are you doing?" asked the father.

"I'm making a little trough," answered the child. "My mother and father shall eat out of it when I grow up."

Then husband and wife looked at each other for a while and soon began to weep. Within seconds they brought the old grandfather back to the table, and from then on they always let him eat with them. Nor did they ever say anything again if he happened to spill a little something here and there.

◈ 79 ◈

The Water Nixie

A LITTLE BROTHER AND SISTER were playing by a well, and while they were playing, they both fell into the water. Down at the bottom of the well was a nixie, who said, "Now I've got you, and now you shall work hard for me." And she took them away with her.

She gave the girl dirty, tangled flax to spin and a bottomless bucket to carry water in. The boy was forced to chop down a tree with a blunt ax, and all they got to eat were dumplings that were as hard as rocks. Eventually, the children lost their patience, and one Sunday they waited until the nixie was in church and then ran away.

When church was over, the nixie found that the chickens had flown the coop, and she pursued them by taking leaps and bounds. However, the children saw her coming from afar, and the girl threw behind her a brush, which formed a huge mountain with thousands and thousands of bristles, and the nixie had great difficulty climbing over them. At last she made it over, and when the children saw that, the boy threw behind him a comb, which formed a huge mountain with thousands and thousands of teeth, but the nixie managed to grab hold of them and eventually climbed over. Then the girl threw behind her a mirror, which formed a glass mountain. It was so very, very slippery that it was impossible to cross, and the nixie thought, I'd better run home and fetch my ax. Then I'll cut the glass mountain in two. But by the time she had returned and had chopped up the glass, the children had long since made their escape, and the water nixie had to trudge back home.

◆ 315 ◆

◈ 80 ◈

The Death of the Hen

ONCE A HEN WENT WITH A ROOSTER TO THE NUT HILL, and they agreed that whoever found a kernel would share it with the other. Soon the hen found a very big nut, but she kept quiet about it because she wanted to eat the kernel all by herself. However, the kernel was so large that she could not swallow it, and it got stuck in her throat. Fearing that she might choke to death, she screamed, "Rooster, please run as fast as you can and fetch me some water or else I'll choke to death!"

The rooster ran as fast as he could to the well and said, "Well, you must give me some water. The hen's lying on the nut hill, and she's about to choke to death."

"First run to the bride," the well answered, "and get some red silk for me."

The rooster ran to the bride and said, "Bride, I need some red silk from you. The silk is for the well, who'll give me some water to take to the hen, who's lying on the nut hill, where she's swallowed a large kernel and is about to choke to death."

The bride answered, "First run and fetch me my wreath that got caught on the branch of a willow."

So the rooster ran to the willow, pulled the wreath from the branch, and brought it back to the bride. In return the bride gave him some red silk, and the rooster brought it to the well, who gave him water in exchange. Then the rooster brought the water to the hen, but by the time he reached her, she had choked to death and lay there motionless and dead. The rooster became so sad that he uttered a loud cry, and all the animals came and mourned for her. Six mice built a little wagon that was to carry the hen to her grave. When the wagon was finished, the mice harnessed themselves to it, and the rooster was to drive the wagon. Along the way they encountered the fox, who asked, "Where are you going, rooster?"

"I'm off to bury the hen."

"May I ride with you?"

"Yes, but since you're heavy, take a seat in the back. If you sat up front, my horses would fall, and the wagon would crack!"

The fox sat down in the back. Then the wolf, the bear, the stag, the lion, and all the animals in the forest took a seat in the back. Thus they continued their journey until they came to a brook.

"How shall we get across?" asked the rooster.

A straw was lying near the brook and said, "I'll lay myself across. Then you can drive over me."

However, as soon as the six mice touched the bridge, the straw slipped and fell into the water, and the six mice went tumbling after and drowned. So the situation was just as bad as it had been before, but a hot piece of coal came along and said, "I'm large enough. I'll lay myself across, and you can drive over me."

Then the coal also laid itself across the water, but unfortunately it grazed the surface a little. Soon it started hissing, and before long it was extinguished and died. When a stone saw that, it took pity on the rooster and offered its help. It lay down across the water, and now the rooster himself pulled the wagon across. When he reached the other side and was already on land with the dead hen, he wanted to help the others in the back out of the wagon, but there were too many of them, and the wagon slipped backward causing everyone to fall into the water and drown. So the rooster was all alone with the dead hen, and he dug a grave for her. He laid her in it and made a mound on top. Afterward he sat down on the mound and grieved until he too died. And then everyone was dead.

◈ 81 ◈

Brother Lustig

ONCE UPON A TIME there was a great war, and when the war was over, many soldiers were discharged. So it was that Brother Lustig too received his walking papers and nothing else but a small loaf of ration bread and four kreuzers in money. With that he set out on his way.

In the meantime, Saint Peter had disguised himself as a poor beggar and taken a place by the roadside, so when Brother Lustig passed by, he begged for alms.

"My dear beggar," Brother Lustig said, "I don't think I have much to offer. You see, I was once a soldier, and now I've been discharged and have nothing but this small loaf of ration bread and four kreuzers in cash. When that's all gone, I'll have to go begging just like you. Still, I want to give you something."

Thereupon he divided the loaf into four parts and gave the apostle one part along with one kreuzer. Saint Peter thanked him and then went farther along the road, where he sat down again, disguised as another beggar, and waited for the soldier to come along. When Brother Lustig approached, Saint Peter begged for alms once again. The soldier responded as he had before and gave him a quarter of the bread and a kreuzer. Saint Peter thanked him and went farther along the road, only to sit down a third time in the disguise of yet another beggar. When he addressed Brother Lustig, the soldier gave him the third part of his bread and a third kreuzer. Saint Peter thanked him, and Brother Lustig continued on his way with nothing more than a fourth of the bread and a kreuzer. Then he went into a tavern, where he ate the bread and ordered a beer for a kreuzer. After he had finished eating and drinking, he moved on, and Saint Peter came toward him once more, now in the guise of a discharged soldier.

"Good day, comrade," spoke Saint Peter. "Could you give me a piece of bread and a kreuzer for a drink?"

"Where shall I get it from?" answered Brother Lustig. "I've been discharged from the army, and they gave me nothing but a loaf of ration bread and four kreuzers in money. Then I met three beggars along the road and gave each one of them a fourth of my bread and a kreuzer. I ate the last piece of bread in a tavern and spent my last kreuzer on a drink. Now my pockets are empty, and if you're broke as well, we can go begging together."

"No," replied Saint Peter. "That won't be necessary. I know something about doctoring, and I'll be able to earn as much as I need by doing that."

"I see," said Brother Lustig. "Well, I don't know the first thing about doctoring, so I'll have to go begging alone."

"Why don't you come along with me?" said Saint Peter. "If I earn something, I'll give you half."

"That's fine with me," said Brother Lustig, and they went away together.

Shortly after, they came to a farmhouse and heard a tremendous crying and groaning from inside. When they entered, they found a sick man lying in bed on the verge of death with his wife weeping and wailing very loudly.

"Stop your weeping and wailing," Saint Peter said. "I'll make your husband well again." He took a salve from his pocket, and in the very next moment he healed the sick man so that he could get up, and he appeared to be quite healthy.

The husband and wife were ecstatic and asked, "How can we reward you? What can we give you?"

Saint Peter did not want to take anything, and the more the farmer and his wife insisted, the more Saint Peter refused. But Brother Lustig nudged Saint Peter and said, "You've got to take something. We need it."

Finally, the farmer's wife brought in a lamb and told Saint Peter that he had to accept it. Yet, he still refused. Then Brother Lustig poked him in the side and said, "Take it, you stupid fool. We need it."

At last Saint Peter said, "All right, I'll take the lamb, but I'm not going to carry it. If you want it, then you must carry it."

"No need to worry," said Brother Lustig. "I'll manage with ease," and he picked it up and carried it away on his shoulder.

After they departed, they came to a forest. In the meantime, Brother Lustig had begun feeling the weight of the lamb, and since he was also hungry, he said to Saint Peter, "Look, that's a nice spot. We could cook and eat the lamb over there."

"That's fine with me," answered Saint Peter. "But I don't know how to cook. If you want to cook, here's a kettle. In the meanwhile, I'll take a look around until the meal's ready. But don't start eating till I get back. I'll return on time."

"Go ahead," said Brother Lustig. "I know a thing or two about cooking, and I'll take care of everything."

So Saint Peter went off, and Brother Lustig slaughtered the lamb, started a fire, threw the meat into the kettle, and cooked it. When the lamb was done and the apostle had still not returned, Brother Lustig took the lamb out of the kettle, cut it up, and found the heart. "That's supposed to be the best part," he said. First he just tasted it, but then he succumbed and ate it up.

At last Saint Peter came back and said, "You can eat the whole lamb yourself. Just give me the heart. It's the only thing I want."

Brother Lustig took the knife and fork and pretended to be busily looking for the heart, but he could not find it. After a while he declared, "There's none here."

"Where do you suppose it is?" asked the apostle.

"I don't know," answered Brother Lustig, "but just think how foolish both of us are! Here we're looking for the lamb's heart, and we've both forgotten that a lamb doesn't have a heart.''

"My word!'' said Saint Peter. "That's something quite new to me! Every animal has a heart. Why shouldn't a lamb have one?''

"That's not so, brother. A lamb doesn't have a heart. If you really think about it, you'll see I'm right. It truly doesn't have one.''

"Very well,'' said Saint Peter. "If there's no heart, then I don't need any of the lamb. You can eat it up yourself.''

"Whatever I can't eat, I'll take with me in my knapsack,'' said Brother Lustig, and he ate half the lamb and stuck the rest in his knapsack.

After they set out again, Saint Peter made a large stream of water rise up and flow directly across their path, forcing them to wade through it.

"You go first,'' said Saint Peter.

"No,'' answered Brother Lustig. "You go first,'' and he thought, If the water's too deep, I'll stay behind.

So Saint Peter waded through, and the water barely touched his knees. But when Brother Lustig began to walk through, the water grew deeper and rose to his neck. Then he called out, "Brother, help me!''

But Saint Peter asked, "Will you confess that you ate the lamb's heart?''

"No,'' he replied. "I didn't eat it.'' Then the water grew deeper until it reached his mouth. "Help me, brother!'' cried the soldier.

Then Saint Peter asked one more time, "Will you confess that you ate the lamb's heart?''

"No,'' he answered. "I didn't eat it.''

Since Saint Peter did not want to let him drown, he had the water sink and helped him across. So they continued traveling and came to a kingdom, where they heard that a king's daughter was sick and on the brink of death.

"Hey now, brother,'' said the soldier to Saint Peter, "this is our chance. If we make her well, we'll be set for the rest of our lives.'' But Saint Peter did not quicken his pace, and Brother Lustig cried, "Pick up your feet, dear brother! We've got to make it there before it's too late.''

However, the more Brother Lustig pushed and shoved, the slower Saint Peter went, and at last they heard that the king's daughter had died.

"You see,'' said Brother Lustig. "That's what we get when you drag your feet.''

"Just be quiet," answered Saint Peter. "I can do more than just heal the sick. I can bring the dead back to life."

"Well, if that's the case," said Brother Lustig, "I'm glad, but I expect you to earn half the kingdom for us at the very least."

Then they went to the royal palace, where everyone was in deep mourning. However, Saint Peter told the king he would restore his daughter to life, and when he was taken to her, he said, "Bring me a kettle of water." After it was brought, he ordered everyone to go outside except Brother Lustig. Then he cut off all the limbs of the dead maiden, threw them into the water, made a fire under the kettle, and let everything boil. After all the flesh had fallen off, he took out the beautiful white bones and placed them on a table, where he arranged them according to their natural order. When that had been done, he stepped up to the table and said three times, "In the name of the most holy Trinity, I call upon you to arise, dead woman!"

At the third time, the king's daughter stood up, and she was alive, well, and beautiful. The king was overjoyed by this and said to Saint Peter, "Name your reward, and even if it's half my kingdom, I shall give it to you."

But Saint Peter replied, "I don't want anything in return."

Oh, you dumb fool! thought Brother Lustig to himself, and he poked his comrade in the side and said, "Don't be an idiot. Even if you don't want anything, think of me."

Although Saint Peter still refused to accept anything, the king noticed that the other wanted something, and he ordered his treasurer to fill his knapsack with gold. Thereupon they continued on their way, and when they reached a forest, Saint Peter said to Brother Lustig, "Now let's divide the gold."

"That's all right with me," he answered. "Let's get to it."

So Saint Peter divided the gold into three piles, and Brother Lustig thought, He's off his rocker with his ridiculous ideas. Why is he making three piles when there are only two of us?

"I've divided everything just right," said Saint Peter. "One pile for me, one for you, and one for the person who ate the lamb's heart."

"Oh, that was me," answered Brother Lustig, who snatched up the gold as quickly as he could. "Believe me, I ate it."

"How can that be?" asked Saint Peter. "A lamb doesn't have a heart."

"Hey, where'd you get that idea, brother? Of course a lamb has a heart, just like all the animals. Why should the lamb be different?"

"Very well, I understand now," said Saint Peter. "Keep the gold for yourself, but I'm not staying with you any longer. I'm going my own way."

"As you wish, dear brother," answered the soldier. "Farewell."

Then Saint Peter turned down a different road, while Brother Lustig thought, Well, I'm glad to see him go. He's certainly a strange sort of a saint!

Now the soldier had plenty of money, but he did not know how to handle it: in the course of time he squandered it and gave it away so that his pockets soon became empty again. Then he came to a country where he heard that the king's daughter had just died.

Hey now, he thought to himself, that can turn out to be a good thing for you. You'll bring her back to life and have them reward you the way one ought to be rewarded. So he went to the king and offered to restore his dead daughter to life. Since the king had heard that a discharged soldier was traveling about and bringing dead people back to life, he thought Brother Lustig was this man. But he did not trust him and asked his councillors for advice. They told him to take a chance because his daughter was dead anyway.

So Brother Lustig had a kettle of water brought to him and ordered everyone to leave the room, whereupon he cut off the limbs, threw them into the water, and made a fire underneath, just as he had seen Saint Peter do. When the water began to boil, the flesh fell off the bones, and he took them out and put them on the table, but he did not know how to arrange them and proceeded to mix them all up. Then he stood in front of the table and said, "In the name of the most holy Trinity, I call upon you to arise, dead woman!" He said that three times, but the bones did not stir. He said it again three times, but it was all in vain. "You stupid woman, get up!" he cried. "Get up, or you'll regret it!"

Just as he was uttering those words, Saint Peter suddenly came through the window in his former guise as a discharged soldier and said, "You godless man, what do you think you're doing? How can this dead maiden get up when you've mixed up all her bones?"

"Brother dear, I've done the best I could," he answered.

"Well, this time I'll help you out of your mess, but I warn you, if you ever try something like this again, you'll suffer the consequences. What's more, I don't want you to ask for or to accept the least little thing from the king." Thereupon Saint Peter arranged the bones in their right order and said to the maiden three times, "In the name of the most holy Trinity, I call upon you to arise, dead woman!"

And the king's daughter stood up, and she was as fit and as beautiful as she was before. So Saint Peter went back out the window, and Brother Lustig was glad that everything had turned out so well. However, he was annoyed that he was not permitted to accept anything. I'd like to know, he thought, what's going on in that crazy head of his. Whatever he gives with the one hand, he takes away with the other. That makes no sense!

Now the king offered Brother Lustig whatever he wanted, but he was forbidden to take anything. Nevertheless, he managed by hints and cunning to get the king to order his knapsack to be filled with gold. Thereafter he left the castle. However, as he was passing through the gate, Saint Peter was waiting for him outside and said, "What kind of a man are you anyway! Didn't I forbid you to take anything? But now your knapsack's filled with gold."

"What could I do?" answered Brother Lustig. "They just stuffed it right in."

"I'm warning you, you'd better not try anything like that a second time, or else you'll pay for it."

"My word, brother! Don't worry. Now that I've got some gold, what would I want with bone-washing?"

"Indeed!" said Saint Peter. "A long time that gold will last! But just so you don't go astray again, I'm going to give your knapsack the power to obtain anything you wish. Farewell now, you won't be seeing me again."

"May God be with you," said Brother Lustig, who thought, I'm glad to see you go, you queer bird. You can be sure that I won't tag along after you. And he did not give even a second thought to the magic power that his knapsack now possessed.

Brother Lustig resumed his wandering, and he also squandered and wasted his gold just as he had done the first time. When he had nothing left but four kreuzers, he stopped at an inn and thought, The money's got to go sometime, and he ordered wine and bread for the four kreuzers. As he was sitting there and drinking his wine the smell of roast goose reached his nostrils. Brother Lustig looked around a bit until he discovered that the innkeeper was keeping two geese warm in the oven. Then he remembered that his comrade had said that he could obtain whatever he wished to be in his knapsack. I might as well try it out with the geese, he thought. So he went outside, stood in front of the door, and said, "I wish the two roast geese would move from the oven into my knapsack." Right after he said that, he unbuckled his knapsack and looked inside, and there they were. "Ah, that's the way," he said. "Now I'm a made man!"

He went to a meadow and set about eating the geese. When he was in the middle of his meal, two journeymen came along and looked hungrily at the goose that had not been touched yet. One's enough for me, thought Brother Lustig, and he called the two journeymen to come over and said, "Here, take the goose and eat it in honor of my good health."

They thanked him and took the goose to the inn, where they ordered half a bottle of wine and a loaf of bread. When they unpacked the goose that they had received as a gift and began to eat it, the innkeeper's wife observed them and said to her husband, "Those two are eating a goose. Why don't you take a look to see if one of ours is missing from the oven?"

The innkeeper went over and found the oven empty. "What! You thieving rascals! So you think you can get a cheap meal off us? You'd better pay at once, or else I'll beat your hides with a green hazel stick."

"But we're not thieves," the two said. "A discharged soldier gave us the goose out there on the meadow."

"Don't try to fool me! The soldier was here, but he went out the door like an honest fellow. I watched him closely. You're the thieves, and you're going to pay!"

However, since they could not pay, he took the stick and beat them out the door. Meanwhile, Brother Lustig went his way and came to a place where there was a magnificent castle with a shabby inn nearby. He went to the inn and asked for a night's lodging, but the innkeeper turned him away and said, "There's no more room here. The place is full of noble guests."

"I'm surprised that noblemen would come to you and not go to that magnificent castle," said Brother Lustig.

"Well," answered the innkeeper, "it's quite difficult to spend the night there. Anyone who's ever tried has not come out alive."

"If others have tried it," said Brother Lustig, "then I'm going to try too."

"You'd better leave it alone," said the innkeeper. "It will cost you your neck."

"I'm not worried about my neck right now," said Brother Lustig. "Just give me the keys and some good food and drink."

So the innkeeper gave him the keys and food and drink. Brother Lustig took everything with him into the castle and enjoyed the meal. Eventually, he became sleepy and lay down on the ground because there was no bed. Soon he fell asleep, but he was awakened in the night by a loud noise. When he opened his eyes, he saw nine ugly devils dancing in a circle around him. "Just dance as long as you want," said Brother Lustig, "but don't any of you come too close to me." Yet, the devils kept pressing toward him and almost stepped on his face with their hideous feet. "Quiet down, you

ghastly devils!'' he cried. But they got worse and worse. Then
Brother Lustig became angry and shouted, ''All right! I'll quiet you
down soon enough!'' So he took the leg of a chair and started
swinging at them. However, nine devils against one soldier was too
much, and when he hit those in front of him, the others behind him
grabbed him by the hair and pulled unmercifully.

''You nasty pack of devils!'' he exclaimed. ''I've just about had
enough of this. Just wait. Into my knapsack, all nine of you!''

Before they knew it, they were inside, and he buckled the knapsack and threw it into a corner. Then all was suddenly quiet, and
Brother Lustig lay down again and slept until daylight. Now the
innkeeper came with the nobleman who owned the castle to see how
things had gone with him. When they saw that he was well and
cheerful, they were astonished and asked, ''Didn't the ghosts do
anything to you?''

''They tried their best,'' he answered, ''but I stuck nine of them
into my knapsack. Now you can move back into your castle and live
in peace and quiet. Nobody will ever haunt it again.''

The nobleman thanked him, rewarded him generously, and asked
him to remain in his employ, where he would be taken care of for
the rest of his life.

''No,'' he answered. ''I'm used to traveling about, and I want to
move on.''

So Brother Lustig set out again, and when he got to a smithy, he
put the knapsack that contained the nine devils on the anvil and
asked the blacksmith and his helpers to flatten it out. They then
pounded with their large hammers with all their might, and the
devils let loose terrible howls. When he opened the knapsack afterward, eight of the devils were dead, but one of them, who had sat in
a crease, was still alive, and he slipped out and went back to hell.

Now, Brother Lustig traveled about the world for a long time, and
anyone who knows about his adventures has a good deal to tell.
However, he eventually grew old and thought about his end. So he
went to a hermit who was known to be a pious man. ''I'm tired of
wandering, and I want to try now to get into the kingdom of
heaven,'' he said.

''There are two paths,'' the hermit responded. ''One is wide and
pleasant and leads to hell. The other is narrow and rough and leads
to heaven.''

Well, I'd have to be a fool, he thought, if I took the narrow and
rough one. So he set out and took the wide and pleasant path and
eventually came to a large black gate, which was the gate of hell.
Brother Lustig knocked, and the gatekeeper looked out to see who

was there. However, when he saw Brother Lustig, he was terrified, for he was the very same ninth devil who had been in the knapsack and who had escaped with a black eye. Therefore, he quickly bolted the gate, ran to the head of the devils, and said, "There's a fellow with a knapsack outside who wants to come in, but whatever you do, don't let him in, or he'll wish the whole of hell into his knapsack. The one time he got me in it, he gave me a nasty beating."

So Brother Lustig was told to move on, for he would not be admitted into hell. Well, if they don't want me there, he thought, I'll go and see if I can find a place to stay in heaven, for I've got to stay somewhere. He turned around and continued on his way until he got to the gate of heaven and knocked. Saint Peter happened to be sitting right there as gatekeeper, and Brother Lustig recognized him right away. Here's an old friend, he thought. Things will go better here.

But Saint Peter said, "Do you think you can make me believe that you really want to get into heaven?"

"Come, let me in, brother. I've got to find a place somewhere. If they had let me into hell, I wouldn't have come here."

"No," said Saint Peter. "I won't let you in."

"Well, if you don't want to let me in, then take back your knapsack, because I don't want to keep anything that belongs to you," said Brother Lustig.

"All right, give it to me," answered Saint Peter.

So Brother Lustig handed him the knapsack through the bars of the gate, and Saint Peter hung it up beside his chair.

Suddenly Brother Lustig said, "Now I wish myself into my knapsack."

Within seconds he was inside the knapsack and inside heaven as well. So Saint Peter was obliged to let him stay there.

◈ 82 ◈

Gambling Hans

ONCE UPON A TIME there was a man who did nothing but gamble, so people called him Gambling Hans. Since he gambled all the time, he eventually lost his house and everything else he owned. Now, on the day before his creditors were to take possession of his house, the Lord and Saint Peter appeared and requested a night's lodging. So Gambling Hans said, "As far as I'm concerned, you can spend the night, but I can't give you a bed or anything to eat."

The Lord said that he had only to provide lodgings and that they would buy themselves something to eat. All that was acceptable to Gambling Hans, whereupon Saint Peter gave him three groschen and told him to go to the baker and fetch some bread. So Gambling Hans departed, but as he passed the house where the other gamblers lived, the same men who had won everything from him, they called out to him, "Hans, come on in!"

"Not on your life," he said. "You just want to win the three groschen from me too."

However, the others did not let up, and they got him to come in and gamble away the three groschen. In the meantime, Saint Peter and the Lord were waiting, and when Hans did not come back after a while, they went out to see what was keeping him. When he saw them coming, he pretended to have dropped the money in a puddle of water and crawled around as if he were looking for it. But the Lord knew quite well that he had gambled the money away. Now Saint Peter gave him another three groschen, and this time he did not let himself be tempted and brought back the bread. After that the Lord asked him whether he had any wine, and he replied, "I'm sorry, sir. The barrels in the cellar are all empty."

Then the Lord told him to go down into the cellar. "The best wine is still down there."

At first Gambling Hans did not want to believe him, but finally he said, "I'll go down, but I know there isn't any."

Yet, when he tapped the barrel, the very best wine came out, and he brought them the wine. The two spent the night there, and early the next morning the Lord told Gambling Hans he would grant him three favors, thinking that he would want to go to heaven, but Gambling Hans asked for a deck of cards that would enable him to always win, dice that would enable him to always win, and a tree that not only had all sorts of fruits, but if anyone ever climbed the tree, he would not be able to get down unless Hans gave the order. The Lord granted him everything he wanted and went on his way with Saint Peter.

Now Gambling Hans began gambling in earnest, and soon he was on the verge of winning half the world. At this point Saint Peter said to God, "Lord, this won't do. Soon he'll win the whole world. We must send Death after him."

So they sent Death after him, and when Death arrived, Gambling Hans was at the gambling table.

"Hans, come outside for a moment," Death said.

"Just wait a little while until the game is over," Hans responded. "In the meantime, why don't you climb the tree outside and pick a few things for us to nibble on along the way."

Death climbed the tree, but when he wanted to get down, he was unable to, and Gambling Hans let him stay up there for seven years, during which time nobody died.

Again Saint Peter said to God, "Lord, this won't do. No one is dying anymore. We shall have to go ourselves."

So they went themselves, and the Lord ordered Gambling Hans to release Death. Hans then went straight up to Death and said, "Get down." And Death seized him and strangled him on the spot. Then they went together to the otherworld, and Gambling Hans went straight to the gate of heaven, where he knocked.

"Who's there?"

"Gambling Hans."

"Oh, we don't need you here. Go away."

Then he went to the gate of purgatory and knocked again.

"Who's there?"

"Gambling Hans."

"Oh, we've got enough misery and trouble here, and we don't want to gamble. Go away."

Then he went to the gate of hell, where they let him right in. There was nobody at home except Lucifer and the hunchback devils (for the straight-back devils were taking care of business on earth). So he sat down right away and began gambling again. Now, Lucifer had nothing to lose but his hunchback devils, and Gambling Hans won them from him because of his deck of cards that helped him always win. After that, he took off with the hunchback devils, and they went to Hohenfurt together and pulled out some hop poles. Next they went up to heaven and attacked the heavenly kingdom with the poles. Soon heaven was about to collapse, and Saint Peter said, "Lord, this won't do. We must let him in, or else he'll overthrow all of heaven."

They let him in, but Gambling Hans instantly began gambling again, and there was such a noise and racket that nobody could hear himself speak. Once again Saint Peter said, "Lord, this won't do. We must throw him out or else he'll cause all sorts of chaos in heaven."

So they seized him and threw him out. His soul was smashed to pieces as a result, and some of the flying fragments worked their way into many gamblers who are still alive this very day.

◈ 83 ◈

Lucky Hans

AFTER HANS HAD SERVED HIS MASTER for seven years, he said to him, "Master, my time is up, and since I want to go back home to my mother now, I'd like to have my wages."

"You've served me faithfully and honestly," said the master, "and I shall reward you in kind."

So he gave Hans a gold nugget as big as his head, whereupon Hans pulled a kerchief out of his pocket, wrapped it around the nugget, lifted it to his shoulder, and set out for home. As he was meandering along, one foot following the other, he caught a glimpse of a rider trotting toward him on a lively horse. The man appeared to be very cheerful and vigorous.

"Ah!" said Hans very loudly. "Riding is such a wonderful thing! All you have to do is sit there as if you were in a chair. You never have to worry about stumbling on stones. You can save on shoes and get wherever you want in a jiffy."

Upon hearing Hans speak this way, the rider stopped his horse and cried out, "If that's so, why in the world are you walking, Hans?"

"I have to," he answered. "I've got to carry this large nugget. Sure, it's gold, but it's so heavy that I can't keep my head straight, and my shoulder's been feeling the weight."

"I'll tell you what," said the horseman. "Let's exchange. I'll give you my horse, and you give me your gold nugget."

"Gladly," said Hans. "But let me warn you, it's a terribly heavy load to carry."

The horseman dismounted, took the gold, and helped Hans get on the horse. The horseman put the reins firmly into his hands and said, "If you want to go at a quick pace, you've got to click your tongue and shout 'Giddyap! Giddyap!' "

Hans was in seventh heaven as he sat on the horse, and he began riding free and easy. After a while he thought he ought to be going faster. So he clicked his tongue and shouted, "Giddyap! Giddyap!" whereupon the horse broke out into such a fast trot that Hans was thrown off and was soon lying in a ditch between the road and the fields. The horse would have run away too if it had not been stopped by a farmer who happened to be coming that way and driving a cow before him. Hans pulled himself together and got up on his feet, but he was very irritated and said to the farmer, "Riding's no fun at all, especially when you wind up with a mare like this one that bucks and throws you off. I'm never getting on that horse again. Now, your cow's a different story. You can walk behind it at your ease. Not only that, you're sure of having milk, butter, and cheese every day. I'd give anything to have a cow like that!"

"Well," said the farmer, "if you really like my cow so much, then I'd be glad to trade the cow for the horse."

Hans agreed with utmost joy. So the farmer swung himself onto the horse and rode off in a hurry. Now Hans drove the cow before him in a leisurely way and thought about his lucky deal. All I need now is a piece of bread—and I'm sure to get some bread—then I'll be able to eat my butter and cheese with it as often as I like. If I get thirsty, I'll just milk my cow and drink the milk. What more could my heart possibly ask for? When he reached a tavern, he stopped and ate up everything he had with great relish, both his lunch and supper, and he ordered a glass of beer with his last few hellers. Then he continued to drive his cow onward toward his mother's village. As midday approached and Hans was traipsing over a heath that would take at least another hour to cross, the heat became unbearable. Indeed, it became so hot that his tongue stuck to the roof of his mouth with thirst. There's a way to remedy this situation, thought Hans. I'll just milk my cow and refresh myself with the milk.

He tied the cow to a withered tree, and since he did not have a bucket, he put his leather cap underneath. However, no matter how much he tried, not one drop of milk came out. And since he was so clumsy in the attempt, the cow finally lost her patience and gave him such a kick in the head with one of her hind legs that he fell down. It took a long time for him to recover and regain a sense of where he was. Fortunately, a butcher happened to come his way at that moment. He was pushing a young pig in a wheelbarrow and called out to Hans, "Somebody's been playing tricks on you!" He helped good old Hans to his feet, and then Hans proceeded to tell him what had happened. The butcher handed him his flask and said, "Just take a drink, and you'll feel better. That cow of yours probably won't give you milk because it's too old. At best it's fit only for the plow or for the slaughterhouse."

"No fooling," said Hans, who stroked his hair. "Who would ever have thought that? Naturally it's a good thing to have a beast around your home that you can slaughter. It'll sure make for a lot of meat! But I don't care for beef that much. It's not juicy enough for me. On the other hand, a young pig like yours has quite a different taste. And, just think of the sausages!"

"Listen, Hans," said the butcher. "I'd like to do you a personal favor, as a friend, and trade the pig for your cow."

"May God reward your kindness!" said Hans, and he handed over the cow to the butcher, who, in turn, got the pig out of the wheelbarrow and gave Hans the rope to which the pig was tied so he could lead it away.

As Hans resumed his journey he thought to himself how everything was going just as he wished. Whenever anything disturbing happened, it was always set right immediately. Soon he met up with a boy carrying a white goose under his arm. They said good day to each other, and Hans began to tell him about his luck and how he always managed to make such advantageous trades. The boy responded and said he was carrying the goose to a christening feast. "Just lift her," he continued, and he grabbed the goose by her wings. "See how heavy she is? They've been fattening her up for the last eight weeks. Anyone who takes a bite of her after she's been roasted will have to wipe the fat from both sides of his mouth."

"I agree," said Hans as he weighed the goose with one hand. "She certainly is heavy enough, but my pig is no lightweight either."

Meanwhile, the boy began looking around suspiciously in all directions and shaking his head. "Listen," he spoke again, "there's something the matter here, and it concerns your pig. Somebody stole a pig from the mayor's sty in the village I just passed through. I fear, yes, I really fear that you've got the pig in your hands. They've sent some people out, and it would be terrible if they caught you with the pig. The very least they'd do to you would be to throw you into a dark dungeon.''

Good old Hans was horrified. "Oh, God!" he said. "Couldn't you help me out of this mess? You know your way around these parts better than I do. Take my pig there and give me your goose.''

"This means my taking a risk too," responded the boy. "But I don't want to be at fault for your getting into trouble." So he took the rope in his hand and quickly moved off with the pig down a side road.

Now good old Hans felt free of his worries and continued his journey homeward with the goose under his arm. "When I really think about it," he said, "I got the better of him in the deal. First there's the fine roast meat, then the large amount of fat that will drip out and supply me with enough goose fat for my bread for the next three months, and finally there are the beautiful white feathers. I'll have my pillow stuffed with them, and nobody will ever have to rock me to sleep again. I'm sure my mother will be delighted about that!''

As he was passing through the last village he came upon a scissors grinder standing next to his cart. His wheel was humming, and he was singing along:

"I sharpen scissors and grind away,
and let the wind guide me from day to day."

Hans stopped and watched him. Finally, he went over to the man and said, ''You feel so well because you like what you're doing, don't you?''

"Yes," said the scissors grinder. "This business has got a solid foundation. A good scissors grinder is someone who always finds money whenever he digs into his pocket. But, tell me, where did you buy that beautiful goose?''

"I didn't buy it, I traded my pig for it.''

"And the pig?''

"That I got for a cow.''

"And the cow?''

"That I received for a horse.''

"And the horse?''

"That I got for a gold nugget that was as big as my head.''

"And the gold?''

"Oh, that made up my wages for seven years' service.''

"Say, you really know how to look out for your interests. Now, if only you could manage it so that you would hear money jingling in your pocket whenever you stood up, your luck would be made!''

"How can I manage that?'' Hans asked.

"You've got to become a scissors grinder like me. All you really need for that is a grindstone. The rest takes care of itself. Now, I happen to have one here for you. It's a little damaged, but you won't have to give me anything for it except your goose. What about it?''

"How can you even ask?'' Hans answered. "You'll make me the luckiest man on earth. If I have money whenever I put my hand in my pocket, I won't have to worry about a thing anymore.'' So he handed him the goose and took the grindstone in return.

"Now,'' said the scissors grinder, as he picked up a plain, ordinary stone that was lying near him on the ground, ''I'm going to give you this solid stone as part of the bargain. You can hit as hard as you want on it and straighten out all your old nails. Just make sure that you take good care of it.''

Hans lifted the stones, put them on his back, and continued

happily on his way. His eyes sparkled for joy. "I must have been born under a lucky star!" he exclaimed. "Everything I wish for comes true. It's as though the gods were looking after me."

In the meantime, since he had been walking all day, he had become tired. In addition he was suffering from hunger because he had eaten up all his provisions to celebrate the great cow trade he had made. It was only with great difficulty that he managed to continue, and even then, he had to stop every other minute. The stones were weighing him down unmercifully, and he could not help thinking how nice it would be if he could get rid of them at that moment. Finally, he saw a well in a field, and as he crawled toward it he resembled a snail. He was hoping to rest and refresh himself with a cool drink of water, and he laid the rocks carefully on the edge of the well, right next to him, to avoid damaging them. After that he sat down and leaned over to drink. But he made a false move and nudged the stones just enough that they fell into the water. As Hans saw the stones sink to the bottom he jumped up for joy. He then knelt down and thanked God with tears in his eyes for showing him such mercy and for relieving him of the stones in such a gracious way. Indeed, those stones had become a great burden for him.

"Nobody under the sun is as lucky as I am!" exclaimed Hans, and with a light heart and free from all his burdens, he now ran all the way home until he reached his mother.

◈ 84 ◈

Hans Gets Married

ONCE UPON A TIME there was a young farmer whose name was Hans. His cousin wanted very much to arrange a marriage for him with a rich wife. So he had Hans sit down behind the stove and then heated it. After that he gave Hans a bowl of milk and a large chunk of white bread and a freshly minted coin that sparkled:

"Hans," he said, "hold on tight to the coin. Take the white bread and crumble it into the milk and stay seated. I don't want you to move from the spot till I get back."

"All right," said Hans. "You can depend on me."

The matchmaker put on an old pair of patched pants and went to the next village, where he called on a rich farmer's daughter.

"Wouldn't you like to marry my cousin Hans?" he asked. "You'll get a forthright, sensible man who's sure to please you."

"How solid is he?" asked the greedy father. "Does he have plenty of bread to break?"

"My dear friend," responded the matchmaker. "My cousin's sitting solidly with both feet on the ground. He's got a pretty penny in his hand and plenty of bread to break. Besides, he's got just as many patches [for that was what they called the pieces of land in that region] as I've got patches on my pants." And he slapped his patches as he said this. "If you want to take the trouble to come along with me right now, I'll show you everything's just as I say."

Since the greedy man did not want to pass up such a good opportunity for his daughter, he said, "If what you say is true, I have no further objections to the marriage."

So the wedding was celebrated on the appointed day, and when the young wife expressed a desire to go out into the fields to see her husband's property, Hans quickly took off his Sunday suit and put on his patched overalls. "I might spoil my good clothes," he said.

They went together into the field, and wherever there was a vineyard, field, or meadow along the way, Hans pointed with his finger and slapped a large or small patch of his overalls and said, "That patch is mine, and that one, too, my dear. Just take a look." By that he meant that his wife was not to gaze at the fields but at his overalls, which did indeed belong to him.

"Were you also at the wedding?"

"Of course, I was there in my finest attire. I had my hair powdered with snow, but the sun came out and melted it. My dress was made from a spider's web, but when I passed through some bushes, the thorns tore it apart. My shoes were made of glass, but then I tripped over a stone, and they went *clink!* and broke in two."

◈ 85 ◈

The Golden Children

THERE ONCE WAS A POOR MAN and a poor woman who had nothing but a little hut and supported themselves by fishing and were living hand-to-mouth. One day, however, as the husband was sitting by the water's edge and casting out his net, he happened to pull in a fish made entirely of gold. His astonishment was great, and while he was examining the fish, it began to speak and said, "Listen to me, fisherman. If you throw me back into the water, I'll turn your little hut into a splendid castle."

"What's the use of a castle," responded the fisherman, "if I don't have anything to eat?"

"I'll take care of that too," continued the golden fish. "There'll be a cupboard in the castle. When you open it, there'll be dishes with the very best food on them and as much as you desire."

"If that's the case," said the man, "I can certainly do you a favor."

"Indeed," said the fish. "But there is a condition attached to this: You're not allowed to tell anyone in the world, no matter who it may be, how you came by your good fortune. If you so much as breathe a single word, all of it will be over."

The man threw the miraculous fish back into the water and went home. However, instead of finding his hut in its usual place, he discovered a great castle and stood gaping at it in amazement. Then he went inside and saw his wife dressed in beautiful clothes and sitting in a splendid room. She was extremely happy and asked, "Husband, how did all this happen so suddenly? I'm really pleased."

"Yes," said the man, "it pleases me too, but I'm also tremendously hungry. Give me something to eat."

"I haven't got a thing," his wife said. "And I don't know where to find anything in the new house."

"No need to worry," said the husband. "Over there's a cupboard. Just go and open it."

When she opened the cupboard, she found cake, meat, fruit, and wine. Everything looked at her enticingly. "What more could my heart desire?" she exclaimed with joy.

They sat down at the table and ate and drank together. After they had finished eating, the wife asked, "Where in the world did all this come from, husband?"

"Ah," said the husband. "Don't ask me about it. I'm not allowed to reveal a thing. If I tell you, then our good fortune will vanish."

"Very well," she said. "If I'm not supposed to know, then I don't want to know." However, she was not being sincere, and she kept thinking about the matter day and night. In addition, she kept tormenting and pestering her husband until he lost his patience and declared that everything had come from a miraculous golden fish, which he had caught, and that he had given the fish back its freedom for the castle. As soon as he said that, the beautiful castle vanished instantly, cupboard and all, and once again they found themselves sitting in the old fishing hut.

Now the man had to start his work all over again, and he went fishing. As luck would have it, however, he caught the golden fish once more.

"Listen," said the fish, "if you throw me back into the water, I'll give you the castle again, and this time the cupboard will be filled with boiled and roast meats. Just be firm, and whatever you do, don't reveal who gave you all this, otherwise you'll lose everything again."

"I'll certainly be on my guard," answered the fisherman, and he threw the fish back into the water. When he returned home, everything had been restored to its former splendor, and his wife was ecstatic about their good fortune. Yet, curiosity got the better of her, and in a few days she began asking questions again about how it all had happened and how he had managed everything. Her husband kept silent for a long time, but eventually she annoyed him so much that he exploded and revealed the secret. In an instant the castle vanished, and they found themselves sitting in the hut once again.

"See what you've done!" said the husband. "Now we'll have to live in poverty again."

"Ah," said his wife. "I'd rather live in poverty than not know who's giving us all that wealth. After all, I want to keep my peace of mind."

The man went fishing again, and after a while the same thing occurred: He pulled in the golden fish for the third time.

"Listen," said the fish. "It's clear to me that I'm bound to keep falling into your hands. So take me home with you and cut me into six pieces. Give your wife two of these to eat and two to your horse. Then bury two in the ground, and you'll reap blessings from them all."

The man took the fish home with him and did as he had been told. Then it came to pass that the two pieces he had buried in the ground grew into two golden lilies, his horse had two golden foals, and his wife gave birth to two children who were all gold. The children grew up and became tall and handsome while the lilies and horses grew along with them. One day the boys said, "Father, we want to mount our golden steeds and go out into the world."

That made the old man very sad, and he replied, "How shall I bear your absence when I won't know what's happening to you?"

"The two golden lilies will stay here," they said. "So you'll be able to tell from them how we are. If they are fresh, then we're doing well. If they wilt, then we're sick. If they perish, then we shall be dead."

They rode away and came to an inn, where many people were seated inside. When the people caught sight of the two golden boys, they began to laugh at them and mock them. Hearing their mockery, one of the brothers felt ashamed and decided that he did not want to see the world anymore. So he turned around and went back to his father. However, the other brother continued his journey and came to a great forest. Just as he was about to ride into it, some people told him, "Don't ride through the forest. It's full of robbers. They'll be rough with you, especially when they see that you're made of gold, and your horse as well. They'll kill you for sure."

But he would not let himself be scared by that and said, "I've got to get through, and get through I shall." Then he took a bearskin and covered himself and his horse with it so that nothing more of their gold could be seen. He then rode calmly into the forest. When he had gone a little way, he heard a rustling sound in the bushes and voices talking together.

"There's one," a voice cried out from one side.

"Let him go. He's just one of those lazy vagabonds, poor as a church mouse. We won't get a thing from him," a voice said from the other side.

So the golden youth rode safely through the forest, and no harm befell him.

One day he came riding into a village and saw a maiden who was so beautiful that he could not imagine any maiden more beautiful than her in the whole world. His love for her was so overwhelming that he went straight up to her and said, "I love you with all my heart. Will you be my wife?"

The maiden took such an immediate liking to him that she, in turn, gave her consent. "Yes, I'll be your wife," she said, "and remain true to you for the rest of my life."

So they held the wedding, and just as the celebration was in full swing, the bride's father came home and was very much surprised indeed to find his daughter married.

"Where's the bridegroom," he asked.

They pointed to the golden youth, who was still wearing the bearskin, and the father was furious and said, "Never shall a daughter of mine marry a lazy vagabond!" And he wanted to murder him.

Then his daughter pleaded as hard as she could. "But, Father," she said, "he's my husband, and I love him with all my heart."

Eventually, the father calmed down, but he could not get over the idea that his daughter might have married a common, wretched beggar, and he woke up early the next morning to see for himself. When he looked into their room, he saw a dazzling golden man in bed, and the discarded bearskin was lying on the floor. Then he went back to his room and thought, It's a good thing that I kept my temper, otherwise I might have committed an awful crime.

In the meantime, the golden youth dreamed that he was out hunting a splendid stag, and when he awoke in the morning, he said to his wife, "I want to go out hunting."

She was anxious and begged him to stay at home. "You could easily have an accident," she said.

But he answered, "I must go hunting, and hunting I shall go." He got up and went into the forest, and before long, a proud stag stopped in front of him, just as in his dream. He took aim and was about to shoot, but the stag ran off. He chased the animal over ditches and through bushes and did not get tired all day. But in the evening the stag disappeared before his eyes, and the youth now looked around him. He saw he was standing before a small cottage, and inside was a witch. When he knocked, the old woman came out and asked, "What are you doing in the middle of the great forest so late?"

"Have you seen a stag?" he asked.

"Yes," she replied. "I know the stag quite well." Now a little dog that had come outside with her began to bark viciously at the man.

"If you don't shut up, you nasty cur," he said, "I'll shoot you dead!"

"What will you do?" the witch cried angrily. "You'd shoot my little dog dead?" Immediately she turned him into a stone, and he lay flat on the ground.

Meanwhile, his bride waited for him in vain and thought, I'm sure that my fears have come true as well as everything else that was weighing so heavily on my heart.

However, the other brother, who was standing near the golden lilies at home, saw one of the lilies suddenly droop. "Oh, God!" he said. "My brother's had a great accident. I've got to go and see if I can save him."

"Stay here," said the father. "What shall I do if I lose you as well?"

"I must go," he replied. "And go I will."

He mounted his golden steed, rode off, and came to the forest where his brother was lying on the ground as a stone. The old witch came out of her house and called out to him. She wanted to trap him too, but he kept his distance from her and said, "If you don't bring my brother back to life, I'm going to shoot you."

Unwillingly, she touched the stone with her finger, and the brother regained his human form at once. There was great rejoicing when the two brothers saw each other again: they embraced, kissed each other, and rode out of the forest together, the one to his bride, the other home to his father.

"I was positive that you had rescued your brother," said the father. "I knew when the other golden lily suddenly straightened up and began to bloom again."

From then on they lived happily, and everything went well for them until they died.

❖ 86 ❖

The Fox and the Geese

ONCE THE FOX CAME TO A MEADOW where there was a flock of nice, plump geese. Then he laughed and said, "I've come just at the right moment. You're sitting there together so perfectly that all I have to do is eat you up one by one."

The geese jumped up and began cackling in fright. They screamed for mercy and begged piteously for their lives. However, the fox closed his ears to their pleas. "No mercy!" he said. "You've got to die."

Finally, one of the geese plucked up her courage and said, "Well, if we poor geese must surrender our innocent young lives, then show us some mercy by allowing us one last prayer so that we won't have to die in sin. After that we'll line up in a row, so that you'll be able to pick yourself out the fattest at your convenience."

"All right," said the fox. "That's a fair and pious request. Go ahead and pray, and I'll wait until you're done."

So the first goose began a good long prayer and kept saying *"Ga!Ga!"* Since she ran on and on, the second decided not to wait for her turn and began repeating *"Ga!Ga!"* Then the third and fourth followed, and soon they were all cackling together.

After they have finished praying, the tale shall be continued, but at the moment they are still cackling away.

❖ 87 ❖

The Poor Man and the Rich Man

IN OLDEN TIMES, when the Lord was still walking upon the earth among mortals, he happened to grow tired, and night descended before he could reach an inn. Two houses were standing in front of him, just opposite one another. The large and beautiful one belonged to a rich man, while the small and shabby one belonged to a poor man. I'm sure I won't be a burden to the rich man, thought the Lord, so I'll spend the night at his place.

When the rich man heard someone knocking at his door, he opened the window and asked the stranger who he was and what he wanted.

"I'd like to have a night's lodging," answered the Lord.

The rich man examined the traveler from head to toe, and since the Lord was dressed very simply and did not look like he had much money in his pockets, he shook his head and said, "I can't put you up. My rooms are full of herbs and seeds. If I were to put up everyone who knocked at my door, then I'd soon have to go out begging for myself. Look for a place somewhere else."

With that he slammed the window shut and left the Lord standing there. So the Lord turned around and went across the street to the small house. No sooner had he knocked than the poor man already had the door open and asked the traveler to enter.

"Stay the night with me," he said. "It's already dark, and you won't be able to go much farther tonight."

The Lord was pleased to hear that, and he entered the house. The poor man's wife welcomed him by shaking his hand. She told him to make himself feel at home and to feel free to use anything they had, even though they did not have much. Whatever they had, he could gladly have. Then she put potatoes on the fire, and while they were cooking, she milked the goat so that they would at least have a little milk with the meal. When the table had been set, the Lord sat down and ate with them, and he enjoyed the meager repast because there were grateful faces around him. When they had eaten and it was time to go to bed, the wife whispered to her husband, "Listen, dear husband, let's make up a bed of straw for ourselves tonight so that the poor traveler can sleep in our bed and rest. He's been traveling the whole day and is probably very tired."

"Good idea," he answered. "I'll go and offer it to him." And he went to the Lord and told him that, if he did not mind, he could sleep in their bed and give his limbs a proper rest.

The Lord did not want to take the old couple's bed, but they insisted until he finally took their bed and lay down in it. Meanwhile, they made a bed of straw for themselves and lay on the ground. The next morning they were up before daybreak and cooked breakfast for their guest as well as they could manage. When the sun began to shine through the little window and the Lord stood up, he ate with them again and got set to continue his journey. As he was standing in the doorway he turned around and said, "Because you are so kind and good, I'm going to grant you three wishes, and they shall indeed be fulfilled."

"There's nothing I want more than eternal salvation," said the man, "and also that we stay healthy and get our daily bread as long as we wish. As for the third thing, I don't know what to wish."

"Don't you want to wish for a new house in place of this old one?" asked the Lord.

"Oh, yes," said the man. "I'd certainly be pleased if I could have that as well."

Right before his departure the Lord gave them his blessings once more, fulfilled their wishes, and turned the old house into a new one. When the rich man got up, it was broad daylight. As he looked out his window toward the other side of the road, he saw a new clean house with a red tiled roof instead of the old shack that used to be there. His eyes popped wide open, and he called his wife. "Can you tell me what's going on?" he asked. "Just yesterday there was a dumpy house standing there, and today there's this new beautiful one. Run over and find out what happened."

His wife went over and asked the poor man, who told her, "Last night a traveler came by looking for a night's lodging, and right before his departure this morning he granted us three wishes, eternal salvation, good health and our daily bread for the rest of our lives, and lastly a beautiful new house in place of our old shack."

The rich man's wife hurried back and told her husband what had happened. Then the man said, "I'd like to beat myself to a pulp. If I had only known! The stranger came to our house first and wanted to spend the night with us, but I turned him away."

"Hurry," said his wife, "and get on your horse. Perhaps you can still catch up to the man and get him to grant you three wishes too."

The rich man followed her good advice, galloped off on his horse, and managed to catch up with the Lord. He used sweet talk with the Lord and begged him not to take it amiss that he had not let him into his house right away; he had gone to look for the door key, but the stranger had disappeared in the meantime. The rich man assured him that, if he passed by again, he would find a place to stay at his house.

"Very well," said the Lord. "If I come back again, I shall stay with you."

Then the rich man asked him whether he also could have three wishes, like his neighbor.

The Lord said yes, but that they would not turn out well for him, and it might be best if he refrained from wishing for anything. The rich man disagreed and asserted that he would be able to choose something to make himself happy if he knew for certain that the wishes would be fulfilled.

"Ride home," said the Lord. "The three wishes you make shall be fulfilled."

Now the rich man had what he wanted. So he rode home and began to contemplate what he should wish for. As he was thus steeped in thought he let the reins drop, and the horse began jumping so much that his thoughts were continually disturbed and he could not collect them. He patted the horse on its neck and said, "Calm down, Lizzy," but the horse kept on bouncing up and down. Finally, he got so annoyed that he lost his patience. "I wish you'd break your neck!" he exclaimed.

As soon as he had said that, he was thrown to the ground, and the horse lay dead as a doornail. Thus the first wish was fulfilled. Since the rich man was greedy by nature, he did not want to leave the saddle behind. So he cut it off, swung it over his back, and proceeded on foot. You've got two wishes left, he thought, and consoled himself with that. As he went walking through the sand under the blazing noonday sun, he got hot and surly. The saddle rested heavily on his back, and he was having a great deal of trouble thinking of a wish. "If I wished for all the riches and treasures of the world," he said to himself, "I'm sure that I'd think of all sorts of other things later on. There'll be this and that, but I'm going to fix things so that I'll cover every wish that one could possibly make."

Then he sighed and said, "If only I were that Bavarian farmer who also had three wishes. He'd know what to do: First he'd wish for a lot of beer, then as much beer as he could drink, and finally a whole barrel of beer." Sometimes he thought he had finally come upon a good wish, but afterward it always seemed to be too little. Along the way he began thinking about how easy his wife had it at home, where she was probably in a cool room and enjoying a fine meal. Just the thought of that annoyed him so much that, before he knew it, he blurted out, "I wish she were sitting on this saddle at home and couldn't get off, instead of my carrying it on my back!" And, just as the last word left his lips, the saddle vanished from his back, and he realized that his second wish had been fulfilled. He became so hot now that he began to run. He was looking forward to sitting down alone in his room, where he would think of something great for his last wish. However, when he arrived home and opened the door to the living room, his wife was sitting on the saddle in the middle of the room. Since she could not get off, she was screaming and complaining.

"Bear with it," he said. "I'm going to get you all the riches in the world with my wish. Just stay where you are."

However, she yelled at him, "What good are all the riches in the world to me if I have to sit on this saddle. You wished me up here, and now you'd better get me off!"

Whether he liked it or not, he had to use the third wish to get her off the saddle and rid of it. His wish was fulfilled at once, and so he got nothing but irritation, trouble, and abuse from the wishes and lost a horse in the bargain. On the other hand, the poor people spent their lives happily, peacefully, and devoutly until they reached their blissful end.

◈ 88 ◈

The Singing, Springing Lark

ONCE UPON A TIME there was a man who was about to go on a long journey, and right before his departure he asked his three daughters what he should bring back to them. The oldest wanted pearls, the second, diamonds, but the third said, "Dear Father, I'd like to have a singing, springing lark."

"All right," said the father. "If I can get one, you shall have it."

So he kissed all three daughters good-bye and went on his way. When the time came for his return journey, he had purchased pearls and diamonds for the two oldest, but even though he had looked all over, he had not been able to find the singing, springing lark for his youngest daughter. He was particularly sorry about that because she was his favorite. In the meantime, his way took him through a forest, in the middle of which he discovered a magnificent castle. Near the castle was a tree, and way on top of this tree he saw a lark singing and springing about.

"Well, you've come just at the right time," he said, quite pleased, and he ordered his servant to climb the tree and catch the little bird. But when the servant went over to the tree, a lion jumped out from under it, shook himself, and roared so ferociously that the leaves on the trees trembled.

"If anyone tries to steal my singing, springing lark," he cried, "I'll eat him up."

"I didn't know that the bird belonged to you," said the man. "I'll make up for my trespassing and give you a great deal of gold if only you'll spare my life."

"Nothing can save you," said the lion, "unless you promise to give me the first thing you meet when you get home. If you agree, then I'll not only grant you your life, but I'll also give you the bird for your daughter."

At first the man refused and said, "That could be my youngest daughter. She loves me most of all and always runs to meet me when I return home."

But the servant was very scared of the lion and said, "It doesn't always have to be your daughter. Maybe it'll be a cat or dog."

The man let himself be persuaded and took the singing, springing lark. Then he promised the lion he would give him the first thing that met him when he got home.

Upon reaching his house, he walked inside, and the first thing that met him was none other than his youngest and dearest daughter: she came running up to him, threw her arms around him, and kissed him. When she saw that he had brought her a singing, springing lark, she was overcome with joy. But her father could not rejoice and began to cry.

"My dearest child," he said. "I've had to pay a high price for this bird. In exchange I was compelled to promise you to a wild lion, and when he gets you, he'll tear you to pieces and eat you up." Then he went on to tell her exactly how everything had happened and begged her not to go there, no matter what the consequences might be. Yet, she consoled him and said, "Dearest Father, if you've made a promise, you must keep it. I'll go there, and once I've made the lion nice and tame, I'll be back here safe and sound."

The next morning she had her father show her the way. Then she took leave of him and walked calmly into the forest. Now, it turned out that the lion was actually an enchanted prince. During the day he and his men were lions, and during the night they assumed their true human form. When she arrived there, she was welcomed in a friendly way, and they conducted her to the castle. When night came, the lion became a handsome man, and the wedding was celebrated in splendor. They lived happily together by remaining awake at night and asleep during the day. One day he came to her and said, "Tomorrow there will be a celebration at your father's house since your oldest sister is to be married. If you wish to attend, my lions will escort you there."

She replied that, yes, she would very much like to see her father again, and she went there accompanied by the lions. There was great rejoicing when she arrived, for they all had believed that she had been torn to pieces by the lions and had long been dead. But she told them what a handsome husband she had and how well off she was. She stayed with them just as long as the wedding celebration lasted. Then she went back to the forest.

When the second daughter was about to be married, she was again invited to the wedding, but this time she said to the lion, "I don't want to go without you."

However, the lion said it would be too dangerous for him because he would be changed into a dove and have to fly about with the doves for seven years if the ray of a burning candle were to fall upon him.

"Please, come with me," she said. "I'll be sure to take good care of you and protect you from the light."

So they went off together and took their small child with them. Once there she had a hall built for him, so strong and thick that not a single ray of light could penetrate it. That was the place where he was to sit when the wedding candles were lit. However, its door was made out of green wood, and it split and developed a crack that nobody saw. The wedding was celebrated in splendor, but when the wedding procession with all the candles and torches came back from church and passed by the hall, a ray about the width of a hair fell upon the prince, and he was instantly transformed. When his wife entered the hall to look for him, she could find only a white dove sitting there, and he said to her, "For seven years I shall have to fly about the world, but for every seven steps you take I shall leave a drop of red blood and a little white feather to show you the way. And, if you follow the traces, you'll be able to set me free."

Then the dove flew out the door, and she followed him. At every seventh step she took, a drop of blood and a little white feather would fall and show her the way. Thus she went farther and farther into the wide world and never looked about or stopped until the seven years were almost up. She was looking forward to that and thought they would soon be free. But, they were still quite far from their goal.

Once, as she was moving along, she failed to find any more feathers or drops of blood, and when she raised her head, the dove had also vanished. I won't be able to get help from a mortal, she thought, and so she climbed up to the sun and said to her, "You shine into every nook and cranny. Is there any chance that you've seen a white dove flying around?"

"No," said the sun, "I haven't, but I'll give you a little casket. Just open it when your need is greatest."

She thanked the sun and continued on her way until the moon came out to shine in the evening. "You shine the whole night through and on all the fields and meadows. Is there any chance that you've seen a white dove flying around?"

"No," said the moon, "I haven't, but I'll give you an egg. Just crack it open when your need is greatest."

She thanked the moon and went farther until the Night Wind stirred and started to blow at her. "You blow over every tree and under every leaf. Is there any chance that you've seen a white dove flying around?"

"No," said the Night Wind, "I haven't, but I'll ask the three other winds. Perhaps they've seen one."

The East Wind and the West Wind came and reported they had not seen a thing, but the South Wind said, "I've seen the white dove. It's flown to the Red Sea and has become a lion again, for the seven years are over. The lion's now in the midst of a fight with a dragon that's really an enchanted princess."

Then the Night Wind said to her, "Here's what I would advise you to do: Go to the Red Sea, where you'll find some tall reeds growing along the shore. Then count them until you come to the eleventh one, which you're to cut off and use to strike the dragon. That done, the lion will be able to conquer the dragon, and both will regain their human form. After that, look around, and you'll see the griffin sitting by the Red Sea. Get on his back with your beloved, and the griffin will carry you home across the sea. Now, here's a nut for you. When you cross over the middle of the sea, let it drop. A nut tree will instantly sprout up out of the water, and the griffin will be able to rest on it. If he can't rest there, he won't be strong enough to carry you both across the sea. So if you forget to drop the nut into the sea, he'll let you fall into the water."

She went there and found everything as the Night Wind had said. She counted the reeds by the sea, cut off the eleventh, and struck the dragon with it. Whereupon the lion conquered the dragon, and both immediately regained their human form. But when the princess, who had previously been a dragon, was set free from the magic spell, she picked the prince up in her arms, got on the griffin, and carried him off with her. So the poor maiden, who had journeyed so far, stood alone and forsaken again, and sat down to cry. Eventually, she took heart and said, "I'll keep going as far as the wind blows and so long as the cock crows until I find him." And off she went and wandered a long, long way until she came to the castle where the two were living together. Then she heard that their wedding celebration was soon to take place. "God will still come to my aid," she remarked as she opened the little casket that the sun had given her. There she found a dress as radiant as the sun itself. She took it out, put it on, and went up to the castle. Everyone at the court and the bride herself could not believe their eyes. The bride liked the dress so much she thought it would be nice to have for her wedding and asked if she could buy it.

"Not for money or property," she answered, "but for flesh and blood."

The bride asked her what she meant by that, and she responded, "Let me sleep one night in the bridegroom's room."

The bride did not want to let her, but she also wanted the dress very much. Finally, she agreed, but the bridegroom's servant was obliged to give him a sleeping potion. That night when the prince was asleep, she was led into his room, sat down on his bed, and said, "I've followed you for seven years. I went to the sun, the moon, and the four winds to find out where you were. I helped you conquer the dragon. Are you going to forget me forever?"

But the prince slept so soundly that it merely seemed to him as if the wind were whispering in the firs. When morning came, she was led out again and had to give up her golden dress.

Since her ploy had not been of much use, she was quite sad and went out to a meadow, where she sat down and wept. But as she was sitting there, she remembered the egg that the moon had given her. She cracked it open, and a hen with twelve chicks came out, all in gold. The peeping chicks scampered about and then crawled under the mother hen's wings. There was not a lovelier sight to see in the world. Shortly after that she stood up and drove them ahead of her over the meadow until they came within sight of the bride, who saw them from her window. She liked the little chicks so much that she came right down and asked if she could buy them.

"Not with money or possessions, but for flesh and blood. Let me sleep another night in the bridegroom's room."

The bride agreed and wanted to trick her as she had done the night before. But when the prince went to bed, he asked his servant what had caused all the murmuring and rustling during the night, and the servant told him everything: that he had been compelled to give him a sleeping potion because a poor girl had secretly slept in his room, and that he was supposed to give him another one that night.

"Dump the drink by the side of my bed," said the prince.

At night the maiden was led in again, and when she began to talk about her sad plight, he immediately recognized his dear wife by her voice, jumped up, and exclaimed, "Now I'm really free from the spell! It was all like a dream. The strange princess had cast a spell over me and made me forget you, but God has delivered me from the spell just in time."

That night they left the castle in secret, for they were afraid of the princess's father, who was a sorcerer. They got on the griffin, who carried them over the Red Sea, and when they were in the middle, she let the nut drop. Immediately a big nut tree sprouted, and the griffin was able to rest there. Then he carried them home, where they found their child, who had grown tall and handsome. From then on they lived happily until their death.

◈ 89 ◈

The Goose Girl

THERE ONCE WAS AN OLD QUEEN whose husband had been dead for many years, and she had a beautiful daughter. When the daughter grew up, she was betrothed to a prince who lived far away. Soon the time came for her to be married, and the princess got ready to depart for the distant kingdom. So the old queen packed up a great many precious items and ornaments and goblets and jewels, all made with silver and gold. Indeed, she gave her everything that suited a royal dowry, for she loved her child with all her heart. She also gave her a chambermaid, who was to accompany her and deliver her safely into the hands of her bridegroom. Each received a horse for the journey, but the princess's horse was named Falada and could speak. When the hour of departure arrived, the old mother went into her bedroom, took a small knife, and cut her finger to make it bleed. Then she placed a white handkerchief underneath her finger, let three drops of blood fall on it, and gave it to her daughter.

"My dear child," she said, "take good care of these three drops, for they will help you on your journey when you're in need."

After they had bid each other a sad farewell, the princess stuck the handkerchief into her bosom, mounted her horse, and began her journey to her bridegroom. After riding an hour, she felt very thirsty and said to her chambermaid, "Get down and fetch some water from the brook with the golden cup you brought along for me. I'd like to have something to drink."

"If you're thirsty," said the chambermaid, "get down yourself. Just lie down by the water and drink. I'm not going to be your servant."

Since the princess was very thirsty, she dismounted, bent over the brook, and drank some water, but she was not allowed to drink out of the golden cup.

"Dear Lord!" she said.

Then the three drops of blood responded, "Ah, if your mother knew, her heart would break in two!"

But the princess was humble. She said nothing and got back on her horse. They continued riding a few miles, but the day was warm, the sun was scorching hot, and soon she got thirsty again. When they came to a stream, she called to her chambermaid once more. "Get down and bring me something to drink from my golden cup," for she had long since forgotten her nasty words.

"If you want to drink," the chambermaid said even more haughtily than before, "drink by yourself. I'm not going to be your servant."

Since she was very thirsty, the princess dismounted, lay down next to the running water, and wept.

"Dear Lord!" she said.

Once again the drops of blood responded, "Ah, if your mother knew, her heart would break in two!"

As she was leaning over the bank and drinking the water, her handkerchief with the three drops of blood fell out of her bosom and floated downstream without her ever noticing it, so great was her fear. But the chambermaid had seen it and was pleased because she knew that now she could have power over the princess. Without the three drops of blood, the princess was weak and helpless. So, as she was about to get back on the horse named Falada, the chambermaid said, "That's my horse. Yours is the nag!"

The princess had to put up with all that. Moreover, the chamber-maid spoke rudely to her and ordered her to take off her royal garments and to put on the maid's shabby clothes. Finally, she had to swear under open skies that she would never tell a soul at the royal court what the chambermaid had done. If the princess had not given her word, she would have been killed on the spot. But Falada saw all this and took good note of it.

Now the chambermaid mounted Falada, and the true bride had to get on the wretched nag. Thus they continued their journey until they finally arrived at the royal castle. There was great rejoicing when they entered the courtyard, and the prince ran to meet them. He lifted the chambermaid from her horse, thinking that she was his bride. Then he led her up the stairs, while the princess was left standing below. Meanwhile, the old king peered out a window, and when he saw her standing in the courtyard, he was struck by her fine, delicate, and beautiful features. He went straight to the royal suite and asked the bride about the girl she had brought with her, the one standing below in the courtyard, and who she was.

"I picked her up along the way to keep me company. Just give her something to keep her busy."

But the old king had no work for her and could only respond, "I have a little boy who tends the geese. Perhaps she could help him."

The boy's name was Conrad, and the true bride had to help him tend the geese.

Shortly after, the false bride said to the young king, "Dearest husband, I'd like you to do me a favor."

"I'd be glad to," he answered.

"Well then, summon the knacker and have him cut off the head of the horse that carried me here. It gave me nothing but trouble along the way."

However, the truth was that she was afraid the horse would reveal what she had done to the princess. When all the preparations had been made and faithful Falada was about to die, word reached the ears of the true princess, and she secretly promised the knacker a gold coin if he would render her a small service. There was a big dark gateway through which she had to pass every morning and evening with the geese, and she wanted him to nail Falada's head on the wall under the dark gateway, where she could always see it. The knacker promised to do it, and when he cut off the horse's head, he nailed it on hard to the wall under the dark gateway.

Early the next morning, when she and Conrad drove the geese out through the gateway, she said in passing:

"Oh, poor Falada, I see you hanging there."

Then the head answered:

"Dear Queen, is that you really there?
Oh, if your mother knew,
her heart would break in two!"

She walked out of the city in silence, and they drove the geese into the fields. When she reached the meadow, she sat down and undid her hair, which was as pure as gold. Conrad liked the way her hair glistened so much that he tried to pull out a few strands. Then she said:

"Blow, wind, oh, blow with all your might!
Blow Conrad's cap right out of sight,
and make him chase it everywhere
until I've braided all my hair
and put it up all right."

Then a gust of wind came and blew off Conrad's cap into the fields, and he had to run after it. By the time he returned with it, she had finished combing and putting her hair up, and he could not get a single strand of it. Conrad became so angry that he would not speak to her after that. Thus they tended the geese until evening, when they set out on their way home.

The next morning, when they drove the geese through the dark gateway, the maiden said:

"Oh, poor Falada, I see you hanging there."

Then Falada responded:

"Dear Queen, is that you really there?
Oh, if your mother knew,
her heart would break in two!"

Once she and Conrad were out in the fields again, she sat down in the meadow and began to comb out her hair. Conrad ran up and tried to grab it, but she quickly said:

"Blow, wind, oh, blow with all your might!
Blow Conrad's cap right out of sight,

and make him chase it everywhere
until I've braided all my hair
and put it up all right.''

The wind blew and whisked the cap off his head and drove it far off so that Conrad had to run after it. When he came back, she had long since put up her hair, and he could not get a single strand. Thus they tended the geese until evening. However, upon returning that evening, Conrad went to the old king and said, ''I don't want to tend the geese with that girl anymore.''

''Why not?'' asked the old king.

''Well, she tortures me the whole day long.''

The old king ordered him to tell him what she did, and Conrad said, ''In the morning, when we pass through the dark gateway, there's a horse's head on the wall, and she always says:

'Oh, poor Falada, I see you hanging there.'

"And the head answers:

'Dear Queen, is that you really there?
Oh, if your mother knew,
her heart would break in two!' "

And thus Conrad went on to tell the king what had happened out on the meadow, and how he had had to chase after his cap.

The old king ordered him to drive the geese out again the next day, and when morning came, the old king himself sneaked behind the dark gateway and heard her speak to Falada's head. Then he followed her into the fields and hid behind some bushes in the meadow. Soon he saw with his own eyes how the goose girl and the goose boy brought the geese to the meadow, and how she sat down after a while and undid her hair that glistened radiantly. Before long, she said:

"Blow, wind, oh, blow with all your might!
Blow Conrad's cap right out of sight,
and make him chase it everywhere
until I've braided all my hair
and put it up all right."

Then a gust of wind came and carried Conrad's cap away, so that he had to run far, and the maiden calmly combed and braided her hair. All this was observed by the old king. He then went home unnoticed, and when the goose girl came back that evening, he called her aside and asked her why she did all those things.

"I'm not allowed to tell you, nor am I allowed to bemoan my plight to anyone. Such is the oath I swore under the open skies. Otherwise, I would have been killed."

Although he kept on insisting and would give her no peace, she would not talk. Then he said, "If you don't want to tell me anything, then let the iron stove over there listen to your sorrows."

After the king departed, she crawled into the iron stove and began to lament and weep and pour her heart out.

"Here I sit now," she said. "Forsaken by the world, and yet I'm a king's daughter. A wicked chambermaid forced me to give her my royal garments, and then she took my place with my bridegroom. Now I must do menial work as a goose girl. Oh, if my mother knew, her heart would break in two!"

Meanwhile, the old king stood next to the stovepipe outside and listened to what she said. Afterward he went back into the room and ordered her to come out of the stove. He had her dressed in royal garments, and it was like a miracle to see how beautiful she really was. The old king called his son and revealed to him that he had the wrong bride, who was nothing but a chambermaid. The true bride, however, was standing there before him, the former goose girl. The young king was extremely pleased, for he saw how beautiful and virtuous she was.

Now a great feast was prepared, and all their friends and the entire court were invited to attend. At the head of the table sat the bridegroom, with the princess at one side and the chambermaid at the other, but the chambermaid was so distracted that she could no longer recognize the princess, who was dressed in such a dazzling manner. After they finished eating and drinking and were all in high spirits, the old king gave the chambermaid a riddle to solve: what punishment did a woman deserve who deceived her lord in such and such a way? Whereupon he told her the whole story and concluded by asking, "How would you sentence her?"

"She deserves nothing better," said the false bride, "than to be stripped completely naked and put inside a barrel studded with sharp nails. Then two white horses should be harnessed to the barrel and made to drag her through the streets until she's dead."

"You're the woman," said the king, "and you've pronounced your own sentence. All this shall happen to you."

When the sentence had been carried out, the young king married his true bride, and they both reigned over their kingdom in peace and bliss.

◈ 90 ◈

The Young Giant

A FARMER HAD A SON no bigger than the size of a thumb. After some years had passed, his son did not show the least sign of getting any bigger or even growing so much as a hair's breadth. One day, when the farmer was preparing to go out to the field to do some plowing, the little fellow said, "Father, I want to go with you."

"You want to go with me?" asked the farmer. "Well, I think you'd better stay here. You're of no use to me out there, and you could get lost."

When he heard that, Thumbling began to cry, so his father stuck him in his pocket and took him along in order to have some peace and quiet. Once he was out in the field, he pulled his son out again and set him down in a freshly plowed furrow. As the boy was sitting there a big giant came over the hill.

"Do you see the big bogeyman over there?" said the father, who just wanted to scare the little fellow so he would behave. "He's coming to get you."

It took the giant only a few steps with his long legs before he reached the furrow. Then he lifted Thumbling up carefully with two fingers, examined him, and carried him away without saying a word. The father stood there so petrified with fright that he could not utter a sound. He was certain his child was now lost to him and he would never set eyes on him again.

In the meantime, the giant took the boy home and let him suckle at his breast, and Thumbling grew and became big and strong like most giants. When two years had passed, the old giant took him into the woods to test him.

"Pull up a stick for yourself," he said.

By now the boy had become so strong that he tore up a young tree right out of the ground, roots and all. But the giant thought, We must do better than that. So he took him home again and nursed him for two more years. When he tested him once more, the boy's strength had increased so much that he could tear an old tree out of the ground. Yet, it still was not enough for the giant, who nursed him another two years, and when he then took him into the woods, he said, "Now, make sure you tear up a stick of decent size!"

The boy tore up the thickest possible oak tree right out of the ground so that it cracked in two, and this was mere child's play for him.

"That's enough now," said the giant. "You've learned all you need to know," and he took him back to the field where he had found him. His father was plowing there as the young giant came over to him and said, "Look, Father, look what a fine man your son has grown up to be!"

The farmer was frightened and said, "No, you're not my son. I don't want you. Go away!"

"Of course I'm your son! Let me do your work. I can plow just as well as you can, or even better."

"No, no, you're not my son. I don't want you, and I don't want you to plow either. Go away!"

However, since the farmer was afraid of the big man, he let go of the plow, stepped aside, and sat down at the edge of the field. Then the young man grabbed the plow and merely pressed his hand on it, but his grip was so powerful that the plow sank deep into the earth. The farmer could not bear to watch all that, and so he called over to him. "If you're so set on plowing, then you've got to learn not to press down so hard. Otherwise, you'll ruin the field."

Then the young man unharnessed the horses and began pulling the plow himself. "Just go home, Father," he said, "and have Mother cook me a large dish of food. In the meantime, I'll plow the field for you."

The farmer went home and told his wife to cook the food, and the young man plowed the field, two whole acres, all by himself. After that he harnessed himself to the harrow and harrowed the field with two harrows at the same time. When he was finished, he went into the woods and pulled up two oak trees, put them on his shoulders, and attached a harrow at each end of a tree and a horse at each end of the other tree. Then he carried everything to his parents' house as if it were a bundle of straw. When he reached the barnyard, his mother did not recognize him and asked, "Who's that horrible big man?"

"That's our son," the farmer said.

"No," she said, "that can't be our son. We never had one that large. Our son was a tiny thing." Then she yelled at him, "Go away! We don't want you!"

The young man did not respond but led the horses into the stable and gave them oats and hay and whatever else they normally had. When he was finished, he went into the kitchen, sat down at a bench, and said, "Mother, I'd like to eat now. Is supper almost ready?"

"Yes," she replied, and brought him two tremendous bowls of food that would have lasted her and her husband a week. However, the young man finished everything by himself and then asked whether she could give him something more.

"No," she said, "that's all we have."

"That was really just a nibble. I've got to have more."

She did not dare contradict him. So she went out and put a large pig's trough full of food on the fire. When it was ready, she carried it in.

"At last, a few more crumbs of food to eat," he said and gobbled up everything that was in it. But that was not enough to satisfy his hunger.

"Father," he said, "I can tell I'll never get enough to eat here.

So, if you'll get me an iron staff strong enough that I won't break it across my knees, I'll make my way out into the world."

The farmer was happy to hear that. He hitched two horses to his wagon and went to the blacksmith, who gave him a staff so big and thick that the two horses could barely pull it. The young man laid it across his knees, and *crack!* he broke it in two, as if it were a beanstalk, and threw it away. His father hitched four horses to his wagon and fetched another staff, one so large and thick that the four horses could barely pull it. Once again his son snapped it across his knees and threw it away. "Father," he said, "this one's no use to me. You've got to harness some more horses and fetch a stronger staff."

Then his father hitched up eight horses to his wagon and brought back a staff so large and thick that the eight horses could barely pull it. When his son took it in his hand, he immediately broke off a piece from the top and said, "Father, I see that you can't get the kind of staff I need. So I won't stay around here any longer."

The young man went away, and he began passing himself off as a journeyman blacksmith. Soon he came to a village that had a blacksmith among its inhabitants. He was a greedy man who never gave anyone a thing and kept everything for himself. The young man went to the smithy and asked him whether he could use a journeyman.

"Yes," said the blacksmith, who looked him over and thought, That's a sturdy fellow. He'll certainly be good at hammering, and he's sure to earn his keep. Then he asked, "How much wages do you want?"

"None at all," he answered. "But every two weeks when the other journeymen receive their wages, I shall give you two blows that you must be able to withstand."

The miser voiced great satisfaction with the terms, because he thought he could save money this way. The next morning the strange journeyman was supposed to hammer first, and when the master brought out the red-hot bar and the journeyman dealt the blow, the iron flew all over in pieces, and the anvil sank so deep into the ground that they could not get it out again. The miser became furious and said, "That's all! I can't use you anymore. You hammer much too roughly. What do I owe you for the one blow?"

"I'll give you just a tiny tap, that's all," said the journeyman, and he lifted his foot and gave him such a kick that he flew over four stacks of hay. Then the journeyman picked out the thickest iron staff he could find in the smithy, used it as a walking stick, and went on his way. After he had been traveling for a while, he came to a large farming estate and asked the bailiff if he needed a foreman.

"Yes," said the bailiff, "I can use one. You look like a sturdy and able fellow. What would you like your wages to be for the year?"

Again he answered that he did not want to be paid, but that the bailiff would have to withstand three blows that he would give him at the end of every year. The bailiff was satisfied with that, for he too was a miser. The next morning the hired workers got up early because they were supposed to drive to the forest and cut wood, but the young man was still in bed. One of the workers called to him, "Hey, it's time to get up! We're going to the forest, and you've got to come with us."

"Not yet," he replied in a rude and surly voice. "You all go. I'll get there and back before the rest of you anyway."

Then the workers went to the bailiff and told him that the foreman was still in bed and would not drive to the forest with them. The bailiff told them to wake him again and order him to hitch up the horses. But the foreman answered just as he had before, "You all go. I'll get there and back before the rest of you anyway."

So he remained in bed another two hours, and when he finally managed to get up, he fetched two bushels of peas from the loft, cooked himself a porridge, and took his own sweet time in eating it. After that was done, he went out and hitched up the horses and drove to the forest. Near the forest was a ravine through which he had to drive. When he drove through it, he stopped the horses, got out, walked behind the wagon, and took some trees and bushes to build a large barricade that would prevent horses from getting through the ravine. When he arrived at the forest, the others were just leaving with their loaded wagons and heading home.

"Drive on," he said to them. "I'll still get home before you."

He did not drive very far into the forest, for as soon as he saw two of the biggest oak trees, he ripped them out of the ground, threw them into his wagon, and turned back. When he reached the barricade, the others were still standing around, since they had been prevented from getting through.

"You see," he said. "If you had stayed with me, you'd have made it home just as quickly, and you'd have had another hour's sleep."

He wanted to drive on, but his horses could not work their way through the barricade. So he unharnessed them, set them on top of the wagon, took hold of the shafts, and whisked everything through as easily as if the wagon were loaded with feathers. Once he was on the other side, he said to the workers, "You see, I got through faster than you." And he drove on, while the others had to stay where they were. At the barnyard he grabbed hold of one of the trees, lifted it by his hand, showed it to the bailiff, and said, "How do you like this nice cord of wood?"

The bailiff said to his wife, "He's a good man, our foreman. Even if he does sleep long, he still makes it home sooner than the others."

So the young man served the bailiff for a year, and when it was over and the other workers received their wages, it was time for him to collect his pay as well. However, the bailiff was afraid of the blows he had coming to him. He begged the foreman to forgo everything and said that, in return, he would make him bailiff and take over the job as foreman himself.

"No," said the young man. "I don't want to be bailiff. I'm foreman and want to stay foreman. And I intend to dole out what we agreed upon."

The bailiff offered to give him whatever he wanted, but it did no good. The foreman rejected everything he proposed, and the bailiff did not know what to do except to ask him for a two-week period of grace. He needed time to think of a way out of his situation. The foreman granted him an extension, and now the bailiff summoned all his clerks together. He asked them to think up a way to help him and to advise him. After they had deliberated a long time, they finally said that nobody's life was safe from the foreman: he could kill a man as easily as he could a gnat. They advised the bailiff, therefore, to order the foreman to climb down into the well and clean it out; when he was down below, they would roll one of the millstones that were lying around there over to the well and heave it on his head. Then he would never see the light of day again.

The bailiff liked the idea, and the foreman was willing to climb down into the well. Once he was standing below, they rolled down the largest millstone they could find and were convinced they broke his skull with it. However, he called up to them, "Chase the chickens away from the well! They're scratching around in the sand and throwing grains into my eyes so that I can't see."

So the bailiff yelled, *"Shoo! Shoo!"* as if he were scaring the chickens away. When the foreman had finished his work, he climbed up and said, "Just look at what a fine necklace I've got on now!" but he meant the millstone that he was wearing around his neck.

Now the foreman wanted to receive his pay, but the bailiff requested another two weeks' grace to think up a new plan. The clerks met again and advised him to send the foreman to the haunted mill to grind grain at night since nobody had ever emerged alive from it the next morning. The bailiff liked the proposal and called the foreman to him that very same evening. He ordered him to carry eight bushels of grain to the mill and grind it that night because they needed it right away. So the foreman went to the loft and put two bushels in his right pocket and two in his left. He carried the other four in a sack that he slung over his shoulder so that half was on his back and half on his chest. And off he went to the haunted mill.

The miller told him he could easily grind the grain during the day, but not at night, because the mill was haunted, and anyone who had gone in there at night had not been alive in the morning to return.

"Don't worry, I'll manage," said the foreman. "Why don't you go and get some sleep." Then he went into the mill and poured the grain into the hopper. Toward eleven o'clock he went into the miller's room and sat down on a bench. After he had been sitting there awhile, the door suddenly opened, and an enormous table came in. Next he saw wine, roast meat, and all sorts of good food appear on the table by themselves, but nobody carried these things in. After that the chairs slid to the table, but nobody came. All at once he saw fingers handling knives and forks and putting food on the plates. Aside from that, he could not see a thing. Since he was hungry and saw all this food, he too sat down at the table, ate along with all those present, and enjoyed the meal. When he had eaten his fill and the others had also emptied their plates, he distinctly heard all the lights being suddenly snuffed out, and when it was pitch dark, he felt something like a smack in the face. Then he said, "If anything like that happens again, I'm going to strike back."

When he received a second smack in the face, he struck back, and so it went the whole night. He took nothing without paying it back generously, with interest, and kept himself busy by smacking anything that came near him. At daybreak, however, everything stopped. When the miller got up, he went by to see how the foreman was, and he was amazed to find him alive.

"I had a very fine meal," said the foreman. "Then I got some smacks in the face, but I also gave some in return."

The miller was happy and said that the mill was now released from its curse, and he wanted to pay the foreman a reward.

"I don't want money," said the foreman, "I already have enough." Then he took the flour on his back, went home, and told the bailiff he had done his job and now wanted to be paid the wages they had agreed upon.

When the bailiff heard that, he really became alarmed and upset. He paced up and down the room, and beads of sweat ran down his forehead. So he opened the window to get some fresh air, but before he knew it, the foreman had given him such a kick that he went flying through the window out into the sky. He flew and flew until he was completely out of sight.

Then the foreman said to the bailiff's wife, "If he doesn't return, you'll have to take the other blow."

"No, no!" she exclaimed. "I won't be able to withstand it," and she opened the other window because beads of sweat were running down her face also. Then he gave her a kick too, and she went flying out the window. Since she was lighter than her husband, she soared much higher.

Her husband called out to her, "Come over here!"

But she replied, "No, you come over here to me! I can't make it there."

So they soared through the sky, and neither could get to the other. Whether they are still soaring, I don't know, but I do know that the young giant took his iron staff and continued on his way.

◈ 91 ◈

The Gnome

ONCE UPON A TIME there was a rich king who had three daughters. Every day they went walking in the palace garden, where the king, who loved trees, had planted many different kinds, but he was most fond of one particular tree, which he protected by placing it under a spell: Whosoever picked one of its apples would be sent a hundred fathoms underground. When harvest time came, the apples on that tree were as red as blood. Every day the three daughters looked under the tree to see if the wind had blown an apple to the ground, but they never found one. Gradually the tree became so full and its branches so heavy that it seemed the tree would collapse.

By then the youngest sister had such a craving for an apple from this tree that she said to her sisters, "Our father loves us far too much to put a curse on us. I think he cast the spell mainly with strangers in mind." So she plucked a nice plump apple, ran to her sisters, and said, "Just taste it, dear sisters! I've never tasted anything so delicious in all my life."

Then the two other princesses also took a bite of the apple, and suddenly all three sank deep down into the earth, leaving no trace whatsoever behind them. At noon the king wanted to call them to the dining table, but they were nowhere to be found. He looked all around the castle and garden but could not find them. Finally, he became so distressed that he made it known throughout the country that whoever brought his daughters back could have one of them for his wife. As a result, more men than you can imagine went out searching for them all over the kingdom, for the princesses were known to be beautiful and kind to all. Indeed, they were loved by everyone in the country.

Among the searchers were three huntsmen who had spent a week looking for them and had eventually come to a great castle. When they went inside it, they found beautiful rooms, and in one of the rooms the table was set with delicious dishes that were still steaming hot, but there was not a living soul to be seen or heard in the whole castle. They waited half a day more, and the food remained steaming hot. At last they were so hungry that they sat down and ate up all the food. Then they agreed to stay in the castle and drew lots to see which one would remain at home there while the other two continued to look for the princesses. The lot fell to the oldest, and the next day he stayed at home while the two youngest went out searching. At noon a tiny little gnome came and asked for a piece of bread. The huntsman took a loaf of bread that he found there and cut off a slice. As he was handing it to the little man the gnome let it drop and asked him to kindly pick up the piece for him. As the huntsman was bending over, the gnome took a stick, grabbed him by his hair, and gave him a good beating. The next day the second huntsman stayed home, and he fared no better. When the other two returned in the evening, the oldest asked him, "Well, how did things go?"

"Very badly."

So the two oldest confided in each other about their plight and did not tell the youngest anything about it, because they did not like him. They always called him Stupid Hans, because he was not particularly worldly-wise.

On the third day the youngest stayed home, and again the gnome came to fetch a piece of bread. When the huntsman handed him a piece, the gnome let it drop again and asked him to kindly pick it up for him.

"What?" cried the huntsman. "Can't you pick the bread up

yourself? If you won't make the effort to take better care of your daily bread, then you really don't deserve to eat it."

Then the gnome got very angry and ordered him to do it. But the young huntsman acted swiftly: he grabbed the gnome and thrashed him soundly. The gnome shrieked loudly and said, "Stop! Stop! Let me go, and I'll tell you where the king's daughters are."

When he heard that, he stopped thrashing him. The gnome told the huntsman that he came from beneath the earth, where there were more than a dozen other gnomes like him, and if the huntsman would go with him, he would show him where the king's daughters were. Then the gnome pointed to a deep well without any water in it and told him to beware of his companions, for they were not to be trusted, and that he would have to save the king's daughters by himself. To be sure, his brothers wanted to rescue the king's daughters too, but they did not want to exert themselves or take any risks. The best way would be to take a large basket, get into it with his hunting knife and a bell, and then have himself lowered down into the well. There he would find three rooms, and in each one he would see a princess picking out the lice from a many-headed dragon. In each room he would have to cut the dragon's heads off.

After the gnome had told him all that, he disappeared, and toward evening the other two huntsmen returned and asked him how his day went.

"So far, so good," he said, and he told them that he had not seen anyone until noon, when a tiny gnome had come and asked for a piece of bread. After he had handed it to him, the gnome had dropped it and asked him to pick it up. When he refused, the dwarf began to spit at him. They had a quarrel, and he gave the gnome a beating. Afterward the little fellow told him where the king's daughters were.

Upon hearing that, the two brothers became so livid that they turned green with envy. The next morning they went to the well together and drew lots to see who would be the first to get into the basket. The lot fell to the oldest again, and he had to get into the basket and take the bell with him.

"If I ring," he said, "you must pull me up quickly."

When he was just a little way down, he rang the bell, and they pulled him up again. Then the second brother got in and did the very same thing. Finally, it was the youngest brother's turn, and he let himself be lowered all the way to the bottom. After he got out of the basket, he took his hunting knife, went to the first door, and listened. When he heard the dragon snoring loudly, he opened the door slowly and saw one of the king's daughters picking lice from the nine dragon's heads in her lap. So he took his hunting knife and cut off all nine heads. The princess jumped up, threw her arms around him, and kissed him many times. Then she took her necklace of pure gold and hung it around his neck. After that he went to the second princess, who was picking lice from seven dragon's heads, and he rescued her as well. Finally, he went to the youngest, who had a four-headed dragon to louse, and he set her free too. Now they were all enormously happy and could not stop hugging and kissing him. Soon he rang the bell very loudly so those above could hear. One after the other, he put the princesses into the basket and had them pulled up. When his turn came, he remembered the gnome saying that his brothers were not to be trusted. So he took a big stone that was lying there and put it into the basket. When the basket was about midway up, the wicked brothers cut the rope so that the basket with the stone inside fell to the ground. Since they thought that he was now dead, they ran away with the king's three daughters and made them promise to tell their father that they were the ones who had rescued them. Afterward the two of them went to the king and asked to marry his daughters.

In the meantime, the youngest huntsman walked around the three rooms morosely, for he thought he was doomed to die. Then he saw a flute hanging on the wall and said, "Why are you hanging there? This is no place for merrymaking!" He looked at the dragon's heads too and said, "You can't help me either." He paced up and down the floor so much that he wore the ground smooth. At last he had an idea: he took the flute from the wall and played a tune on it. Suddenly many gnomes appeared, and with each note he played, another would emerge, and he kept on playing until the room was full of them. They asked him what he desired, and he said that he would like to return to the top of the earth again and see the light of day. Then they each grabbed a strand of his hair and flew up to earth with him. When he was above, he went straight to the king's castle, where one of the princesses was soon to be married. Next he found the room in which the king was sitting with his three daughters. When the princesses saw him, they fainted. The king got very angry and immediately had him put in prison. He thought the huntsman had harmed his daughters, but when the princesses regained consciousness, they begged the king to release him. When the king asked them why, they said they were not allowed to tell him the reason. However, their father said they should tell it to the stove. Meanwhile, he left the room, listened at the door, and heard everything. Shortly after, he had the two older brothers hanged on the gallows and gave the youngest daughter to the young huntsman for his wife.

When the wedding took place, I was wearing a pair of glass shoes and bumped into a stone. The stone said, *"Clink!"* and my slippers broke in two.

◈ 92 ◈

The King of the Golden Mountain

A MERCHANT HAD TWO CHILDREN, a boy and a girl, who were still infants and could not walk. About this time the merchant had invested his entire fortune in richly laden ships that had gone out to sea. Just when he was about to make a lot of money through this venture, he received news that the ships had sunk. So now, instead of being a rich man, he was a poor one and had nothing left but a field outside the city. In order to take his mind off his troubles somewhat, he went out to his field, and as he was pacing back and forth a little black dwarf suddenly stood beside him and asked him why he was so sad and what was gnawing at his heart.

"If you could help me," said the merchant, "I'd certainly tell you."

"Who knows," answered the black dwarf, "maybe I can help you."

Then the merchant told him that he had lost his whole fortune at sea and had nothing left but the field.

"Don't worry," said the dwarf. "You shall have as much money as you want if you promise to bring me in twelve years the first thing that brushes against your leg when you return home. And you must bring it to this spot."

The merchant thought, What else can that be but my dog? Of course, he did not think of his little boy and so said yes. Then he gave the black dwarf a signed and sealed agreement and went home.

When he returned to his house, his little boy was so happy to see him that he held himself up by some benches, toddled over to his father, and grabbed him around the legs. The father was horrified, for he remembered the agreement, and he knew now what he had signed away. Still, he thought the dwarf might have been playing a joke on him since he did not find any money in his chests and boxes. One month later, however, when he went up into his attic to gather some old tinware to sell, he saw a huge pile of money lying on the floor. Soon he was in good spirits again and bought new provisions, with the result that he became an even greater merchant than before and trusted in God to guide his destiny. In the meantime, his son grew and learned how to use his brains wisely. As he neared his twelfth birthday, however, the merchant became so worried that one could see the anxiety written on his face. His son asked him what was bothering him, and the father did not want to tell him. But the son persisted until he finally revealed everything to him: how without thinking he had promised him to a black dwarf and received a lot of money in return, and how he had given the dwarf a signed and sealed agreement to deliver him to the dwarf on his twelfth birthday.

"Oh, Father," said the son. "Don't be discouraged. Everything will turn out all right. The black dwarf has no power over me."

The son had himself blessed by the priest, and when the hour arrived, he went out to the field with his father. There he drew a circle and stepped inside it with his father. The black dwarf came then and said to the old man, "Have you brought what you promised me?"

The father kept quiet, but the son said, "What do you want here?"

"I've come to discuss matters with your father, not with you."

"You deceived my father and led him astray," replied the son. "Give me back the agreement."

"No," said the black dwarf. "I won't give up my rights."

They bickered for a long time until it was finally agreed that, since the son no longer belonged to his father, nor did he belong to his archenemy, he was to get into a little boat and drift downstream on the river. His father was to shove the boat off with his foot, and the son's fate was to be decided by the river. The boy said farewell to his father, got into the little boat, and the father had to shove it off with his own foot. The little boat soon capsized with the bottom up and the top facedown. The father thought his son was lost, and he went home and mourned for him.

However, the boat did not sink but continued to drift calmly downstream with the boy safely inside. Finally, it touched down upon an unknown shore and stood still. The boy went ashore, saw a beautiful castle lying before him, and went toward it. When he entered, he realized it was enchanted. He went through all the rooms, but they were empty except for the last chamber, where he found a snake all coiled up. The snake was an enchanted princess, who was glad to see him and said, "Have you come at last, my savior? I've been waiting now twelve years for you. This kingdom is enchanted, and you must release it from the magic spell."

"How can I do that?" he asked.

"Tonight twelve black men wearing chains will come and ask you what you're doing here. You must keep quiet and refuse to answer them. Let them do whatever they want with you: they will torture you, beat you, and stab you. Let them do that, just don't talk. At midnight they must go away. The second night twelve other men will come, and the third night there will be twenty-four, who will chop off your head. But at midnight their power will be gone, and if you have held out until then and have not uttered a single word, I shall be saved and shall come to you carrying the Water of Life. I shall rub you with it, and you shall be alive again and as healthy as you were before."

Now, everything happened just as she had said: the black men could not force a word out of him, and on the third night the snake turned into a beautiful princess who came with the Water of Life and brought him back to life. Then she embraced him and kissed him, and there was joy and jubilation throughout the castle. Soon thereafter they celebrated their wedding, and he was king of the Golden Mountain.

Thus they lived happily together, and the queen gave birth to a handsome boy. After eight years had passed, the king's thoughts turned to his father. His heart went out to him, and he wished he could see him again. But the queen did not want to let him go and said, "I can tell that this will bring me bad luck."

Still, he gave her no peace until she consented to let him go. Upon his departure she gave him a wishing ring and said, "Take this ring and put it on your finger; with it you can transport yourself immediately to wherever you want to go. But you must promise me never to use it to wish me away from here to your father's place."

He promised her, put the ring on his finger, and wished that he was home, outside the city where his father lived. Before he knew it, he actually found himself there and started to walk toward the city. However, when he reached the city gate, the sentries would not let him enter because he was wearing such strange clothes, even though they were rich and splendid. So he climbed a hill where a shepherd was tending his flock, changed clothes with him, and put on the shepherd's old coat. This time when he went into the city, the sentries did not challenge him. After he got to his father's house, he revealed his identity, but his father would not believe he was his son and said that, to be sure, he had had a son, but he was long since dead. Nevertheless, the father offered the man a plate of food since he saw he was a poor, needy shepherd.

"I'm really your son," said the shepherd to his parents. "Don't you remember any birthmarks you'd recognize me by?"

"Yes," said his mother, "our son had a raspberry mark under his right arm."

He pulled up his shirt, and when they saw the raspberry mark, they no longer doubted that he was their son. Then he told them that he was king of the Golden Mountain and that he had a princess as his wife and a handsome seven-year-old son.

"Now that can't possibly be true," said his father. "What kind of a king would run around in a tattered shepherd's coat?"

Immediately the son got angry, and not thinking of his promise, he turned his ring and wished both his wife and son there, and within seconds they were with him. But the queen wept and accused him of breaking his promise and making her unhappy.

"I did it without thinking. There was nothing underhanded about my actions," he kept saying, and he eventually convinced her. Indeed, she appeared to be satisfied, but there was evil on her mind.

Shortly thereafter he led her outside the city to the field and showed her the spot on the riverbank where the little boat had been shoved off. While they were there, he said, "I'm tired now. Sit down next to me. I'd like to sleep a little on your lap."

He laid his head on her lap, and she loused him a bit until he fell asleep. While he was sleeping, she took the ring off his finger and drew her foot out from under him, leaving only her slipper behind. Finally, she took her child in her arms and wished herself back in her kingdom. When he awoke, he was lying there all alone. His wife and child were gone, and the ring as well. Only the slipper, as a token, had been left behind. "You can't go back home again to your parents," he said to himself. "They'd only say you were a sorcerer. You'd better pack up and get back to your kingdom."

So he went on his way and finally came to a mountain where three giants were standing and quarreling because they could not decide how best to divide their father's inheritance. When they saw him riding by, they called to him and said that since little people were shrewd, they wanted him to divide the inheritance among them. This inheritance consisted of three things: First, a sword that chopped off everyone's head except that of the person who held it and said, "All heads off except mine!" Second, a cloak that made one invisible if one put it on. Third, a pair of boots that carried the person who wore them to any spot he wished in a matter of seconds.

"Give me the three objects," said the king, "so I can see if they're in good condition."

They handed him the cloak, and when he had put it on his shoulders, he was invisible and then turned into a fly. After that he resumed his true form and said, "The cloak is good. Now give me the sword."

"No," they said. "We won't give it to you. If you say, 'All heads off except mine!' we'd lose our heads, and you alone would keep yours."

Nevertheless, they gave it to him on condition that he try it out on a tree. He did that, and the sword cut the trunk of a tree in half as if it were made of straw. Now he wanted to have the boots, but they said, "No, we won't give them away. If you put them on and wish yourself on top of the mountain, then we would stand here below with nothing."

"Oh, no," he said, "I would never do anything like that."

So they gave him the boots as well. But, when he had all three objects, he could think of nothing but his wife and child and sighed to himself, "Oh, if only I were on top of the Golden Mountain!" And he vanished right before the eyes of the giants. Thus their inheritance was divided.

When he drew near the castle, he heard cries of joy and the sounds of fiddles and flutes. The people at the court told him that his wife was celebrating her wedding with another man. So he got angry and said, "That faithless woman! It was she who duped me and then left me while I slept!" He hung his cloak around his shoulders and went unseen into the castle. When he entered the hall, there was a large table covered with delicious food, and the guests were eating and drinking, laughing and joking. The queen was sitting in a royal chair at the center of the table. She was wearing magnificent clothes and had her crown on her head. He went over to her, took a place right behind her, and nobody was aware of his presence. When they put a piece of meat on her plate, he snatched it and ate it. And, when they gave her a glass of wine, he snatched it and drank it. They kept giving her food and wine, but she would always end up with nothing because her plate and glass would vanish immediately. She became so upset and distraught that she left the table, went into her chamber, and began weeping, while he stayed behind her all the time.

"Has the devil got me in his power?" she asked. "I thought my savior had come."

Then he smacked her in the face and said, "Your savior came!

Now he's got you in his power, you faithless thing! Did I deserve to be treated the way you treated me?''

He made himself visible, went into the hall, and announced, "The wedding is over! The true king has arrived!"

The kings, princes, and ministers who were assembled there began jeering and mocking him, but he wanted to make short work of them and said, "Will you leave or not?"

At that they charged and tried to capture him, but he took out his sword and said, "All heads off except mine!"

Then their heads rolled to the ground, and he alone was master and king of the Golden Mountain.

◈ 93 ◈

The Raven

ONCE UPON A TIME there was a queen who had a daughter that was still so little she had to be carried in her mother's arms. One day the child was very naughty, and no matter what the mother said, she would not keep quiet. The mother became impatient, and as she looked at the ravens flying around outside the castle, she opened the window and said, "I wish you were a raven and would fly away! Then I'd have my peace and quiet."

No sooner had she said those words than the child was changed into a raven and flew from her arms out through the window. She headed for a dark forest, where she stayed for a long time, and her parents heard nothing more from her.

Some time later, a man was making his way into this forest and heard the raven call. He went toward the voice, and as he came closer the raven said, "I am a king's daughter by birth and have been cursed by a spell. However, you can set me free."

"What am I to do?" he asked.

"Go deeper into the forest," she said, "and you'll see a house. There's an old woman sitting inside. She'll offer you something to eat and drink, but you must not touch a thing. If you eat or drink anything, you'll fall into a sleep and won't be able to release me from the spell. In the garden behind the house there's a big pile of tanbark. You're to stand on it and wait for me. I shall come three days in a row at two o'clock in the afternoon with a carriage. The first time my carriage will be drawn by four white stallions, the second time by four bay stallions, and the last time by four black ones. But if you fail to stay awake, I won't be set free.''

The man promised to do everything she had demanded, but the raven said, ''Oh, I can already tell you won't set me free. You'll take something from the old woman.''

Again the man assured her he would touch neither food nor drink. However, once he was inside the house, the old woman went over to him and said, ''Poor man, you're all worn out. Come and refresh yourself. Have something to eat and drink.''

''No,'' said the man. ''I don't want to eat or drink.''

But she would not leave him in peace and kept saying, ''Well, if you don't want to eat, just take a sip from the glass. One little sip won't count.''

Finally, he let himself be persuaded and drank. Toward two in the afternoon he went outside into the garden and climbed onto the pile of tanbark to wait for the raven. As he stood there he suddenly felt so tired that he could not help himself and had to lie down and rest a little. He did not want to fall asleep, but no sooner had he stretched himself out than his eyes closed by themselves, and he fell asleep. He slept so soundly that nothing in the world could have wakened him. At two o'clock the raven came driving up in a carriage with four white horses, but she was already in full mourning and said, ''I know he's asleep.'' When she drove into the garden, he was indeed fast asleep. She climbed out of the carriage, went over to him, and shook him and called him, but he did not awake.

At noon the next day the old woman came to him again and brought him food and drink, but he did not want to take anything. However, she refused to leave him in peace and kept talking to him until he took another drink from the glass. Toward two o'clock he went into the garden and climbed onto the pile of tanbark to wait for the raven. Then he suddenly felt so tired that his limbs could no longer support him. Since he could not help himself, he lay down and fell into a deep sleep. When the raven drove up in her carriage drawn by four bay stallions, she was already in full mourning and said, ''I know he's asleep.'' She went over to him, but he lay asleep and could not be wakened.

The next day the old woman asked him what the matter was and why he was not eating or drinking. Did he want to die?

''I don't want to eat or drink,'' he replied. ''Nor am I allowed to.''

In spite of this, she set a bowl of food and a glass of wine in front of him, and as the smell reached his nostrils, he could not resist and took a deep draft. When the time came, he went outside into the garden and climbed onto the pile of tanbark to wait for the princess. Yet, he was even more tired than he had been on the previous days. So he lay down and slept like a log. At two o'clock the raven came, and her carriage was drawn by four black horses. The carriage and everything else were also black, and she was already in full mourning. "I know he's asleep," she said, "and he won't be able to set me free." When she went over to him, he was lying there sound asleep. She shook him and called him, but he could not wake him up. So she put a loaf of bread beside him, then a piece of meat, and lastly a bottle of wine. No matter how much he took from any of them, they would always replenish themselves. After that she drew a gold ring from her finger and placed it on his finger. Her name was engraved on it. Finally, she left him a letter on the ground in which she explained that the things she had given him would never run out, and she concluded her letter by saying, "I clearly see that you can't set me free in a place like this. But if you still want to save me, then come to the golden castle of Mount Stromberg. It's within your power. That I know for sure." And after she had given him all those things, she climbed back into her carriage and drove off to the golden castle of Mount Stromberg.

When the man woke and saw that he had slept through everything, he was terribly sad and said, "I'm sure she's been here, and I haven't set her free." Then he noticed the things lying beside him, and he read the letter that explained everything that had happened. So he stood up and set out for the golden castle of Mount Stromberg, even though he did not know where it was. After he had wandered about the world for a long time, he finally came to a dark forest and continued wandering for fourteen days. When he realized that he could not find his way out, he lay down exhausted on the fourteenth evening and fell asleep under a bush. The next day he moved on, and in the evening, as he was about to lie down under another bush, he heard such a moaning and groaning that he was unable to sleep. When the hour came for people to light their lamps, he saw a light glimmering in the distance, got up, and went toward it. Shortly after, he came to a house that appeared to be very small because a big giant was standing in front of it. If you try to go inside, he thought to himself, and the giant catches sight of you, he'll put an end to your life. Finally, he decided to risk it and stepped toward the door. When the giant saw him, he said, "It's good that you've come. I haven't had a thing to eat for a long time. So I'm going to gobble you up for supper.''

"You'd better not," said the man. "I don't like to be gobbled up. If you want something to eat, I have enough here to fill your stomach."

"If that's true," said the giant, "you can rest easy. I wanted to eat you only because I had nothing else."

They went in and sat down at the dinner table, and the man took out the bread, wine, and meat that never ran out.

"I like this very much," said the giant, and he ate to his heart's content.

After supper the man asked him, "Can you tell me the location of the golden castle of Mount Stromberg?"

The giant said, "I'll look it up on my map. It shows all the cities, villages, and houses." He got out a map that he kept in the room and looked for the castle, but it was not on it. "Don't worry," he said. "I've got even larger maps in the closet upstairs. We can look for it on them." Yet, it was all in vain.

Now, the man wanted to move on, but the giant begged him to stay a few more days until his brother returned. He had merely gone out to fetch some provisions. When the brother came back, they asked him about the golden castle of Mount Stromberg.

"When I'm finished eating," he answered, "I'll look it up on the map."

A little later he climbed upstairs with them to his room, and they looked for it on his map but could not find it. Then he got out other maps that were even older, and they kept on looking until they finally located the castle. However, it was thousands of miles away.

"How will I ever get there?" asked the man.

"I've got two hours to spare," said the giant. "I'll carry you as far as I can, but then I must return home and nurse our child." So he carried the man until he was about a hundred hours' walk from the castle and said, "You can go the rest of the way by yourself."

Then the giant turned back, while the man went on day and night until he finally came to the golden castle of Mount Stromberg. But the castle was up on a glass mountain, and he saw the enchanted maiden drive around the castle in her carriage and go inside. He was happy to have caught a glimpse of her and wanted to climb up to her. Yet, whenever he tried, he slipped down again on the glass. Once he realized that he could not reach her, he was very distressed and said to himself, "I'll stay down here and wait for her." So he built a little hut for himself and stayed there for one year. Every day he watched the princess drive around on top of the mountain, but he could not climb up to her.

One day he peered out of his hut and saw three robbers fighting. When he called out to them "God be with you!" they stopped fighting, listened to see where the cry came from, and then resumed fighting when they could not see anyone. It was dangerous just to be near them, but again the man called out "God be with you!" Again they stopped, looked around, and resumed their fighting when they could not see anyone. Finally, he called out for a third time "God be with you!" and this time he thought to himself, You'd better go see what these three are up to. So he went out to them and asked them why they were fighting. One of them said he had found a stick and that whenever he struck a door with it, the door would spring open. The second said he had a cloak and that whenever he hung it over his shoulders, he would be invisible. The third said he had caught a horse and that one could ride it everywhere, even up the glass mountain. However, they did not know whether to share these things or to part ways. Then the man said, "I'll make an exchange with you. I'll take those three things, and to be honest, I don't have any money, but I do have other things that are worth more than money. First, however, I must test your things to see whether you've told me the truth."

They let him sit on the horse, put the cloak over his shoulders, and handed him the stick. As soon as he had all three objects, they could no longer see him. So he gave them all a good beating and cried out, "Now, you lazy scoundrels, you've got what you've deserved. Are you satisfied?"

The man rode up the glass mountain, and when he got to the top, he found the castle door was closed. So he struck the gate with the stick, and it immediately sprang open. He entered and went up the stairs until he came to a hall. There sat the maiden, and she had a goblet filled with wine in front of her. However, she could not see him because he was wearing the cloak. When he went over to her, he pulled off the ring that she had given him and dropped it into the goblet so that it rang out.

"That's my ring!" she exclaimed. "Then the man who's going to set me free must be here somewhere."

They searched all over the castle, but they could not find him. Indeed, he had gone outside, mounted the horse, and thrown off the cloak. When they finally saw him out by the gate, they rejoiced. So he dismounted and took the princess in his arms. She kissed him and said, "Now that you've set me free, we shall celebrate our wedding tomorrow."

◆ 94 ◆

The Clever Farmer's Daughter

ONCE UPON A TIME there was a poor farmer who had only a small house and one daughter but no land. One day the daughter said, "I think we should ask the king for a little piece of farming land."

When the king learned about their poverty, he gave them a small field, which the farmer and his daughter cleared so they could sow a little wheat and plant some kind of fruit. When they had almost finished their work, they found a mortar of pure gold on the ground.

"Listen," said the farmer to his daughter, "since the king was so gracious as to give us this field, we ought to give him this mortar in return."

But the daughter did not agree and said, "Father, if we give the mortar without the pestle, then we'll have to find the pestle as well. I think we'd be better off if we kept quiet about the whole thing."

However, the farmer did not listen to her. He took the mortar, carried it to the king, and said that he had found it on the heath. Now he wanted to offer it to the king in his honor. The king took the mortar and asked the farmer if he had found anything else.

"No," replied the farmer.

Then the king asked him about the pestle and told him to bring it to him. The farmer replied that there was no pestle, but that was like talking to the wind. He was thrown into prison, where he was to stay until he produced the pestle. The servants brought him bread and water every day, the usual fare in prison, and every day they heard the farmer sighing "Oh, if only I had listened to my daughter! Oh, if only I had listened to my daughter!" Finally, the servants went to the king and told him how the prisoner kept crying "Oh, if only I had listened to my daughter!" and how he refused to eat and drink. The king ordered the servants to bring the prisoner before him, and he asked the farmer to tell him why he kept sighing "Oh, if only I had listened to my daughter!"

"What did your daughter tell you?"

◆ 378 ◆

"She told me not to bring you the mortar; otherwise, you'd want to have the pestle as well."

"If you have such a clever daughter, I want to see her."

So she had to appear before the king, who asked her if she really was so clever and said that he wanted to give her a riddle to solve, and that if she solved it, he would marry her. She replied right away that she would solve it. Then the king said, "Come to me, not dressed, not naked, not on horse, not by carriage, not on the road, not off the road, and if you do, I'll marry you."

The farmer's daughter went home and got undressed until she was completely naked, so that she was not dressed. Next she took a large fishnet and wrapped it completely around her so that she was not naked. Then she took some money, leased a donkey, and tied the fish net to its tail. The donkey had to drag her along so that she neither rode nor drove. And, since the donkey had to drag her along the wagon tracks, only her big toes could touch the ground so that she was neither on the road nor off it. Thus, when she appeared before the king this way, he said she had solved the riddle and had fulfilled all the conditions. He released her father from the prison, took her as his wife, and ordered her to look after all the royal possessions.

Now, some years went by, and one day, when the king was out reviewing his troops, a group of farmers happened to stop in front of his castle. They had been selling wood, and some of the wagons were drawn by horses, others by oxen. One of the farmers had three horses, and his mare gave birth to a foal that ran away and lay down between two oxen hitched to another farmer's wagon. When the two farmers came together, they started bickering, throwing things at each other, and making a lot of noise. The farmer with the oxen wanted to keep the foal and claimed that the oxen had given birth to it. The other said no, his horse had given birth to it, and the foal was his. The quarrel was taken before the king, and he declared that wherever the foal had laid itself down, there it should stay. So the farmer with the oxen got the foal, even though it did not belong to him. The other farmer went away, wept, and grieved over his foal. However, since he had heard that the queen came from a farmer's family and was compassionate, he went to her and asked whether she could help him get his foal back.

"Yes," she said. "But you must promise not to tell that I've helped you. Now, here's what you have to do: Early tomorrow morning when the king goes out to review his guard, you're to place yourself in the middle of the road where he has to pass. Bring a large fishnet with you and pretend to fish with it. You're to keep

fishing and shaking the net out as though it were full.'' Then the
queen also told him what to answer the king when he questioned
him.

The next day the farmer got up and went fishing on dry land.
When the king rode by and saw that, he sent his messenger to ask
the foolish man what he was doing.

''I'm fishing,'' he replied.

When the messenger asked how he could fish without water, the
farmer answered, ''If two oxen can manage to give birth to a foal,
then I can manage to catch a fish on dry land.''

The messenger brought the farmer's answer back to the king, who
summoned the farmer and said he knew that the farmer had not
thought up the answer himself. The king wanted to know, on the
spot, who had helped him with the answer. But the farmer refused to
talk and kept repeating, may God help him if he did not think up the
answer himself. So they laid him down on a bundle of straw, beat
and tortured him until he confessed that he had got the idea from the
queen.

When the king returned home, he said to his wife, ''Why did you
dupe me? I no longer want you for my wife. Your time is up! Go
back to the farmhouse where you belong.'' However, he granted her
one last request: she could take the dearest and best thing that she
could think of with her, and that was to be her parting gift.

''Very well, dear husband,'' she said. ''Your wish is my command.'' Then she embraced him, kissed him, and asked him to drink
to her parting. He agreed, and she ordered a strong sleeping potion.
The king took a big swig, but she only drank a little. Soon he fell
into a deep sleep, and when she saw that, she called a servant, took
a beautiful white linen sheet, and wrapped him in it. The servant had
to carry him outside and put him into a carriage. Then she drove him
to her house and put him to bed. He slept a whole day and night,
and when he woke up, he looked around him and said, ''My God!
Where am I?'' He called his servants, but nobody came.

Finally, his wife came to the bed and said, ''Dear King, you
ordered me to take the dearest and best thing with me from the
castle. Since you are the dearest and best thing I know, I took you
with me.''

Tears began to well up in the king's eyes, and he said, ''Dear
wife, you shall be mine, and I shall be yours forever.'' Then he took
her back with him to the royal castle and married her again. And I
am sure that they are still living together even today.

Old Hildebrand

ONCE UPON A TIME there was a farmer and his wife. The village priest had taken a liking to the farmer's wife and kept wishing he could spend one whole day alone with her in pleasure. The woman would have liked that too.

One day he came to her and said, "Listen, my dear, I've figured out a way we can spend a whole day together in pleasure. Here's the plan: On Wednesday you must take to your bed and tell your husband you're sick. You'd best moan and groan as much as possible and keep it up until Sunday, when I'm to hold my sermon. Then I'll preach that if anybody has a sick child at home, a sick husband, a sick wife, a sick father, a sick mother, a sick sister or brother, or whoever else might be sick at home, he should make a pilgrimage to Mount Cuckold in Italy. There one can purchase a peck of bay leaves for a kreuzer. Then the sick child, the sick husband, the sick wife, the sick father, the sick mother, the sick sister, or whoever else might be sick will get well at once."

"That's fine with me," replied the farmer's wife.

On Wednesday, as was agreed, the farmer's wife lay down in bed and moaned and groaned as if the world were coming to an end. Her husband brought her everything he could think of, but nothing helped. When Sunday came, the farmer's wife said, "I feel just miserable, as if I were going to die any minute. But before my end comes, I'd like to do just one more thing: I'd like to hear the priest hold his sermon today."

"Oh, no, my sweet," answered the farmer. "Don't do that. If you get up, you could make things worse. Look, I'll go to church, listen to the sermon carefully, and then I'll return home and tell you everything he's said."

"Well, all right," said the farmer's wife. "Go and pay close attention and tell me everything he says."

So the farmer went to church, and the priest began to preach the sermon and said, if anyone had a sick child at home, a sick husband, a sick wife, a sick father, a sick mother, a sick sister or brother, or whoever else might be sick, he should make a pilgrimage to Mount Cuckold in Italy, where a peck of bay leaves costs a kreuzer, then the sick child, the sick husband, the sick wife, the sick father, the sick mother, the sick sister or brother, and whoever else might be sick would get well at once. Any person wanting to make the journey was to come to the priest after mass, and he would give them the sack for the bay leaves and the kreuzer. Nobody was happier than the farmer when he heard that, and after the mass he went straight to the priest, who gave him the sack and the kreuzer. Then the farmer went home, and before he even got through the door of his house, he shouted, "Hurray, my dear wife, now you're as good as cured! The priest preached that if anyone with a sick child at home, a sick husband, a sick wife, a sick father, a sick mother, a sick sister or brother, or whoever else might be sick makes a pilgrimage to Mount Cuckold in Italy, where a peck of bay leaves costs a kreuzer, then the sick child, the sick husband, the sick wife, the sick father, the sick mother, the sick sister or brother, or whoever else might be sick would get well at once. I've already got the kreuzer and the sack for the bay leaves from the priest, and I'm going to start out on my journey right away so you can get well that much sooner."

He then departed. However, he had hardly left when his wife got up, and the priest lost no time in getting there. Now, let us leave the two of them alone for a while and go on with the farmer.

Once the farmer was on his way, he walked at a rapid pace so he could reach Mount Cuckold all the sooner. Along the way he met his neighbor, an egg dealer, who was returning from the market, where he had sold all his eggs.

"Praise the Lord!" said the egg dealer. "Where are you off to in such a rush, neighbor?"

"To all eternity, neighbor," said the farmer. "My wife's sick, and I heard our priest preach today that if anyone had a sick child at home, a sick husband, a sick wife, a sick father, a sick mother, a sick sister or brother, or whoever else might be sick and that person makes a pilgrimage to Mount Cuckold in Italy, where a peck of bay leaves costs a kreuzer, then the sick child, the sick husband, the sick wife, the sick father, the sick mother, the sick sister or brother, or whoever else might be sick will get well at once. Then I got the kreuzer and the sack for the bay leaves from the priest, and now I'm off on my pilgrimage."

"Hold on, neighbor!" said the egg dealer to the farmer. "Are you so simpleminded that you believed him? Don't you know what's happening? The priest wants to spend a pleasant day alone with your wife. That's why they cooked up a plan to get rid of you."

"Goodness gracious!" said the farmer. "I'd surely like to know if that's true."

"Well," said the neighbor. "I'll tell you what: You just get into my egg basket, and I'll carry you home. Then you can see for yourself."

So that is what they did. The neighbor put the farmer in his egg basket and carried him home on his back. When they got there, believe you me, there was a lot going on! The farmer's wife had already slaughtered whatever she could find in the barnyard and had also baked a lot of pancakes. The priest had also arrived and was strumming on his fiddle. When the neighbor knocked, the farmer's wife asked who was outside.

"It's me, neighbor," the egg dealer said. "I need a place for the night. I wasn't able to sell my eggs at the market, and now I've got to carry them home. But they're much too heavy for me, and I won't be able to make it home before darkness."

"Well, neighbor," said the farmer's wife, "you've come at a very bad time, but since there's nothing we can do about it, come in and sit down on the bench by the stove."

So the neighbor took a seat on the bench by the stove and set the basket down. In the meantime, the priest and the farmer's wife continued having a merry old time. Finally, the priest said, "Listen, my dear, since you have such a fine voice, I want you to sing me a song."

"Oh, I can't," said the farmer's wife. "I used to be able to sing all day long in my youth. But those days are gone forever."

"Oh, c'mon," said the priest again. "Just a little song for me." Then the farmer's wife began to sing:

"I sent my husband far away
to cuckold's mountain for the day."

The priest joined in:

"I wish he'd spend the whole year there
and keep the sack for all I care.
                    Hallelujah!"

Now the neighbor, who was sitting back by the stove, began to sing (but I must tell you first that the farmer's name was Hildebrand):

"Hey, Hildebrand, your wife's a wench!
How can you watch this from the bench!?
          Hallelujah!''

And now the farmer inside the basket started singing:

"Oh, I can't stand this anymore!
I'm getting out, for I'm quite sore!
          Hallelujah!''

So he jumped out of the basket, gave the priest a good beating, and drove him out of the house.

◈ 96 ◈

The Three Little Birds

MORE THAN A THOUSAND YEARS AGO there were many petty kings in this country, and one of them lived on the mountain called Köterberg. He was very fond of hunting, and one day, when he left his castle and went down the mountain with his huntsmen, he came upon three maidens tending their cows. When they saw the king with his men, the oldest pointed at the king and called to the other two, "Hallo, hallo! If I can't have that man over there, I don't want any at all.''

Then the second responded from the other side of the mountain and pointed at the fellow walking on the king's right. "Hallo, hallo! If I can't have that man over there, I don't want any at all.''

Finally, the youngest pointed at the fellow on the king's left and called out, "Hallo! hallo! If I can't have that man over there, I don't want any at all.''

The two men were the king's ministers, and the king had heard what the maidens had said. After he returned from the hunt, he summoned the three maidens and asked them what they had said the day before on the mountain. They refused to answer, but the king asked the oldest if she would take him for her husband. She said yes, and her two sisters also married the two ministers, for the maidens were all beautiful and had fine features, especially the queen, who had hair like flax.

The two sisters did not bear any children, and once when the king had to take a trip, he asked them to stay with the queen and cheer her up, for she was with child. While he was away, she gave birth to a little boy who had a bright red star as a birthmark. But the two sisters decided to throw the pretty baby boy into the river. After they had thrown him in (I think it was the Weser), a little bird flew up in the air and sang:

"Get ready for your death.
I'll see what I can do.
Get ready for the wreath.
Brave boy, can that be you?"

When the two sisters heard that, they feared for their lives and ran off. Later the king returned home, and they told him the queen had given birth to a dog, and the king responded, "Whatever God does is always for the best."

However, a fisherman lived by the river, and he fished the little boy out of the water while he was still alive. Since his wife had not given birth to any children, they fed and cared for him.

After a year had passed, the king went on another journey, and the queen gave birth to a second boy during his absence. The two wicked sisters again took the baby away and threw him into the river. Then the little bird flew up into the air once more and sang:

"Get ready for your death.
I'll see what I can do.
Get ready for the wreath.
Brave boy, can that be you?"

When the king came home, the sisters told him the queen had again given birth to a dog, and he responded as before, "Whatever God does is always for the best."

However, the fisherman fetched this baby out of the water too, and he fed and cared for him.

Once again the king went on a journey, and the queen gave birth to a little girl, whom the wicked sisters also threw into the river. Then the little bird flew up into the air once more and sang:

"Get ready for your death.
I'll see what I can do.

Get ready for the wreath.
Brave girl, can that be you?''

When the king came back home, the sisters told him the queen had given birth to a cat. This time the king became so angry that he had his wife thrown into prison, where she was forced to stay for many years.

In the meantime, the children grew up, and one day the oldest went out fishing with some other boys, but they did not want him around and said, "You foundling, go your own way!"

The boy was very upset by that and asked the old fisherman whether it was true. Then the fisherman told him how he had been out fishing one day and had found him in the water. The boy then said he wanted to go out and search for his father. The fisherman begged him to remain, but there was no holding him back. At last the fisherman gave in, and the boy went forth. He walked for many days until he came to a large and mighty river, where he found an old woman standing and fishing.

"Good day, grandma," said the boy.

"Why, thank you kindly."

"You'll be fishing there a long time before you catch any fish."

"And you'll be searching a long time before you find your father. How are you going to get across the river?" asked the old woman.

"God only knows."

Then the old woman picked him up and carried him across on her back. Once he was on the other side, he continued his search for his father a long time, but he could not find him.

When a year had gone by, the second boy went out looking for his brother. He too came to the river, and the same thing happened to him as with his brother. Now only the daughter was left alone at home, and she grieved so much for her brothers that finally the fisherman had to let her go too. Soon she came to the large river also and said to the old woman, "Good day, grandma."

"Why, thank you kindly."

"May God help you with your fishing."

When the old woman heard that, she treated the girl in a friendly way. She carried her across the river, gave her a stick, and said, "Now, my daughter, just keep going straight ahead, and when you come to a big black dog, you must be quiet. Don't be afraid or laugh or stop to look at it. Then you'll come to a large open castle. You must drop the stick on the threshold and go right through the castle and out the other side, where you'll see an old well. A big tree will be growing from the well, and on the tree a cage with a bird inside will be hanging. Take the cage down and get a glass of water from the well. Then carry both things back the same way you came. When you come to the threshold, pick up the stick, and when you come to the dog again, hit it in the face with the stick, but see to it that you don't miss. Then come back here to me."

The girl found everything just as the woman had said, and on her way back from the castle she met her two brothers, who had been searching half the world for each other. They went on together to the spot where the black dog was lying. Then she hit it on the face, and it turned into a handsome prince who accompanied them to the river. The old woman was still standing there and was happy to see them. She carried all four of them across the river, and then she departed, because she had now been released from the magic spell.

The others traveled back to the old fisherman, and they were all glad to have found each other again. Once inside the house, they hung the birdcage on the wall. But the second son was still restless. So he took a bow and went hunting. When he became tired, he took out his flute and began playing a little tune. The king, who was out hunting too, heard the music and went toward it. When he saw the boy, he said, "Who's given you permission to hunt here?"

"Nobody."

"Who're your parents?"

"I'm the fisherman's son."

"But he doesn't have any children."

"If you think I'm lying, come along with me."

The king did so and asked the fisherman, who told him all that had happened. Suddenly, the little bird in the cage began to sing:

"Oh, King of noble blood,
your children are back for good.
But their mother sits in prison
with nothing much to live on.
Her sisters are the wicked ones,
who took away your daughter and sons
and left them to the river's fate,
but the fisherman came 'ere it was too late."

When they heard the song, they were all astounded. The king took the little bird, the fisherman, and the three children with him to his castle, where he had the prison opened and his wife released. However, she had become very sick and was haggard. So her daughter gave her a drink of water from the well, and she regained her health. But the two wicked sisters were burned to death, and the daughter married the prince.

◈ 97 ◈

The Water of Life

ONCE UPON A TIME there was a king who was sick, and nobody thought he would live. His three sons were very saddened by this and went down into the palace garden, where they wept. There they met an old man who asked them why they were so distressed, and they told him that their father was so sick that he would probably die. Nothing seemed to help.

"I know of a remedy," the old man said. "It's the Water of Life. If he drinks it, he'll regain his health. But it's difficult to find."

"Well, I'll find it," said the oldest, and he went to the sick king and requested permission to leave and search for the Water of Life, for that was the only cure for his illness.

"No," said the king. "The danger is much too great. I'd rather die instead."

But the son pleaded so long that finally the king had to give his consent. Deep down the prince felt, If I bring him the water, I'll be my father's favorite and shall inherit the kingdom.

So he set out and, after he had been riding for some time, he came across a dwarf, who called to him and said, "Where are you going in such haste?"

"You meddling twirp," the prince said contemptuously, "that's none of your affair!" And he rode on.

But the little dwarf became furious and put a curse on him. Meanwhile, the prince found himself traveling through a mountain gorge, and the further he rode, the more the mountains closed together until the way became so narrow that he could not proceed. Nor could he turn his horse or get out of his saddle. He sat there as if he were in a prison.

The sick king waited a long time for the prince, but he did not come back. Then the second son said, "Father, let me go and search for the Water of Life," and he thought to himself, If my brother's dead, then the kingdom will fall to me.

At first the king did not want to let him go either, but finally he gave in. So the prince set out on the same road that his brother had taken and met the dwarf, who stopped him and asked where he was going in such haste.

"You meddling twirp," said the prince, "that's none of your affair!" And he rode off without turning around.

But the dwarf put a curse on him, and he ended up in a mountain gorge, where he became trapped like his brother. Indeed, that is what happens to arrogant people.

Now, when the second son also failed to return, the youngest offered to set forth and fetch the water, and eventually the king had to let him go too. When he met the dwarf and was asked where he was going in such haste, he stopped and answered, "I'm looking for the Water of Life because my sick father is on the brink of death."

"Do you know where to find it?"

"No," said the prince.

"Well, since you've behaved yourself in a proper manner and are not arrogant like your faithless brothers, I'll tell you how to get to the Water of Life: you'll find it gushing from a fountain in the courtyard of an enchanted castle, but you'll never make your way inside unless I give you an iron wand and two loaves of bread. You're to knock three times on the castle gate with the iron wand, then it will spring open. Inside are two lions lying on the ground. They will open their jaws, but if you throw a loaf of bread to each of them, they will be quiet. Then you must hurry and fetch some of the Water of Life before the clock strikes twelve. Otherwise, the gate will slam shut, and you will be locked in."

The prince thanked him, took the wand and the bread, and went on his way. When he arrived there, everything was just as the dwarf had said. After the third knock the gate sprang open, and when he had calmed the lions with the bread, he entered the castle and went into a big beautiful hall, where he found enchanted princes sitting all around. He took the rings from their fingers and also grabbed a sword and loaf of bread that were lying on the floor. Then he moved on to the next room, where he encountered a beautiful maiden, who was delighted to see him. She kissed him and said that he had set her free and could have her entire kingdom as reward. If he would return in a year's time, their wedding would be celebrated. Then she also told him where to find the fountain with the Water of Life, but that he had to hurry and draw the water before the clock struck twelve. So he went on and finally came to a room with a beautiful, freshly made bed, and since he was tired, he wanted to rest a little. Once he lay down, however, he fell asleep. When he awoke, the clock was striking a quarter to twelve, and he jumped up in a fright, ran to the fountain, and drew some water in a cup that happened to be lying on the ledge. Then he rushed outside, and just as he was running through the iron gate, the clock struck twelve, and the gate slammed so hard that it took off a piece of his heel.

Nevertheless, he was happy that he had found the Water of Life, and on his way home he passed the dwarf again. When the little man saw the sword and the bread, he said, "You've managed to obtain some valuable things. With the sword you'll be able to defeat whole armies, and the bread will always replenish itself."

But the prince did not want to return home to his father without his brothers, and so he asked, "Dear dwarf, could you tell me where my two brothers are? They went out looking for the Water of Life before me and never came back."

"They're trapped in between two mountains," said the dwarf. "I put them there with a magic spell because they were so arrogant."

Then the prince pleaded until finally the dwarf decided to release them but not without a warning. "Beware of them," he said. "They have evil hearts."

When he was reunited with his brothers, he was happy and told them all that had happened: how he found the Water of Life and was now bringing back a cupful to their father, how he had rescued the beautiful princess and was going to marry her after waiting a year, and how he would receive a vast kingdom after their marriage. Once his story was told, he rode on with his brothers, and they came to a country plagued by war and famine. The king was already convinced that he would soon perish because the situation was so desperate. But the prince went to him and gave him the bread, which he used to feed his people and satisfy their hunger. After that the prince also gave him the sword, which he used to defeat the enemy armies, and he was then able to live in peace and quiet. So the prince took back the loaf of bread and the sword, and the brothers rode on. However, they passed through two other countries plagued by famine and war, and on each occasion the prince gave the king his bread and sword. In this way he was able to help save three kingdoms.

Later on they boarded a ship and sailed across the sea. During the trip the two older brothers plotted together against their brother. "The youngest found the Water of Life, and we are empty-handed. So our father will give him the kingdom that is ours by right, and our brother will deprive us of our happiness."

Overcome by a desire for revenge, they planned to put an end to their brother. They waited until he was sound asleep. Then they poured the Water of Life from his cup into their own and replaced it with bitter salt water. When they arrived home, the youngest brought the cup to the sick king and told him to drink it and he would get well. No sooner did the king drink the bitter salt water than he became sicker than ever. And as he began to moan the two oldest brothers came and accused the youngest of wanting to poison the king, while they, on the other hand, had brought the true Water of Life, and they handed it to their father. As soon as he drank some, he felt his sickness on the wane and became as strong and healthy as in the days of his youth. After that the two older brothers went to the youngest and belittled him. "Oh, we know you found the Water of Life," they said, "but we're the ones who've received the reward for all your trouble. You should have been smarter and kept your eyes open. We took the water from you when you fell asleep at sea, and in a year's time one of us will fetch the beautiful princess. Still, you had better not expose us. Father will not believe you anyway, and if you breathe a single word about it, your life will be worth nothing. If you keep quiet, we'll let you live."

The old king was angry at his youngest son because he believed that his son had wanted to take his life. So he summoned his ministers and ordered them to sentence his son to be shot in secret. So, one day, as the prince went out hunting, suspecting no danger, one of the king's huntsmen had to accompany him. When they were all alone out in the forest, the huntsman looked so sad that the prince asked him, "Dear hunter, what's the matter?"

"I can't say," answered the huntsman, "and yet I should."

"Tell me," said the prince. "Whatever it is, I'll forgive you."

"Ah," said the huntsman. "The king has ordered me to kill you."

The prince was taken aback by this news and said, "Dear huntsman, let me live. I'll give you my royal garments, and you give me your common ones in exchange."

"I'll gladly do that," said the huntsman. "I couldn't have shot you anyway."

They exchanged clothes, and the huntsman went home, while the prince went deeper into the forest.

After a while three wagons loaded with gold and jewels arrived at the king's castle for his youngest son. They had been sent by the three kings who had defeated their enemies with the prince's sword and who had nourished their people with his bread. The wagons were an expression of their gratitude, and when the old king saw that, he began to think, Perhaps my son was innocent? And he said to the people at his court, "If only he were still alive! Now I regret that I ordered him to be killed."

"He's still alive," said the huntsman. "I didn't have the heart to carry out your order," and he told the king what had happened.

The king felt greatly relieved, and he had it proclaimed in all the surrounding kingdoms that his son was free to return and was back in favor with the king.

In the meantime, the princess had decided to build a glittering gold road that would lead up to her castle. She told her guards that whoever came riding to her straight up the middle of the road would be the right man and they should let him enter. However, whoever rode up on the side of the road would not be the right man, and they were not to let him enter.

When the year of waiting was almost up, the oldest son thought he would get an early start and pass himself off as her savior. Then he would get her for his wife and the kingdom as well. So he rode forth, and when he came to the castle and saw the beautiful road, he thought, It would be a terrible shame if you rode on it. So he turned off to the right and rode along the side. But when he got to the castle gate, the guards told him that he was not the right man and he had better go away. Soon thereafter the second prince set out, and when he came to the gold road and his horse set its hoof down on it, he thought, It would be a terrible shame if you damaged the road. He turned to the left and rode along the side. However, when he reached the gate, the guards told him he had better go away, for he was not the right man.

When the year was completely over, the third son prepared to ride out of the forest and hoped to forget his sorrows in the company of his beloved. As he set out he kept thinking about her and wishing he were already with her. When he arrived at the gold road, he did not even notice it, and his horse rode right down the middle of it. Once he reached the gate, it opened, and the princess welcomed him with joy. She pronounced him her savior and lord of the realm, and they were blissful as they celebrated their wedding. When it was over, she told him his father had sent for him and had pardoned him. So he rode home and explained to his father how his brothers had deceived him and why he had kept quiet about it. The old king wanted to punish them, but they had taken flight on a ship, sailed away, and never returned as long as they lived.

Doctor Know-It-All

ONCE UPON A TIME there was a poor farmer named Crab, who drove a cord of wood into town with his two oxen and sold the wood to a doctor for two talers. When the farmer went inside to get his money, the doctor was just about to sit down to dinner, and the farmer admired the fine food and drink at the doctor's table. His heart yearned for something like that, and he thought how nice it would be if he were a doctor. He lingered there awhile and finally asked if it was possible for someone like him to become a doctor.

"Of course," said the doctor. "There's not much to it."

"What do I have to do?" asked the farmer.

"First, you must buy yourself an ABC book, the kind with the picture of a rooster in it. Second, you must get cash for your wagon and two oxen and purchase some clothes and other things that doctors tend to need. Third, you must have a sign painted with the words 'I am Doctor Know-It-All' and nail it above your front door."

The farmer did everything he was told, and when he had doctored for some time but not very long, a rich and mighty nobleman was robbed of some money, and he heard about Doctor Know-It-All, who was living in such and such a village and would probably know what had become of the money. So the nobleman had his carriage hitched up, drove out to the village, and inquired at the farmer's house whether he was Doctor Know-It-All.

Yes, that was he, the farmer responded. Then the nobleman requested that he return with him and help him get back his stolen money. The farmer agreed, but added that Greta, his wife, had to come along too. The nobleman gave his approval, offered them both a seat in his carriage, and they drove off together. When they came to the nobleman's mansion, the table was already set, and Doctor Know-It-All was to eat with the lord, but he wanted his wife, Greta, to eat with them too. So they all sat down together at the table.

Now, when the first servant arrived with a dish of delicious food, the farmer nudged his wife and said, "Greta, that was the first," and he meant that that was the man with the first course. But the servant thought he meant "that's the first thief," and since he really was the thief, he got scared and went out to tell his accomplices, "The doctor knows everything. There's trouble ahead. He said I was the first."

The second servant did not even want to go in, but he had no choice. When he entered with his dish, the farmer nudged his wife and said, "Greta, that's the second." This servant too got scared and hurried out. The third fared no better. Again the farmer said, "Greta, that's the third." The fourth had to carry in a covered dish, and the nobleman asked the doctor to demonstrate his skill and guess what lay under the cover. Crabs were being served, and when the farmer looked at the dish, he was at a loss for words. "Poor Crab!" he finally cried.

When the nobleman heard that, he exclaimed, "There, he knows! I'm sure he must also know who has the money."

The servant was frightened to death and winked at the doctor to step outside for a moment. When he got outside, all four servants confessed to him that they had stolen the money. They proposed that he take charge of it and offered a large sum in addition if he would not expose them. Otherwise, they would soon be dangling from the gallows. Then they led him to the place where they had hidden the money. The doctor was satisfied, went back inside, sat down at the table, and said, "Sir, now I intend to look in my book to see where the money's been hidden."

In the meantime, the fifth servant had crawled into the stove to see if he could hear what else the doctor knew. As the doctor sat there at the table, he opened his ABC book and turned the pages back and forth looking for the rooster. Since he could not find it right away, he said, "I know you're there. I'm bound to find you."

The servant in the stove thought that the doctor was talking about him, and he jumped out of the stove in fright and said, "That man knows everything!"

Then Doctor Know-It-All showed the nobleman where the money was, but he did not reveal who had stolen it. As a reward he received money from both sides and became a famous man.

◈ 99 ◈

The Spirit in the Glass Bottle

ONCE UPON A TIME there was a poor woodcutter who worked from morning until late into the night. When he had finally saved up some money, he said to his son, "You're my only child, and I want you to have an education. So I'm going to give you the money that I've earned by the bitter sweat of my brow. If you learn something honest and decent, then you can support me in my old age, when my bones are stiff and I must sit at home."

The boy went off to a university and studied so hard that his teachers praised him, and he stayed there for some time. After he had studied at a few universities and was still trying to master everything he could, his father's small earnings ran out, and he had to return home.

"Ah," said the father sadly. "I have no more to give you. In these hard times I can just about earn enough for our keep and not a farthing more."

"Dear Father," answered the son, "don't even think about it. If this is God's will, then it will all turn out for the best. I know I can adjust."

As the father was getting ready to go out into the forest and earn something by chopping and piling up cordwood, his son said, "I want to go and help you."

"But that will be too difficult for you, my son," said the father. "You're not used to the hard work, and you won't be able to take it. Besides, I have only one ax and no money to buy another one."

"Just go to our neighbor," answered the son. "He'll lend you an ax until I've earned enough money to buy one myself."

So the father borrowed an ax from the neighbor, and the next morning at daybreak they went out together into the forest. The son helped his father and was quite cheerful and alert. When the sun was overhead, the father said, "Let's rest and eat our lunch. After that the work will go twice as fast."

The son took his bread and said, "Why don't you rest, Father?
I'm not tired. I want to take a walk and look around the forest a little
to see if I can find birds' nests."

"Don't be so foolish," said the father. "What do you want to run
around for? Later on you'll be tired and won't be able to lift an arm.
Stay here and sit down with me."

But the son went out into the forest and ate his bread. He was
happy and gay and gazed up at the green branches to see if he could
discover a nest. He searched all over the forest until he came to a
huge dangerous-looking oak. It must have been hundreds of years
old at the very least, and it would have taken more than five men to
span it. He stood still, looked at the tree, and said, "I'm sure that
many birds have built their nests here." Suddenly he seemed to hear
a voice. He listened and heard a muffled voice calling, "Let me out,

let me out!" He looked around him but could not detect a thing. It appeared as if the voice were coming out of the ground. So he called out, "Where are you?"

"I'm stuck down here in the roots of the oak," the voice answered. "Let me out, let me out!"

The student began to clear away the brushwood and search among the roots until he finally found a glass bottle in a little niche. Then he lifted it in the air against the light and saw something jumping up and down inside that resembled a frog.

"Let me out, let me out!" it kept crying, and since the student suspected no harm, he pulled the cork out of the bottle. Immediately, a spirit rose out of the bottle and began to expand itself. It grew so fast that in a few moments a horrible fellow, half as big as the tree, stood before the student.

"Do you know what your reward will be for letting me out?" the spirit asked in a frightening voice.

"No," the student answered fearlessly. "How should I know?"

"Well, I'll tell you," cried the spirit. "You're going to get a broken neck."

"You should have told me that in the first place," responded the student, "then I would never have let you out. But my head's going to stay right where it is until we consult a few more people."

"I don't care about more people!" exclaimed the spirit. "You're going to get your just reward. Do you think that I was being held prisoner in there for such a long time because people felt pity for me? No, I was being punished, for I'm the almighty Mercurius, and I must break the neck of anyone who lets me out of the bottle."

"Take it easy," said the student. "Not so fast! First you must prove that you were really in that little bottle and that you're not a fake. If you can really get back inside, then I'll believe you, and you can do whatever you like with me."

"That's as simple as pie," said the spirit contemptuously, whereupon he proceeded to shrink himself and make himself as thin and as small as he was before. Then he went back through the opening and down the neck of the bottle. No sooner was he inside than the student took the cork he had pulled off and shoved it back on the bottle. After that he tossed the bottle into its old place among the roots, and the spirit saw that he had been outwitted.

Now the student started back to his father, but the spirit cried out pitifully, "Oh, let me out! Let me out!"

"No," answered the student. "Not a second time. I'm not about to let anyone free who's already tried to take my life once, especially after I've got him where I want him."

"If you let me go," called the spirit, "I'll give you enough money to last you as long as you live."

"No," responded the student. "You'd only trick me just as you did the first time."

"You're throwing away a golden opportunity," said the spirit. "I won't harm you. On the contrary, I'm offering you a generous reward."

I'll risk it, thought the student. Maybe he'll keep his word. Besides, he can't harm me. So he pulled out the cork, and the spirit rose up as high as he had the previous time and expanded himself until he became as big as a giant.

"Now you'll receive your reward," he said, and handed the student a little patch of cloth that resembled a bandage and said, "If you rub a wound with one end, the wound will heal. And if you rub steel or iron with the other end, it will turn into silver."

"I must try it first," said the student. He went over to a tree, sliced the bark with his ax, and rubbed the slit with one end of the patch. The bark closed immediately, and the wound healed.

"Now everything's settled," the student said to the spirit, "and we can part company."

The spirit thanked him for setting him free, and the student thanked the spirit for his gift and went back to his father.

"Where have you been keeping yourself? Did you forget that we've got work to do? I told you you'd never be able to finish the job."

"Don't worry, Father. I'll catch up."

"Catch up!" said the father angrily. "That's no way."

"Watch me, Father! I'm going to chop that tree right down, and it's going to make a big crash." He took his patch, rubbed his ax with it, and gave the tree a tremendous blow. However, since the ax had turned to silver, the blade bent. "Father, just look at the bad ax you gave me! It's all bent."

The father was taken aback and said, "Oh, look what you've done now! I'll have to pay for the ax, and I don't know where I'll get the money. You're useless!"

"Don't be angry," answered the son. "I'll pay for the ax all right."

"You dumbhead," cried the father. "What are you going to pay with? You've got nothing except what I give you. Your head's full of ideas from studying, but you don't understand the first thing about wood chopping."

After a while the student said, "Father, I can't work anymore. Let's call it a day."

"What's this now?" he answered. "Do you think that I want to sit with my hands in my lap like you? I've still got work to do, but you can head home if you want."

"Father, this is the first time I've been in this forest. I don't know the way home. Please come with me."

Once the father's anger had subsided, he let himself be persuaded to go home with his son. Then he said, "Go and sell that damaged ax and see what you can get for it. I'll have to earn the rest to pay back our neighbor."

The son took the ax and brought it to a goldsmith in the city, who tested it, put it on the scales, and said, "It's worth four hundred talers, but I don't have that much in cash."

"Give me what you have," said the student, "and you can owe me the rest."

The goldsmith gave him three hundred talers and owed him a hundred. After that the student went home and said, "Father, I have the money. Go and ask our neighbor how much he wants for the ax."

"I already know that," answered the old man. "One taler and six groschen."

"Then give him two talers and twelve groschen. That's double the amount and should more than do. See, Father, I have money to spare," and he gave his father a hundred talers and said, "You'll never want for money, and now you can live in comfort."

"My God!" said the old man. "How did you ever come by this fortune?"

Then the student told his father how everything had happened and how he had struck gold by trusting in his luck. Now he took the rest of the money and went back to the university, where he continued studying. And since he was able to heal any kind of wound with his patch, he became the most famous doctor in the world.

The Devil's Sooty Brother

A DISCHARGED SOLDIER had nothing to live on and no longer knew what to do with his life. So he went out into the forest, and after walking for a while, he met a little man who was actually the devil himself.

"What's the matter?" the little man said to him. "You look so gloomy."

"I'm hungry and have no money," said the soldier.

"If you hire yourself out to me and will be my servant," the devil said, "you'll have enough for the rest of your life. But you've got to serve me seven years, and after that you'll be free. There's just one other thing I've got to tell you: you're not allowed to wash yourself, comb your hair, trim your beard, cut your nails or hair, or wipe your eyes."

"If that's the way it must be, let's get on with it," the soldier said, and he went away with the little man, who led him straight to hell and told him what his chores were: he was to tend the fires under the kettles in which the damned souls were sitting, sweep the house clean and carry the dirt out the door, and keep everything in order. However, he was never to peek into the kettles, or things would go badly for him.

"I understand," said the soldier. "I'll take good care of everything."

So the old devil set out again on his travels, and the soldier began his duty. He put fuel on the fires, swept and carried the dirt out the door, and did everything just as he was ordered. When the old devil returned, he checked to see if everything had been done according to his instructions, nodded his approval, and went off again. Now, for the first time, the soldier took a good look around hell. There were kettles all about, and they were boiling and bubbling with tremendous fires under each one of them. He would have given his life to know what was in them if the devil had not strictly forbidden it.

Finally, he could no longer restrain himself: he lifted the lid o
first kettle a little and looked inside, only to see his old sergeant
sitting there.

"Aha, you crumb!" he said. "Fancy meeting you here! You used
to step on me, but now I've got you under my foot." He let the lid
drop quickly, stirred the fire, and added fresh wood. After that he
moved to the second kettle, lifted the lid a little, and peeked inside.
There sat his lieutenant. "Aha, you crumb!" he said. "Fancy
meeting you here! You used to step on me, but now I've got you
under my foot." He shut the lid again and added a log to the fire to
make it really good and hot for him. Now he wanted to see who was
sitting in the third kettle, and it turned out to be his general. "Aha,
you crumb! Fancy meeting you here! You used to step on me, but
now I've got you under my foot." He got out a bellows and pumped
it until the fire of hell was blazing hot under him.

And so it was that he served out his seven years in hell. He never
washed, combed himself, trimmed his beard, cut his nails, or wiped
his eyes. The seven years passed so quickly that he was convinced
that only six months had gone by. When his time was completely
up, the devil came and said, "Well, Hans, what've you been doing
all this time?"

"I've tended the fires under the kettles, and I've swept and
carried the dirt out the door."

"But you also peeked into the kettles. Well, you're just lucky that
you added more wood to the fire; otherwise, you would have
forfeited your life. Now your time is up. Do you want to go back
home?"

"Yes," said the soldier. "I'd like to see how my father's doing at
home."

"All right, if you want to get your proper reward, you must go
and fill your knapsack with the dirt you've swept up and take it
home with you. And you must also go unwashed and uncombed,
with long hair on your head and a long beard, with uncut nails, and
with bleary eyes. And if anyone asks you where you're coming
from, you've got to say 'From hell.' And if anyone asks you who
you are, you're to say 'I'm the devil's sooty brother and my king as
well.' "

The soldier said nothing. Indeed, he carried out the devil's instructions, but he was not at all satisfied with the reward. As soon as
he was out in the forest again, he took the knapsack and wanted to
shake it out. But when he opened it, he discovered that the dirt had
turned into pure gold. "Never in my life would I have imagined
that," said the soldier, who was delighted and went into the city. An

... standing in front of his inn as Hans approached, and
... aught sight of Hans, the innkeeper was terrified because
... her looked so dreadful, even more frightening than a scare-
... . He called out to him and asked, "Where are you coming
... om?"

"From hell."

"Who are you?"

"The devil's sooty brother and my king as well."

The innkeeper did not want to let him inside, but when Hans
showed him the gold, he went and unlatched the door himself. Then
Hans ordered the best room and insisted on the finest service. He ate
and drank his fill but did not wash or comb himself as the devil had
instructed. Finally, he lay down to sleep, but the innkeeper could not
get the knapsack of gold out of his mind. Just the thought of it left
him no peace. So he crept into the room during the night and stole it.

When Hans got up the next morning and went to pay the innkeeper before leaving, his knapsack was gone. However, he wasted
no words and thought, It's not your fault that this happened, and he
turned around and went straight back to hell, where he complained
about his misfortune to the devil and asked for help.

"Sit down," said the devil. "I'm going to wash and comb you,
trim your beard, cut your hair and nails, and wash out your eyes."

When he was finished with the soldier, he gave him a knapsack
full of dirt again and said, "Go there and tell the innkeeper to give
you back your gold; otherwise, I'll come and fetch him, and he'll
have to tend the fires in your place."

Hans went back up and said to the innkeeper, "You stole my
money, and if you don't give it back, you'll go to hell in my place
and you'll look just as awful as I did."

The innkeeper gave him back the money and even more besides.
Then he begged him to be quiet about what had happened.

Now Hans was a rich man and set out on his way home. He
bought himself a pair of rough linen overalls and wandered here and
there playing music, for he had learned that from the devil in hell.
Once he happened to play before an old king in a certain country,
and the king was so pleased that he promised Hans his oldest
daughter in marriage. However, when she heard that she was supposed to marry a commoner in white overalls, she said, "I'll go
drown myself in the deepest lake before I do that." So the king gave
Hans his youngest daughter, who was willing to marry him out of
love for her father. So the devil's sooty brother got the king's
daughter, and when the old king died, he got the whole kingdom as
well.

Tales 1-100

There were seven major editions of the *Children's and Household Tales* of the Brothers Grimm, known in German as *Die Kinder- und Hausmärchen*. The first edition appeared in two volumes; thereafter the tales were always published in one volume:

1st edition	1812, vol. I	86 tales
	1815, vol. II	70 tales
2nd edition	1819	170 tales
3rd edition	1837	177 tales
4th edition	1840	187 tales
5th edition	1843	203 tales
6th edition	1850	203 tales
7th edition	1857	210 tales

There was also a small edition that included 50 of the more popular tales, which went through ten editions from 1825 to 1858. Beginning with the second edition of the complete tales in 1819, Wilhelm Grimm was chiefly responsible for revising and expanding the collection of tales, and most of the additions after 1819 came from literary rather than oral sources.

During the initial stages of their collecting, the Grimms relied mainly on people within the region of Kassel and on the so-called Bökendorfer Circle in Westphalia. Wilhelm Grimm visited the estate of Freiherr Werner Adolf von Haxthausen in Bökendorf and became friendly with a group of young people there who provided him with numerous tales. Contrary to popular belief, the Grimms obtained most of their oral and literary tales from educated members of the middle and aristocratic classes. Indeed, the majority of their informants were women, and the Grimms did not travel widely to collect their tales.

A complete list of contributors can be found at the end of the Notes. The following were the key oral contributors: Dorothea Viehmann (35 tales); Family of Rudolf Wild (altogether they contributed 36 tales); Johann Friedrich Krause (7 tales); Friederike

Mannel (8 tales); Ferdinand Siebert (13 tales); Family Hassenpflug (altogether they contributed 41 tales); Bökendorfer Circle (altogether they contributed 66 tales).

In the notes that follow, after each story's German title I have indicated in parentheses the date of a tale's first publication in the Grimms' collection. In those instances where Wilhelm Grimm combined two or three tales, I have indicated that the tale is a mixed version. Wherever possible, I have tried to provide the place and date of publication of the literary sources.

For further information about the sources of the Grimms' tales, one should consult:

Brüder Grimm, *Kinder- und Hausmärchen,* 3 vols. edited by Heinz Rölleke (Stuttgart: Redlam, 1980).

Dieter Hennig and Bernhard Lauer, eds., *Die Brüder Grimm. Dokumente ihres Lebens und ihres Wirkens* (Kassel: Weber & Weidemeyer, 1985).

1. **The Frog King, or Iron Heinrich** "Der Froschkönig oder der eiserne Heinrich" (1812). Source: Family Wild

2. **The Companionship of the Cat and the Mouse** "Katz und Maus in Gesellschaft" (1812). Source: Gretchen Wild

3. **The Virgin Mary's Child** "Marienkind" (1812). Source: Gretchen Wild

4. **A Tale About the Boy Who Went Forth to Learn What Fear Was** "Märchen von einem, der auszog, das Fürchten zu lernen" (1812). Source: Originally published under the title "Gut Kegel- und Kartenspiel" ("A Good Game of Ninepins and Cards"), this tale was revised and expanded in 1819 with material from Ferdinand Siebert, Dorothea Viehmann, and a story from Mecklenburg.

5. **The Wolf and the Seven Young Kids** "Der Wolf und die sieben, jungen Geisslein" (1812). Source: Family Hassenpflug

6. **Faithful Johannes** "Der getreue Johannes" (1819). Source: Dorothea Viehmann

7. **The Good Bargain** "Der gute Handel" (1819). Source: Family von Haxthausen

8. **The Marvelous Minstrel** "Der wunderliche Spielmann" (1819). Source: From Lorsch near Worms. Informant unknown.

9. **The Twelve Brothers** "Die zwölf Brüder" (1812). Source: Julia and Charlotte Ramus

10. **Riffraff** "Das Lumpengesindel" (1812)). Source: August von Haxthausen

11. **Brother and Sister** ''Brüderchen und Schwesterchen'' (1812). Source: Family Hassenpflug

12. **Rapunzel** ''Rapunzel'' (1812). Source: Story by Friedrich Schultz in *Kleine Romane* (Leipzig, 1790), which was based on the tale ''Persinette,'' in *Les Fées, Contes des Contes,* (1692) by Mlle. Charlotte-Rose de la Force.

13. **The Three Little Gnomes in the Forest** ''Die drei Männlein im Walde'' (1812). Source: Dortchen Wild

14. **The Three Spinners** ''Die drei Spinnerinnen'' (1812). Source: Originally published under the title ''Von dem bösen Flachsspinnen'' (''A Tale About the Evils of Spinning Flax'') conveyed by Jeanette Hassenpflug. In 1819 it was replaced by Paul Wigand's version.

15. **Hansel and Gretel** ''Hänsel und Grethel'' (1812). Source: Family Wild

16. **The Three Snake Leaves** ''Die drei Schlangenblätter'' (1819). Source: Johann Friedrich Krause and Family von Haxthausen. Mixed version.

17. **The White Snake** ''Die weisse Schlange'' (1812). Source: Family Hassenpflug

18. **The Straw, the Coal, and the Bean** ''Strohalm, Kohle und Bohne'' (1812). Source: Dorothea Catharina Wild

19. **The Fisherman and His Wife** ''Von dem Fischer un syner Fru'' (1812). Source: Philipp Otto Runge. Written in a Pomeranian dialect (*plattdeutsch*).

20. **The Brave Little Tailor** ''Das tapfere Schneiderlein'' (1812). Source: Martinus Montanus, *Wegkürtzer* (c. 1557).

21. **Cinderella** ''Aschenputtel'' (1812). Source: From an anonymous woman in the Elizabeth Hospital in Marburg. Obviously influenced by Charles Perrault's ''Cendrillon,'' in *Contes du Temps passé* (1697). This version from Marburg was mixed with additional versions, in particular, one by Dorothea Viehmann. The term *Aschenputtel*, or Cinderella, appears in other tales to characterize a young woman obliged to do the dirty work in the house.

22. **The Riddle** ''Das Rätsel'' (1819). Source: Dorothea Viehmann

23. **The Mouse, the Bird, and the Sausage** ''Von dem Mäuschen, Vögelchen und der Bratwurst'' (1812). Source: Hans Michael Moscherosch, *Gesichte Philanders von Sittewald* (1650).

24. **Mother Holle** ''Frau Holle'' (1812). Source: Dortchen Wild

25. **The Seven Ravens** ''Die Sieben Raben'' (1812). Source: Family Hassenpflug

26. **Little Red Cap** ''Rotkäppchen'' (1812). Source: Jeanette and Marie Hassenpflug. Influenced by Charles Perrault's ''Le petit chap-

eron rouge,'' in *Contes du Temps passé* (1697), and Ludwig Tieck's drama *Leben und Tod des kleinen Rotkäppchens* (1800).

27. **The Bremen Town Musicians** ''Die Bremer Stadtmusikanten'' (1819). Source: Family von Haxthausen and Dorothea Viehmann. Mixed version.

28. **The Singing Bone** ''Der singende Knochen'' (1812). Source: Dortchen Wild

29. **The Devil With the Three Golden Hairs** ''Der Teufel mit den drei goldenen Haaren'' (1819). Source: Dorothea Viehmann. The German term *Glückskind*, which literally means ''fortune's child,'' is translated here as ''fortune's favorite.''

30. **The Louse and the Flea** ''Läuschen und Flöhchen'' (1812). Source: Dorothea Catharina Wild

31. **The Maiden Without Hands** ''Das Mädchen ohne Hände'' (1812). Source: Marie von Hassenpflug, Dorothea Viehmann, and Johann H. B. Bauer. Mixed version.

32. **Clever Hans** ''Der gescheidte Hans'' (1812). Source: Family Hassenpflug

33. **The Three Languages** ''Die drei Sprachen'' (1819). Source: Hans Truffer

34. **Clever Else** ''Die kluge Else'' (1819). Source: Dortchen Wild

35. **The Tailor in Heaven** ''Der Schneider im Himmel'' (1819). Source: Jakob Frey, *Gartengesellschaft* (1556), and Hans Wilhelm Kirchhoff, *Wendunmuth* (1563). Mixed version.

36. **The Magic Table, the Golden Donkey, and the Club in the Sack** ''Tischendeckdich, Goldesel und Knüppel aus dem Sack'' (1812). Source: Jeanette Hassenpflug

37. **Thumbling** ''Daumesdick'' (1819). Source: From Mühlheim, a town near Cologne. Informant unknown.

38. **The Wedding of Mrs. Fox** ''Die Hochzeit der Frau Füchsin'' (1812). Source: The first tale is from either Frau Gottschalk or Jacob Grimm himself. The second is from Ludovica Jordis.

39. **The Elves** ''Die Wichtelmänner'' (1812). Source: Dortchen Wild, all three tales.

40. **The Robber Bridegroom** ''Der Räuberbräutigam'' (1812). Source: Marie Hassenpflug

41. **Herr Korbes** ''Herr Korbes'' (1812). Source: Jeanette Hassenpflug. According to a letter written by the Grimms to the first English translator of the tales, Edgar Taylor, the name *Korbes* is supposed to mean ''bogeyman.''

42. **The Godfather** ''Der Herr Gevatter'' (1812). Source: Amalie Hassenpflug, expanded by a tale with the same title in Ludwig Aurbacher's *Büchlein für die Jugend* (Stuttgart, 1834). Mixed version.

43. **Mother Trudy** "Frau Trude" (1837). Source: Meier Teddy, "Klein Bäschen und Frau Trude, Ammenmärchen," a poem in *Frauentaschenbuch* (1823).

44. **Godfather Death** "Der Gevatter Tod" (1812). Source: Marie Elisabeth Wild and Friedrich Gustav Schilling. Mixed version.

45. **Thumbling's Travels** "Daumerlings Wanderschaft" (1812). Source: Marie Hassenpflug

46. **Fichter's Bird** "Fichters Vogel" (1812). Source: Friederike Mannel and Dortchen Wild. Mixed version. The influence of Charles Perrault's "La barbe bleue" ("Bluebeard"), in *Contes du Temps passé* (1697), is also apparent. The word *Fichter* is taken from the Icelandic *Fitfuglar*, which is a kind of web-footed bird.

47. **The Juniper Tree** "Von dem Machandelboom" (1812). Source: Philipp Otto Runge, written in a Pomeranian dialect (*plattdeutsch*).

48. **Old Sultan** "Der alte Sultan" (1812). Source: Johann Friedrich Krause

49. **The Six Swans** "Die sechs Schwäne" (1812). Source: Dortchen Wild and the tale "Die sieben Schwäne," in *Feenmärchen* (Braunschweig, 1801).

50. **Brier Rose** "Dornröschen" (1812). Source: Marie Hassenpflug. Also influenced by Charles Perrault's "La belle au bois dormant" ("Sleeping Beauty"), in *Contes du Temps passé* (1697).

51. **Foundling** "Fundvogel" (1812). Source: Friederike Mannel. Originally entitled "Fündling." A literal translation of *Fundvogel* would be "The Found Bird."

52. **King Thrushbeard** "König Drosselbart" (1812). Source: Family Hassenpflug

53. **Snow White** "Schneewittchen" (1812). Source: Family Hassenpflug

54. **The Knapsack, the Hat, and the Horn** "Der Ranzen, das Hütlein und das Hörnlein" (1819). Source: From Lower Hessia. Informant unknown.

55. **Rumpelstiltskin** "Rumpelstilzchen" (1812). Source: Dortchen Wild and Lisette Wild. Mixed version.

56. **Sweetheart Roland** "Der liebste Roland" (1812). Source: Dortchen Wild

57. **The Golden Bird** "Der goldene Vogel" (1812). Source: Gretchen Wild

58. **The Dog and the Sparrow** "Der Hund und der Sperling" (1812). Source: Gretchen Wild and Dorothea Viehmann. Mixed version.

59. **Freddy and Katy** "Der Frieder und das Katherlieschen" (1819). Source: Dorothea Viehmann

60. **The Two Brothers** "Die zwei Brüder" (1819). Source: Family von Haxthausen

61. **Little Farmer** "Das Bürle" (1812). Source: Family Hassenpflug and Dorothea Viehmann. Mixed version.

62. **The Queen Bee** "Die Bienenkönigin" (1812). Source: Albert Ludwig Grimm, "Die drei Königssöhne," in *Kindermärchen* (1808).

63. **The Three Feathers** "Die drei Federn" (1812). Source: Family Wild and Family Hassenpflug. Mixed version.

64. **The Golden Goose** "Die goldene Gans" (1812). Source: Family Hassenpflug

65. **All Fur** "Allerleirauh" (1812). Source: Dortchen Wild. A more literal translation of the title would be "All Kinds of Fur."

66. **The Hare's Bride** "Häsichenbraut" (1819). Source: Hans Rudolf von Schröter

67. **The Twelve Huntsmen** "Die zwölf Jäger" (1812). Source: Jeanette Hassenpflug

68. **The Thief and His Master** "De Gaudeif un sien Meester" (1819). Source: Family von Droste-Hülshoff. Written in Münster dialect.

69. **Jorinda and Joringel** "Jorinde und Joringel" (1812). Source: Johann Heinrich Jung-Stilling, *Heinrich Stillings Jugend* (Berlin, 1777).

70. **The Three Sons of Fortune** "Die drei Glückskinder" (1819). Source: Family von Haxthausen

71. **How Six Made Their Way in the World** "Sechse kommen durch die ganze Welt" (1819). Source: Dorothea Viehmann

72. **The Wolf and the Man** "Der Wolf und der Mensch" (1819). Source: Family von Haxthausen

73. **The Wolf and the Fox** "Der Wolf und der Fuchs" (1819). Source: From Hessia. Informant unknown.

74. **The Fox and His Cousin** "Der Fuchs und die Frau Gevatterin" (1819). Source: From Bohemia. Informant unknown.

75. **The Fox and the Cat** "Der Fuchs und die Katze" (1819). Source: From Switzerland. Informant unknown.

76. **The Pink Flower** "Die Nelke" (1819). Source: Dorothea Viehmann. *Die Nelke* can also be translated as "The Carnation."

77. **Clever Gretel** "Das kluge Gretel" (1819). Source: Andreas Strobl, *Ovum paschale oder neugefärbte Oster-Ayr* (Salzburg, 1700).

78. **The Old Man and His Grandson** "Der alte Grossvater und der Enkel" (1812). Source: Johann Heinrich Jung-Stilling, *Heinrich Stillings Jünglings-Jahre* (Berlin, 1778).

79. **The Water Nixie** "Die Wassernixe" (1812). Source: Marie Hassenpflug

80. **The Death of the Hen** "Von dem Tode des Hühnchens" (1812). Source: Clemens Brentano and Wilhelm Engelhardt. Mixed version.

81. **Brother Lustig** "Bruder Lustig" (1819). Source: Georg Passy. Tale from Vienna. The word *Lustig* means "merry" or "funny."

82. **Gambling Hans** "De Spielhansl" (1819). Source: Simon Sechter. Tale from Lower Austria written in dialect.

83. **Lucky Hans** "Hans im Glück" (1819). Source: Oral tale recorded by August Wernicke in the journal *Wünschelruthe* 33 (April 23, 1818).

84. **Hans Gets Married** "Hans heiratet" (1819). Source: Johannes Praetorious, *Wünschelruthe* (Leipzig, 1667).

85. **The Golden Children** "Die Goldkinder" (1812). Source: Friederike Mannel

86. **The Fox and the Geese** "Der Fuchs und die Gänse" (1812). Source: Family von Haxthausen

87. **The Poor Man and the Rich Man** "Der Arme und der Reiche" (1815). Source: Ferdinand Siebert

88. **The Singing, Springing Lark** "Das singende, springende Löweneckerchen" (1815). Source: Dortchen Wild

89. **The Goose Girl** "Die Gänsemagd" (1815). Source: Dorothea Viehmann

90. **The Young Giant** "Der junge Riese" (1815). Source: Georg August Friedrich Goldmann

91. **The Gnome** "Dat Erdmänneken" (1815). Source: Ludowine von Haxthausen. Written in Paderborn dialect.

92. **The King of the Golden Mountain** "Der König vom goldenen Berg" (1815). Source: Based on a tale told by a soldier.

93. **The Raven** "Die Rabe" (1815). Source: Georg August Friedrich Goldmann

94. **The Clever Farmer's Daughter** "Die kluge Bauerntochter" (1815). Source: Dorothea Viehmann

95. **Old Hildebrand** "Der alte Hildebrand" (1819). Source: From Austria, perhaps Georg Passy.

96. **The Three Little Birds** "De drei Vügelkens" (1815). Source: From a shepherd in Köterberg. Written in dialect.

97. **The Water of Life** "Das Wasser des Lebens" (1815). Source: From Hessia and Paderborn. Mixed version.

98. **Doctor Know-It-All** "Doktor Allwissend" (1815). Source: Dorothea Viehmann

99. **The Spirit in the Glass Bottle** "Der Geist im Glass" (1815). Source: From a tailor in Bäkendorf (Paderborn).

100. **The Devil's Sooty Brother** "Des Teufels russiger Bruder" (1815). Source: Dorothea Viehmann

Wherever possible the dates and professions of the contributors have been indicated.

Achim von Arnim (1781–1831), romantic writer and close friend of the Grimms. It was he who encouraged the Grimms to publish their collection of tales in 1812.

Friedmund von Arnim, author of *Hundert Mährchen im Gebirge gesammelt* (1844).

Ludwig Aurbacher (1784–1847), writer and collector of folk and fairy tales, author of *Büchlein für die Jugend*.

Johann Henrich Balthasar Bauer (1792–1835), friend of the Grimms in Kassel, provided a version of "The Maiden Without Hands."

Albrecht Dietrich, author of *Historia von einem Bawrenknecht* (1618).

Jenny von Droste-Hülshoff (1795–1859), member of the Bökendorfer Circle.

Annette von Droste-Hülshoff (1797–1848), member of the Bökendorfer Circle and Germany's most famous woman poet of the 19th century.

H. Eckstein, Viennese bookdealer.

Heinrich Georg Ehrentraud, author of the "Old Rinkrank" version printed in the journal *Friesisches Archiv* (1849).

Wilhelm Engelhardt (1754–1818), a colonel from Kassel.

Eucharius Eyering, author of *Proverbiorum Copia* (1601).

Jakob Frey, author of *Gartengesellschaft* (1556).

Karl Goedeke (1814–87), professor of German from Celle.

Georg August Friedrich Goldmann (1785–1855), sent the Grimms several different versions of tales from Hannover.

Frau Gottschalk, wife of a doctor in Steinau, used to tell the Grimms folk tales.

Anne Grant, author of *Essays on the Superstitions of the Highlanders of Scotland* (1811).

Karl Gotthard Grass (1767–1814), painter and poet.

Albert Ludwig Grimm, (1786–1872), writer of fairy tales and teacher, author of *Kindermährchen* (1808). No relation to the Brothers Grimm.

Herman Grimm (1828–1901), son of Wilhelm Grimm, became a folklorist.

Eberhard von Groote (1789–1864), acquaintance of Jacob Grimm from Cologne.

Joseph Haltrich, editor of *Deutsche Volksmärchen aus dem Sachsenlande in Siebenbürgen* (1856).

Georg Philipp Harsdörffer, author of *Der grosse Schau-Platz jämmerlicher Mord-Geschichten* (1663).

Family Hassenpflug, a magistrate's family in Kassel with a Huguenot background, very close friends of the Grimms. Dorothea Grimm married Ludwig Hassenpflug, and the Hassenpflugs as a group provided numerous tales for the Grimms, many of which were originally French.

Marie Hassenpflug (1788–1856).

Jeanette Hassenpflug (1791–1860).

Amalie Hassenpflug (1800–1871).

Moriz Haupt, professor of German.

Family von Haxthausen, their estate in Westphalia became the meeting place for the Bökendorfer Circle. Contact was first made with the von Haxthausen Family when Jacob made the acquaintance with Werner von Haxthausen in 1808. A warm friendship developed between the Brothers Grimm and most of the Haxthausens in the ensuing years.

Marianne von Haxthausen (1755–1829).

August von Haxthausen (1792–1866).

Ludowine von Haxthausen (1795–1872).

Anna von Haxthausen (1800–1877).

Philipp Hoffmeister, collector of folk tales from the region of Schmalkalden.

Ludovica Jordis-Brentano (1787–1854), a sister of the German romantic writer Clemens Brentano. She lived in Frankfurt am Main and provided the Grimms with two tales.

Johann Heinrich Jung-Stilling (1740–1817), whose significant autobiography *Heinrich Stillings Jugend* (1777) and *Heinrich Stillings Jünglings-Jahre* (1778) contained tales, which the Grimms used in their collection.

Friedrich Kind (1768–1843), German poet and librettist who wrote the libretto for Carl Maria von Weber's opera *Der Freischütz*.

Fräulein de Kinsky, a young woman from Holland.

Hans Wilhelm Kirchhoff, author of *Wendunmuth* (1563).

Johann Friedrich Krause (1747–1828), a retired soldier who lived near Kassel.

Legier du Loiret, author of *Traditions et Usages de la Sologne* (1808).

Hans Luft, editor of *Auslegung des 101. Psalms* (1534), containing an interpretation by Martin Luther, which served as the basis for *The Clever Servant*.

Friederike Mannel (1783–1833), daughter of a minister in Allendorf.

Karl Hartwig Gregor von Meusebach (1781–1847), an old school friend of Jacob Grimm and later a professor in Berlin.

Martin Montanus, author of *Der Wegkürtzer* (1557).

Hans Michael Moscherosch, author of *Gesichte Philanders von Sittewald* (1650).

Karl Müllenhoff, editor of *Sagen, Märchen und Lieder der Herzogthümer Schleswig, Holstein und Lauenburg* (1845).

Carl Friedrich Münscher (1808–73), informant of "The Life Span."

Johann Karl August Musäus (1735–87), writer and author of one of the first, significant collections containing adapted legends of folk tales, *Volksmährchen der Deutschen* (1782).

Karl Nehrlich, author of the novel *Schilly* (1798).

Elisabeth Charlotte von Orleans, author of *Briefe 1676–1722* (1843), edited by W. Menzel.

Georg Passy (1784–1836), librarian in Vienna.

Jean Paul (1763–1825), renowned German author. Part of his novel *Die unsichtbare Loge* (1793) served as the basis for "The Star Coins."

Johann Pauli, author of *Schimpf und Ernst* (1522).

Theodor Pescheck, author of "One-Eye, Two-Eyes, and Three-Eyes" (1816).

Johannes Praetorius, author of *Wünschelruthe* (1667) and *Der abentheurliche Glückstopf* (1669).

Heinrich Pröhle (1797–1875), minister and writer, primarily of religious books, author of *Märchen für die Jugend* (1854).

Charlotte R. Ramus (1793–1858), friend of the Grimms in Kassel.

Julia R. Ramus (1792–1862), friend of the Grimms in Kassel.

Philipp Otto Runge (1777–1810), famous romantic painter.

Hans Sachs (1494–1576), leader of the Nürnberg Meistersinger and prolific author of folk dramas, tales, and anecdotes.

Friedrich Gustav Schilling (1766–1839), poet and novelist who wrote *Neue Abendgenossen* (1811), a collection of stories.

Friedrich Schmid, teller of two Swiss oral tales, "The Griffin" and "The Peasant in Heaven."

Wilhelm Schröder, recorder of "The Hare and the Hedgehog," told to him by a forester in Bexhövede.

Hans Rudolf von Schröter (1798–1842), professor of old German literature in Rostock.

Andreas Schuhmacher, author of *D'Ganshiardarin* (1833).

Friedrich Schultz, author of *Kleine Romane* (1790).

Johann Balthasar Schuppius, author of *Lehrreiche Schriften* (1663).

Simon Sechter (1788–1867) from Weitra in Lower Austria, recorder of the dialect tale "Gambling Hans."

Ferdinand Siebert (1791–1847), teacher in Kassel.

Emil Sommer, editor of *Sagen aus Sachsen und Thüringen* (1846).

Karoline Stahl (1776–1837), writer of children's books and author of *Fabeln und Erzählungen für Kinder* (1818).

Friedrich Stertzing, author of "The Master Thief" (1843).

August Stöber (1808–84), teacher and researcher of folklore in Alsace, author of *Elsässisches Volksbüchlein* (1842).

Andreas Strobl, author of *Ovum paschale oder neugefärbte Oster-Ayr* (1700).

Sylvanus, author of *Das verwöhnte Mutter-Söhngen* (1728).

Meier Teddy, poet, whose poem "Klein Bäschen und Frau Trude," in the journal *Frauentaschenbuch*, served as the basis for "Mother Trudy."

Hans Truffer (1774–1830), a lawyer from Visp.

Dorothea Viehmann (1755–1815), wife of a village tailor near Kassel.

Anton Viethen, author of *Beschreibung und Geschichte des Landes Dithmarschen* (1733).

Josef Franz Vonbun (1824–1870), folklorist and editor of *Volkssagen aus Vorarlberg* (1847).

Wilhelm Wackernagel (1806–68), professor of German in Switzerland.

Burkard Waldis, author of *Esopus* (1548).

August Wernicke, recorder of the oral tale "Lucky Hans."

Jörg Wickram, author of *Rollwagenbüchlin* (1555).

Paul Wigand (1786–1866), close friend of the Brothers Grimm, who studied with them in Kassel.

Family Wild, a pharmacist's family in Kassel, who were all very close to the Family Grimm. Wilhelm eventually married Dortchen Wild, who supplied the brothers with numerous tales.

Dorothea Catharina Wild (1752–1813).

Lisette Wild (1782–1858).

Gretchen Wild (1787–1819).

Marie Elisabeth Wild (1794–1867).

Dortchen Wild (1795–1867).

Johann Rudolf Wyss (1782–1830), Swiss writer, author of the poem "Die Brautschau" and *The Swiss Family Robinson*.

Martin Zeiler, author of *Miscellen* (1661).

Franz Ziska, editor of *Österreichische Volksmärchen* (1822).

About the Translator

JACK ZIPES is professor of German at the University of Minnesota, in Minneapolis and has previously held professorships at the University of Florida, New York University, the University of Munich, the University of Berlin, the University of Frankfurt, and the University of Wisconsin–Milwaukee. In addition to his scholarly work, he is an active storyteller in public schools and has worked with children's theaters in France, Germany, Canada, and the United States. His major publications include *The Great Refusal: Studies of the Romantic Hero in German and American Literature* (Frankfurt, 1970), *Political Plays for Children* (St. Louis, 1976), *Breaking the Magic Spell: Radical Theories of Folk and Fairy Tales* (London, 1979), *Fairy Tales and the Art of Subversion* (New York, 1983), *The Trials and Tribulations of Little Red Riding Hood* (South Hadley, 1983), *Don't Bet on the Prince: Contemporary Feminist Fairy Tales in North America and England* (New York, 1986) and *Spells of Enchantment: The Wondrous Fairy Tales of Western Culture* (New York, 1991). He coedits *New German Critique,* an interdisciplinary journal of German studies, and has written numerous articles for various journals in the United States, Great Britain, Germany, Canada, and France.

A Note on the Illustrations

John B. Gruelle (1880–1938) is known primarily as the creator of
Raggedy Ann and Andy, but in fact, he was one of the more
versatile and gifted American illustrators of the first half of the
twentieth century. Born in Arcalo, Illinois, Gruelle spent his childhood largely in Indianapolis, and the Midwest took a strong hold on
his imagination. Throughout his works there are friendly, open-
hearted country characters, idyllic farm scenes, and placid natural
settings reminiscent of the late nineteenth-century American Midwest. His father, Richard B. Gruelle, a noted landscape painter, also
exercised a major influence on the young Gruelle, who developed
rapidly as an artist. While still in his teens, Gruelle became a
cartoonist for the *Indianapolis Star,* and by the time he turned
twenty, he had found a position on the *Cleveland Press.* Gruelle was
such a talented artist that he could draw any kind of cartoon or
illustration for advertisements or articles, and in his spare time he
began writing and illustrating his own children's stories.

In 1910 Gruelle won a contest sponsored by the *New York Herald,*
and he soon moved to Connecticut to live in an artists' colony called
Silvermine, where he hoped to benefit from the exchange with
like-minded painters and writers. It was then that his career as
commercial artist, illustrator, and cartoonist suddenly began to soar.
Due to his versatility, he was able to produce an incredible amount
of material for a variety of newspapers and magazines such as
Physical Culture, Judge, and *Life,* and he continued to write and
illustrate children's stories for *Good Housekeeping* and *Woman's
World.*

During this time he was commissioned to illustrate the Margaret
Hunt translation of the Grimms' tales by the publishers Cupples &
Leon. The book appeared in 1914, and unfortunately Gruelle's
artwork did not receive the attention it deserved. Although the color
illustrations are often sentimental, Gruelle's black and white
drawings—most of which have been reproduced in this volume—

add a new dimension to the tales because of his introduction of American motifs and settings that would be familiar to his readers. Gruelle also sought to emphasize the humor and optimism of the Grimms' tales by choosing scenes that captured both the mood of each tale and the manner in which a child might view the scene. As in his Raggedy Ann and Andy books, Gruelle contrasted the figures of good and evil in his line drawings in a way that induced an atmosphere of hope. For Gruelle, a fairy-tale illustration always had to point to the possibility of attaining a happy end.

It is interesting to note that only after he had finished the illustrations for *Grimm's Fairy Tales,* in 1914, did he go on to create the Raggedy Ann stories, in 1918. From this point on until his death, in 1938, Gruelle composed twelve Raggedy Ann and Raggedy Andy books as well as his various original fairy-tale collections. Numerous motifs from the Grimms' tales can be found in Gruelle's own tales and their illustrations, and so it is fitting that, in this new American edition of the Grimms' fairy tales, Johnny Gruelle's artwork is once again exhibited and can receive the attention that it deserves.

J.Z.

Don't miss these classic tales of high adventure from master storytellers

____21190-0	CAPTAINS COURAGEOUS, Rudyard Kipling	$3.95/$5.50 in Canada
____21332-6	KIM, Rudyard Kipling	$3.95/$5.50
____21338-5	THE WAR OF THE WORLDS, H. G. Wells	$4.95/not available in Canada
____21011-4	THE RED BADGE OF COURAGE, Stephen Crane	$3.95/$4.95
____21399-7	THE ODYSSEY, Homer	$4.95/$5.95
____21326-1	IVANHOE, Sir Walter Scott	$5.95/$7.95
____21232-X	GULLIVER'S TRAVELS, Jonathan Swift	$3.95/$4.95
____21376-8	THE PHANTOM OF THE OPERA, Gaston Leroux	$4.95/$5.95
____21370-9	THE HUNCHBACK OF NOTRE DAME, Victor Hugo	$5.95/$7.95
____21271-0	DRACULA, Bram Stoker	$4.95/$6.95
____21178-1	PETER PAN, J. M. Barrie	$4.95/$6.95
____21311-3	MOBY DICK, Herman Melville	$4.95/$6.95
____21247-8	FRANKENSTEIN, Mary Shelley	$3.95/$5.50
____21079-3	THE ADVENTURES OF HUCKLEBERRY FINN, Mark Twain	$3.95/$5.50
____21329-6	THE LAST OF THE MOHICANS, James Fenimore Cooper	$4.95/$6.95
____21225-7	THE SEA WOLF, Jack London	$3.95/$4.95

Ask for these books at your local bookstore or use this page to order.

Please send me the books I have checked above. I am enclosing $____ (add $2.50 to cover postage and handling). Send check or money order, no cash or C.O.D.'s, please.

Name _____

Address _____

City/State/Zip _____

Send order to: Bantam Books, Dept. CL 18, 2451 S. Wolf Rd., Des Plaines, IL 60018
Allow four to six weeks for delivery.
Prices and availability subject to change without notice. CL 18 1/99